The Dance Card— Copyright © 2016 by Shay Lawless

ISBN-10: 1-940087-13-9
ISBN-13: 978-1-940087-13-9

21 Crows Dusk to Dawn
Publishing, 21 Crows, LLC

Cover image: Simon Hack

S. LAWLESS

Chapter –1

Note to Self: 1) Funeral. Delbert. 11:00   2) Piss off Delilah by getting kicked out of funeral

"It is a junk shop, sweetheart. Just let it go. Get a real job—"

"Delilah, stop—"

"I will when you listen. But you can't leave things for chance. You're never going to make any money there—"

"Delilah, please stop. We are at a funeral—"

"—and if you don't make wise decisions, the river will never give you up."

"Oh, my God, *Mom*," I whisper-scream. "STOP!"

Yes, that's me gnashing my teeth together furiously inside my jaws. I am staring steel-hard at the back of the seamless black formal dress of the woman in front of me who made the remark, followed by one of her many sayings that simply make no sense at all. "What does that mean?" I hiss between my teeth. *"Don't leave things for chance. Make wise decisions or the river won't give me up?* You're speaking riddles."

"Journey Dawn, I am saying that your silly dream of making money at your antique shop is never going to fly. And if you grind your teeth like that, you'll waste five-thousand dollars of your grandfather's hard-earned money invested in your orthodontics. Stop."

And yes, my name is Journey Dawn. Unsuitably, so. It seems to imply a life of excitement and adventure. I live in the small town of Bacon Valley, Ohio. And if you haven't heard of it, there is a reason why. It isn't exciting. It is so downright boring sometimes, it is mind-numbing. Nothing ever changes here.

There is a rundown downtown with tree-lined street after tree-lined street of little white houses with the paint shedding off on to dried-grass ground like dandruff settling on the shoulders of a little old woman.   I am a product of this shoddy small town. I went to a small community college, returned home to a nagging mother and a high school sweetheart boyfriend who intends to marry me.

I actually live in one of those tiny, brick ranch houses on a cul-de-sac on the edge of town. It looks exactly like the twelve others on my street, settled into each other like sleepy puppies in a big, safe basket. It can't get any less adventurous than this. In fact, I could compare my life to the cheap paperback novels tossed in a bin by the grocery store registers and cut down to half-price. Every chapter is defined by one of the old, sappy country music songs that make everybody cry. The contents, uninspiring, are written like all the others, and with the same cliché-ridden ending where the two lovers ride into the sunset together and you've got no idea where they are heading other than west.

So— "Yes," I croak, soft and gruff to the comment about my dental work. It's my mother's back along with a few stray tendrils of her red hair dangling on her neck that I am glaring at while she tosses the words over her shoulder at me. She is also the one who named me Journey Dawn after a Transcendental Meditation group she was a member of in some California desert during the 1960s. And we are at Delbert Johnson's funeral. The funeral is outside in the tiny Bacon Valley Memorial Cemetery.

There are sixty-two dark umbrellas lifted into the air against the misty haze of early May rain falling. This umbrella-cave is like a big black and clammy circus tent complete with three-hundred pound Elsa Scranton as the fat lady sitting three rows up. Dickie Roberts, from the tattoo shop, with his purple-painted hair is the bandleader.

He plays his battery-operated piano keyboard. Stoic-faced Reverend Wilson is the ringmaster. He uses his hands in a wild melee to stress every point he makes about Delbert's incredibly long life.

Then there is me, his bleach blonde sidekick who croons out little jingles from the Bacon Valley United Church hymnal between appearances, unsure how to react because there's no applause after each sad song. After my last awkward song, I move back to the second row behind my mother and beside Delbert Johnson's pack of surly twenty-something grandkids who have been sneering at me long before the fight with my mother began. *Get a real job.*

My mother's whisper dangles between the two of us like her pinched forefinger and thumb wiggles enticingly in front of her cat, Sugar Baby, while she coaxes him to take his diabetes pill. She wraps his prescription pill in a tiny ball of cheddar cheese tucked into a sandwich of two chunks of tuna. She expects me to take her advice with the same lusty slurp of lips that Sugar Baby gives while he greedily laps at her fingers. I want to. I really do. In spite of my mother's efforts, even the damn old cat has figured out how to outfox the thin, but daunting creature in front of me. Fourteen and a half year-old Sugar Baby has enough dignity to hack up the little pink pill on to the shag carpet behind mother's leather couch once his furry fat butt rounds the corner of the kitchen and knows she is out of sight.

I, on the other hand, stand there quietly without a bit of dignity. I make a hard swallow of my mother's bitter pill like it is a prescription drug I have to take to survive. She doesn't even bother to wrap her words into something rich and delicious like fresh deli cheese and canned tuna fish. She just stuffs the damn pill down my throat, bare and bitter. It settles there waiting for me to choke on it, a big ball of ache stuck near the back of my tongue.

"Did you hear me, *sweetie*?" she asks just to rub it in, gloat in my unease. She turns slightly and her eyes dip downward. She squints at my dress near my waist. Her eyes widen. "Oh, honey."

She wiggles a well-manicured fingernail like a witch casting a spell. My eyes plunge, thinking for a millisecond my mother just might be able to pull it off, an incantation to make me completely disappear. She doesn't. Instead, I see a small piece of canary yellow paper dangling there. It is one of my little Post-it note reminders I call Notes to Self and sticking everywhere to remind me of things, or to jot down words to songs I make up before I forget them. It says: Funeral. Delbert. 11:00 I miss him. So bad.

"Yes, Delilah, I hear you," I answer in my hoarse, less -enthusiastic voice while I tug the note off. Could she not have seen it before I sang? "Everyone within a quarter mile radius can hear you. Even deaf people can hear you."

I pause, hear a chair squeak and turn my head to the right. An entire section of about eighteen people who have overheard my retort are giving me what I call THE LOOK. I seem to be the only one who ever gets this expression. It is head cautiously tipped to the side, brow furrowed and lips casually pursed as if trying desperately to keep from correcting whatever faux paus I had blurt out.

Our neighbor's dog has the same expression when he's getting ready to poop. However, those staring at me are not getting ready to poop. They are just trying to figure out how I could come up with something so stupid that it is able to fully surpass all the other stupid things I have said in the past. All the while, they are wondering how the hell such a bright and intelligent woman like Delilah Bacon could have given birth to such a harebrained twit like me.

I puff out my lips and give them all a cold, hard glare. Even Patty Hutchinson who—oh-shit, is hard of hearing, is giving me the stink eye. I turn my head and slump down a little to make myself small. Then, I stare at Delilah's back. My mother. If you haven't already figured it out, she is an intimidating figure even in her size four and a half high heels and elegant black hat. Her name is Delilah Bacon and she has never allowed me to call her Mama, Mom or Mother out loud.

I call her Delilah, although I secretly call her Mother and Mama just to feel like a normal daughter once in a while. She has lived in Bacon Valley all but four years of her life just like me. We are the fifth generation of Bacons living here and as the name implies, by old money and new condo stocks, we pretty much own everything.

Everybody knows Delilah Bacon. Beyond the old money, she is pretty much the only celebrity who came out of here. Mother had been the Bacon Valley Summer Sizzlin' Queen for four years straight back when she was still in high school. She probably would have kept on winning the local contest if she hadn't moved on to regional beauty contests, then state, and Midwest. She spent two years in California as a teen movie star in some G-rated beach movies.

She probably would have been a household name, except for one minor problem. Delilah got pregnant with me. Now my mother just spends most of her days hanging out with a wine in one hand and a cigarette in the other at the Bacon Valley Golf Club.

She reminds me how far she could have gone if she hadn't gotten homesick in Tennessee and slept with some idiot one hot July night at a festival in Nashville. *Some idiot.* That's what she calls the guy who got her pregnant. I never get to call him daddy because Delilah never revealed his identity to me.

I only know that I am half her and half him and so I remind my mother of this all the time when she calls him an idiot. She just rolls her eyes and tells me the apple never falls far from the tree. When I give her my stupid look (which is widening my already too-big, too-blue eyes and blinking them five times fast), she sighs loudly. Then Delilah explains, with a roll of her own eyes, that what she means is that I inherited her good looks. Yet, I got the idiot's brains.

"So we are on the same page then?" My mother turns slightly to expose a perfect, tiny nose, high cheekbones and wide, blue eyes. "You'll get a job at the bank? You'll stop this nonsense."

I clench my fists tightly to prevent my hands from working their way upward, sliding across the shoulders and choking the woman in front of me. I narrow my eyes and cock my head slightly to the right. I have long bleach-blonde hair stuck upon top of my head in a bun and hidden beneath a short black hat and lace veil. I imagine I am some masked assassin sent to murder her. My hands rise gently upon the neck in front of me, then my fingers begin to clench the soft skin, strangling the woman to death.

"What are you doing, dear?"

I realize my imagination has gotten away with me while Delilah cranes her neck just a bit to glare at me. My hands have actually made it to her shoulder. I pretend I am batting away a bug and tell her the same. "You had a fly on you," I lie. "A big, fat one." I know that getting away with murdering my mother in cold blood in front of a hundred people at a funeral would be nil to none. I picture Reverend Wilson diving over the crowd and wrestling me to the ground while Delilah spills out her last words: *She was never a perfect daughter. But don't give her the death penalty. The prisoner execution chair might muss her hair.*

"Well?"

I blink and shove away the image of me in an orange jumpsuit staring out of a jail cell, my skinny freckled arms resting on the bars. Instead of murdering my mother, I gnaw a manicured cherry-red thumbnail to aggravate her.

"Well—I can't remember the question," I say, looking up toward the sky. "What was it again?" I know everyone within hearing range is rolling their eyes. I hear one of Delbert's nephews growl out a: " *God, what a ditz.*"

I get this treatment all of the time. It is what is expected from Delilah Bacon's half-witted, bleach-blonde-haired daughter. I've spent the better half of my life with Delilah dragging me around to beauty pageants. I learned a long time ago, the small town hicks who run the pageants aren't looking for a pretty face with a soul and a brain. The same judges who liked to reduce my ego down to a negative twenty while they openly discussed my flaws (like breasts that a man with small hands could even cup), also liked the thought that they could cup my teeny weeny breasts, too, behind the stage if they could.

"I know you heard me." Delilah almost screams it. "Do not make me say it again."

I can see a few lips tighten in the row I am standing in. Raymond Wilson is performing the service. The minister has given us both warning gazes twice. Each time he does, he takes a white kerchief from his pocket and rubs away another layer of sweat from his forehead. Then, he scrubs it upward until it stops just short of the last remaining ring of hair at the top of his head.

"There are no jobs in Bacon Valley," I finally whisper -spit out, "unless you own a vacant building that used to be a hotdog factory." Oh, I imagine Delilah's eyes opening wide. It diminishes the itch of goose pimples of irritation creeping up from wrists to elbows for the moment.

It is true. Bacon Valley's only claim to fame is the Appalachia Hot Dog Company started by a local farmer by the name of Judson Bacon. The National Hot Dog Association claimed Bacon Valley had the world's largest factory for ninety-two years. It is actually only ninety-one years. In 1936, Grandma and Grandpa got a divorce. Grandma got the factory. She closed it down for eleven months out of spite. When Grandma found out she couldn't afford to buy a new pair of shoes through the Sears Catalog every other day during the Depression, she started doing some soul searching. She forgave Grandpa whatever sins he had made and they lived happily ever after. They had Delilah. Then Delilah and her idiot had me.

"Let me just say this—"

I groan really loudly when I hear this. My mother has an opinion on everything. It means the fight is over and she has to get the last word in. She cranes her neck around and looks at me, eyeing me from the tip of my high heels to the top of my veiled head.

I cringe. I see Delilah pause momentarily at my bare legs. I am wearing a super-short, little black dress with spaghetti straps that exposes the pale skin more than a few inches between knee and upper thigh. I also have on a tiny hat with a lacy veil settling just below my eyes. I look up. Sharp, blue eyes meet sharp blue eyes and an angry stare meets an angry stare. It is the only thing matching on us, the glare.

Delilah Bacon's pursed lips bedecked in funeral-appropriate bland pink meet pursed lips adorned with my defiant cherry red lipstick. A crackle of thunder creeps across the sky. If anyone is looking at the moment the bolt of lightening lingers there moments later, they would think it has erupted from the fiery stares between mother and daughter. Perhaps, they are right.

"Say it, Delilah," I mutter, feeling a little defiant. I might be able to best her once like her damn cat does all the time with a hairball behind the couch. I really think I can spit out the pill she is handing me. Surely Delilah will not actually say what she is feeling in front of most of the town right now. I am wrong.

"Okay, I will. How do you ever expect to get married, much less keep a husband if you are sitting in that old, god-forsaken building all day long staring at a bunch of old, rusted junk covered in dust?" Delilah says it. And she says it in the loudest whisper her voice can hold. "Do you think Robert wants to introduce you to his peers one day with: *This is my wife. She owns a junk shop?* No. Do you want to be alone?"

I blanch. Now the first row of the funeral goers are snapping to attention, eyes scanning down the rows until they stop on me. Ah, they do love the Bacon drama. I feel my throat tighten, my cheeks turn hot and bright pink. "I don't care what they think," I stutter. "Alone sounds good. I feel like I am already standing on the threshold of hell living here, Delilah."

"Speak of the Devil, and he will come," Delilah hisses toward me. My mother is always coming up with these odd quotes and old wives tales to keep me from making the same mistakes she made. *Don't count your chickens before they hatch*, she would tell me before every pageant so I wouldn't get my hopes up for winning. *Feed a cold, starve a fever,* I always hear when I feel a cold coming on. *Don't swallow gum. It takes seven years to digest.*

"Oh, my God!" I fan my face with my hand frantically. "No, he won't."

"Do not say the Lord's name in vain!" she retorts.

"You do it all the time!"

Reverend Wilson can hear us. Every head is turning to my own. His cool brown eyes are drawn nearly closed in a scathing, scolding gaze. He is balding and the top of his head turns an angry, fiery red. He makes a double swipe with his kerchief across his high forehead, cheeks, and chin. I let out a deep groan. He sighs, drops his bible down to his waist. He jabs his thumb toward the tiny gravel parking lot at the front of the cemetery.

"Oh, my God, I'm getting kicked out of a funeral," I say. I peer left to right, realize my escape route is blocked by the knees of Delbert's family who are sitting in green or black fold-up chairs to my right. I try to rub away the heat of embarrassment in my cheeks with my palms, give Reverend Wilson one last pouty, wide-eyed gaze with my eyes to see if he has changed his mind. His glare tells me he has not. Even Delbert's family is scooting their legs to the sides of their chairs, parting a way for me to trudge through.

It is a huge family. Delbert had thirty-two grandchildren who went all through school with me. Farm kids. I remember them wearing cowboy hats and old barn boots with manure on them even to high school dances. Boots with manure are never in style.

Of course, when the Wells and the Johnsons (wearing twenty-dollar overalls from The Farmer's Market in Byers Village twenty miles away) made up the bulk of the class size, my one-hundred and thirty-dollar skirts (from Caitlin Smythe's Boutique in New York City) became the object of their ridicule.

I wiggle sideways through the wall of Delbert's family, down the aisle and bump along the irritated glares. *The Bacons always have to make it about themselves.* I hear one say. *Even at a funeral.* I wince like I am biting down on pieces of ice when I look up to see who said it.

I hone in on a freckled face and flawless, fine red-blonde hair parted in the center and with bangs hanging in his eyes. At first I don't recognize the slender frame, nor the delicate slant of nose and jawline of the man staring back at me. I would have thought him a stranger as my bare knees skim along the cloth knees of the voice saying those words.

Then, he shakes his head ever so slightly to the right and pushes the bangs from his eyes with one hand. It strikes me dumber than usual while I catch the beautiful, vibrant blue glare now unhidden slicing hard into my own.

"What are you staring at, Bacon?" he whispers loudly. "Get an eyeful?"

"N—Nothing," I stutter. "And no."

His lips part in a mocking grin at my fumble of words. He resituates himself on his chair and crosses his arms over his chest defensively.

Brody Wells. Delbert Johnson's wild child grandson. The boy could always manage to make me feel socially awkward and incredibly hideous. Still—damn, he was so pretty. He was never the type of boy I would actually date, even if he was the type I *wanted* to date. Brody Wells was wild, like a pretty pony that didn't want to be tamed, although lots of girls tried. Brody burned down his dad's barn when he was eighteen and got kicked out of the house. I haven't seen him since.

"You are a piece of work, Bacon," he tells me under his breath, his voice floating over the heads and through the tarp of umbrellas with a gritty stare and a flat voice. I sniff a grunt while trying to slip gracefully past the last four people with grave stares on the row.

One of them is Bella Johnson, Brody Wells's cousin and self-appointed bodyguard. Bella played football in high school. I saw her tackle a guy once twice her size, catch him from halfway down the field. Bella's legs were chubby.

However, they were toned and muscled. I swore Bella flew that chilly night in September, her feet off the ground before the boy was left in a crumpled heap on the field. He got up after five minutes. I heard he cried like a newborn baby, her tackle hurt so bad. The Bacon Valley EMS wheeled him away in a gurney.

Bella stands up from her chair as if to allow me to pass, tugging down on her pants like men do when they sit up. Her hair is black and she keeps it cut short. She rolls her hand through it all the time as if she is pressing it back against her head. She puffs out her chest, narrows her eyes, slicing into my own. Her voice is soft and husky while she leans hard into me nearly touching nose to nose.

"Keep looking over your shoulder, Piece of Bacon. 'Cause I'm going to kick your ass just when you least expect it and all the way to Cleveland, O-Hi-O."

I flinch. She must catch a whiff of pure terror coming off my skin. She licks her lips, wetted pink tongue rolling slowly and deliberately from left to right and back again.

"Hey," she murmurs a wisp of warm, mint-gum-smelling air burning my ear lobe. "You stay away from my family. You forget about the stupid promise. You forget about the old dance card thing my grandpa gave you."

I see Brody Wells smirking at me. It makes me so irritated. I realize, then, everybody in town knows about The Promise. I bring up my hand, expose my middle finger to him. Someone gasps. I feel the blood drop from my cheeks while the hushed crowd glances back at me. And the only thing I can do is slide my way down the aisle and stare down at the ground, tears falling hot and hard while I escape.

Chapter −2

You stand there, tell me to dance to a different song. The steps I'm taking, they're all wrong—

The promise. The real promise Delbert Johnson forced me to keep wasn't what everyone was whispering from one ear to another. The real promise started with a canary yellow cardboard cigar box with a raggedy lid barely clinging to the top. KING JOHN REGAL CIGAROS was printed boldly on the lid and along two sides. A giddy looking man with a crown sitting half kilter on top of his head is smoking a thick cigar beneath the letters. The box smells like mothballs, Delilah's spice cabinet, and the torn books in the historical section of the library you can't check out because they are so old.

Delbert Johnson gave me the little cardboard cigar box one hot and muggy afternoon two weeks earlier. He brought it from where it sat on the top shelf in his closet.

"Happy Birthday, Red," Delbert had announced with a grin from ear to ear. He always called me Red even though my hair was bleach blonde and nearly white. Underneath ten years of Hair Flavor Number 10-Pale Honey hair color, though, my hair was the rusty color of guardrails after they had been out in the rain for ten years. I always told Delbert to quit pointing my true hair color out. He always told me I was hiding the true me behind a bottle of bleach. I had propped myself up on the counter with my back to the wall and my guitar on my lap. I had placed an oscillating fan at the far end of the counter so the breeze from the paddles spread air from my feet, straight up my skirt, and then to just above my chin. I had been humming a new song, trying to figure out words matching my mood, match the notes I plucked on the strings.

It just wasn't coming to me, the song. The weather was hot. And I was miserably dealing with the sweat trickling tiny streams down between my shoulders and between the spaghetti straps of my top.

I hadn't been surprised to see Delbert. I jumped up, though, quickly catching the last seven foot tall shelf of five in the room and closest to my counter. If the door slammed hard enough against the wall holding the front bay window, the rickety shelves started to wiggle back and forth. I was terrified one day, they would fall like a long line of Dominoes until they crushed someone to death coming in the front door.

Delbert was the worst culprit of slamming the door. I was so used to it, I would slip from whatever position I was in, automatically clinging to the last shelf until it made its jarring impact with the wall. He always mumbled an apologetic toothy-grin and helped me place a wadded up piece of paper at the bottom to level out the shelf. It was only a matter of time, the paper would get squished and wiggle its way out so a new gob would be shoved beside it as a replacement.

There were a lot of wads of paper under the shelf. Delbert visited every day from eight in the morning until I left at four in the afternoon. His daughter, Gayle Wells, runs the post office on the corner of the block. She would drag him with her to work every day so she could keep an eye on him. He'd gotten a little forgetful. On a daily basis, the police would get a call an old man was wandering up the road toward town. It was always Delbert.

So he used to sort the mail for Gayle, putting the letters into the postal boxes for all the rural folks who picked up their mail in town. He got bored with it one day and he wandered into my shop, sat down, and opened a bottle of pop with his bent-knuckled hands.

He started telling me about a little dull scout pocketknife I had on my desk. He gave me an explanation for all the uses of the little tools on it that had been a mystery to me until he poked a gnarled finger at it and divulged all its secrets. Delbert told me he was a scout for most of his boyhood and a good one too. I was fascinated, dug out three more antiques I couldn't identify. He examined them carefully, poked them, prodded them, then sighed, and revealed their purposes—a can opener, a wooden frog lure and a water witching tool.

After the first day, Delbert Johnson said he saw something shine in my eyes each time he recognized and named an item, told me its use. I felt like he was opening a little treasure box, shoving a key into a long-locked padlock, and opening the container with all its secrets exposed to me. I saw the light in his eyes when he had found out he was still useful, not some old man who had to be babysat by his daughter or the too-bubbly young girls at the senior center on Main Street.

So Delbert hung out with me instead of all the other old guys with hearing aids, old-fashioned glasses, and aluminum walkers at the makeshift senior center at the Bacon Valley Bibleway Church two blocks north. He never gave me The Look when I said something silly. Sometimes, he would laugh, though, and tell me *That's a good one!* Much to my mother's dismay, I hung out with him instead of the local women at the ice-cream/coffee shop gossiping about their boyfriends over their soy chocolate mocha lattes.

The day Delbert brought in the cigar box, I leaned up from where I had been stuffing a thick bundle of old newspaper under the shelf. I gritted my teeth and felt the pockets of perspiration prickle in my armpit.

"It's not my birthday, Mister Johnson," I told him. I was wearing my thick, black glasses instead of my contacts. They are designer Mattie Lanes. Delilah insists I buy nothing less than the most expensive, most fashionable. When I can't afford them, she flips out her credit card to pay for them. I detest those glasses because of this reason. It is belittling having her persist in still choosing my clothes and accessories like I am the sixteen year-old dress-up doll she dragged to beauty pageants. But even more, I hate wearing them because they slip down the bridge of my nose, a moist descent only curtailed by my forefinger. But I have lost my contacts again. It is no secret I lose stuff a lot. Stuff like my car keys, cell phone and, of course, my glasses. And I can't see shit without them.

"Oh, well, we'll celebrate it anyway," Delbert told me. "Because I got you something. And I can't wait until your birthday." He had a funny walk, a kind of limp to his left side. When he took a step up to the counter, he dipped hard to the left and latched on to the edge to help him straighten his stance.

I waited, intrigued. Usually, as soon as Delbert would plop some mysterious item he had dug up at a yard sale or found in the attic, he would start with something like— "When I was a kid—" because when Delbert brought something in for me, he always had a story to go with it.

He poked his finger at the counter and said something about the building being there when Bill Gillespie gave him the cigar box. 1939. He was cleaning the store out, getting ready to sell the building. There was something about the year. I knew it was a hardware store because the old and worn wooden sign with W.G. GILLESPIE'S HARDWARE STORE - 1914 painted in faded white letters was still tacked to the building above the front door.

"I was sixteen the year Junior Fenton's dad bought the old Gillespie Hardware Store," Delbert told me while he poked a gnarled finger at the counter. "Back then, it had a blacksmith shop out back. But folks were driving cars. Nobody needed a blacksmith anymore. I was standing right here when Bill shook Andrew Fenton Senior's hand and sealed the deal. Bet you didn't know I raced cars down on Goose Creek Road with Junior Fenton, too, did you?"

"I did not," I answered, realizing Delbert was leading into one of his stories—*long* stories, that is. And I really wasn't in the mood for one of his lengthy life chronicles complete with a consequence that he believed would parallel my life at some point. I stifled a fake yawn, hoping he would pick up on my impatience. It was too hot. I just wanted to go back to playing my guitar. I wished for just a moment that at least one of his forty-five nieces, nephews, and grandkids would take up an interest with him so I didn't have to be the only one he had to impart his lifetime of wisdom. He must have sensed my lack of enthusiasm.

"That's where they used to see the ghost," he tried to entice me with an eerie wail right after. I rolled my eyes up to his, sighed. The ghost. Every teen in town for the last seventy-five years has made the ride along Goose Creek to see The Ghost. It is a rite of passage, I suppose. A girl was killed in a car crash there, so the story goes. Her ghost walks the road, a figure in white, no less. If you call out her name three times, she will come to you. We always called her 'Molly.'

The only confrontation I had with the ghost was Delbert's grandson, Brody, and his best friend Zach Metzler jumping out at my best friend, Andrea, and me one night when we drove down there in my car to scare ourselves. The boys had been hiding in a little meadow. We got out of our car, walked down the road. I started chanting *Molly, Molly, Molly.*

All of a sudden, the two boys came screaming out of the brush with sheets over their heads. Andrea screamed and peed her pants. I ran head first into the side of my car and had a golf-ball size bump on my head.

I didn't divulge this to Delbert. I figured he had probably heard the telling and retelling of our horrible confrontation. I know everyone at school did. Instead, I just nodded with a certain boredom. "I don't believe in ghosts."

"I imagine you don't. Open the cigar box." He rapped the lid with his knuckles. I thought I saw a bit of that excited light go out of his eyes. I felt a jab of guilt.

I had nodded, none-the-less, if not a bit grateful I didn't have to listen to him drone on today with the naivety of those who think their best friends lives will go on forever. I dug in with my forefinger and popped open the lid. I leaned both elbows on the counter, peered inside.

The first thing catching my eyes was a little bag made of tan feed-sack cloth. Curious now, I snatched up the pouch, pushed a finger inside the bag and wiggled the strings loose until it opened. With a gentle twist of my fist, the bag was upside down and the object spilled within my outstretched hand.

It was the size of my hand from wrist to fingertips, palm laying flat. It looked like a tiny and dull sterling silver purse with floral swirls etched into the design and a four inch chain dangling at one corner. There was a clasp closure holding the two sides together much like the opening of my mother's old purses.

I held it aloft to study it, noting the delicate way it set so easily in my palm. I turned it around, examining it from top to bottom, running my finger along the cool exterior. Then I pushed upon the clasp. It opened wide to expose a tiny mirror compact, two change holders, two small doors for storing things, and a compartment for a dance card.

"That there is a dance card holder," Delbert told me. He reached out and fingered the top, tapped it with a gnarled knuckle. "At least, that's what we used to call it. Freddy called it something else. Can't quite remember."

"Freddy Johnson," I grunted the name with the same lack of exuberance as my mother's cat farts when he rounds the corner of the kitchen after a good meal. "What would Freddy know about something like this? This is the same nephew who tried to pawn your wife's gold wedding glasses off to me as something he found at a yard sale?"

Delbert mumbled noncommittally, shrugged. "That's him. And the one who was puttering around my closet looking for it." He steadied himself against the counter, looked forlorn. "That boy just ain't right. It's not worth much money." Delbert huffed. "But it's worth a million in memories."

"Memories," I smiled, tried to coax the same out of Delbert's suddenly sad face. "Okay, what's the story today?"

"I was hoping you'd ask that," he said. He told me how he had been hanging around outside this very store one hot day like today back in the 1940s. He was just about to get into his old farm truck when a boy dressed in city clothes came by in a brand new car. The city boy bet Delbert he could beat him in a race. Whoever won would get the papers on the loser's car.

"I raced him," Delbert said. "But it was for a stupid reason. The guy had the most beautiful girl in his car I had ever seen. She had wide eyes as big as oranges just like yours. I bobbed my head up and down like an idiot when he asked. Then I didn't have a choice."

"My eyes are not as big as oranges," I laughed and asked him if he won the race.

"Um, yeah, I did. My truck was old, but the other guy put his tire too far on the side of the gravel road," he said.

"It went off into the grass." Delbert rubbed his palm across the last remains of his gray hair. "But I didn't win the car. The guy said there was no way in hell my car was worth anything close to his. Instead, he reached over and snatched something from the girl's hands and tossed it to me." Delbert poked a finger at the dance card purse. "The purse. I tried to give it back to her, but she just shook her head. Still, I got the best part of the deal. I didn't get his car, but three weeks later she came back to the hardware store to find me. She wanted to give me something else."

That was when Delbert Johnson handed me the dance card. It was old, worn, smelled like mothballs. The outer cover was a pale white, thick like a postcard. While I rolled my fingers down the delicate material, I realized the picture of two dancers on the front was hand painted. The woman wore a 1920s hat adorned with a real feather.

Carefully, I took the upper corner of the cover and pulled it back to expose the contents within. It was a small booklet of old, tan paper. On the first page was printed: *Winford Senior Ball - March 1940*. There were nineteen dances listed down two pages with a line for a signature next to each. They were all blank. It appeared the book never got used.

"This is what the girl brought me." Delbert drew in a raspy breath, jabbed a bent finger at the book. "The girls used to carry these cards at all the dances. We boys would sign up for dances with the girls we wanted to get to know. Her school was having a formal dance. She gave me the book and told me she'd save every dance for me. All's I had to do was show up with the dance card and the purse."

I was intrigued, almost to the point I had not breathed. "Did you take her to this dance?" I huffed, rubbing my finger on the card. "What happened? The whole thing doesn't have a single signature on it."

Delbert Johnson didn't say anything for a stifling long time. Such, I wrestled with the urge to apologize for all my questions. I didn't need to. Delbert pursed his lips, let a little air slide out of his lips.

"Naw, I didn't take her. Something came up," he sighed. "Then I met my wife and I forgot all about it. Made a different choice, walked a different path." He scratched his head, looked thoughtful, maybe a little melancholy. "She was a beauty, though. Red, those were the good old days."

I stared at him, watched a smile play on his lips. Then he cleared his throat and sighed. "But that's not why I gave it to you, sweetie. When I found this in my closet, I realized you're sitting in this old building every day, talking to an old man. You should be out having good ol' days too. You need to fill your dance card."

"And it isn't going to be anytime soon. Robert's not so big on dancing." I joked. "He wouldn't even do the Hokey Pokey at Jenny Smith's wedding and he was drunk. I would probably have to drug him to get him on the floor."

"But you like to dance, right?"

"Of course," I answered.

"Then maybe—maybe you could find a different partner to dance with you."

My eyes shot up, stunned. It occurred to me right then what he was implying. He wasn't talking about dancing at all, but spending my life with someone.

"Delbert, I've got Robert. We were meant to be. Just like you and your wife. You were meant to be with each other that's why you didn't reunite with the pretty girl. Heck, even Robert's last name is Ironwood. So I'll be Journey Ironwood. You know, like Journey—onward with a southern twang. It's cool."

Delbert was lowering his eyes at me like I had just said something completely stupid. I shrugged it off. "Whatever. But if he won't dance, I just won't dance. No big deal. He doesn't make me watch football. And I certainly don't need to dance with anybody else."

"Then you are going to miss out, I suppose." Usually, Delbert Johnson simply shut his mouth and smiled kindly when he didn't agree with me. Not so today. Perhaps he was hot and grumpy, too, with sweat pooling in his armpits.

"So what's going to happen when he tells you he doesn't want you to sing?" he told me instead, nodding toward the guitar. "You gonna stop singing in the choir at church, at the restaurant, and right here in your shop? Red, you have a beautiful voice. I heard you sing at the Senior Center Christmas party last year."

"Robert wouldn't stop me from singing. And it scares me to get in front of people, you know that. I have to think out every word or I stutter."

"Stutter, butter. Then think every word out. Everybody's got something they worry about. Your songs, they make people know they're normal with those things just like you. Anyways, you don't stutter when you sing. You always take the easy route, Red. Sometimes you've got to buy a ticket and take the long road to see the sights. You can't stay cooped up here like a little songbird in a cage. You've got to set yourself free, soar above the trees. Sing to anybody who'll hear you."

"I like shortcuts," I tell him.

"I'm an old man, Journey Dawn," Delbert told me flatly. His face bore no smile, his gaze was steady, deeply penetrating into my own. "If I die tomorrow, I want to know that at least someone learns from my mistakes. I'm just an old fart with Alzheimer's as far as everybody else is concerned. No one listens to me anymore. Nobody," he said.

"Except you. So, unfortunately, you get to hear me out because you seem to be the only one with ears."

I wanted to tell him I would fill out that card for him. I couldn't. It was just the way it was. Everybody talked about how I couldn't get any better than Robert Ironwood. He was such a good hometown boy. He was nice. He had money in the bank.

"Mister Johnson, I have obligations," I said instead. I really didn't think I could get anyone better. It wasn't like anybody else ever asked me out on a date. "I get what you are saying. But I've been with Robert since my sophomore year of high school. I just don't think anybody else would put up with me."

"Yeah, because that good-for-nothing boyfriend of yours won't let anybody else get past." Delbert nodded solemnly. A little bit of light had gone out in his eyes. He had said nothing more about the subject that day. He stayed for just a little while. Then he snatched up the cigar box. He said something about having a doctor's appointment and left.

Chapter −3

You stand there, tell me to dance to a different song. The steps I'm taking, they're all wrong—I hold out my arms to dance with you and you're gone. I didn't know you meant I'd be dancing alone.

Maybe he didn't think he was going to die so soon. Delbert Johnson didn't bring up the subject of Robert for the next two weeks passing. Then one afternoon, he came strolling in with his usual loping steps. I had been leaning with my elbows on the counter at the shop. I was halfway listening to an old country music song playing out a staticky beat on the radio and halfway reading a well-worn 1922 Suave Movie Star Confessions magazine.

I looked up, caught Delbert in my eyes. He was pale, so pale. His fine, gray hair was strangely askew on his head. His shirt was not tucked into his pants. Delbert looked like he had just rolled out of bed, stuffed himself into his clothing. He was always so particular about sticking his carefully-ironed shirt into his pleated, pressed pants. Yet, at that moment, he had wrinkles on his shirt. It was buttoned incorrectly. Something was wrong. And he had that damn cigar box in his hand, plopping it on the counter.

"Promise me you won't marry that no good boyfriend of yours until you try somebody else out." Delbert had taken three steps, came to a jerky halt when he had gutted me with his words. I thought the conversation was over, figured he had moved on. I could only stare at him, blue eyes darting back and forth at Delbert's bloodshot stare. He reached out one hand, latched on to the edge of the counter and leaned hard against it.

"You," he pointed hard at me with the wrinkled-knuckle forefinger of his free hand. "You have to promise me." His face was both flushed and pale at the same time, a bit of sweat had pooled on his brow.

"Huh?" I had tipped my head to one side, started around the counter, watched Delbert collapse there. The next thing I knew, he was sliding down the rough wood and his rear was planted on the floor.

I would later completely forget dialing 9-1-1. I wouldn't remember how excruciatingly long it took before I heard the wail of life squad siren piercing the air.

"Sweetie, I'm old," he finally worked up enough air to tell me. "Old people die."

"You can't die," I told him. I sounded five years-old while my mouth twisted into a grimace to stop the tears. I sat with him, his wrinkled hand patting my own, thinking this was maybe just a really, really bad dream.

Eddy Walters of the Bacon Valley EMS swept in, hovered over Delbert, trying to stick a sterile plastic air mask over his nose and mouth. Eddy checked the blood pressures down at the senior center on Fridays. Delbert always said he made the cuff puff up too tightly and he called him EMS Eddy.

"What the hell is that boy doing?" Delbert had grunted, irritated.

"He's giving you oxygen," I had answered while eyeing EMS Eddy cautiously. Delbert's hand tried to swat the kneeling man away. "So you can breathe better."

"It ain't my breathing that's bad, Red," Delbert complained. "It's my heart. I'm almost a hundred years old and the heart's got to go sooner or later. I'm thinking it is sooner even though I planned on getting a haircut this morning. I suppose it'll cost more for a mortician to do it."

I had looked at Delbert horrified, then at EMS Eddy with the narrowed eyes of the untrusting. If Delbert didn't want the oxygen, there was going to be a fight. If there was going to be a fight, I figured I would have Delbert's back. I wasn't quite thrilled I was revolting against the Bacon Valley township EMS. The Bacon Valley police had *their* backs. But *I* would take a blow for Delbert, watch *his* back.

EMS Eddy was three years older than me. He was always one of those boys who sat in a dark cubby in the library at school with a few others just like himself, debating which battle of the civil war was the turning point or discussing the particulars of a tabletop fantasy role playing character he would become the same evening while he and a choice few of his friends rolled dice on a card table in his mom's dank basement. He pronounced everything clearly, concisely like his life depended upon it, his deep pink lips accentuated with each syllable. And he never washed his hair, his greasy bangs swinging over one eye. Whenever I would walk into the room, he and his friends would stop talking like I was some robot spy in their fantasy roll playing games who deciphers their secret codes just by walking by them. They would stare at me with wary gazes until I passed.

EMS Eddy still had greasy black hair. He was always in the shop with the same bunch of boys who played fantasy games in school and who were now grown men, digging through my stuff looking for antiques they could use in their Civil War reenactments on the weekends. When I found him something from 1861 to 1865, he would get so excited he would rub his fingers through his sleek, oiled-down bangs and get a sparkle to his brown eyes.

His eyes weren't sparkling now. They were anxious, darting around toward the door like he was waiting for more help to arrive.

"Mister Johnson," EMS Eddy was shoving the mask at Delbert, trying to hold back his hand with his own. "You have to let me give you oxygen."

"Does he?" I interjected. "I mean, is it —*the law*?" I gave a little leeway before the last part and stressed the words just a bit for effect.

EMS Eddy was the kind of guy who had a higher than 4.0 average in school. He gave me THE LOOK. Then he went straight to a glare in the same way the Bacon Valley policeman who sits on the main road outside town looks at me when I answer his question about the reason I am going ten miles over the speed limit again. I stare at Officer Andy McGee the 35 miles per hour sign four feet from the car, scratch my head and ask him what the speed limit is.

"No, it isn't the law," EMS Eddy muttered. "But if he doesn't, he might die. And if he dies, do you want his death on your hands? I think not. That might get you arrested."

"Oh, don't do that to her." Delbert managed to give EMS Eddy a decent shove back with one hand. I let him, pretending I lost my balance while I sat on my heels on the floor.

"You have to fill up the dance card. You do it for me."

"Mister Johnson, I can't," I whined, adamantly shook my head back and forth. "I mean, I don't even know whose names I would use to fill the card if I can't use Robert."

"How about him?" Delbert pointed a finger at EMS Eddy. My eyes veered upward, my head shook back and forth. Yuck and awkward both at once.

"Mister Johnson, please!" I pushed out a hand.

"Then how about my grandson. I thought about that one last night." Delbert took in another painfully gruff breath. Oh, he was pale.

"Billy is probably eight years younger than me." I wondered when this conversation was going to end. "He's still in high school. Do you want me to get arrested?"

"Brody's your age," EMS Eddy offered with a shrug.

"Even if he is my age, he isn't my type," I gurgle.

Then EMS Eddie added, "Listen, Journey, Mister Johnson has to get this oxygen mask on. Can you help me out? I have to get him in a stretcher. We have to get him to the hospital—pronto." He was calm, so calm to my hands shaking. His eyes were telling me what I really knew, what I didn't want to realize. *Delbert Johnson is dying.*

So I nodded and saw EMS Eddy give me the faintest wisp of a smile of relief. "Thank you."

But Delbert grabbed my hand. "Listen to me and listen to me well. Sweetie, you're the one who needs the oxygen in that silly little ginger head of yours. Take this damn card. Fill it up. But not with that good for nothing louse you've got now. Go out and try a few dances with some other nice gentlemen. Fill up the card. For me."

"Okay," I said, knew my eyes were too wide. "Delbert Johnson, put on the oxygen mask, do what EMS Eddy says and I'll fill up the card, alright? I'll go out with EMS Eddy, here, or Billy or Brody or the stinky guy at the Pump and Dump Gas Station if you want."

"You promise? Journey Dawn. Dates. There are nineteen dances on the card. Fill up your dance card of life. Promise me."

"I will," I said to Delbert while he stared at me long and hard. "I promise." Then the light flickered out of those gentle orbs. And just like that, Delbert Johnson had died.

Chapter −4

She's a rebel child. Daddy's little girl gone wild.
Sweet Sixteen. Small town.
Gonna take some poor redneck boy down.

The locking mechanism inside the knob of the back door to my little antique shop is broken. It has been for as long as I remember. Everybody in town knows it is busted because they are always dropping off little boxes of their collectibles on the back porch just inside the door. Some leave notes with their names asking me to sell the items for them on consignment. Others just drop off old stuff they don't want anymore.

Gayle Wells knows it is broken. After five o'clock, I always lock the front door. If Delbert was still there after closing, she would come down the alley between the post office where she worked and the store to pick her father up to go home.

I have a little hole in the floor in the front room where they used to conceal their daily cash in the 1930s during the Depression and when the banks went bust. It is large with a built−in lockbox, about two feet by two feet. It has a little door with a lock and key. Delbert showed it to me. He said Junior Fenton showed it to him when Junior's dad owned the store.

I keep my daily cash in the lockbox. There's room for extra keepsakes. I'm somewhat of a packrat when it comes to sentimental things. I've kept my first valentine, my favorite old Barbie Doll, and a couple hundred grocery receipts, Post-it notes and tiny pieces of whatever paper is nearby I use to jot down words to songs I write. A section of red, fluffy remnant carpet lays overtop.

Gayle probably thinks I am gone for the day when she sends her son to drop off some of Delbert's things for me. I usually leave around four o'clock on Thursdays to get to my job at Hobie's Bar and Grille. However, I am running behind today because my boyfriend, Robert, walks in just as I am about to lock the front door.

"Where do you think you are going?" Robert asks me. I am not very quick with retorts with him. I have learned to hesitate, measure his many moods by the way he narrows his eyes, the way he purses his lips. He folds his hands at his waist defensively when he is coaxing a fight, leans forward when he wants me to be agreeable. When he's mad at me, he comes stomping across the floor with his head bent. I have this habit of reaching out my hand when he comes at me like this, wiggling my fingers at him. *What are you doing?* He spats each and every time. He knows what I'm doing. Like I can read the ways he tests me with his confrontational gestures, he knows my own motions of submission and surrender. I am fending off a fight in the only way I know how to a six foot and four inch man who weighs a hundred and sixty pounds.

His chin is cocked to one side and pushed upward now. He is big and well-built like a husky St. Bernard pup. He doesn't always, however, have the same happy-go-lucky disposition as this particular breed of dog. My boyfriend's character would be equivalent to one of those nippy little Chihuahua dogs mixed with the over-protectiveness of an untrained, vicious German Shepherd.

I watch as he hones in on a couple pieces of torn paper on the counter, pieces of songs partially written, ideas that may go to the wind, but may someday be songs.

"Baby, these creep me out, you know?" he says, picking up a fistful. "It's weird all your notes. Weird."

I don't answer. Maybe they are weird. They don't sound much like songs just jotted down on the paper. At least not until I add in music from my guitar.

I can be quite obsessive with them. I was in the middle of an order a couple months ago waitressing at Great Escapes Restaurant. I found I had written down a song where I should have been writing: *2 Pizzas PP.* Instead, I handed this to the kitchen staff:

She's a rebel child. Daddy's little girl gone wild.

Sweet 16. Small town. Gonna take some poor redneck boy down.

Down, down, gonna go down tonight.

No fears. It's alright. Gonna get him without much fight.

"Hey, you in there?" Robert asks me now, knuckling up and banging softly on top of my head. "What is up with you today? Did you forget there was something important? You completely missed your job interview at the bank."

His smile says he is teasing me gently. However, his stance tells me he is in a taunting, irritated mood. It is conflicting, yes. It is difficult to read him when he is like this. I stand there clasping and unclasping my hands knowing he can read my nervous stance just as easily as I can read his confrontational posture by the way he holds his clinched fists at his waist. He works in his dad's bank loan office and he sees this posture all the time when someone comes in to ask for a loan that is much too large for what they can afford. But I tell him the truth. I didn't forget.

"I do not want to work at the bank, Robert. I won't. It smells like elementary school in there—like crayons, boxes of modeling clay and old books. I don't want to sit behind a desk. I like my shop. I like taking off in my car and—"

"And this place smells like old, dead people's stuff," Robert tosses back. He has these buggy eyes and he lets them roll across the front room until they pause momentarily on a corner of the back room. "Holy shit, what did you waste your money on this time?"

My own eyes follow. They land on the pale blue dress settled perfectly on the dressmaker's dummy. It is beautiful and a genuine dress from the Civil War era, flouncy and wide and complete with all the undergarments. I paid over eight-hundred dollars for it. But I have a buyer from a little museum two towns up that already wants to purchase it sight unseen.

"It's a dress, Robert, for a museum," I start to say, but his eyes have already rolled to an old rusted bottle opener on a shelf. He walks across the room and picks up the bottle opener.

"Baby, what's this worth, huh? Fifty-cents? You'd have to sell a thousand of these a day to make enough to buy those fancy dresses your mom gets you now." He tosses it back, rolls his eyes. "And, yes, you will work at the bank," he snorts. "Sooner or later, I'm the one who is gonna be stuck buying you the dresses. I can't afford to pay for this place and your clothes. We've talked about this before. Your mom agrees." It hurts my feelings so I take a step back and turn my attention to the wall over his shoulder.

"C'mon don't look at me like that," he goes on, tossing his hands into the air. "This place is a piece of shit. It is falling down around you." Robert grunts and snickers. I remember these two sounds from somewhere. However, I cannot quite pinpoint where I heard them until he finishes it off with a deep, full-bellied sigh. Then I drudge up the memory. These are the same sounds he makes when we have sex. He taps me on the shoulder and wiggles a finger in a little circle.

He nudges me over on my belly for a five minute bounce, then finishes his last lap with a grunt and that strange little snicker. Most would consider his noises that of simple pleasure. I honestly believe it is a sigh of relief he simply got the job done and is ready for whatever comes next —late night TV shows, a beer and plain potato chips.

"What is up with you, huh?" he continues, completely unaware I am cringing inwardly thinking about his sex-grunts. "Dad told you from the start renting the place was temporary. It is just too expensive to do it as a favor just for you for— this."

"*This*?" I am sounding whiny now, too. "I like *this*."

"Well, you're going to have to stop liking—*this*. You've got no choice. And the bank job is your only option. Who the hell else is going to hire somebody who loses their cell phone at least three times a day? Who has been out of college five years and still hasn't gotten a real, big girl job?"

"This is a real job, a *big girl* job," I tell him, knowing I will never win this battle. I wonder why I even try. "It is no different than working at a bank."

"Are you actually comparing *my* work with what you do here?" There is deep laughter, sarcastic laughter. "Setting up a yard sale in an old building is not a job. Baby, you can't make a living doing this."

"Yes, I can. I can prove it with that dress back there."

"You know what?" Robert looks at the dress, rolls his eyes. "I've got to be honest. Going out with you is like going out with a frigging twelve year-old because of *this*. You never answer your phone, you stay out half the night. You forget shit all the time. And it isn't just because you are such a ditz. And, sweetie, you are one big ditz. You've got to take some responsibility. That means going to bed at a decent hour. Now, you run around all over the place collecting this crap, don't get home until two in the morning," he grunts.

"You have got to grow up, Journey. At some point in your life, you are going to have to quit dragging around that stupid pawn shop guitar with you like you're going to be a rock star. You're not going to make a dime on that shrilly voice of yours or this ridiculous junk store—and quit looking at me like I'm giving you a spanking, would you?"

There is a bang in the back room, the kind of creak a foot makes when it scuffs across an old wooden floor. My shoulders tighten because I know someone is back there and I know whoever it is can hear us fighting.

"You have somebody here?" Robert asks.

I turn my head slightly, shake it back and forth. "No," I answer. "It might be somebody dropping something off."

"Great, more junk," Robert lowers his voice, peers toward the crack in the door between rooms. "Dad's selling this building. They are closing down the post office here. Renting that section was the only money he made off of this entire block."

"I pay rent."

"Baby, Dad doesn't charge you shit to rent this place because you're with me, you know that, right?"

"Well, I'll buy the shop from him then." I was counting my savings in my head, realizing I needed a lot more than the $23,552.28 I had secretly stashed over the last five years working three jobs to buy this place.

"You're going to buy this place." It wasn't a question. He lobs the words toward the ground like he is tossing a freshly-used, snotty tissue into a garbage can. "Well, that's not going to happen. I can guarantee that, baby. You're not going to buy this place because I won't allow it. And my dad wouldn't give you a loan for it. He's the only bank in town—"

"Daddy, I got to go pee pee."

The voice wafts through the doorway soft and gentle.

It is followed by the deeper voice of a man I recognize instantly as Brody Wells. Shit. Of all the people I want to hear me fighting with my boyfriend, it is certainly not him. Brody Wells could sniff out my weaknesses in high school like a beagle sniffs out a bunny trying helplessly to duck beneath the two-inch grass of a freshly mowed lawn. Then he would drag me out and display my flaws in his sharp little teeth for all to see.

"Sweetie, I'm almost done," Brody is saying. "Can you hold it until we get back to grandma's?"

I walk over and pull the door open enough to see inside. Brody Wells is standing with a crate in both his hands. A little girl is behind him, one hand resting on the back door knob, her body between the door and frame. They match, those two, like all the Wells kids do. Red-blonde hair and fiery blue eyes. She is holding the crotch of a pair of old jean pants cut off just above the knee, bouncing from one leg to the other making a tap-tap on the wooden floor with mismatched pink and blue flip-flops.

"No, daddy, I got to go."

Just as her words fade, Brody turns. He looks painfully uncomfortable, a cat cornered on a kitchen table with a fresh cup of milk toppled over to one side and dribbling down to the floor. I see his jaw working back and forth, see him eye the child's white t-shirt with brown smudges on the front right before he turns to me. I see him bounce his fingers on his leg. Brody's always done this quirky tap on his leg six times, stop, then six times again when he's nervous. I remember he used to do it before all the math tests in high school.

The fire in his eyes fades away to the kind of defeat a soldier has in the movies right before his enemy sends a dagger into his heart.

For just a moment, I feel like the beagle, see Brody Wells as the bunny rabbit. Then I hear Robert shuffle his feet.

"Is there somebody back there?" Robert thunders the words, makes a show of coming around the corner and fixing his tie. I jolt, his voice is so loud. I'm the bunny again.

"Just one of Delbert Johnson's grandsons dropping off some stuff," I answer. I turn back and shift my attention to the little red-haired girl.

"The bathroom is right over here." I lean to the left, flip on the light, opening a second squeaky door to expose a small sink with a white porcelain bowl and a mismatched light green toilet. I am afraid to move. She looks terrified with wide eyes. "Do you need help?"

The little girl neither answers nor moves. Her feet are rooted to the spot, her body motionless and her mouth slack like she has started to say something and freezes right at the moment her lips part. She stands there unblinking, staring past Brody's shoulder, eyes dead set on me.

"Is she okay?" I ask, turning my attention to the man behind her, trying to keep my voice soft so I don't frighten her more.

"She's fine," Brody shoots back gruffly, defensively. His eyes are like this ocean-colored blue now with sharp anger at me. He pauses as if to access the situation, looks at his daughter whose gaze at me is like a doe caught in the headlights of a semi-truck. "She's just—" Brody starts to justify her behavior, pauses as if he cannot. "I don't know." So Brody coaxes her with a gentle tap. "Cayce, go on." It seems to break some kind of spell. She blinks, looks up at Brody with fist-size eyes and nods dumbly, mouth slack. Slowly, she scoots across the room, her eyes not once leaving mine.

"Are you sure she's alright?" I ask again. "She doesn't look alright."

Now she has turned at the restroom door to walk backward into the room so she doesn't take her eyes away from me. Her knobby-kneed legs start jumping up and down again until she bumps her back into the sink.

"Cayce, go to the bathroom." Brody chides softly, but firmly. His face is red while he takes a quick glance over at Robert. "She's not stupid," he spurts out, "if that is what you are implying."

"No, I didn't mean that at all." I snap my eyes from the bathroom.

Robert chuckles softly and sarcastically beneath his breath. His jeering is not aimed at the child, but me. "That's what it sounded like to me, sweetheart."

I feel the awkward silence surround me. It is a pressure I cannot stand so I clap my hands together suddenly, remembering a box of stuff Delbert saved for his grandson. "Oh, I have something for you. I put your action figures and comic books in a few crates for you." I point across the room to the dim recess behind the door. "Your grandpa saved them from one of your mom's yard sales."

"Huh?" Brody winces. I walk across the room, tug back the door a bit and nudge a metal crate with the toe of my shoes.

"These are all your action figures and comic books," I announce. "It was so funny. Your mom was going to have a yard sale. Your grandpa found your comic books in with the sale stuff in the barn. He got this idea in his head that we could hide them somewhere so she didn't get rid of them. So he spent an entire Saturday planning out a way we could sneak them out on Sunday while everybody was at church and stash them here —"

"God, babe, you are such a ditz," Robert is shaking his head when I look up.

I realize from his embarrassed cock of his head and Brody's confused furrow of brow, I have done one of my knee-jerk reactions that pop up clear out of nowhere. "He doesn't want to hear all that, Journey." Robert grunts from where he has not moved. I feel my cheeks get as cherry-red as my lipstick. By the confusion written on their expressions, neither Robert nor Brody have a clue what I am talking about with my sudden outburst.

"You're right," I stutter and pretend to fix my hair.

"I've got a meeting in two minutes." Robert is good at wiping away my embarrassing flare ups. He shoves them under a rug with an excuse to leave. "Dammit, why can't anything ever go smoothly?" Then he snaps his head up, points a finger across the room at Brody. "You're almost done, right? I assume you'll drop the junk, head on back to your mom's house." Ouch, that was a jab. Brody winces.

"Yeah, I just have to drop off three more crates." Brody is standing there. He is tall, taller than Robert, but thinner. Both are staring at each other, maybe sizing each other up like they used to in high school. Brody looks more bored than ready to fight. He shrugs, kicks one of the crates with his foot.

"Good, then, I'm leaving." Robert mutters. He walks across the expanse between us, nudges me with a knuckle and gives Brody a warning glare before he turns back to me. "I put your phone on the counter. Keep an eye on him. He's probably drugged out or something. Call me when what's-his-name is done so I know you're alright. And make sure he doesn't try to burn the place down."

I nearly keel over dead when he says that. I know Brody can hear the comment about the barn burning. I watch Robert walk across the room and pretend to rub some dirt off my skirt before I, too, turn. "You know, he isn't always like that. I'm sorry if you heard— anything."

"He has always been like that." Brody stares at me. "And I didn't hear anything." But I know he is lying. Everybody is still whispering about that old barn.

"I didn't mean that at all about your little girl," I tell him. "I know she isn't stupid. I mean, I just don't know when kids start doing these things by themselves. She looked scared like I was going to eat her or something."

"She's been doing these things for two years," he mutters. Then he sighs, loses a bit of the anger in his eyes. "It— it's usually a lot more straightforward, I suppose."

I'm not sure if he is joking. He doesn't smile, just scoots around me with a wide berth and helps his daughter wash her hands. Still, I know he is here for a reason. I had not even gotten to my car at the funeral when Freddy Johnson came stealthily bustling up behind me as if he had come to help me open my door. Freddy's dad is one of Delbert's nephews and owns the used car lot in town— Johnson's Used Cars. Freddy sells cars there, but he's always looking to make another buck doing odd jobs.

Freddy cornered me at the funeral with his knee between us. "Hey, girl, you never called me back." Freddy had leaned into me like I'm his best friend, pawing at my back but never quite touching it. "I left three messages." He is tall, dark-haired and skinny and wears suits all the time. They aren't the cheap ones either like his dad buys at the local retail stores. They are like five-hundred dollar suits.

I told him I wasn't making any sales at his grandpa's funeral, holding out my hand and keeping him at bay. And I told him I wasn't selling a gift his grandpa had given me.

But he won't listen. He keeps leaving calls on my answering machine. And after Bella had threatened to beat me up, it just isn't worth it. Now, I got a good idea that is what Brody has come to get. Freddy probably gave him ten bucks to get it from me.

"Hang on. I got what you came for," I say.

I go into the front room, open the cigar box. Inside, I tug out the dance card holder Delbert gave me. My heart aches a bit thinking I am letting Delbert down. I blink the thought away, close the box. Then I grab fifteen dollars from the cash register, walk back to the dark room where Brody is standing.

I hold out my hand palm up. "Your grandpa gave me the dance card purse for my birthday. He told me to sell it, fix up the shop with it, maybe get enough to buy a coffee machine so folks would come in and chat it up with me. Then he died." I take in a breath, shrug. "He gave it to me with the dance card. Those are the two things Bella was talking about that she says I stole from your grandpa. I'm sure Freddy told her it was worth a million bucks. It isn't. I'm keeping the dance card. It's worth fifteen bucks which I will pay you," I tell him. "But the dance card holder, it is real silver, you can keep. I'm sure it's worth something. I got a call yesterday from some guy who saw my posting online. I told him it wasn't for sale now. Your grandpa asked me to find out what is was worth. Your cousin, Freddy, has called me six times trying to talk me out of it. Now you're here. I suppose he talked you into trying to talk me out of it too. So here it is. Take it and we can call a truce. No more bullying me."

"Bullying *you*?" Brody takes the purse absently.

"Yes, like putting glue in my chair, calling me 'Piece of Bacon' and howling like a dog when I sang in choir."

"That was Bella."

"No, it was you," I say flatly. "You called me J—J—Journey when I stuttered."

"You called me a dumbass redneck cowboy," he says in defense. His voice is low, his head slightly cocked as if listening for his daughter. "You—"

"I did," I interrupt. "I laughed at your torn up shirts and your cowboy boots that always had dried brown manure on them."

Brody holds up his hands, shakes his head. "I don't want your dance thing. I don't want to have anything to do with the whole lot of this dumbass town. I just want to get the hell out of here as soon as I can."

"Well—I'm sorry." I say it too late. Brody has already turned, my voice is soft and it is muted by the skid of the door against the gritty floor. It probably doesn't matter. It was ten or fifteen years too late. He doesn't take the dance purse when he leaves. It is sitting on the shelf in the back room. The last thing I hear before he slams the door shut to the car is his little girl asking if I am a real princess. It is soft and sweet and cut off by the rumble of the truck engine. I wonder what he tells her. I am glad I don't hear it.

Chapter −5
Note to Self: Work at Hobie's 5:00

"If Robert knew you were asking me out, he would probably kick your ass." I am hovering over the big aluminum bar sink at Hobie's Bar and Grille just off the highway. It is always dark back here and smells like bleach and mildewed dish rags. I have my blouse sleeves rolled up to my elbows. My arms are deep in water and suds, my fingers probably look like wrinkly peach pits from washing the evening dishes. I have to yell over the sound of a band out on the stage and the crash of water falling into the aluminum sink.

"I'm thinking it'd be worth the ass-kicking."

I look over my shoulder to the shadow behind me. I can't see much, just the side of an arm while Drew Billings slings a box of hamburgers back into the freezer. I sigh wishing I was doing anything but washing dishes in an old dirty bar. At least I've got Drew for company although sometimes he just stares at me with a faraway gaze when I talk to him, and I don't know if he is even listening at all.

Still, he's a quiet guy when he is working in the kitchen, doesn't say much at all until he gets a shot up on the stage. I don't blame him. He hates being the cook on Friday nights. But he loves being on stage. I see him turn sometimes while he's cooking hamburgers on the grill. He has this sad, longing gaze that reminds me of a puppy at the pound looking out of its cage. But the owner of the bar lets him sing from seven to seven forty-five Friday and Saturday as long as Drew cleans out the grease vats under the grill.

The bar used to just be Hobie's Bar and Grill. A year ago, Hobie went to Dayton and noticed all the new bars had added an 'e' to the end of the word *grill*. Now the rickety sign outside has all but one faded letter and it is a lopsided 'e' in deep blue.

Blue was the only can of paint not dried up that he had in the shed behind the bar.

A half-assed attempt at changing the bar's name doesn't change the fact Hobie's isn't much more than one step up from being an old shack. It used to be part of a slaughterhouse before Hobie's uncle bought it sixty years ago. Now, it is the downtown ghost town of Coalville's only business besides an all-night diner, a gas station with bars on the window and the backside of Midwest College of Rendville.

It sits fragilely between the past and the future and is about to get gobbled up by subdivisions to the north. To the south, there's nothing for miles but more old, defunct towns and deep cuts of forest. It doesn't stop folks from crowding in to see the bands on Friday and Saturday night. Old Hobie might have owned a crappy building in the middle of nowhere, but he used to run bars in Nashville and New Orleans. He knows every country band from here to Texas. They come for a visit once in a while and play like they are lounging back in somebody's living room.

I look up again at Drew Billings who is now leaning with his butt against the dials of the grill. His arms are up in the air and his fingers have snatched the shoulders of the clean white t-shirt he wears when we get to go out and sing our five or so songs between the bands. I watch him slip the shirt off, can't help but notice in the shadows of the kitchen the kind of tight muscles that come naturally to guys who actually work for a living.

"You know Witt used to sing a song that kind of went like that. Girl meets guy in a parking lot. Boyfriend goes around trying to find them to kick the boy's ass."

Witt. Drew is always talking about Witt. It is short for Josh Wittler and, when shortened, the name of the band.

Drew idolizes the band even though they split up a few years ago. Their lead singer went solo, then fell off the map. It doesn't matter to Drew. In his mind, some days he thinks they are all still together and maybe they'll show up at his trailer to strum a few tunes with him.

"I've heard it," I lie. I haven't.

Drew stands there a moment with his shirt half-on and half-off, just covering his arms as if he knows I'm taking him in like this guy named Billy Gentry contentedly, but longingly, squeezes out the last few sips of the one beer Hobie allows him before he plays with his band.

You see, Billy is the singer in the lead band playing on the weekends. Hobie said he used to play with a really big band in Nashville, even got a contract to make an album. He had it all—big house, pretty wife, money. Then Billy started drinking too much, lost his job, lost his wife and a couple girlfriends he had on the side, lost it all. Now, he plays guitar at Hobie's, sneaks one beer after the other when nobody is looking, and growls at everybody over everything.

Whenever Billy comes in the door, he always yowls over at me: "Be a good girl, Ditzy, get me a damn beer and be quick about it." Then he sits on a stool by the stage, tickles his fingers on the guitar to warm up, talks to Hobie and makes little comments about my bleach blonde hair, the shape of my ass, and how useless waitresses and women are. I tell Hobie that he ought to be nice to me and tell Billy Gentry to watch his mouth. One day, I just might get big. I'd be his bread and butter. So Hobie always calls me Bread and Butter to tease me.

Billy always laughs like it's a joke. He keeps an old bat by his drum set just in case a fight breaks out. When he laughs at me, I wish I could pick up that bat and beat him in the knee with it.

When I tell Bailey the Bartender that's what I'd like to do, she always tells me I need to grow some balls and just do it for every woman who has ever been treated like shit by a man. I agree. But I don't do it.

So I'm staring at Drew while he waits for an answer. It isn't that I really have a crush on him or anything. I'm just kind of curious. Robert is built like a big semi-truck. Drew is built like a farm truck. I've always liked the look of farm truck boys better. I just never had a chance to drive one. Robert always seemed to be there, blocking my view of them, never letting me take them out for a test drive.

But not now. Drew tosses off his shirt and grabs his old one up laying across the sink. He grins when he asks me out and he is grinning again now, his eyes twinkling like they do when he is able to hit the right note singing over his grilling hamburgers and not burning them all at once. Hobie's is thirty-two miles from Bacon Valley, but word of my promise to Delbert has already made it up the main highway, down three asphalt county streets that hadn't been paved in fifteen years, two gravel township roads and then across the old railroad tracks to the now defunct town of Coalville.

Drew tosses the towel at me, hits me in the shoulder. "But I would suspect if Robert knew you worked here," Drew shrugged his thin shoulders, scratched the scrubby beard on his chin, "he'd kick *your* ass."

I'm not sure if he is kidding or not. Yeah, he is right. Robert would not approve of me being in this bar, much less singing with a bunch of old drunks looking up my dress while I'm up on the raggedy old stage. There are always fights and once in a while, the beer bottles smash over my head. Hobie's is a greasy old diner/bar in the middle of nowhere. I don't think Robert even knows these types of places exist.

Or if he did, he would drive past them fast with a wary, distant look to his eyes and a foot pressed hard to the accelerator pad.

"You're probably right," I answer, knowing Robert wouldn't really kick my ass. But Drew smiles and he is cute with his dark hair rolling in his eyes.

"You need to grow a set of balls, girl."

"Why does everybody tell me that?" I moan. I hate that saying. It is coarse, sexist, and rude. It is difficult, however, to mumble a quick retort when Drew is teasing me with those eyes of his. Blue eyes, that is, and the kind the girls dancing on the worn wooden floor of the bar ogle over every night. I have to admit when Robert and I are fighting, I sometimes wonder what it would be like to toss my leg over Drew's motorcycle seat behind him, wrap my arms around his waist, and take off in the middle of the night wild and free.

Drew never gives me THE LOOK. He just laughs at the loopy things I say like a child giggles at even the most bungled knock-knock-who-is-there joke. It isn't mean. He thinks it is funny. He has tattoos running down both his arms and a tiny moon-shaped scar on his upper lip. In more than a couple daydreams, I have wondered what it would be like waking up in his arms some morning, tracing the tiny scar with my finger, asking him where he got it. I figure it was a fight over some girl at a bar or something raunchy like that. Maybe his mama threw a beer bottle at him.

Still, Drew is not really my type. It isn't necessarily his bad-boy appearance. He always talks about going south and being a country music star. I like the safe feeling of being embraced by Bacon Valley. I think if anybody has a chance to be famous, it will be him.

He has a voice like all the new pop and country singers have now, even if Hobie doesn't appreciate anything but the old stuff. Drew likes getting up on stage. I don't. I throw up every time after I sing. However, I'm sure he has his suitcases shoved into the closet of his trailer like I have some tucked into the trunk of my car, just waiting for the right moment.

Drew always seems to have some band manager or booking agent in the bar checking him out. Nothing ever seems to pan out, but I think most of them just want free beer. More than likely, like me, he will never go far. I mean, how many good agents ever come to some little poop hole in Ohio? And me, I really hate singing in front of people. Okay, I do it with my dress hiked up at Hobie's Bar on the weekends, wearing old country music star dresses at Billy Wright's Bar and Grille on Tuesdays, and donning a Halloween-made princess outfit at The Great Escapes Family Restaurants on Wednesday weeknights. But there is a reason for this. I want to buy my Knick-Knack Shop.

Still, I get pretty good tips waitressing and on Friday and Saturday, Hobie pays me fifty bucks a night to sing old country songs for an hour with Drew before the real bands show up at eight and ten o'clock. He stands in the dark shadows of the bar with his beefy, freckled arms crossed one over the other. I can see him nodding his thick red head of hair to the beat of the songs. He likes them, says my voice reminds him of the sultry nights he used to sit behind the pig barns with his girlfriend and make out at the Bacon Valley Fair. He closes his eyes on the soft songs I sing and when a truck of beer comes in, me and Drew step it up and get a little wild with the crowd until Hobie comes back in.

"Hey, you okay in there?" Drew interrupts my thoughts.

"Um," I blink, realizing I am staring at Drew while my mind is riding a back road with my forehead pressed to his warm back. My mind gets jammed often. Drew is kind enough not to remind me of it and give it a loving kick like he does his motorcycle when it won't start. He simply reaches out a knuckle and nudges me gently.

"So the rumor is true?" Drew asks me, flipping the towel from hand to hand. "The old man's last request was that you go out with his grandson?"

I groan out loud because I see Drew smirking. He thinks it is funny, a big joke. I can't get mad at him though. He doesn't ever judge me. He never asks why I hide from Robert that I work at Hobie's. Or even why I stick with him. I think Robert and I are just there like the two back to back signs on the road just within the boundaries of Bacon Valley that say: *WELCOME TO FRIENDLY BACON VALLEY, OHIO* facing those coming in *AND HOPE YOU COME BACK SOON, WE'LL MISS YA'* facing those who drive out. We are together and will always be together.

I hear the sound of Billy warming up by the stage, look up and see him wiggling his fingers toward me. "Hey, Ditzy," his mouth forms the words, "get me a cool one, would ya'?"

"You should tell him to go to hell," Drew says. "You're too good to be treated like that."

I roll my eyes. "Why don't you tell him that?" I ask him with a smack of my lips, knowing he won't. "Go ahead, Drew. Hobie will fire your ass like he would fire mine."

Hobie says Billy is an icon, a true hero of what country music used to be back before it turned to pop and rock. He says Billy is probably the only reason this dump even stays open nowadays, folks coming to see an old country music star sing and bring his friends back to play here.

But Drew, he isn't looking at me then. His blue eyes are looking toward the front door and the shadow slipping inside. "I wouldn't worry so much about Hobie, Journey," he says, his voice low. "But I'd keep my eye out on that old guy."

I lean back from the sink, my hands dripping while Drew tosses the dirty towel at me. I catch it half-heartedly and look out through the kitchen door and over the counter and ready myself to get Billy his beer.

Chapter –6

Note to Self: 1) Don't let Pervert Cop Walk me to My Car 2) Drew's Show—Saturday

That 'old guy' coming through the front doors in full uniform is the township police, Andy McGee. I groan, drop my shoulders.

"Smalltalk," I curse the nickname I have given him, blowing out a defeated puff of air from my cheeks. "Officer Smalltalk."

"Yeah, and dammit, I wanted to practice some on our show for this Saturday," Drew bangs the grill with his fist. He looks unnerved and I understand the reason. "You're going to be there, right?"

"Yeah, I promised you." I tell him. "I will."

"Because this is a once-in-a-lifetime for me." Drew is looking at me hard. "I can't do it without you. I am relying on you with my heart and soul. Can you write it on a couple of those little posty notes and stick them to your car windshield?"

"Yes, I already have. I will be there."

On Saturday, he has a couple agents coming in to listen to him sing. Drew has half his family and part of his home town coming to listen and to show he could bring in good crowds. He doesn't want to mess up.

"Journey, we have got to work on this or I'm never going to get out of this shithole."

"Drew, you aren't going to screw it up," I console him. "We sing together twice a week. We got the songs down. Besides, you don't need me. I'm just backup."

"Yeah, I'm not so sure about that, Journey." And he doesn't look so sure while he stares at Officer Andy McGee.

Yet, I don't think it is his singing worrying him right then.

Like clockwork, the Bacon Valley Township police officer comes in every Friday and Saturday night at the exact time I just happen to get off work.

He is a tall man with deep strawberry blonde hair cut short and thick-muscled shoulders. He never says a whole lot, just nods at Hobie whose cheeks take on a certain pasty paleness when the cops come around. Then my boss makes a wide-eyed, nervous double-check around the bar to make sure everybody looks 21 years-old and above. Then he tells me as soon as Smalltalk gets his usual hamburger and fries, my shift is over, and get out of there before the uniformed officer scares everybody off.

I do what Hobie says. Officer Smalltalk won't leave until he walks me to my car, shuts it tight behind me with both hands on the open window. He steps away with arms folded across his chest, waiting for me to leave. He never says much, just asks how I am doing in a gruff, grumpy voice and asks how my shop is going, just small talk. Small Talk. That's the nickname I gave him. Sometimes he leans a little close and tries on a scary, flirty smile. Once he even mentioned he would like to buy me a new dress.

"You be careful of him, girl," Drew mumbles. He wags a finger at me, turns around and walks to the refrigerator at the far side of the room, gets Billy's cold beer and turns his attention to me. Then he shoves it into my hands. "You don't think it's weird the police guy walks you to your car every weekend night?"

I do. He never touches me, though, never tries to ask me out or makes me get into his car. I don't say anything like that to Drew. I just shrug. "I'm not naive. My mama told me about men like that, Drew," I say, taking the plate with a roll of my eyes. "But he seems harmless, right? He's always giving me advice like —"

"How to leave your front door unlocked at night?"

"No, goofy," I tell him. "Like if some pervert jumps in the car with me. I should put my seatbelt on and then drive right into the closest wall."

"That sounds safe."

"He says I would have an airbag and my seatbelt on. The carjacker would go through the windshield." I'm not as stupid as my blonde hair and wide eyes imply. I cannot count on the fingers of my hands the amount of times old fart, pageant judges would make hot whispers in my ear that they would be more than happy to give me a few extra points if I would meet them in their hotel room at night. Besides, I watched a few Saturday afternoon movies on the women's network where they found cute young women dead, duct-taped, and tied up in the trunks of scary, old small town police cars.

I tell Drew that. But I didn't tell him when I was little, Smalltalk's mother used to babysit me when Delilah needed to got to yoga classes and church meetings. Smalltalk used to take me fishing back behind his mama's house, put worms on my pole and talk about fish and tackle boxes and the tools he kept in his garage. I played with the worms or stared at the red and white bobber. I listened to the old Bluegrass music songs he liked sometimes and let my bare toes dabble in the water. Then he took me for a can of soda at the gas station and we added it to a little cup of the ice cream he dug out of the freezer at the store to make it into a root beer float. He did this until I was fifteen and Delilah said I was too old for a man to take me behind his mama's house alone. I miss sorting out the stuff in his tackle box, asking Smalltalk what this lure was and why he didn't get lead poisoning when he bit down on the little sinkers to tighten them on the line.

"Did she tell you about men like me?" Drew jokes.

I turn. "Uh huh," I say back to him. "That's why I'm thinking about going out with you. Maybe I just will. We'll take off one day, never come back." Then I wink, start away.

"You know, Journey Dawn, you sound like a young Mary Dixon."

I stop, tip my head. "Who is that?" I figure she is some singer I don't know. I listen to the radio a lot in the background at the shop. I am never interested in the names that go with the songs.

"Exactly," Drew answers to my back. I turn, give him a questioning stare.

"I don't get it. I asked who she was."

"And that's what I'm telling you. She's a nobody, never went anywhere," Drew wiggles the spatula in his hand, pretends to play it like a guitar. "She had one song that made it to the country music charts back in the 1950s, then just faded away to nothing. She could have been great. Her voice was just like yours—soft and sweet and strong all at once. It strokes a man inside—" he stops like he is going to say more. I am surprised he even says as much as he does. "You're just too good to be in a place like this singing songs to a bunch of old, horny drunk guys."

I look him straight in the eye, tell him the truth. "I kind of like singing to a bunch of old, horny drunk guys. After six or seven beers, they tell me I look like Marilyn Monroe before she went on drugs and I sing like Patsy Cline before she died. It makes me feel good."

Drew just stares at me a minute with a funny look on his face. "I'm not joking, Journey," he says, but shrugs and smiles. "So does it make you feel good when they puke all over your feet while you're serving them beer?" he retorts.

Drew is quick. That's another reason I think he's got what it takes to make it as a musician.

I laugh. "I'm here, aren't I?" I answer. "It's what I've got."

I hear Hobie clear his throat, look across the bar to where he is nodding at the police officer. Before I clear the door, though, Drew's voice flows over the gentle roar of the freezer in back.

"I could take you away. To *there*, you know."

There. I was pretty sure I know where he was talking about. It was anywhere but here and maybe another shitty bar a couple states over. Or maybe it was having five songs on the radio. This time I don't stop, just step out to the bar with Smalltalk's hamburger plate in one hand and Billy's cold beer in the other wondering, in the back of my mind, if I want to be *here* at all.

Twenty minutes later, Smalltalk dusts off the last of the hamburger bun from his mouth, wiggles his Smokey Bear hat on his head. The way he is staring at me, I wonder if he wants to take me in the back of his police cruiser right then. He nods to Hobie. It seems to be the custom between the two. Hobie is swiping off the bar with one of his musty-smelling washrags and bobs his head up and down in return.

"Time to go, Bread and Butter," he mutters to me in a gruff, soft voice when I pass. Then he wags a finger at me, leans in a little close. His breath smells like stale beer and cigarettes. "Birth certificate. Journey Dawn, you've promised me sixteen times you'll get me a copy." I am rounding the bend with a tray full of empty beer bottles juggling in my right hand and my own sticky washcloth in the other. I bob my head up and down like I have the last sixteen times he has asked me for it. The twenty times before that, he told me he needed my driver's license.

"I'll get it. I told you I would."

"You'll get it by next Tuesday or you're not picking up tips next week or going onstage with your boyfriend on Friday."

"Aw, c'mon, Hobie," I whine. "For one thing, Drew's not my boyfriend. Two, I have tried six times to get my birth certificate uptown. They can't find it. I'm over twenty-one. Everybody knows that."

"Well, you look fourteen. So, you heard what I said," Hobie grunts. "Now get your scrawny little ass out of here."

I am getting a jumpy feeling in my belly like Hobie and Smalltalk have a secret between the two along with a drawer of duct tape and an empty car trunk. I feel like ol' Hobie is my old man handing off his little girl to be a child bride to his old friend. Then maybe, he gets seconds.

"I'm going to miss a bunch of tips," I gripe to Hobie. "Cripes, you act like I'm twelve." But he shakes his head and Bailey the Bartender who helps him serve drinks takes the tray from my hands. Maybe she is in on the kidnapping too.

I groan and wiggle a bit of crinkled receipt out of my pocket. I have jotted down a couple words for a song while I was passing out beers. I take it and slip it into Drew's back pocket. "Oh, my God, you've got to quit this, girl," he tells me. "You right me these notes and my girlfriend thinks I'm screwing around with another woman."

She's a rebel child. Daddy's little girl gone wild.
Sweet 16. Small town. Gonna take some poor redneck
boy down. Down, down, gonna go down tonight.
No fears. It's alright.
Gonna get him without much fight.

I get my usual escort to the car. Halfway there Smalltalk, who is walking one step behind me, takes a step forward and pushes out a hand and stops me in my tracks.

The moment he does this, I feel my face flush. The officer carries a black baton at his belt beside his gun. I can almost hear him slip it from his place and bring it up in his hand before he clobbers me hard enough on the head to knock me out, but not enough to kill me. I saw this on TV the other night, too. Officer McGee doesn't seem like the type who would want to desecrate a cold corpse. He is more the abduction type. He will kill me after he and Hobie pass me around a bit.

I stop in my tracks, feel my heart beating hard while I turn to look up at the police officer. He isn't holding a baton, instead something white in his hands. "First, you should carry this on you at all times." He hands me a little metal container. I don't have my glasses so I squint at it. ECONO-SIZE BEAR AWARE BEAR REPELLENT, it says on it. I look up. "What? Are there bears here?"

His eyes work upwards like I have said something utterly stupid. "No, this is in case I get a call and cannot walk you to your vehicle." Smalltalk pokes a finger at the bottle. "It is protection from humans too. Men who might be drunk and follow you out to the parking lot. I have found this works a little better than the standard pepper spray on humans. You just pull the little safety here and aim for the eyes and nose. You might get some on you. It makes it hard to breathe and see. Just wait it out, run as fast as you can. Better not leave things up to chance. "

"Oh." I nod, repeat his saying. "Better not leave things up to chance. My mother always says that."

He tells me to put it in my purse, keep it handy so I am prepared. I absently stick it in the center pocket.
The bottle is big and bulky.

"And second. Here," he says, thrusting a white envelope toward my belly. I look up at him and then down to the envelope. "Open it up," he demands.

I figure he has a traffic ticket in his hands. I passed him doing sixty-eight in a fifty-five zone last Tuesday. Or it could be a request to find one of the little scout pins he collects. My heart is still racing and I'm wondering if perhaps it is some sort of poison on the envelope that will put me to sleep. Still I take the envelope in my hands and flip up the lip. Inside, I can see a wad of money an inch thick— tens, twenties and fifties.

"What—what is this?" I ask. I never really address him by any name. I'm not sure what to call him. Police Officer Smalltalk? Mister McGee? When I was little and he would come in and talk about avoiding drugs in middle school, we used to call him Officer Andy, so I finish with that: "So what is this, Officer Andy?"

He kind of smiles funny when I call him this, then pokes a finger at the envelope. "I was thinking maybe instead of waitressing here on Friday nights, you and me, we could hook up— together."

Hook up? Together? I just stand there, feeling a little tingle slip over my lips, my temple. "Hook up?" I ask, my eyes darting upward. Oh, God, he heard about the dance card and Delbert and the nineteen dates. Or maybe he had come in last Friday when Hobie had gone out to get an order of meat from the Don's Steaks truck. I had done a silly dance with the pole on the bar while I sang for extra tips.

"Yeah, maybe you could use that to help fix up your shop and we could do things—together. Just you and me." He stops, cocks his head to one side, and gets a little grin on his face while he winks. "Hook up? It's the right word you kids use today?"

Holy shit. "Oh," I say with dry lips. My heart starts pounding a pulpy beat. I'm thinking I just might have to reach in my purse and grab out that bear spray or maybe he is just giving it to me to make me feel safe.

Maybe there isn't really even anything in the container.

I wonder if he would give a wave to Hobie, have him reach into the drawer in the back room, and grab up the silver duct tape. Or maybe the police officer will start giving me tickets and taking me down to some dark jail cell on Friday nights if I don't *hook up* with him.

"I really loved watching your mama sing back in the day," he says a bit shyly like he is a first date waiting for a kiss. "I loved to hear her sing, Journey Dawn, loved to watch her sing. You're just like her, aren't you? You remind me so much of her, it makes me ache."

And I imagine where it makes him ache. I feel my belly lurch. No. No, I am not. I am not anything like my mother, hanging out with boys at the festivals, flirting with the judges, trying to find some old man to make me a millionaire. I work at the bar so I can sing, so I can get some extra money for rent.

"Oh, no, I don't do that," I mutter in a huffed breath. My eyes must have been wide because his mirror my own when I trip backward and nearly fall on my rear. I shove the envelope back at him and set my eyes to my car, my feet pounding pretty hard on the gravel parking lot.

My face is burning hot and my hands are shaking. I decide to take the chance and just put Smalltalk on my list of people to avoid like Bella Johnson and Brody Wells. But I can hear Smalltalk yelling behind me to stop. I just don't listen and he doesn't pull me over on the way home.

Chapter −7

Note to Self: 1) Send thank you note to John Wells for changing my tire.
2) Find out if mom is right if I cross my eyes they will stick that way

I find stuff. It is my job. I have to say I'm pretty good at it as long as I keep a hundred little Post-It notes with reminders on them. When my mom first started harassing me about finding a real job instead of running my antique shop, I went down to fill out an application at the local real estate office. I drew a blank when asked on the application to state my current employment. I put in *shop owner* first. I erased that because it didn't sound important enough. So then I wrote in *self employed.* I think I about rubbed the eraser end of the pencil off with ideas before I finally just wrote in FIND STUFF in big letters.

When I got to the interview, Janice Long who ran Bacon Valley Real Estate asked me what I meant. She looked bored and detached beneath her fake smile when I told her I was just good at finding things for people. She poked her blonde hair back behind her ear and nodded a bland 'oh, uh huh' like she didn't care in the least and looked over my shoulder and out the window.

It was a sunny eighty-five degrees outside and I knew she would rather be bronzing her too-tan skin in her above ground pool right then. So I pointed a finger at the little fair -haired, 1962 Missy Me Baby Doll she had plunked on a cherry wood shelf.

"I can find the male counterpart to that 1962 Missy Me doll. It is mint condition and has the original clothing and included golf club set that came out in February of that year, I have seen them go for up to seven-hundred dollars.

I have a business contact that may be able to get it for about two-hundred and eighty bucks."

I looked from the doll to Janice Long who had stopped mid-swipe of the hair above her right ear. She narrowed her gaze at me, trying to look cool. I could read the anxiousness in a quiver of her fingers. Because along with being good at finding stuff, I could also read the desire of a person for wanting what I could find.

Her little finger quivered with anticipation. Janice Long wanted the doll a lot. "Okay, you say you can find stuff," she said coolly. "I figure if you can *find* that doll for me for a reasonable price we can agree upon, you might be good at *finding* houses for prospective customers. If you get me the doll for less than three-hundred, you've got the job."

I did not take the job, but I got Janice the doll for two -hundred and forty dollars. It seems everybody in the real estate office heard about the doll and one by one, they each have something they need found from old baseball cards and collectible spoons to miniature die-cast cars and expensive tarnished silver coins off old pirate ships. Word got around the town. When somebody needed something old or lost or collectible, they came to me to locate it. I have not failed yet. Well, almost.

As luck would have it, the one thing I have never been able to locate is the one thing everyone seems to require to confirm my very existence—my birth certificate. It is just a piece of paper, but not even my own mother has been able to exhibit the original document.

"Delilah, I need a copy of my birth certificate." I finally work up the nerve to ask her about it a week after the funeral. But she skirts my question as only Delilah can do. I hear nothing but silence on the other end of the line for twenty seconds.

Then she says this: "When were you going to tell me about Delbert Johnson's last request, Journey Dawn?"

It seems everybody in town knows about Delbert Johnson's last words. And my mother is no exception. She actually found it posted on the church Facebook page when she was checking the Bacon Valley Women's Society North Coast Ohio Winery/Autumn Leaf Tour itinerary.

I can almost hear Delilah blinking hard on the other end of the phone, her thick mascara clacking together with the upraised brow. It is what she does when someone annoys her. "Now, look what you've done, sweetie. Call that lovely boyfriend of yours and let him know you won't go through with such a silly notion. I'm sure he's heard about it. And with, of all people, that miscreant of a boy, Brody who burned down his poor father's farm—by the way, what are you doing home so late?"

"Okay, first of all," I groan. I cross my eyes, an old habit I've done since I was two years-old whenever she irritates me. "What you read online or heard from your friends is not really the whole story. Delbert Johnson just *requested* I date someone else before I got married. I really don't think he expected me to follow through."

"That Wells boy has a child. Isn't he married? Are you crossing your eyes at me over the phone? Because your eyes will stick like that, you know."

"No, Delilah, I am not crossing my eyes," I lie. I wonder if my eyes will really stick that way. "You do know people don't have to be married to have babies, don't you, *mother*? Oh, that's right. You weren't married when you had me with *the idiot*." Oh, double whammy with a gut kick by calling her *mother*. She says nothing. Then I change the subject, tell her I had a flat tire on the way home. There is silence again.

"Did you call one of the Belcher boys from the garage to change it?" she asks me. "I didn't get a call from them to add it to my bill."

No, she had not. I did not need to call Belcher Auto Service at all. It had started storming just past the Pump and Dump Gas Station on the outskirts of town on my way home from the funeral. The Pump and Dump is a little gas station and RV septic dump station right outside the city park and campground.

The rain was streaming down buckets on the windshield while I pressed my face toward the glass. I tried to see past the scummy smear left on the windshield by the worn out wipers. If it wasn't for the old wipers, I would have seen the piece of muffler dropped off the bottom of the pickup in front of me. I didn't.

My passenger-side tire had made a loud pop and deflated until it was making a thump-thump-thump all the way to the curb. I had started crying long before I started to dig the spare tire out of the trunk. I was sobbing by the time I dragged my guitar and three suitcases out of the back of my car, an old aluminum milk crate of baseballs I had bought off a guy at a flea market, and a bag of clothes I needed to take to my mom's to wash. I laid them on the wet asphalt.

I managed to get the jack under the car. However, my palms were wet and the handle kept slipping. Five times, I texted Robert. He didn't answer. About five minutes of grunting over the tire, I started kicking it. I hadn't heard the truck pull up behind me. Suddenly, John Wells and his son, Brody, were standing next to me.

Brody shoved a wet umbrella in my hand, didn't say anything about me crossing my eyes trying to see past the water streaming down my black veil.

"Hold this up." Meanwhile, he and his father battled with the tire at my feet. Water was streaming down Brody's hair, rivulets making tiny droplets along the bridge of his freckled nose.

I had done as he said, holding it over their matching red-blonde heads, listened to them grunt and make small talk while their Sunday best suits and trousers were doused in muddy street water.

When Robert finally called, he was halfway through lunch with Andrea at the restaurant in town. I was sopping wet and ankle-deep in a puddle. I knew he was digging his fork into his hamburger which he always eats with a knife and fork like it's a steak. I hear the ting-ting the fork tongs make when they hit the bottom of the plate. I could hear Andrea laughing and talking through a mouthful of salad in the background. Robert offered to call a tow truck. I declined.

John Wells nodded sternly when they were finished. Brody had stared at me without a trace of expression on his perfect face.

"Help her put her stuff back in the trunk, son." He got up and made a half-hearted attempt to swipe the fresh layer of water streaming down his cheeks with one hand. Their white shirts were smattered with the gritty splashes of the kind of smooshed up asphalt they have on the country roads here, a tar and pebble mixture that falls away like two day old apple pie crust after six months or so.

I had muttered a sob-huff thank you, saw Brody Wells look up at me and shake his head like he had just thrown a half-dead catfish back into the creek. "You flipped me off in front of a hundred people, church girl, and at my grandpa's funeral," he muttered. "I think you had it coming to you."

Brody looked upward toward the thick gray clouds over our heads like he was staring toward the heavens and thanking God for answering a prayer that he had probably made against me when I flipped him off. *Dear God, I know it sounds bad, but please let her have a flat tire on her car when she leaves. She is such a bitch.* And still, all I'm thinking is that he had the bluest eyes I'd ever seen on anybody. They were like chlorinated swimming pool water before it turns green in late summer.

"I told Dad to keep driving on past just so you know." He grunted something else, walked to the back of the car, snatched up the suitcases.

"Heading out of town soon?" he grunted. For some reason, the moment I caught his hard gaze, I knew Brody had heard about Delbert's last request. He looked insulted, like he thought I was leaving town because of his grandpa's request and by God, he was far too good for that. There was a heart-sinking feeling in my chest. There was no way in hell I was going to go out with Brody Wells.

"—Journey, are you there?" Delilah interrupts my thoughts. "Did you call Belchers?"

"No, Mom, John Wells stopped in his suit and tie and jacked off on the tires."

"*Jacked off on the tires?*" she repeats. "Oh, my God, Journey Dawn, I hope you didn't say that to anyone else. Don't say that," she gasps into the phone. I know I am getting THE LOOK on the other end of the phone. "If things could go wrong for you, they would go wrong." She always tells me that. I think those words are her motto for me.

"The apple doesn't fall far from the tree," I spit back. "Isn't that what you always tell me?" But by then, I am already shamed out of begging her to dig my birth certificate out of some box in the attic.

Chapter −8

Note to Self: Pick up Birth Certificate and Get Blackmailed by Zach Metzler

So it is three-thirty in the afternoon when I trudge over to city offices for the fifth time this year. I am hoping I can sweet-talk someone in the Clerical Documents Office to dig out my birth certificate so I can keep my job at the bar.

It is a big stone building with a clock tower on Main Street and two blocks from my shop. Over the last two weeks, I have spent more time inside the stuffy-smelling building than I would prefer. Over the last few years, the city has cut back. All of the agencies inside are combined into three different departments and run by just a few people. This is unfortunate for me because Dottie Brubaker and Zach Metzler are the two staff persons who oversee the Clerical Documents branch having to do with the health department, marriage licenses, and birth certificates.

Dottie Brubaker is a stoic woman in her late sixties with pinched lips, a searing gaze, and a bitter attitude because she would rather be sipping cocktails on a beach in Honolulu with her 40 year-old lover. I know the latter because she has six huge calendars of Hawaii on the walls above her desk and she has Scotch-taped pictures of well-muscled young men to each of them.

Dottie also sings soprano in the choir at the Valley View Church on the northern side of town and takes the job seriously. Delilah sings soprano in the choir at Bacon Valley United Church. The Christmas eve of 1997, the two churches combined for a midnight service and there was a bit of a tussle over who would be the keynote soprano. Delilah was chosen. Since then there has been a coolness between the two which has flooded over to me.

This is actually only secondary compared with the fact Zach Metzler has been the best friend of Brody Wells since high school. Zach loves nothing better than giving me a hard time whenever I come in the door.

"*Ba—con!*" he says when I come through the doors, drawing it out like my last name is two words.

"Metzler," I say back, but my voice is flat. I would like to say I could describe Zach in three words—annoying, pudgy, and immature. I know everybody felt sorry for him because his dad was really rough on him. Sometimes, he came to school with bruises. I felt no sorrow for him. He picked on me way too much.

"So—" he starts off, dropping his voice low and looking back to where Dottie is bent over her computer keyboard and poking each key with the forefinger of her right hand. He snaps his gaze back and watches me come to a stop at the wooden counter between us.

"I hear you and my best friend are getting married, huh?" He actually reaches out over the counter between us and pokes me in the shoulder. "Ha ha! Guess who I heard that from."

"No," I say. I am jabbing the counter with one finger. "I won't. I just need my birth certificate like you promised me three weeks ago, then two weeks ago and last week."

"I heard it from Ashley Walters, that's who."

Ashley Walters used to hang around Brody and his gang. I think Brody had a mild crush on her although he dated her best friend, Kylee Thurston. Brody used to walk around school with his arms around both girls like some slumlord gigolo toting around his favorite prostitutes. It didn't surprise me Ashley was passing around gossip. She knew every scandal, every juicy piece of hearsay hovering around the dark nooks and crannies of Bacon Valley.

If she didn't have any sleazy chitchat to pass around on any particular day of the week, she would make something up.

"Ashley Walters is the same girl who told everybody somebody exchanged hair remover for my shampoo in the gym showers and my hair fell out. I never took a shower after gym class, much less washed my hair there," I say. Already, my voice is getting angry.

"Yeah, because people like you don't sweat?" he asks me sarcastically. Then he shakes his shoulders like he is shoving his words aside. "So when are you two setting the date?" He wiggles his eyebrows. "Because if I was you, I'd do it quick. Kylee Thurston's been calling him every ten minutes. In fact, they went out last night."

I stare at him long and hard. I can feel a stress headache coming on. "Stop. Please." I have two days to get the birth certificate or I am going to lose my job and he thinks it is funny. So I tell him that.

"It is so much fun to watch you squirm." He sits back, looks pleased with himself.

I ignore him. He has watched me squirm from fourth grade through high school while he and his best friend picked on me.

"Listen, if you do not get me my birth certificate, I will march right down to your supervisor and tell her you are offensive and threatening. It is my right to have it. I want it now, you idiot."

"My supervisor is three steps away and listening to every word you say, Miss Bacon." Zach looks smug with a condescending tip to his chin while he leans back and taps his finger on the counter. He turns his head slightly, looks at the woman sitting at the desk behind him. "Dottie, she called me an idiot. Did you hear that?"

"I did." Dottie looks up with a warning gaze. "Should I call security and have her escorted from the building?"

I could feel my blood pressure rising, feel an ache just above my temple.

"Journey, I told you we are working on it." Zach looks quite pleased he has backup and I don't. I wish I had Robert here right now. He would put a stop to their bullying. But I can't ask Robert to help. I would have to explain why I needed the birth certificate, including having to divulge I worked at a bar. I think his head would explode.

"Listen, Zach," I hiss. "I need my birth certificate. I know it isn't that difficult to get one. I have seen people come in and out while I am in line and have a birth certificate in two minutes. I tried two years ago and I got the same answer. My mother had to use a hospital certificate so I could get my driver's license. Why is it so difficult for you to come up with it?"

"Maybe your mother needs to come in and supply us with more information."

I stop, close my eyes, grit my teeth. "I am over eighteen. I do not need my mother to obtain my birth certificate. Why are you doing this?" I ask, my hands coming out to my sides. "Do you give everyone who walks in here a difficult time?"

"Young lady," Dottie snips, "if you want to be waited on courteously, you need to keep your voice down or I will have to ask you to leave."

I couldn't tell him I didn't want my mother to know I was working at Hobie's. But I had to. The odds are slim to none he would have any interaction with my mother. The odds were good I would get fired if I didn't supply the birth certificate.

"I need it for a job."

"You can use your driver's license."

"No, I can't," I tell him. "Because I lost it. And the license bureau is now requiring my birth certificate to get a copy."

"That's not true." He shook his head.

Did he really think his office had the monopoly on giving me a difficult time?

"Okay," I mutter between clenched teeth. I don't realize it, but my hands are on my head in infuriation. "What is it going to take to get a copy of my birth certificate?" Then I let a little air flow out of my lips, start to turn. Obviously, I am going to have to drive to Mexico and get a fake driver's license and birth certificate. "Hey, wait!" It is like a light goes off in Zach's chubby little head. Ping! He gets a sly smile and taps a forefinger on the counter. Then he leans in. But he's giggling to himself, stifling a bit of laughter and getting a dirty look from Dottie. He wiggles his finger at me, enticing me forward.

"What?"

"I might be able to dig something up."

"Uh huh?" I ask warily.

"Uh huh," he answers. "I have waited years for this," he tells me. He leans up on the counter, rests his elbows on the top. His voice drops low and I can barely hear it over Dottie's tap, tap, tapping on the keyboard. She picks up a pair of old-fashioned ear phones and plugs it into an outdated boom box. "I have waited so long to have something over on you so I can return a favor."

"That is probably illegal considering you are a public servant." I heave a sigh.

"We prefer to call ourselves public service employees. And yes, it probably is —improper," he answers. "But who is gonna tell on me, you?"

"I could."

"How badly do you want your birth certificate?"

I glare at him. He glares back.

"Journey Bacon, queen of the bitches, I have waited a long time to settle a score with you."

I should have been taken aback. I'm not. It is not the first time Zach Metzler, Brody Wells and his posse of friends and family have tossed those words in my face.

"What score is this?" I ask him dully. "I really thought we were even when you and Cowboy nearly gave me a heart attack at his grandpa's old farm." I feign a look at a watch that is not on my wrist. "Make it quick. I would like to grab a quick lunch after my blackmail."

"Um, that was almost enough." He looks to the ceiling as if recalling the moment and sighs contentedly. "But no, I think you know that little trick was not even close to the one you did."

"I think I *don't* know, Metzler." I shake my head, finger a tendril of hair laying on my shoulder. But I know exactly what he is talking about while I bring my hair over and nibble it between my lips. He holds up both hands, touches his forefingers and thumbs together to form a jagged heart-shape. "Does this help?" he spats at me. "Do the words: 'code-word-heart' ring a bell?"

And for just a wisp of a moment, I am taken back to a place both awkward and heart-wrenching. Where even now, the burnt-electric scent of a copy machine or newly-inked printer warming up will make my eyes get teary and my tummy ache. Because that was where my locker was in twelfth grade, next to the office where Patty Mills, school secretary, ran a million copies a day.

After all the copies, the entire hallway outside her office smelled like an old burnt-down house. On the day a skinny seventeen year-old boy was standing there with a red teddy bear with a heart in its paws, Miss Mills had run four-hundred and twelve copies of the Bacon Valley High School newspaper. The copy machine was smoking when she came outside to fan some of it in the hallway.

I had been tardy and just signed in at the office, ducked under her arm in just enough time for Brody Wells to stuff the bear in my arms and mumble something about liking me too. The joke was supposed to be on me. Brody was just collateral damage.

I stood there while people started laughing in the hallways. I thought at first, he was making fun of me like he usually did. I started to laugh too. It wasn't funny. I just learned early on in my pageant days that crying and running off the stage when I fell on my ass during a routine didn't get me points with the judges. But a smile and a wink could at least dig me out of a hole. So I did just that. It was at the wrong person, Robert, who was dating my best friend, Andrea. I found out two days later, the two had orchestrated this whole prank with tiny, secret love notes in Brody's locker that were allegedly from me. They kept holding up their hands making a heart when they passed each other, a secret language they had made up as they planned it: code-word-heart. I had thought it was just some silly display of telling each other I love you. Of course, the principal thought I was the mastermind behind the prank because the little notes all appeared to be signed by me.

"I think getting suspended from school for two days was enough justice," I mutter, feeling my tummy gurgle.

"I want you to ask Brody out. Just like his grandpa asked you to do," Zach said straight out. "You're going to walk right up to him and right in front of everybody, you're going to ask him out."

"Not happening," I say, hands out, pushing the words away. "I have a boyfriend and when he finds out I asked Brody out, he'll go berserk. Brody'll make me feel like an idiot turning me down and you all will make a joke of it."

"Alright." Zach just shrugs. "I'll let it rest. But who knows how long it will take for us to get that birth certificate? Might be months, might be years."

"So if I ask Brody out in front of a bunch of his friends and you all get a big laugh out of it, you'll figure out where my birth certificate is?"

"Yeah," Zach agrees. I can't see him. But I know he is grinning behind me. I nod my head. And I leave.

Chapter −9

Note to Self: Work at Great Escapes 6:00 Don't Freak Out Because Zach shows up with half of Bacon Valley

Still—it wasn't the promise to a dying man's ears landing me in front of Table 8 at Great Escapes Family Restaurants with pencil and order pad, wearing my too-pink and too-puffy twelfth grade prom dress as Princess Scarletta Rose and trying to avoid eye contact with Brody Wells.

"Hey, you've got a special request," another waitress named Summer Adams tells me four minutes earlier while she pokes a pencil in the air to a dark corner of the room.

I can barely hear her over the noise of people laughing and talking, plates banging and kids loudly playing the video games in the recreation room. It is raining out tonight and so it is packed with everybody who had outside plans and had to move somewhere inside. Summer is only about two years older than me. She dyes her hair pitch black and pencils-in her eyebrows. She has this dark look and I think some of the daddy's choose her to serve their family's booth because they have some inner fantasy about taming the wicked witch in all the story tales.

"Little girl's birthday," she goes on. "The uncle said he wanted the skinny bleach-blonde Barbie in the ugly pink bridesmaid dress. The little girl's name is Cayce. The uncle ordered a Daddy-Daughter Number 3."

A Daddy-Daughter Number 3. I groan inwardly. A Number 3 was three pizzas, eight drinks and a small, $9.99 pre-dressed generic doll from a shop called the Great Escapes Dream Doll Room holding dolls and the owner's wife's own doll clothing line.

Girls could choose from twenty-seven different dolls, depending upon how much daddy could afford, and a wide array of princess outfits to suit the mood of the daughter.

It also includes one three-minute waltz on the dance floor with the daddy, a bizarre inspiration by the owner of the restaurant forty years ago that never faded away. While daddy is ambushed with a dance with the princess, another server escorts daddy's little girl to the Great Escapes Doll room to pick out her doll, and hopefully talk her into something much larger than daddy's pocket can probably afford. Of course, we accept credit cards.

Still, I usually got a good tip on the Daddy-Daughter's. So I chuck away the inward moan and exchange it for a mental image of me someday paying off the Knick-Knack Shop. I nod reluctantly, eyes working toward the wall Summer had pointed out. Then it hits me like a brick to glass. I can see Zach Metzler scooting around the table.

"You can't take it?" I ask Summer hastily, knowing there really is no chance I'm getting out of this one. I assumed Zach was going to corner me at the coffee shop in town for his blackmail. I never expected him to make me eat my part of our date-versus-birth certificate bargain at Great Escapes Restaurant. However, there he is doling out the chairs to friends and family right before my eyes.

There is a large wooden booth with two tables added on, seating for twenty-two. They have added another chair on the end to make it twenty-three. In the chair is plopped Brody's little girl who is propped up with a plastic booster seat. A red-checkered tablecloth dons the booth. Cayce is wearing a pink diamond birthday tiara. There are leftover cups and plates from the last party sitting there. All the seats are filled with the under-thirty crowd of the Johnson and Wells clan.

Suddenly my stomach twists remembering the walk-throughs I used to make in my tight, itchy fair queen attire through the barn stalls. Me in my high heels, puffy dress and thick makeup buttered with sweat that soaked in the wood shaving dust everybody kicked up from the stalls.

It was tradition for me to pass out the placement ribbons for the Bacon Valley Fair doled out to me by the fair board. When I got to the piggy and cow barn, it was filled with the same crowd that is assembled at Table 8 in the Great Escapes Family Restaurant now. It was so humbling in that stinky barn to take in their muffled clucks, hoots, and wolf whistles while they lounged against the pens in their comfortable old shorts and t-shirts and the big barn fans blowing at them. All the while, I had to stand there with a smile plastered to my face and crisp taffeta dress stuck awkwardly to my sweaty, dusty-covered flesh.

I can see Zach looking at us, his hand waving me over, his mouth making the kind of haughty smirk only seen on evil comic book villains.

"Excuse me, miss," he is mouthing while his finger dips down to point out the leftover plates and pizza pan, "this is not our food. We need our table cleaned, pronto. The candles aren't even lit." It is almost all adults at his table, except Brody's little girl and two pudgy little boys fighting over a seat. I don't want to tell him we're not allowed to light candles at the tables with kids under ten. I'm scared he's going to complain. I smile stiffly at him, then turn to beg Summer with my eyes. "I'm begging you," I plead with her. "I've got six tables and I've got to sing the princess birthday song for Table 3."

"Not on your life," Summer holds up her hands, feigns me away. "I get off in an hour."

I wish I had never told Zach I would ask Brody out. I mean, I know it is only going to be three minutes of humiliation while he torments me with one of his arrogant, self-righteous half-grins. He will probably blurt out a loud *Not on your life, Piece of Bacon* while his friends laugh at me and the other customers give us curious gazes. Perhaps there will be an excruciatingly long pause before and after, adding another thirty or forty seconds.

Then, I have to finish serving them. They'll make fun of my old stutter, my dress, my hair. It seemed much easier when I was still hearing the echo of Hobie's voice yelling in my ear and was desperate to get my birth certificate while standing in the cramped Bacon Valley Clerical Documents Office feeling like a Chihuahua caught between a big Rottweiler and a couple beagles. Now, it isn't so simple.

Still, I muster up my courage and just as I'm getting to the table, I see Brody Wells snapping his head up and his eyes meet with mine. I could have come over to the table completely naked and gotten the same surprised reaction, I think. Stunned. Horrified? I can only think of myself extending my middle finger at the funeral. I can only see his lips, that day, upturned like he had come upon a skunk lying dead and bloated on a hot asphalt road.

It is only for a second, but his baby blues open wide with a shocked, knee jerk reaction. Boom, then it is gone. His gaze skims away. I watch him mumble something to the girl sitting next to him and I realize this is Kylee Thurston who he dated in high school. She is still skinny and cute, wearing a pink t-shirt and tight blue jeans. Her hair is longer, but her eyes still hold distaste towards me. *Oh-my-God, can things get worse?* Kylee scoots closer to Brody's little girl who leans away hard from her.

At the moment, I just want to run and know I can't. I have to go up and clear away the napkins and dirty plates.

I snatch up the matches near the candle by Brody and his daughter. I see everyone look at me. I don't know why until it gets suddenly quiet. *Matches. Fire. Barn.* It looks like I am taking them away from him. I watch Brody say something to his daughter, get up, leave the table. He heads toward the restrooms. I hear Zach somewhere near the center of the booth complaining about the tabletop being sticky.

"Wow, so this is what happens to prom queens after high school?" I hear Kylee say to Ashley Walters who is sitting to her left. It is loud enough for me to hear. I vaguely remember Ashley. She has darker blonde hair and eyes that turn up at the corners like an elf. She twirled baton and played in the band. Both of them laugh and the soft giggles of those near enough to hear the remark echo around the table. My face burns. I know they can see the two big apple red circles on my cheeks. They all seem surprised to see me here, maybe a bit full of themselves that I was the one scooping up the dirty pizza pan and piling it with the pizza-encrusted plates and glasses. I feel humbled. It isn't anything new. I know this is just like whip cream on a sundae to Zach who would love to reduce me as low as he could. I'm not sure you can get much lower than cleaning up somebody else's mess. So I ignore them and I scurry off to the kitchen and drop the plates into the sink.

I supposed at the moment I walk back out of the kitchen with a cloth to wipe the tables in my hand, I have already decided I don't need my birth certificate that much. Drew's worried eyes keep coming back to haunt me, though, along with the guilt. If I don't get my birth certificate, Hobie is not going to let me sing next Saturday. I have promised Drew for six months I will be there for him.

That was when I see Brody Wells coming toward me, his steps hard and heavy on the flowered maroon carpet. His arms are held tensely at his side. One is tapping six times on his knee over and over. I feel my heart racing, feel the adrenaline pouring into my wrists. I realize he scares the crap out of me like step-daddy did. He looks mad, maybe. I don't know. He stops two steps away and tips his chin upward.

"Alright, what's going on?" he throws at me. He has a suspicious furrow to his brow and I'm caught off-guard by how deep his voice is now. I just stand there a minute, the tepid washcloth dangling from my hand, thinking about step-daddy.

I usually like stormy days because it rained the morning my step-daddy left. He was Delilah's only husband and I don't remember much about him. I always try to push him out of my head when somebody like Brody Wells angrily stomping toward me sets it off. Sometimes, though, on the nights I can't sleep, his image pops uninvited to my head—a clenched-teeth smile, the stomp of footsteps when he walked my direction and his arms held tense at his sides.

What I do recall the day he left was peering out the window at the police car sitting in our asphalt driveway. I was only seven. And I don't remember much else about being seven except for being scared all the time. And feeling little welts of hurt that would show up black and blue in places my teachers wouldn't see like where he would snatch my shoulder and dig his nails in deep. They were always places Delilah would think I had fallen off my bike or bumped my shoulder on a door.

When step-daddy left, rain had pattered on the window. I had used my fingers to push away the condensation on the inside and watched a fuzzy policeman escorting a fuzzy step-daddy to his car.

Maybe I was too little to really imagine the old rain had washed away the scared I always got when step-daddy was around. The day he left, I still had a little brown and green bruise where his fingernails had bitten in two days earlier around the back of my neck when I was too loud coming down the stairway.

I had touched the bruise softly with my finger where it was hidden beneath my hair. Well, almost hidden. Missus McGee was babysitting me while Delilah and step-daddy went to the movies. She saw it when she started to braid my hair.

"Why didn't you tell me he was hurting you, Journey Dawn?" Delilah had asked me while she stood at the window staring out at the cars driving away. I imagine now it must have been a hard pill to swallow hearing it from the babysitter. Back then, I didn't turn and I didn't answer her, just shrugged liked kids do when they don't know. Because I didn't know. I suppose inside I thought she would be mad at me for saying something to make him have to leave.

"Well, he is gone now," she told me with the same lackadaisical tone she used when she told me it was time for bed. "He won't be coming back. Missus McGee's son, is escorting him out of town with his cruiser. But it won't be Andy who will shoot him if he comes knocking on the door," she went on. I turned around thinking she would be mad at me. "It will be me." She smiled, instead. But I saw she was smudging the tears away from her mascara-stained eyes with a Kleenex. It was right then, I felt the rain wash him away.

While I stand there realizing my hand has involuntarily come up to rub the bruise long-gone on my shoulder, I feel like I am staring at step-daddy again. My hand starts to come out to fend him off in the same way I wiggle it at Robert.

Brody takes note of my reaction, takes a step back. I stop, embarrassed.

"Okay, fine, don't answer me," he says gruffly, if not looking a little flustered at my reaction to him. "But I have my kid over there and whatever is planned, I don't want her to be a part of it. I know you don't have kids, Journey Dawn, but —" he paused. I watch his teeth clench. Then he opens his mouth like he is going to say something. He just shakes his head slowly back and forth, throws up his hands lazily. "I don't know." But his churning jaws aren't like step-daddy's at all. Nor are his eyes dark and glazed. They just look—bruised, pleading, broken. "Please—I don't want Cayce to see her daddy a part of whatever joke is getting laid on me again. I'm all she's got." I just stand there not sure why he thinks the joke will be on him.

"I guess things will never change, then," he sighs, turning to walk away. "I knew I should have stayed at home."

But I reach out, grab a swatch of his shirt at the elbow and tug. "Zach-is-making-me-ask-you-out-in-front-of-all-your-friends-or-he-won't-give-me-my-birth certificate." I blurt out. I see him stop and realize this is my chance.

"Oh no, not this again," he curses and turns. He is tall and has to look down at me. I feel like a little kid who got caught with her hand in the cookie jar because I'm still clinging to his sleeve.

"Brody, I don't want to do it," I heave it all out. I can't believe I am doing this, submitting to the enemy. "It's like the thing with the teddy bear all over again, but this time it's *your* friends doing it. It isn't *you* who is going to look like the idiot this time. It is me. I don't want to be laughed at. I'm tired of being laughed at by your friends," I tell him and sigh. "It hurts and I really don't want to be laughed at anymore."

I turn to look back toward the table where Zach Metzler is sitting, but we are hidden from view. I forgot how reserved Brody had always been. He doesn't say much, just sits back with angry eyes watching the world go by. He is just staring down at me like he's waiting for me to say something. So I do.

"But—but I'll make you a deal," I mumble. I finally let my hand fall off his arm. I feel like an idiot I am clinging to him so long. "If you just say something like—I don't know—maybe something like 'I'm sorry, but I've got a girlfriend' or anything that won't make me the butt of the joke, I'll buy your kid any doll she wants in the gift shop. I get a good discount. We'll call it even."

"Okay." That's all Brody Wells says while he nods his head up and down. His face is expressionless, his eyes just narrow a bit while he looks down at me like he's reading my mind. Then he leaves and I'm standing there with the tepid washcloth in my hand, now terrified he's going back to laugh at what I did because maybe he knows what is going on in the first place.

I try to relax when I take the order between singing a birthday song at another table and mopping up a spilled drink at Table 11. I didn't know how to ask a guy out. *Will you go out with me?* I'd never done it before. *Hey, want to go to a restaurant with me?* It wasn't really going to happen. I had Robert. And it occurred to me that if I asked Brody out in front of 23 of his closest friends, would word get back to Robert? Oh, no, what had I gotten myself into?

I nearly drop the pizza on Ashley and have to go back twice for the wrong drinks. Everyone stares suspiciously at me, those same eyes staring at me in high school watching every move I make, eyes eager to pick out my flaws, my mistakes.

"Can I get you anything else?" I finally stand there, pen tapping nervously on the check presenter. My heart is racing and I feel a bead of sweat getting ready to dribble down my forehead. I can't think of the best time to blurt out my end of the deal. It should be so easy. It is getting harder every second ticking by. Heads wag back and forth, more interested in the chatter they are having with each other.

"Okay, so in about ten minutes everybody gets a chance to go play games and daddy gets to dance with any of the princesses," I look at Brody and he's just doing the same head bob above the chatter. His fingers are tapping on his knee. Then I round the table, kneel down next to Brody's little girl.

She isn't fidgeting like the two boys who are devouring the game room with their eyes. She is staring at me with those wide eyes and poking at her half-eaten piece of pizza with a smudged forefinger. Brody's little girl is tiny like I used to be, skinny, freckly and wearing a little polka-dot cotton dress with spaghetti straps. Well-worn pink flip flops nearly fall off her feet while she bangs her legs against the booster seat.

"Cayce," I say, while her eyes get wider looking over at me. She must be incredibly shy by the way her mouth clamps tightly and her thumb slides up to her mouth. "You get to pick out a doll." I have a coupon in my hand that I wriggle between finger and thumb between us. She stares at it, blinking her daddy's eyes at me. I have to smile because I remember the same squinty-eyed twinkle in Brody's eyes when he was out on his horse at the fairgrounds riding it around and around the pen.

"I get a doll?" she whispers, her voice soft and husky.

"You do," I say and start to rise to tell her she must wait in lines already forming with the rest of the daddies and daughters for the dance and doll.

It is my usual spiel so I can go line up with the other waitresses at the dance floor at the far end of the room. But she suddenly comes alive, a tiny feral kitten and wiggles from her chair lugging a little book. She latches on my arm with her free hand, trembling and tugging me and nearly knocking me over to get to the doll room.

And I'm okay with it because my manager is always telling me to do everything I can to make the customer happy. And I hate dancing with sweaty, pizza-breath men I don't know. I hear Brody half-heartedly trying to stop her. I think he isn't expecting her to hop up so quickly and his own reaction is delayed like my own.

I certainly had not anticipated her to jump from withdrawn to wild child in a matter of two seconds. The entire time she has been here, she hasn't done anything more than rest her head to her daddy's shoulder and cling to his arm.

"I know what doll I want," she announces as we blow through the Great Escapes Dream Doll Room.

I try to gather up my skirts so I can make it through the door without catching it on the frame. She stops, takes in the room around her, then points to the large display where girls can build dolls to look like themselves.

There goes my paycheck, I am thinking while she marches me over there and sizes me up and down. These are the least purchased, most prized and also the most expensive dolls in the store. "I want my baby doll to look just like you." She releases my arm, tugs up her book and opens it. Then she flips through the pages slowly until she points to a page with a cartoon princess. It does, in an absurd way, look like me with long hair and puffy dress.

"This is you. I want it to be just like you."

She is beaming up at me, a smile from ear to ear. It is hard to say no to this freckle-nosed little girl with red-blonde hair tucked behind big ears. She really thinks I'm a princess beneath all the makeup and sweaty costume. I still say to her, "You know, you are supposed to get a doll that looks like you." The smile starts to fade so I reach out a finger and tap her nose. "You know, you do look like me when I was five or so," I tell her. "I had red-blonde hair and freckles. I was tiny like you."

The smile returns, the same cock-eyed, half grin her daddy used to have. The entire time we put together her doll, it is almost like staring Brody Wells in the face in kindergarten after he would mischievously slug me in the arm. I laugh to myself. He gave me a valentine in first grade with I LOVE YU handwritten in bold letters above his name. It was soft and had a velvet lion on it. I kept the valentine in my treasure box and used to stroke my finger along the furry-feeling lion until it was nearly rubbed off. Heck, I still have it in the lockbox at my shop.

"And I want the horse," she tells me pointing up above her head to the stack of stuffed Pretty Princess Combo package stallions. A white placard announces the horse with brown and white markings is only $29.99 more with the purchase of a princess doll. "Daddy had to leave his horse. I want to get him one of those to remember him."

I want to tell her that I would like to keep my next two paychecks, but I can't. Her little blue eyes are lighting up like she has won the lottery so I let her pick a brown one off the bottom layer and she looks pleased with herself.

"Aw, that's way too much."

I don't know how long Brody has been standing above us. I look up to see him staring uncomfortably at the prices. I just tell him a deal is a deal and that's what Cayce wants. He looks torn for a minute.

I think he believes I'm doing this for something more sinister, I suppose. I watch him, though, looking at Cayce and her sparkly eyes meet his and I think something passes between them because they both smile slightly at each other. Then Brody looks back at me and the smile breaks into nothingness.

Ten minutes later, I'm standing at his table, picking up the check presenter with an assorted array of cash everyone has tossed in to cover the food. I am trying to hurry. I am late getting to the Daddy-Daughter dances. I don't want to get fired tonight. Everyone just stares at me with the same bored faces, tidying up their areas while they ready themselves to leave. So this is the moment I've been dreading. I look at Zach at the far end of the table who is tapping on his cell phone.

Then I turn to Brody who is pushing his wallet back into his back pocket, getting ready to rise.

"You know, I still have that valentine you gave me in first grade," I burst out to him, my voice shaky and a little too loud. My pen is tapping anxiously on the book again, *tap-tap-tap*. I can't stop it and Kylee is staring at it with an annoyed purse of her lips. *Tap-tap-tap*.

I see Brody glance up and his jaws working hard. His fingers are tapping hard on his knee, too.

"It had a little velvety lion on it and said, um—" I look up and try to remember. It is quiet at the table, only the raucous sound of dance music banging out a beat behind me. "It said, *I'd be lyin' if I said I didn't like you.*" *Tap-tap-tap*. I feel like I am going to throw up. "I always wondered what it would have been like if I hadn't been too shy to tell you I liked you too. Hey, you wouldn't want to go out sometime would you?"

Twenty-three sets of eyes blink stunned at me. I hear Zach sniffle a laugh, but nobody else follows. I realize then by the dark expression bubbling up on Kylee's face, no one but Zach knew about this little payback he was taking out on me. Ashley looks at Brody, then looks at me. Everyone else follows her gaze back to Brody who is sitting back in his seat and seems to be listening intently to me.

"Yeah, sure, I'd like that," he says and I swear to God, he smiles sincerely at me.

Chapter –10

Note to Self: Don't dance with Men in the parking lot.

I like to swirl a peppermint candy cane in my coffee while I drink it. It is strange and people tell me so. Still, it isn't the reason I didn't sit down and drink my coffee at The Coffee Shoppe on Main Street today. I've got to be honest, I was really worried everybody in town, including Robert, had heard about me asking Brody Wells out on a date. Worse yet, they found out about the dance.

Yeah, okay, I forgot about a few things last night because I was so frazzled about Zach's bribe. I forgot to give Table 11 their check. I forgot to clean three tables, change out of my dress before I left the back door of the restaurant and, I forgot about the daddy-daughter dance with Brody Wells.

Well, Cayce didn't forget. When I walked out to my car in the dimly lit parking lot at ten-fifteen there was an old red truck parked next to my car. Next to it, Brody Wells was leaning against the passenger side door with his hands in his pockets.

"You forgot something," he told me while I stopped just short of the bumper of his truck and jiggled the keys in front of me. He was staring at me strangely. I let my eyes fall.

"Aw, crud, you're right," I muttered, snapping my eyes down to my dress. My hand went to my forehead in disbelief. "I didn't change my dress." But I was wondering why he is waiting for me outside. I thought I lived up to all my deals this night.

"Well, no," he answered. I think he started to grin when he realized what I had done. His voice was low.

He pressed a finger to his lips before he jabbed his thumb toward the truck. I peered over his shoulder. Inside, I could see his little girl sound asleep in her car seat, doll hugged tightly to her chest.

"You forgot the daddy-daughter dance," he said. "Cayce remembered. She wanted to tell you so. But you lucked out. She just fell to sleep."

"Oh," was all I could muster. I fumbled with my purse, zipped open the top preparing to barter what I thought a dance was worth. If he went inside and told my boss, I think he just might be really angry. "I guess I can pay you back." I told him as I rummaged through the uncounted crumpled dollar bills of tips I had gotten tonight. "Will ten work? I can't afford to lose the job."

"I don't want your money, Journey," he said, both hands out in front of him, halting my offer. He looked a bit perturbed that I said such a thing.

"Then what do you want?" I asked.

"I don't know." Brody shrugged. "I guess I just want everything to be perfect for her—everything hasn't always been perfect for her."

"I'm so sorry," I told him. "I was just—stressed out. I forgot. I didn't mean to ruin her birthday." I felt a rush of embarrassment. Robert was right. I am an idiot. There is nothing worse than ruining some little girl's dreams. It was her birthday. I botched it up.

"Oh, God, no," he was shaking his head back and forth. "It wasn't you at all. I shouldn't have come. I should have known Zach was up to something. Cayce was upset about the dance so I figured we'd stick around so maybe she could get a hug or something. Hell, that sounds stupid. I don't know. I was hoping she'd fall asleep before you came out. I was just getting ready to leave because she did.

Then you came out. I didn't want to just up and leave with you wondering why I was standing here next to your car like some creep. Maybe I can just tell her we danced after she fell to sleep."

"Princess Scarletta Rose!"

I heard the voice from inside the truck. I leaned to my left, peered around Brody who was groaning to himself, his head falling back. "Could this night not get any worse?"

I saw Cayce kicking her legs out of her car seat and walking across the seats to the open window. Her skinny arm waved at me like a pageant queen, hand cupped.

"Daddy didn't get to dance with you. He said he'd wake me up. I woke up by myself." She beamed proudly.

"Yeah, sweetie," Brody said, turning slowly. "That's not going to happen now. The restaurant is closed. Maybe another time."

She wiggled two little fingers around in a circle just outside the door. "You can dance out here."

"Honey, we can't," I lied to her. "It is illegal to dance in the parking lot."

"Don't tell her that." Brody turned around. I glared at him, held up my arms.

"Okay, Cowboy, do you want to dance out here?" I asked him in a low voice. "I don't."

"Then just tell her that."

"No, Brody Wells," I growled. "You tell your daughter that you don't want to dance out here with me. Considering she waited this long." I wasn't going to be the one breaking her heart.

"Little Punkin'," he said, turning and leaning his elbows on the window. Cayce reached out her hands and held his head. He gave her a little peck on the nose. "I don't want to dance with Princess Scarletta Rose, alright?"

Poof. The little face went from slap-happy to angry-sad in less than two seconds, lips screwed into a horrible pucker and eyes splashing over with tears.

"How'd that work for you?" I asked him smugly, crossing my arms. "*Just tell her that.*" I repeated his words, making my voice whiny and high. "Do you have any concept of how women think at all?"

"I guess not," He turned with his hand in the air in surrender, scowled. "She's tired."

"I'm tired. I want to go home and take off this itchy dress." I sighed with resignation, held out my arms, one high and one low, offering up a dance. "You do know how to dance, don't you?"

"I know how to dance," he grumbled, gave me a stone-cold face.

"You don't have to be such a hardass about it." I was getting more than annoyed. "I'm trying to be nice. What little girl doesn't want her daddy to dance with a princess? I know I wanted my mother to dance with a prince."

"You're wanting to get your birth certificate, Journey, I'm not an idiot," he returned. Still, he reluctantly leaned in, put one hand around my waist and one around over my shoulder. It wasn't as awkward as it could be. He's a close dancer and I didn't mind that so much with him. His body was warm against me, his arms led me without making me feel like I was on a leash.

"Then you'll talk to Zach for me?"

"Sure," he nodded. "And you'll quit telling everybody that you promised Grandpa Delbert I'd go out with you."

I tipped my head to the side, eyed Brody warily. Close. We were so close, I could see the specks in his eyes. "Uh, Let me make one thing clear. I did not tell anyone I promised your grandpa that."

"Sure, Journey, we'll go with that," he acted like he was laughing it off like I was lying. It irked me. He looked all smug right then like I embarrassed him for even making people believe he would go out with me.

"Just stop telling everybody. That's all I ask. It's humiliating."

I wanted to scream. I didn't. Instead, I gritted my teeth. "Listen, Cowboy, I didn't tell anyone what happened in my shop the day your grandpa died."

"Don't call me Cowboy."

"Enough," I said quietly and stepped away. Cayce was smiling and wiping away her tears with her fists. I made a big curtsy for her sake.

"Bow, daddy," Cayce told Brody. He closed his eyes and shook his head, then did as she told him.

"You are mean and bitter," I said between clenched teeth. I could still feel the warmth of his body against me even though we had pulled away. I saw his eyes staring down at me, saw something both sad and sensual in the way he looked at me. I still smelled the scent of him lingering on my clothes. It was nice so it pissed me off.

I turned toward my car, steps hard as I walked to the driver's side door. My fluffy skirts made a loud swishing sound against my legs. I just wanted to cry. I knew my eyes were getting red and puffy. I missed Delbert so much, my chest ached right then.

"Eddy, your mom, and a couple guys from the firehouse were there. It has to be one of them starting the rumor. Let me make it clear. I did not tell anyone about the promise. I don't want to talk about this anymore." I let the irritation surround me and bit down hard on my lip before I slipped into the car. "And you know what? I'll call you Cowboy or Dumbass or whatever I want."

I was bawling after I got into my car. I heard Brody knock on the window. I locked the doors and drove away. Now, a day later, my eyes are all red and puffy. I drink my coffee alone. To make matters worse, something happened that frazzled my nerves one hour earlier.

I was just sitting in the shop, sorting through a dusty, torn cardboard box filled with old dolls I had bought at an auction. I had just laid them out in a row, started to search online to see if I could figure out what kind of dolls they were when the door to the shop opened wide.

Two men stood there. One was short, the other tall. The short one was balding and had beady eyes. The tall one had bushy red-brown hair and kept rubbing his nose with the knuckle of his right hand. Both were dressed in suits and ties. I blinked up at them, smiled. Usually, I would greet folks coming into the store and tell them they were more than welcome to look around. I just sat there instead. I don't know why. There was something in their stance making me believe they weren't here to poke around the shelves for an antique tool that looked like their grandpa's, or find an old toy that brought back childhood memories.

"We're here about the dance card purse."

I stand there in an awkward silence, thinking somewhere in the back of my mind that it's strange they know about the dance card purse. I rolled my hands along my dress, pressed it down nervously, looked down at my high heel shoes.

"The dance card purse?" I looked up and repeated back to them. The shorter of the two rolled his eyes. I get that a lot, the impatient gaze. It isn't just the blonde hair and blue eyes, but my voice that comes out a little child-like sometimes like the ditzy blondes on TV.

"You've got a dance card purse for sale," Bushy Hair said. "A friend of ours stopped by the other day, took some pictures. We're looking to buy it."

"It isn't for sale," I told the man. Yes, their friend had stopped by. He was an old man in khaki pants and a suitcoat. He came in while I was talking to the mailman. He said he liked to collect pieces from the 1930s and 1940s. I showed him a couple things including the purse, as an example. I told him the purses were easy to find and I could get him one. He said he would think about it. He took some pictures and then, he left. It didn't occur to me he was trying to buy it. "I told him mine wasn't for sale. I just listed it online to get a price quote on it. I'm not selling it."

"We'd like to look at it." Beady Eyes stepped right up to the counter. He held out his hand and wiggled his fingers. "I may be able to give you a price. I might even give you a price that will make you decide to sell it."

I hesitated before I reached beneath the counter and tugged out the cigar box from the little shelf holding it. I gingerly popped open the lid and pulled the dance card purse from where it lay between Delbert's dance card and a couple tissues I laid in there to protect it.

The men came at it like two kittens eagerly awaiting to lap up a bowl of warm milk I had just set out in front of them. They said not a word while Beady Eyes turned the purse over in his hands, paused long enough to roll a finger across the initials before he opened it wide and peered inside.

Silence. Then Beady Eyes looked up and tugged out a checkbook. He opened it wide and told me he was going to write a check for five-hundred dollars for the dance card purse. I stuck out my palm, shook my head. "It isn't for sale. My friend gave it to me before he died. It is priceless to me."

Something changed in Bushy Hair's eyes while he gently held the purse. They got dark, angry. Beady Eyes tugged an asthma inhaler from his pocket. He took a deep swig of its contents. "You will sell it," he told me. His hard gaze was odd as if he saw himself as a hypnotist and expected me to fall under his spell and dumbly hand the purse to him.

"I will not," I told him, untangling his fingers from the purse before I snatched it away to my chest. It must have been two minutes they stared at me. Maybe it was only a few seconds, but it seemed an eternity. Bushy Hair jabbed a thumb in the air and Beady Eyes nodded.

"We'll be back," Bushy Hair said. With one more deep gulp from Beady Eye's inhaler, the two simply turned and walked out the door.

I had waited until I heard their steps fade away, then I walked to the door and peered outside. The two were getting into a compact, black sports car. It looked expensive. The windows were tinted. In a matter of moments, the car pulled away. I could just barely make out a green and white sticker on the back: *when guns are outlawed, only outlaws have guns.* But I stayed there at the door feeling vulnerable and a bit scared they would come right back. They didn't. I thought about locking the front door, then decided I was only a scream away from the sidewalk. About four minutes and six cars later, I saw Brody Wells's truck making its way down Main. For a moment, the two strangers left my mind.

It would be another five minutes before I left the door and got back to work. It is sweltering and dust seems to sit in the air, a million twinkles flitting and floating in the two beams of light coming through the windows. A shadow flits across one beam and the door slams open.

I have to do my usual, automatically grab the rickety shelves with my hand. I think of Delbert Johnson and my tummy makes a melancholy flip-flop. I look up to see Brody Wells sauntering in. My breath sticks in my lungs. I am surprised, but try to keep my cool while I listen to his steps make their way across the squeaky floor boards. He is wearing tan cargo shorts and a nice button up shirt with stripes. His hands are deep in his pockets and he is nibbling on his lower lip. "Hey," I greet him. But it sounds more like it has a question mark attached to it. I look behind him, waiting for his entourage of friends. But he is alone.

"Hey," he says in return. Brody stops just short of the counter while I sit back on the bar stool I use for a chair. Brody knocks on the counter with a knuckle and pushes out a smile. It isn't quite genuine, but I get the feeling he's a little uncomfortable. "I'm sorry I made you cry last night."

"You didn't make me cry."

"Okay, whatever," he says offhandedly. "I suppose that sound coming from your car was just the engine squealing like a newborn pig."

"What the heck, Cowboy?" I grouse at him, hands coming out to my sides. "Why are you being so mean. You trying to make me cry again?" He's got a funny smirk to his face while he shrugs.

"So you *were* crying."

I sit there thinking there must be something about the shop today bringing in idiots with an attitude. I shake my head, pretend I'm opening a drawer at the counter near my knee. "Get out of my shop, Brody."

"I talked to Mom last night. She said you weren't lying. Grandpa made you promise you'd go out with somebody else before you got married."

"Yeah, so what? That isn't a newsflash for me."

"She also said I should ask you out so you wouldn't be stuck forever worrying you didn't live up to Grandpa Del's last request. And you know what I told her?"

"I don't even want to guess," I answer, feeling a trickle of anger goose-pimples rise on my arms.

"I told her it would be like going on a date with Satan. A date from holy hell." He doesn't change his straight -lipped expression, just stares at me like he is sizing me up, waiting for some comeback. But I've got none. I just stare at him, lack of words only veiled by the tiniest of thoughts flitting through my mind. The day of the funeral, I found a little note Delbert had left me hidden in my lockbox hole in the floor. It was hastily written in his old man scrawl. It said: *A date consists of 1) holding hands for a minimum of five minutes 2) pleasant conversation where the eyes meet more than once 3) A slow dance beneath the stars 4) A kiss goodnight.*

Delbert had somehow tucked it in there amidst all my little knick-knacks when I wasn't looking. It was underneath the little red teddy bear his grandson had given me in high school and beside my first R-rated movie ticket I bought myself. He was so stubborn when he got something set in his mind. And he was dead set Robert wasn't the right man to become my husband. Obviously, stubbornness was passed down in the family.

"You've changed. You're like—an old dead-broke horse. I can't believe you're not going to say anything?" He asked, taunting.

I've been compared to many things. But I have never been equated to an almost-dead horse. "Yes," I say. "I grew up. And I told you to get out of my store. You aren't welcome here."

I stand up as if to escort him out, push my hands in front of me like I'm sweeping him toward the door. "You, however, haven't changed. You are mean and hurtful and I don't have to be around people like you."

"Then why do you hang around with Robert and Andrea?"

"GET OUT!" I scream it with a husky throat. "How dare you come in here and criticize me, then turn around and belittle my relationships. Get out!"

Then it was like all of a sudden, he deflates like a cheap, plastic beach ball with a hole poked into it. He curses loud beneath his breath and his head drops. That's when I realize Brody Wells isn't here to apologize at all. There is always an ulterior motive. He has the look of a little boy who has gotten socked in the nose, then after he punches back, he has to apologize to the bully who started the whole fight.

"You find things." He reaches up and grabs at the cowboy hat that isn't there. Then he slaps his palm on his pants. "I was talking to Zach the other day. He said the same thing."

"I do," I answer suspiciously. Zach Metzler grew up with Brody. Back in high school, he was a big, red-haired farm boy who used to chew tobacco and spit it out just a few inches from my bare-toed, sandaled feet. You hardly saw one without the other. When Brody left town right after high school in disgrace and with his tail between his legs, Zach stuck around looking as lost as a goldfish tossed from the tiny bowl he had lived in all his life into the wild, blue ocean.

"And you keep it confidential?" His eyes work up to mine. They are still angry down there deep.

"Of course," I say with a bob of my head. "Lots of folks are looking for stuff they would rather no one knew about." And I wonder why I am being so civil. He is right. I am like a dead-broke horse. There was a time I would say something mean to him in return. But it just isn't there anymore.

Brody scrubs a hand over his cheeks, looks like he would rather be anywhere but here. "I need to find a piece of jewelry, a specific kind. Do you know how to look for really hard stuff like that?"

"Brody, I've found an old oil can in an antique shop in Kentucky for Joey Ratcliff at the drugstore that his dad actually used when he was little. I found a pair of boots worn by Jake Little's great, great grandpa in the Civil War. For heaven's sakes, I paid some old man a hundred bucks to dig up half an old dump behind his house in Cleveland to get an old medicine bottle for somebody from a company that used to be where the old man's yard is now. Spit it out, Brody," I state impatiently. "What is it you need?"

"When I left, I took my grandma's engagement ring from my mom's jewelry drawer," he tells me flatly, chewing on his bottom lip. "I gave it to my girlfriend because I thought we were going to get married." He stops cold, gives me a hard gaze, shrugs. "Mom didn't give it to me, Journey. I took it. The bank foreclosed on the farm and we've got to be out in two weeks. Mom's getting everything packed away yesterday and she notices the ring gone. Now she's going nuts trying to find it."

"You are selling your farm?" I almost gasp. His words strangely hit me hard. I see the farm in my mind and I can only see the Wells and the Johnsons living in it. I remember Robert mentioning that Brody's dad had a couple bad years with his cows and crops one day in early summer.

I just thought it was talk, though. Robert is always spitting out things that his dad mentions at the dining room table, hearsay, chitchat, and half-truths that may or may not occur.

We had been sitting on his mom's porch swing and Robert had burst out with the news like a greedy bird who had just found a bird feeder full of seed. *I think we're getting the old Johnson Farm*, he had told me. *Dad can make a mint on it, sell it in packages for a subdivision—*

Now Brody is giving me such an angry glare as if *I* am taking his farm.

"I'm sure you've heard about it," Brody says sarcastically and low beneath his breath. "Not selling it, Journey. Robert's dad is foreclosing on the farm now Grandpa is dead. After the fire, they never could catch up."

"Oh, I'm sorry." What else am I supposed to say? I just stand there, staring at him. Finally I tap my finger on the table.

"Yeah, I bet you are." Brody sniffs. "But it isn't your mom sobbing around the house all day, looking for her ring. It is like she is banking everything on this ring. She's losing her family farm and if she doesn't find grandma's ring, she's lost everything."

I'm still in shock. You see, I can't imagine Bacon Valley without the Johnson farm, without the whole lot of them nearly taking over the town. They fill half the school bus.

Piece of Bacon, I remember Brody calling me in the hallway at school. Actually, it was P—P—Piece of Bacon. I stuttered sometimes when I was nervous in grade school. It made me feel small, vulnerable like everyone there had seen me in my underwear.

Piece of Bacon.   Brody Wells had given me the nickname in third grade and he stuttered it out just like he and his friends would stutter out J—J—Journey when they said my name.

He made fun of me all through elementary school, junior high and the first three years at the Bacon Valley High School. He called me chicken legs, church girl, ditzy and dumb blonde. He would sit back in his chair, all cool and with a cocky half-grin on his lips, and give me a wink whenever I walked into a classroom with him. Then he would take on a really high-pitched girly-girl voice and say something like: *Well, look who it is. It is J—J—Journey Dawn Bacon, church girl with a porn star name. Are you lost, darlin'? Do you need somebody to walk you to your special class?*

Everybody would laugh at his clowning around at my expense. My face would turn red and my eyes would dart around like a kitten treed by a Rottweiler. Even the teachers would chuckle beneath their breath while I fumbled around with my books. Then Brody would pull something like standing up, tipping his hat and pulling out the chair for me. I swayed there wondering if he was going to pull it out from beneath me. Just when I sat down, Brody Wells would just stare tough and unsmiling into my eyes as if he was saying, *Bitch, you ain't no better than us.*

Brody is staring at me just like that now. He shakes his head and looks at his shoes. So I bite down hard on my lip and ask him: "Do you have a picture of the ring?"

His eyes shoot up, his gaze working back between my own. I know he is expecting me to toss some rubbish back at him. Maybe, I think, it is more hurtful if I simply say nothing mean at all.

"Journey, my mom didn't know I took the ring. Now that she's moving stuff out for the sale—" He stops, looks to the ceiling and chews on his lip. "The only thing I can tell you is that it's gold. The engraving says: *To Grace, my love.* Grace was my grandma. For now, I'll walk you over so you can get your birth certificate from Zach."

"You don't have to," I tell him. "Everything doesn't have to be a deal. I made the promise to your grandpa because I really loved him—like a friend. I mean, he was like my best friend. Because—" *He was my only friend.* I don't say that. "I don't like hanging around Andrea and yes, Robert can be a shit. I'm trying not to lose sleep over the promise. But I've got obligations. I can't just go out with other people. I can't just ask anyone out, they'll get the wrong idea. Cowboy, what I'm saying is that I'll look into the ring. There is no deal."

"No, it has to be a deal or no deal," he says a little more softly. "I lost my job when I moved back home. I've got hardly fifty bucks right now until we figure out where we're moving and I can get a job. I already feel like an idiot that you bought my kid the doll and horse last night. I don't want to owe anybody."

"Especially me."

"Yeah, whatever." he nods. "I need the ring. I'll make payments, do what I need to do. Take you out to lunch, make us both stop losing sleep."

I can't imagine why Brody would lose sleep over the promise. I shrug his remarks off. But here is where things start going wrong. I can't quite pinpoint the exact moment it occurs. Maybe it is when I nod my head reluctantly or maybe it is when Brody opens the door for me and we slip out into the hot afternoon air. I'm not sure. I don't feel any different from the point we walk the three blocks from the Knick-Knack Shop to the city offices. But it happens here.

Zach's head snaps up from his desk and he nearly giggles in delight when Brody and I walk awkwardly into his office. Smugly, he gets up, tapping a bundle of papers in his hand I thought surely were my birth records. I was wrong. Zach had been prepared. He tugs on his tie, scrubs a hand through his mostly-shaved head.

"Oh!" he says with a grin showing a snaggletooth-tooth usually hidden behind his tightlipped smile. His breath smells like stale mint gum. "Are you the couple coming in to get married today?" Then he starts in on an entire spiel of a wedding ceremony and won't stop until we play along no matter how much both Brody and I protest. Red-faced, I can't look at Brody and can't figure out why I'm so mortified. So I just shut up and listen to Zach rant on.

A couple workers in the office are watching intently, two baby-faced girls fresh out of high school and sporting flip flops, tan city polo shirts, knee-length cargo skirts and latex gloves. One is holding a clear plastic garbage bag so the other could empty the gray trash cans in Zach's office into it. The two must have been summer interns because they both suddenly burst into smiles even though Brody keeps holding up his hand for Zach to stop.

Brody finally turns to me and flatly tells me to play along because Zach won't stop until he is done. I know he isn't lying. I once watched Zach give an hour speech at a pep rally at the end of the day on the reason we shouldn't stick gum under our desks just so we didn't have to go back to class. I play along unenthusiastically. I even sign the fake marriage documents he slaps in front of us.

The interns clap when Zach is done. They even sign as witnesses before they turn to get back to work. I poke my finger at the papers and tell him this stack better be for my birth certificate. He nods, then sighs.

"I know, I know, Journey, we can't find your documents here, but we can order them online," Zach tells me, his face now more serious. I stare at him, numb faced and dazed.

"You can't do this to me, Metzler," I tell him fiercely. My face is now hot with anger. "You didn't even bother to look. I've got to have my birth certificate. I'm tired of excuses."

"I'm telling you the truth." Zach has both hands up. He's got another smile on his face, though. "I really can't find it. It would be easier for you right now to buy a fake one for a couple hundred bucks—"

"Aw, come on," Brody doesn't look like he believes him and now I'm not sure if Zach is just pulling my leg again. "Don't lie to her. Just get her birth certificate, Zach."

So Zach turns to Brody, tosses out his hands. He smiles, but it is a bit more solemn. "Bro, honestly, we've never had this happen before. I'm telling the truth. The certificate isn't showing up online or in our system. She doesn't exist."

Chapter −11

Date 1

Note to Self: Put a Spare Car Key in my purse

"Well, for one thing, you were going twenty miles over the speed limit. Two, your GPS was begging you to *not* turn right and you did anyway. Twice. The second time, it was on a road that doesn't even exist."

Okay, that is Brody Wells yelling at me. It is three-thirty on Thursday afternoon and my car had come to an abrupt stop twenty minutes earlier on a road that used to be County Road 12.

Obviously, the road isn't there anymore because the asphalt and gravel have been replaced by grass and trees. A bent and gnarled guardrail shields a small ditch between the main roadway and the old County Road 12. I should have come out unscathed; my car did not come into contact with the guardrail. Instead, it slipped over a bolt loosened by the last poor soul to come to a skidding halt here because he had not updated his car's satellite navigation system. My right front tire made a loud pop when it slid to a terrifying halt only six inches from the rail.

So now we are a few miles from my car without a house in site. Both our phones are locked in my car along with my keys because while we were shouting at each other, we both shut the doors and they automatically locked. It is Brody's bright idea to walk until we find a home or business that has a phone.

"It told me to turn right, I heard it," I tell him. I wasn't quite telling him the truth. But I didn't want to divulge to Brody that I thought we were being followed by the little black car with the two impolite men who had stopped in my shop.

I made the first turn off the asphalt highway to see if they followed. They slowed, but did not turn. When I saw the second tiny road pop up on the screen, I tried to make a quick getaway like they do on TV. Then the tire popped. Of course, I have not seen the car since. I am trying, in high heels, to keep up on the old dirt road. He is five long strides ahead of me and not slowing down.

"It was screaming for you to follow the curve. There is no road there, Journey. It was pretty obvious."

"Okay!" I scream at his back. "I made a mistake, but whose brilliant idea was it for us to walk, huh?"

"Me. What are you going to do, Journey? Even if you break a windshield which was no brilliant suggestion in the first place, you don't have a spare tire because you never got the tire fixed the last time it was busted after Grandpa's funeral. And, there is no cell phone service here anyway even if we wanted to call somebody." Brody throws back his head. "Why? Why did I agree to do this?"

Nor should I have agreed to it. But a couple hours earlier, Gayle Wells walked into my shop. The door is propped open with a wooden wedge to let the breeze slip through. Had I not looked up, I wouldn't have seen her she was so quiet. But she cleared her throat and I jumped. She was on her lunch break at the post office and she had a brown paper bag in her hand. I was reaching down into a box and tugging out some old baseball cards I got at an auction, readying to place them on a shelf.

"Hi, honey," she said with a slightly worn smile. Her strawberry blonde hair was up in a pony tail that bounced as she walked. She was wearing tan capris, a button-up shirt and tennis shoes. I can't help but note how different she dresses from Delilah. There is such a stark contrast between Gayle's $12.99 retail outfits versus Delilah's $200.00 tailor-made dresses. I don't feel bad for comparing the two.

I wished sometimes that I could don a pair of raggedy second-hand blue jeans and an old t-shirt. However, if I did, I think Delilah would disown me.

"Hey," I returned, smiling. I like Gayle. She's always been nice to me, even though she has probably known for some time that Robert's family is the one who will buy her family farm. She stopped just short of the shelf and looked around the room. "I think what I like about your shop, Journey, is that it is always changing and evolving," she told me. "Like the cooking shows on the cable channels where they take an old family recipe and add some spark to it. There is always something new—well, old, every time I come in." Then she walked to the counter and set the sack down. "I brought some lunch over. There are a couple peanut butter and jelly sandwiches inside," she told me. "Brody is coming to pick me up early. I told him to stop in here and bring another milk crate of Dad's stuff for you. I thought maybe you two could share a lunch."

"Oh," I mustered. I see where this is going. "I appreciate the thought," I told her, "but I am actually leaving in about ten minutes. I know a guy who owns a pawn shop in Midland and he is going to give me a quote on the dance card purse your father gave me."

"You're going to sell it?" she asked slowly, carefully. She fingered a little doll I have laying on the counter, didn't look at me.

"No," I replied. "It was a gift from your father. But I've had a few people come in to ask about it. They are a bit shifty. I'm wondering if I need to stick it in a safety deposit box."

"It might be worth a lot?"

I turned and faced her, but she was still fiddling with the doll. "Honestly, I see these online once in a while for about fifty bucks." I told her honestly, watching her fiddle.

"It doesn't look any different from a hundred others." I walked over to the back of the counter and pulled out the cigar box. While Gayle stepped over, I reached in and tugged out the dance card and purse and put it on the counter between us.

I asked her if she had ever seen it before and she put it in her hand and opened it up. She traced the M.L. initials on the front, then shook her head and told me, no, she hadn't. "I don't know where Dad got this. Not sure whose initials these would be either."

"He said he won it in a race," I said. "Maybe he didn't tell you because a girl gave it to him. He told me it was before he met your mother."

Her head popped up. She laughed like the idea was funny. "I hope he didn't have any skeletons in the closet." Gayle waved away a fly and looked around. "Who knows. Things change, I suppose." Then she sighed deep in her chest. "You're going to miss this place when they tear it down. I'm not sure if I'm going to miss seeing these old rundown buildings or if I'm glad they are getting rid of them. I keep expecting Dad to come walking down the sidewalk. Maybe if they are gone, I won't have that memory all the time."

I was tipping my head as she talked, soaking in her words. "Who—who told you they were tearing down the buildings?" I asked.

"Oh." She kind of held on to the word a long time like she was realizing she had said something maybe she shouldn't. "Why, Big Bob Ironwood told us he was having the buildings demolished in a couple weeks when we went in to sign over the farm papers to him. They are moving the post office, too."

She must have seen my face fall. I felt like the blood was draining from my cheeks.

Robert had spoken about removing the buildings, but I thought it was just one of his idle threats because I forgot to do one thing or the other. But while she apologized, I just gritted my teeth and smiled. Maybe she misunderstood Big Bob.

"Sweetie, maybe he was just talking." She opted for small talk, then looked me straight in the eyes. "But on another note, I'm just going to say something. I know this date thing that Dad made you promise has been kind of hard on you. I know you had a special friendship and it was really wrong of him to put you on the spot. You don't have to do it, you know. Nobody's going to think any less of you. Everybody will forget it in a couple months or so. And my family certainly doesn't hold you to anything. Just forget about it and go on."

My eyes darted back and forth between Gayle's eyes. I shake my head because at that very moment, I believed she was the only one in the world who might understand. Because my mother certainly didn't. Nor does Robert or Andrea. They thought it was strange I hung out with Delbert.

"I don't think I can," I divulged to her. "I don't just miss your dad. I am torn between feeling obligated to him and being mad at him for putting me in this position. "

"Why don't you take Brody along with you to Midland?" she offered. "It would be good for both of you to get out, get away." She sniffed a laugh. "He keeps telling me how bad he hates this place. Between you two, you can call it a date for the sake of Dad's request."

"Mom, she doesn't want to take me to Midland," Brody's voice swept across the room at the same time his shadow blocked the light from the doorway. "I don't want to go to Midland. I'm supposed pick up Kylee tonight and go somewhere. Me and Journey already worked this out.

She's got a boyfriend who would murder me if I took her out. Do you want me dead? Will you please stop meddling in my stuff?"

Gayle did stop meddling. But after six kids, she had acquired a certain flair in the fine art of persuasion. She threw a slight wrench into my own and Brody's plans by nodding her head, dropping the smile on her face.

"Brody, I have enough on my mind trying to move and trying to find grandma's wedding ring before we have to get out of the house. I don't need one more worry that Grandpa's final wishes were not met. If you don't do it for Journey. Do it for me."

And so here we are in the middle of nowhere, walking toward Midland that is thirty miles away.

"You could have at least had the keys in your hand so you didn't lock the phones in the car," he spats back at me. "Or better yet, you could have gone down and bought a new spare tire for your car."

I would've had my keys in my hand if Brody hadn't jerked open his door so the bit of wind picking up along the woods around us hadn't sent about thirty of my little pieces of random paper sitting on the dashboard with songs on it flying out the door. Instead of helping, he had slammed his door, made a rude comment about all the little pieces of trash in my car. "Songs." I tell him. "Or at least future ones." He just rolls his eyes.

I toss my hands in the air. "Do you know where we are anyway? We could walk for days without finding a house."

He comes to a complete halt and turns. I'm forced to stop three steps away and look up at him. A dribble of sweat has formed on his temple and he swipes it away angrily.

His eyes are squinting against the sun and have turned a bright sea blue, almost the color of the sky right before dusk. They are stunning and it catches me off-guard. He looks hot and annoyed both at once, but I'm just kind of lost in his eyes.

"And it would be better to sit at your car and rot while we wait for somebody to drive by two weeks from tomorrow—?" he asks me. Then he stops abruptly and tips his head to the side. "How the hell do you manage to look so damn beautiful, so damn perfect like you haven't even broken a sweat after walking an hour in ninety degree temperatures?"

I tug my eyes away from his and stare at Brody's irritated face. I am actually sweating bullets down my back. I can feel a couple droplets lingering near my shoulder blades. But he called me beautiful. *Beautiful.* I don't hear that often or at least not with so much passion in the voice.

Robert tells me I am pretty sometimes, but it just comes out of his mouth in the same way he flips up his shoe to reveal the bottom, asking me if he had poop on it from his neighbor's dog using his grass as a toilet. I honestly don't think he really believes I am pretty at all because he usually has an addendum attached like:—*but that dress kind of makes you look like your mother.* There is something genuine about somebody who hates you telling you are beautiful. Between that and taking in Brody Wells's eyes, I feel something jump in my tummy like I have just crested a hill in my car and came off the other side a little too fast.

"Was that a compliment?" he asks me with a sarcastic twist of his lips. "Because I didn't mean it like I was judging you for one of your beauty pageants. It just isn't normal you're not sweating. It isn't normal to be a real person and not—sweat."

"I am sweating," I tell him in return. My heart sinks. Now my feelings are hurt. I hate Brody Wells. My stomach topples over like I just bit into the brown side of a rotten banana.

So I wag a finger toward the road in front of us. "Will you please walk? I hate you. You're mean. I just want to be done with this. I'm not stupid, Cowboy, I know the only reason I ever won was because everybody was afraid if they didn't choose me that Delilah or Big Bob would be mad. You don't need to rub it in. You don't need to be a shit about it."

He looks both stunned and has a new, funny twist to his lips. It is almost a smile. I'm not sure I have ever actually seen Brody Wells with a genuine smile.

"Ha ha," he laughs. "Church girl just said a naughty word."

"Oh, you want to hear a naughty word?" I ask him. Now I am really sweating and my face is red hot to boot. I lift up my middle finger and aim it right toward him. Then I let off the foulest oath I can imagine and ending with a firm "off." Brody doesn't say anything at all, just turns on his feet and walks on. Another hour passes on the deserted gravel road, this one is totally silent. It is excruciating. I am getting lonely, so I pipe up with this: "I think we were being followed," He is walking beside me, maybe a half stride in front of me. He stops in mid-step, starts to turn and I nearly slam into him.

"What?" Brody's face is all scrunched up, his head tipped to one side and his forehead furrowed like I had just told him I thought the world was flat. I jab a thumb behind us.

"A couple guys came into my shop and wanted to buy the dance card purse your grandpa gave me," I tell him. "I told them I didn't want to sell it. They were—"

I chew on my thoughts for a moment. "They were pushy, didn't want to take 'no' for an answer. I swear I saw their little black car behind me for about the last fifteen miles."

I think Brody is going to shuck me off with a laugh, toss his hand into the air, and call me a ditz. He doesn't. "In a black Jaguar." Brody says, his eyes narrowing slightly. I shrug. I didn't know one type of car from another.

"Yeah, I saw it," he goes on. "It passed me on Main in town. I noticed it because it was a damn nice car. Then I saw it sitting down the street in front of the courthouse. I figured it was just some rich attorney. It didn't quite occur to me when it was heading out of town at the same time we were, it was anything more than coincidence."

"Well, me either for a while," I tell Brody. "But I made so many twists and turns on wrong roads to see if they would go another direction, it couldn't be anything else. I finally passed a couple cars and turned before they could see me."

He taps my arm and takes a step so we keep walking. "So is that dance card purse worth enough to make somebody want it bad enough to—?" he stops right there and kind of lets his words dangle in the air. I know what he wants to say, something like 'kill someone' or the likes.

"I looked it up online and they run about fifty bucks and up to a couple hundred," I tell him honestly. I can't help notice how blue his eyes look against the dark of the trees around us. "From experience, the only time something's worth enough to threaten someone is if it has sentimental value."

"Hmm," he sniffs. "I think my mom would kill me if she knew I took her ring. I hope they aren't smashing in your car window as we speak to get the purse."

He rubs a hand across his cheek and I feel a smile crawl up on my lips. Delbert used to do the same thing when he was thinking something out. Then I thought about the little note Delbert had left for me in the cash register drawer.

"Can you hold my hand for five minutes?" I blurt out. I get a questioning chin-cocked, eyes narrowed gaze that screams: *how stupid is this woman?* I see Brody's mouth working like he has no clue how to answer such a weird request and especially from one who just told him off. He stops long enough to shrug, "Are you scared?"

"Scared?" I ask, now the confused one, my eyes roaming around to the deserted roadway, then the bland forest of trees. "No, I don't think so. Scared of what?"

"I assumed the guys who were following us in the car," he answers slowly. "That's what you were talking about when you asked me to hold your hand."

"Oh," I draw it out, nod my head slowly in understanding. "No, that's not why I asked. This is supposed to be kind of like our—" I almost can't say the word, "—date, right? Because—" I stutter, "Your grandpa told me, um, that it wasn't a real date unless you hold hands for five minutes."

"Are you kidding me? You call this a date?" Brody's expression changes from baffled to impatient. He looks around, tosses out his hands to his side. "I had more fun picking up trash on the side of the road to pay for a parking ticket last year. And how the hell have you survived this long with a brain that can't hold a damn thought for more than five seconds?"

"Screw off, dumbass," I tell him hotly. I push around Brody and start walking again. My feelings are hurt again along with the humbling rejection. I feel like crying, but I don't. My back is sweaty because the sun is beating down on the black dress.

I can even feel a dribble rolling from my brow down to my temple. I wish I was just back at my dusty shop, plucking on the guitar strings and singing to the stray cat that shares my lunch with me.

I think ten minutes pass before Brody comes up beside me. He doesn't say anything and tries to hold my hand. My palms are all sweaty and his fingers are cool, but I tug my hand away.

"Aw, come on, I'm trying to say I'm sorry," he mutters. It took him three tries and a groan before I let him hold my hand. We walk in silence, me feeling his sweaty fingers clasped in my sweaty hand and thinking it is really weird even though I have goosebumps on my arm. I don't like it, don't like Brody. In the uncomfortable silence, I count to ten, then twenty, then thirty before I mumble, "This is really awkward."

"Yeah, I feel like I'm holding hands with my little sister." Brody's head bobs up and down and we let go at only forty-five seconds.

I hope Delbert would have been proud that we had held on that long. So I paid my dues with Brody. It shuts him up for a while until we come out into the open and find an old farm house and a field with a horse grazing. He stops and whistles the horse over, a sad tip to his lips while he pats her head and scratches her neck. It occurs to me I haven't seen him smile at all since he has come home—not an actual smile, that is. He just always looks like a lonely, sullen cowboy without a hat or a horse. I tell him I'll take a hike up to the farmhouse, ask if I can use the phone to call Andrea to pick us up while he flirts with the mare. Brody just shrugs indifferently.

Five minutes later, I come back with a surprise for him. I hold up a pair of boots, an old pair of jean shorts, and a t-shirt.

"Um, those are too small for me," he tells me.

I roll my eyes. "They're for me," I tell him. "The lady who lives there said I can't clean a stall in a dress."

Brody looks at me bewildered. "Can you clean a stall at all?" he asks, looking me up and down like I'm too stupid to know how to push a shovel into horse poop and scoop it out. "And why are you mucking a stall?"

"I'm not mucking it. I'm cleaning it."

"Mucking a stall is cleaning the manure out of the stall."

"Oh, then I guess I'm mucking it."

Again, I get a puzzled stare. But he just shrugs and says, "Okay, have fun. Did you call Andrea?"

He must have misconstrued the sly smile on my face for coming up with his surprise. I sigh and shake my head. "No, Cowboy, the lady did not have a phone," I tell him. "But she says there is a saddle and bridle in the barn and if I clean the stall, you can ride the horse. You do like horses, don't you? I mean, you looked like you were going to cry a minute ago when you saw the horse."

I think for a minute he is going to give me one of his classic sour retorts. *The only thing that would make me cry is those shoes you're wearing.* Instead, Brody just stares at me with this long, serious face like he is thinking really hard about what I am saying, like he thinks there is some joke attached. I can see him carefully trying to read my face, eyes working back and forth between my own, guarded like a pup that's been slapped hard by the same hand that pets it gently.

"Your grandpa told me I needed to try new things, things that weren't easy," I say a little quietly. "He always said I go the easy route. So I'm trying something new, something hard." I say it while I nod toward the barn.

"I've never cleaned shit out of a stall. It is new. I've never gone out of my way to be nice to you. That's hard."

He props his elbows up on the fence, rubs one hand on the horse's head and kicks the bottom board with his tennis shoe. "Well, okay, if Grandpa told you to do it," he said solidly. "You muck. I'll ride."

Chapter –12

Found myself outside your bedroom window last Friday after school Thinking about those crazy, silly little things we used to do— But it was all in my head—

I remember watching Brody ride his horse at the Bacon Valley Fair. It was a brown and white Paint, tall and graceful. He called it Jack. He always looked like the cowboys on the old western movies my mom watched on Saturday afternoons, not the dumb actors that bounced around a lot, but the stunt doubles who came in and rode away smooth and cool into the sunset at the end. Around the fields, he would ride, once in a while looking up to the pack of girl-admirers that followed him around the horse rings and barns, but usually just focused on his horse.

Now that I think about it, it was the only time I would see him truly smiling. Don't get me wrong. I don't think Brody was really an unhappy kid. I just think he was more caught up in other things. When he was with his horse, he got to relax. That is what I am seeing after I get done cleaning the stalls. I am sitting on Emma Pine's front porch with a cool lemonade in my hand. She has long dark hair and lots of wrinkles, and a funny laugh that echoes off the walls. She is telling me about her daughter who is in the military and can't come home for another three months. She is the one who usually mucks the stalls, rides the horses. But after she gets out, she gets a scholarship to the local college.

I am wearing her daughter's t-shirt and jean shorts and a borrowed pair of cowboy boots that are nice and worn in and fit me just right. She has a chest full of old books and while Brody rides up to the front lawn, I tell her I can sell them for her.

"You want to ride?" Brody asks while the horse nibbles at the grass. I laugh.

"No," I tell him. "I don't think I've ever ridden one except at summer camp one year. It was a pony and bucked me off."

"Come on," he says. "It's just like a car. I'll do the driving. You can just ride along behind."

"No, thank you. I'll bounce off the back."

"Suit yourself," he tells me. He thanks Emma and starts to turn the horse toward the barn. And I do something way out of the ordinary for me and stand up, yell out: "Hey, okay, I'll do it."

Brody Wells looks neither pleased nor irked while he turns the horse back around, stretches out a hand for me to climb aboard. Awkwardly, I place my foot into the stirrup and he tows me up. But instead of setting me in behind him, he slides over the back of the saddle and places me in front.

"You won't bounce off now," he tells me, easing up a bit so I feel his chest against my back.

I know I must smell like horse stalls. Sweat is still drying on my back from shoveling the manure into the old metal wheelbarrow Emma gave me to toss it out behind the barn. He doesn't comment on this impropriety and instead brings his arms around me to snatch up the reins. I'm not sure I'm comfortable being this close to Brody Wells. I can feel his soft breath on the nape of my neck. Although it is difficult, I decide not to think about the way he rests his hands on my bare legs just where the fringe of the cutoff shorts pause at the top of my thighs.

"It is a really nice thing for you to do, Journey," he tells me. "I miss my horse."

"Cayce said you couldn't get him from the barn where you boarded him," I told him. "You had to leave him and you were sad."

"That's not the only thing I screwed up and left behind," he sniffs a bitter laugh. "I left my mom's ring. And I'm the dad who lost his daughter's best friend somewhere between the town of Petigo, Kentucky and Bacon Valley."

I tip my head with a slight turn, questioning, but I can only see his eyes.

"Her doll. It was all she had left of her mom," Brody explains. "She wasn't a good mom, but that's not why it never made it to Bacon Valley. I don't think Cayce remembers the bad stuff that much. I met her mom while I worked at some rodeos and fairs when I first left home. I didn't have a job or a place to stay. It's rough out there by yourself. I moved into her trailer, got her horse ready to ride, cleaned and stuff. I didn't have a choice. I had nothing but the clothes on my back. Not much love there, just—well, you know."

I didn't say anything, just look up at him. He kind of gives me a funny lop-sided smile. "You probably don't know," he says. "You've never left Bacon Valley except to go to college." It isn't mean. Nobody knows how scared I am of Robert all the time, how much I wish I could just leave.

"Her mom took off with her when she was a few months old," he goes on. "June sixth. I remember the date. I hate that stupid number—six. No phone calls. No letters. Nothing. Just a note she was going to another rodeo. Then she dropped her on my step about eleven months later, full of bruises and—stuff. Mom and Dad sent me money to go to court and get custody of her." He stops abruptly like he has said too much and simply huffs a breath. "Probably another reason they are losing the farm. Regardless I lost the doll on our drive home to Bacon Valley and my head was in such a fog, I didn't even notice. I assumed Cayce told you about her doll at Great Escapes Restaurant." He looks away slightly.

"She's been freaking out since. That's why Zach wanted to take her there, to get a new one. He's not really a bad guy."

"She didn't say anything about the doll. Just your horse. Jack."

"Yeah, old Jack. There wasn't a day I wasn't out riding him for the last ten years," he says softly. "Money's been tight the last few months. They cut my hours at the barn where I worked when I broke up with my girlfriend. Then they started charging me for the boarding fees. I couldn't afford them. The same ex-girlfriend who told me she sold my mom's ring online sold the horse to pay for the boarding I was past-due."

"A cowboy without his horse," I say quietly staring out at the fields in front of us. I feel the wind in my face and turn enough to tousle Brody's hair with my fingers. "And without his old cowboy hat," I go on. "It sounds like a sad country song."

He sighs deep in his chest. "Yeah, right now my life feels like a sad country song, Journey. Her parents own the stables and the farm at Petigo. That's her last name, Petigo. Jolanna Petigo. I get kicked out of there and come back home to find out we're losing the farm. God, I just want to stop and plant my feet somewhere. I'm too young to be this tired."

"Jolanna Petigo," I repeat, trying to store the name in my memory. It might be useful in finding the ring.

"I do miss that horse."

"But not the girlfriend," I chuckle.

"Definitely not the girlfriend," he agrees. He nudges me with his shoulder and I look up to see a grin still sitting on his lips. I swear I see something in the way those blue eyes linger on mine screaming he knew first-hand exactly how I feel about Robert sometimes. Then, it is gone.

We must have ridden an hour and a half. Brody shows me how to use the reins and my knees to guide the horse. Then a little quicker than I would have liked, we are done and walking the lonely road again.

Emma tells us it is about an hour and a half walk to the closest town—Jacobs. It will be getting dark by the time we get there. Between, there are three houses that might have people home where we could make a call. We aren't so lucky. Nobody is home.

And so we make it into Jacobs at about eight-thirty. Brody is getting antsy. He doesn't gripe about being late for his date with Kylee. However, when we get to a bar/ restaurant called Thirsty Al's Family Restaurant and Tavern, which is the only place open in the teeny-weeny town, he uses the phone to call her. He does this between me calling Andrea who doesn't pick up her phone and Billy Belcher of Belcher's Tire and Service Station who grunts a gruff reply that for my mother's sake, he will record the baseball game he is watching. He will be out in about a half hour to fix my tire. Brody finally calls Zach to come pick us up and take me back to my car. I tell him where my spare key is inside my shop. I have three because I lock myself out so much.

And so we sit at a rusty umbrella table outside Thirsty Al's, without a dime to our names and with a restaurant/bar full of people waiting in line and staring at us while they do. I finally go inside and ask the bartender if I can wait on a couple tables. On the way in, a girl about my age flags me down in the line.

"I know you," she tells me. My mind churns. Her face is not familiar, nor are the others in the line bobbing their heads up and down. I smile, none-the-less.

"You sing at Hobie's," the man standing next to her says. He waves his hand around. "We all went there a couple Saturdays ago. We saw you sing."

I nod and smile. "Yeah, that would be me and Drew." Now I'm freaking out, hoping Brody can't hear them. I'm terrified Delilah or somebody from church is going to find out I sing there.

"You two are singing tomorrow, right?" another girl asks. She gets into her purse, pulls out a folded paper and pushes down the flaps. It is one of the advertisements Drew placed at the college behind Hobie's. It says: DREW'S JOURNEY. FRIDAY NIGHT. HOBIE'S BAR AND GRILLE. 7:00 PM. Thank God, he made my name sound like part of the band.

"We'd planned on coming if you were. You waited on our table last time too. That was so cool."

"We'll be there."

I chit-chat for another minute while the line kind of folds in on me. Everybody seems to have heard about Hobie's and wants to know about the gig tomorrow. I finally excuse myself, sideways glancing at Brody and praying he didn't overhear. Worry sets in. I try not to see the horrified gaze I will get from Delilah if she knows where I work.

I work my way to the bar and ask the manager if, in exchange for something to eat, I can wait some tables. Who would have thought he would say a hearty "yes." A couple of the waitresses are running late getting into work tonight.

I grab the tables the others aren't waiting on and make about fourteen bucks in tips. Twenty-five minutes and until his other waitress shows up to take my place is enough for a petite sirloin steak dinner for Brody and a side salad with bread and butter for me.

"What's this?" Brody asks while I plop the plate down in front of him.

"It is the Little Al Petite Steak with mashed potatoes and gravy, corn and a dinner roll." I say, pointing at each of the side orders, one at a time. "I hope it is enough. I couldn't order the Big Al steak. It was five bucks more. I waited some tables so they could catch up the line outside. If I took more tables, I'd have to stay longer and I didn't know what time Zach would be here. I'm starving, are you?"

He is just staring at the food, then he looks up at me. "Is that what you've been doing?"

"Yeah, I'm resourceful," I joke as I dig into my salad. "But you have to be with a mother like Delilah. If she didn't think I should have something, I didn't get it. Anything from cut-off shorts like I am wearing to a guitar. So I have always managed to work around it. She didn't want me taking music classes in college, so I snuck them in and paid for them by waitressing tables and singing on the side. One of many creative ways I learned to go around my mother."

"I thought you got lost in the bathroom," he says really seriously. I think this is really funny because I can't tell if he is joking or not.

"For a half hour?" I am holding my fork mid-air, trying to stifle a giggle with my fist so I don't spit out lettuce on Brody.

"I thought there might be a line," Brody says with a serious shrug. Then, he smiles. "No, I'm just kidding. You seem to know everybody here. I assumed you were chatting it up inside too."

"Not really. They just remember me from Great Escapes."

Brody looks up at the crowd with a bit of uncertainty. "I wouldn't have thought they were the type to go to a doll restaurant."

Ug. I need to think things out. "They have good pizza at
Great Escapes. But, I guess it could have been a wedding I
sang at." He dismisses the conversation with a shrug of
shoulders.

Our whole dinner goes like this, awkward but not
embarrassing. I feel like we are clumsily avoiding anything
that might provoke a fight. Like two warring countries who
are just too darn tired to fight anymore, we make simple
small-talk and mumble apologies when we think we
accidently cross the war-zone line.

At somewhere close to 9:00 p.m., Zach has still not
shown so we go to the parking lot and take turns leaning
into a dimly lit lamppost. I suppose there is only so much
two strangers who have known each other a lifetime can
talk about because we both become quiet shortly into our
move outdoors in the cooler night air. I kick the dirt with
the boots Emma said I could just keep. Brody stuffs his
hands in his pockets and stares up at the half-moon.

"I guess since you bought supper we could call this a
date," Brody finally mumbles. "I think Grandpa Del would
give us that."

I roll my eyes. "Well, he had some criteria for a real
date and it was more than just yelling at each other while
we walk down an old road and then eating a meal together.
But even if he didn't, as far as I'm concerned, what we have
done today could have passed as a business meeting."

"It wasn't that bad," he tells me, forcing a smile.

"Fine for you, Cowboy." I sigh deeply, "Probably in
his eyes you are released from his request. But he wanted
me to fill up a dance card full of dates before I married
Robert. Even if I count this one, I've got eighteen more to
fill up the card. I really don't think Robert would support
my desire to date nineteen guys before we get married.
Twenty if we call this a business meeting gone bad."

I roll my eyes. "Your grandpa was kind of sappy. He told me a date had to include holding hands and kissing. I can guarantee Robert would have a problem with that."

"Are you two engaged?" he asks.

"Well, no," I say. I almost feel like I should give an excuse for Robert and my own procrastination on getting married. But right then, I can only think that I don't have a choice but to eventually marry him. We had been dating so long.

"Um," Brody nods, looks at the ground. He stuffs his hands in his pockets and shuffles his feet. It is sexy, this stance, like a cowboy in a movie. I try not to think about it. Silence follows and I nibble my lip.

"You know, when Andrea and I were in middle school we had this secret code," I say right out of the blue. Brody is giving me THE LOOK. He has no clue what I am talking about. I know I just burst out with it. I am nervous. I hate awkward silence. "Um, we used to always put X's and O's on all the little messages and notes we sent each other. When Robert was around, he'd always snatch them up and try to read them. So if I knew he was going to read it, I wrote the opposite and put O's and X's."

"What's your point?"

"I don't know. I'm just making conversation."

Silence again. We both stare at the ground. Then Brody reaches out and pokes my arm with his forefinger.

"So we held hands," he says slowly, his eyes had caught mine just a moment, then drop again. "If I kissed you, you would only have eighteen dates left to fulfill his promise?"

"Something like that," I laugh, thinking Brody Wells is just looking at the number. I never think he is contemplating something else.

"Can I kiss you then?"

I have been staring at Brody's feet just like he is staring at them. One is kicking the ground in front of the lamppost, a gritty gravel mixed with hard pieces of asphalt. I look up at the same time he does, our eyes catching for just a moment. He has a guarded expression, his eyes are wary and his lips are pressed hard together.

"Okay." It was that easy. I didn't ask if he would tell Robert. I didn't think about how many years I had gone without kissing anyone else. There were probably five or six other things I didn't think out then because I caught a flash of those blue eyes of Brody Wells and I honestly forgot everything else. I just went—stupid. And he simply took a step, leaned in and gave me a brush along the lips.

A kiss and a quick one. Nothing more, nothing less. In some countries, I understand, folks greet with a kiss even for business meetings. It could have been appropriate there. But it doesn't just end right then. I feel the softness of his lips, then they touch mine a bit harder. I'm not sure if Brody expects to go any farther than a simple one second peck, but his lips are right there and soft and cool and wet and I grab his shirt with my fingers and I tow him toward me. He doesn't grunt an excuse and shove me away. So we did have a big kiss like the kind in the movies that lasts about a minute, maybe a minute and a half.

"Holy shit," Brody breathes out. I'm thinking, *oh, no,* I screwed up. He hates me worse now and he thinks the kiss was awful. Because I get the feeling Robert hates my kisses because he avoids them when we are getting hot and heavy on the couch.

I'm standing here feeling a little dizzy from the kiss and a little woozy from the realization of what I have done. Then the next thing I know, Brody is sliding his hand behind my neck, warm against the cooler night air.

He pulls me forward with a gentle tug of his arm and I feel his lips, feel my tummy wiggling around like I've got a hundred butterflies inside trying to get out. I feel his heart beating and my heart beating and I'm wishing it would never stop because I've never been kissed like this before. Never.

"Hey, lovebirds, you going to stay here and make out all night or do you want a ride?"

I think I could have died right then as Zach hollers out his car window about a stone's throw away in the parking lot. Brody jerks away like I am on fire. I step back. Both our faces are red.

"Oh, no," is all I can mutter. I am running my hand through my hair nervously while Brody mumbles something about making sure Zach doesn't say anything. It is a quiet ride back to my car. Brody sits in the front with Zach and I sit in the back while Zach tells stupid jokes and Brody laughs a little too heartily.

"Well, at least your car isn't broken into," Brody says while I shove my extra car key into the driver's side that Zach found in my office. He reaches in, snatches up his phone and waits for me to get in and drive off. And I watch Zach's car in the rearview mirror and hope to God he doesn't tell everybody about the kiss.

I can't sleep when I get home. The kiss. I can only think about not hating Brody Wells anymore after his damn kiss and maybe hating him more. And guilt. It is flooding over me what I had done. I kissed a guy and it wasn't Robert.

I can't sleep so I get out my guitar, find myself working on an old song I tried to write but never got done. More little pieces of paper with words on them, more little bits of song in the trash can, on the floor, on my desk, on my bed. I bang it around and while I think about Brody and the kiss, it starts coming to me. I remember a song I wrote in high school and I toss into the trash a hundred times.

I write it all down again, then stop because my head is getting fuzzy from being so tired. *Found myself outside your bedroom window last Friday after school Thinking about those crazy, silly little things we used to do. The time you stood up in front of everybody at the county fair. You said I was yours. Your friends gave you crap and you said you didn't care. There was the time we stood on the train tracks screamed at the train, Riding your horse into the sunset. Dancing in the rain, jumping on your bed. There were a hundred other things before I realized it was all in my head. All in my head, all in my head, all in my head, head, head.*

The house is silent and there are twelve messages on my answering machine from Robert and three from Andrea. They have texted me about twenty times each—*where are you?* I just send a quick message telling them I went to meet a customer and I had a headache. I will call them tomorrow. I am terrified I will blurt out my secret, just accidently toss it out there before I have time to think things out.

But I am working. It isn't a lie. To prove it, I start a search on Brody's ex-girlfriend and online auctions. Then I search the social networks and boom! I get a hit.

Jolanna Petigo has about a thousand pictures of herself posted online along with the horses she sells and trades. Right smack in the middle of the page is the pretty paint horse I remember Brody used to own. JACK. REGISTERED PAINT. 15 HANDS. WILL TRADE.

I stare at it thinking it is unfair she gets the horse. Not that I don't think Brody probably doesn't warrant it. He can be a hardass. Still, I send her a message, ask what she is wanting for the horse. I don't expect a reply, but while I am brushing my teeth, I hear a soft *ting* on my computer and go to check my e-mail.

Here is what it says: *I'm asking $1200.00. Firm. I got a trader coming in tomorrow afternoon to take twelve geldings to auction. If you're interested, you would have to be here before noon. He's dead broke just like his former owner.*

I sit there chewing my lip. Dead broke. Brody was anything but 'dead broke.' It irritated me even though *he* called *me* the same thing. I pushed it aside. I was here about the ring. The ring. How can I include the ring in the message without implying I know Brody?

I write back: *I might be interested. Getting the horse for my fiancé. But not sure if I have enough for horse and a ring for us. Thanks, but got to think of the ring first.*

It isn't four minutes before I get the message that she has a ring her ex-boyfriend had given her and he was a shit and she wants to get rid of it. It has some engraving on the inside, but she says I can scratch them off, probably, with a nail file. A picture displays a small diamond ring. I have to assume it is the right one. I don't want to ask what it says and push the issue. She tells me for fifty bucks for the ring and $1200.00 for the horse, her memories of the jerk will be gone.

I sit there at my dark desk staring at the screen. I am just a few keyboard strokes away from making Delbert's daughter, Gayle, happy and Brody happy. At a cost, that is, of $1250.00 out of my bank account that I am sure I am not going to get returned to me anytime soon. And I have to get back to Hobie's to work by 7:00 p.m. What if it is the wrong ring? And what the hell am I going to do with a horse? But my desire to make a deal outweighs prudence just then. That and the damn kiss was still lingering on my lips. While I sit there numbly, my fingers begin to type:

Hold the horse and the ring. I'll be there by noon. Need an address.

And, oh shit, where am I going to get a horse trailer at midnight?

Chapter –13

Date 2

Note to Self:

1) Drew's show 7:00   2) Get money for horse

I didn't forget Bella Johnson's threat about kicking my ass at Delbert's funeral. It has been hanging in the air around me since she said it. Her words leave me feeling like I have to constantly peer over my shoulder in case we cross paths and she decides to make good on her word. Every dark-headed, thick-set person over six feet tall that walks my way makes me recoil. I think I am getting a twitch in my eye from it. But my fears don't stop me from calling Bella at a little past midnight. My desire to find something for someone else overrides it.

Bella is grumpy at 12:30 at night when awakened from a dead sleep. I have a good idea it might increase my chances of getting my butt kicked more sooner than later. Still, she is the only person I know who has a pickup truck and a horse trailer and can drive it.

"This is Journey Bacon. Can I ask you for a favor?" I inquire in my softest, sweetest voice.

"Can I kick your ass for waking me up at 2:00 in the morning?" she answers like a black bear awakened from a winter sleep.

"No," I tell her. I assume the odds of denying Bella the authority to kick my ass and her actually putting off the task in the immediate future are slim. However, it is worth a try. I do not correct her and tell her it is closer to midnight, nor do I remind her that if I die from any of her punches in the court of law, my murder will have been premediated. "I need you to drive your horse trailer to Kentucky for me and pick up a horse."

"No."

"Bella, please," I appeal to her.

It has never bothered me a bit to beg under the right circumstances. I am thinking I should probably get used to it anyways because when she starts pounding me with angry fists, I will be pleading for my life. "It isn't for me. It is for Brody."

There is silence on the other end of the line for a good thirty seconds. I can hear her moving around in her bed like she is sitting up. "Why would anything you are doing have something to do with my cousin?"

I knew it would come up in the conversation, I just haven't quite settled on what I will say. "Okay, Brody and I —"

"*Brody and I?*" she growls a hoarse snarl. "Bacon, don't ever use your name, even applied as a pronoun with stupid in front of it, and my cousin's name in the same sentence."

"Okay," I say amicably, thinking out my words carefully. "Brody's horse is for sale online. Jack. You remember Jack? His ex-girlfriend is selling it. I found it. It is getting sold at auction tomorrow if I don't get it by noon."

Nothing. For a moment I think she has hung up. I chew my thumbnail, then tell myself I will count to a hundred and back again before I hang up and call her back. Then, I hear her taking in a deep breath and grunting it out again.

"Jack," she mutters. Then she curses. "Damn, he loves that horse. It is all he talks about." Then there is another long pause. "You know, Bacon, that woman isn't going to sell that horse back to Brody. There's no way he can show up there tomorrow and she's going to hand him over that horse."

Bella is quiet, seems to mull it over. "She might have a gun in her hand," she goes on. "But she ain't handing over that old horse's reins. I'm not even going to ask how and why you know about this horse for sale. Or why you care."

"Well," I start instead. "Brody isn't going and she doesn't know I even know him. Does she know you?"

"I've never met her face to face," she tells me. "She never let Brody come home when they were dating. Bacon, you really don't know what you're getting into. This woman's the biggest, controlling bitch anybody's ever met."

It was my turn to pause, take in a breath. I clamp my jaws shut. "Well, Bella, you're the biggest, controlling bitch I've ever met," I say frankly. "Especially when it comes to Brody. I bet you could take her on. It would be like Godzilla and Mothra fighting it out." I had this sudden vision of Bella and Brody's ex-girlfriend lashing out at each other like two monsters from a B-rated Japanese movie.

"You know, you really need to think things out before you say them, Bacon," she answers in a flat tone. "You know you just insulted me, right?"

"Did I?" I ask, my voice rising a bit like I'm confused at her insinuation. "Oh." I *had* actually thought it out.

"Yeah, and don't pull that 'I'm cute and ditzy' shit on me. I'm not a guy. I don't think with my crotch. So don't let it happen again," she tells me in the old gruff voice. "God, I want to kill you," she groans. "I'll be there at seven. It's probably a five hour drive."

I breathe out, hadn't realized I'd been holding my breath waiting for an answer. I am surprised she doesn't pursue the question why I'm doing this for Brody. It wouldn't matter anyway. I can't quite figure out if I just like the quest to find something for somebody so badly, I'll go to any extent. Or maybe it is still that damn kiss.

Regardless, I make Bella promise to keep this a secret between us. If Brody's ex-girlfriend gets a whiff of what I am doing, she isn't going to sell the horse or the ring to me.

The problem is, Bella doesn't listen well or keep secrets. At seven in the morning, I am standing in the driveway waiting for her. I have already made a trip to town to withdraw the cash I need. I haven't done my wash in three days, so I snatch up the jean shorts and a t-shirt from my closet floor. The cowboy boots fit so well yesterday, I figured I'd wear them again too. Emma said she had them in a bag headed for Goodwill. But they look in great shape to me. As I look up, I can see a huge black truck coming around the curve of my street. The windows are tinted and I stand there unsure until the passenger window rolls down and I see one of the two inside wearing a cowboy hat.

"What the heck?" I toss my hands in the air and point right at Brody when Bella swings the truck and trailer around, then rolls down the window. Bella leans across the seat.

"I'm not good at secrets," she says smugly and with an evil twist to her lips.

"Naw, she's not," Brody adds before he pops open the door and scoots to his left. He is just staring at me, no smile on his face. He leaves just enough room for me to slide in along the weathered vinyl seat. It is cramped and I try hard to hug my purse on my legs and lean hard into the door. The truck is loud when it takes off and Bella flips a switch so the radio is blasting country music.

I eagerly grab my phone and earplugs out of my purse, but Brody stops me just before I turn on some music.

"You know I don't have the money she's asking for the horse," Brody nearly has to yell over the radio. He looks cramped, uncomfortable.

It is probably the last thing he wants to say to me. He doesn't mention the ring, so I am assuming Bella doesn't even know this little secret of his.

"I know," I say. "I've got it covered."

"He tried to talk me out of doing this for an hour," Bella is yelling too. I can foresee a headache coming on soon.

"I *don't* want to do this," he said, looking peeved.

"You don't want the horse?" I ask. I'm ready to put my hand out, stop this charade when I see Bella shaking her head back and forth behind him.

"He wants the horse," she says, then elbows Brody hard in the ribs. "You want the damn horse. Let her pay for it. We'll worry about paying her back later."

"I've got no place to keep him," Brody mutters. "I mean, I find it really hard to waste the money on horse feed and hay when my mom and dad can't even afford to make the house payments."

"He's going to stay at my dad's farm," Bella tells him. "You deserve the horse. *She* doesn't deserve shit." She jabs a thumb toward me. "Let her make up for the crap her family's put us through. She's part of the problem, Brody."

"I didn't do anything," I sit up a bit, lean toward Brody and toss out a hand in my defense. "Hey, I'm trying to help."

"Well, if you really want to help, you should tell old Ironwood to look over his bank books again," Bella spits at me. "Because I don't think Grandpa Del or Uncle Johnny ever missed a damn payment."

"Bella, stop," Brody is shaking his head back and forth. I can tell he is embarrassed. He won't even look at me.

My phone beeps. It is Drew. Again. He messages me twice, reminding me to be at Hobie's on time. He sends a picture of himself looking worried. Then he sends another one looking mad. Then he sends a third looking all cocky and happy. *Which Drew do you want to see?* He messages me. *Because the first one is me now because you haven't called. The second is me if you stand me up. The third is if you tell me you promise you won't be late. Write that one back and it better be the happy one.*

I laugh and look up to see Brody looking over my shoulder, eyeing me carefully before he slumps in the seat.

"Maybe we shouldn't do this," he states, looking right at me. I think his cowboy hat must be like the consoling blanket I used to carry around when I was three. He pokes it, caresses it when he talks to me.

"It's your call," I tell him while I stick out my tongue and make a silly face at my phone and take a picture. *Late for what? Do we have a date?* I text Drew with an emoji of a smiley face with eyes crossed. Brody doesn't answer. Instead, he goes back to grumbling at Bella. I listen to Brody and Bella bicker for the first half hour. Then I slowly sink down in the seat and shove my earplugs in and let the music take me away.

Four minutes from Brody's ex-girlfriend's stables, Bella bangs on my leg and asks me if I have a plan. Of course, I don't. "Well, I did until you brought Cowboy, here," I tell her, tugging off my earplugs. "It would have been pretty simple just driving right up to the house, paying her and driving away. But since you've got Brody, I'm all ears to what we're going to do with him. You don't have a trunk to stuff him in."

"You would stuff me in a trunk?" It is the first time Brody has talked to me in the four hours and forty-five minutes since I shoved my earplugs in.

I look up and he's tugging his hat down to hide his eyes and he looks really cute.

I never really fell in love with country music until I started playing it hard at Hobie's bar. Delilah only listens to classical music and the religious stuff she sings in the choir. But when I eyed Brody right then in his pale blue t-shirt, sleeves tight against his work-muscled arms and his head tipped to see me beneath his hat, I decide I just might want to be a country music star just so he might take a look at me. Of course, I won't let him know that.

"I would," I answer. "And not just because I'm thinking if your ex-girlfriend finds out I tricked her, she will be fighting with Bella over which one is going to beat the crap out of me. The odds are pretty good with you sitting in this truck, she's going to see you, get her shotgun out and kill us all." I bring up my hand and make it into a gun with forefinger pointing at Brody. "Bang, bang," I say in almost a whisper.

I don't have time to wait for his answer or see his expression. We pull into a huge u-shaped gravel drive and Brody's face turns a shade of putrid green-white I have never seen on any living person. There is a huge farm looming before us—barn after barn, stable after stable and a luxury resort hotel-like house plopped in the middle. It is certainly not even close to what I had imagined.

"When you said you worked at an old stable, Brody, I thought you meant rundown, not historical," I tell him. "Delilah would be right at home here and the idea that the milk she drinks comes from a living animal makes her queasy," I say with more truth than I would like to divulge. Brody laughs nervously, turns enough to point a finger at one barn in particular.

"I lived in a mobile home out back." He shifts in his seat. "She's waiting for you," he says, pointing out the windshield. "Along with her pack."

"Pack?" I ask. What did I get myself into? I see Bella giving Brody a knowing gaze.

"Yeah, those women are like wolves. They work for the Petigos," he says. "And they'll do anything they say, attack on command. Most of them are my ex's friends from high school. Try not to piss her off." he adds, then laughs as I stare hard at him. "You know, I'm just kidding."

But his eyes are lying. I look up, see a bunch of girls sitting on a fence and one breaking free from the group and hopping off. They all look big and mean to me. The one jumping off is built like Bella, but has long brown hair and a less-round face.

"Is there anything I need to know before I do this, Cowboy?" I ask quickly. "I've never bought a horse. I have no idea in hell what your ex-girlfriend is like or if she is going to bargain."

"It isn't much different than what you do with your store. How much you got and how much is she asking?" he says really fast.

"I got $2000.00 out of the bank. She is asking $1200.00."

"Um, she's going to expect that you to take a look at him, then maybe check out a few others," Brody divulges to me. "When she asks if you want to ride him—"

"She's going to ask me to ride him?" I huff. "I can't ride a horse!"

"Yeah, well, just tell her you hurt your back or something and can't ride now. Offer a thousand even though he is worth more."

I'm blinking at him, taking it all in and wishing I had a garbage can to puke in. I see Jolanna walking toward the trailer with heavy strides and her hands in her jeans pockets. I'm a little worried she'll get close to the truck and see Brody so I jump out and start towards the woman.

"Hey," I hear Brody yell-whisper to me. "Um, her name's Jolanna, but they call her Jolie," he says. "And even though she's got a hard right swing, it starts really slow at first."

I have my back to him, but snap my head upward, and make an uncertain and wide-eyed glance back toward the truck. Is he kidding? Surely, he is kidding. I start to question him with a hazy sense of impending doom in my tummy and a silent "*what?*" slipping from my lips but he is already sliding into the recesses of the truck, hidden behind the tinted windows.

I groan inwardly, thinking I am making this much harder than it really has to be. I barter and trade antiques every day. I make a beeline toward Jolanna and three steps away, she stops.

"You're here to look at the horse?" she asks. "The girl I texted last night?" She has a certain confidence I lack and while I look up at her, I realize she is nearly six inches taller than me. But she is pretty with doe-brown eyes. Bitch or not, as Bella described her, it was easy to see that perhaps even if she has flaws, Brody wouldn't have been an idiot if he had overlooked them.

I give a quick nod, stick out my hand to shake hers. Damn, she has a hard grip that kind of sticks there a moment while she peers over my shoulder, then latches hard on my eyes.

Beautiful, self-assured and cool, she was in comparison to my dopey, cowardly and timid.

"You got somebody to help load him if you want him?" she says. "He's a good horse, but he's a hard loader."

I nod when she waves me forward. I follow her two steps behind, past the eight girls balancing on the fence with their rears on the wood and their feet dangling toward the ground. They don't seem to have much interest in me. They are all sucking on soda pops and digging chips out of a couple bags like they are taking a break. One asks Jolanna if she needs help, but she doesn't even bother to answer, simply waves the girl away.

I'm nervous. Jolanna keeps eyeing me and then the truck even while she gets to the small stall where the horse is hanging out his head. She holds out her hand toward him. She yaks away about the horse, telling me things I already know about him because I've seen Brody riding him down the road or at the fair. And it is old Jack, I even recognize him. Still, I almost feel like Jolanna can scent out my fear like a hound dog smells a scared rabbit in the brush. Or maybe it is the Ohio license plates—or maybe it is just a trap and she knows it is Brody all along.

"Do you want to take him out for a ride?"

"No," is all I say and I just want to get this over with because the longer she talks, the more I'm getting anxious. Besides, I had to get back home by 6 o'clock so I could get dressed and meet Drew for his singing debut at Hobie's.

"It's for my fiancé. He either likes him or he doesn't. If he doesn't, he'll trade him in for another, I suppose. I'm not really big on horses like he is."

"Suit yourself," she shrugs. "It's one less I got to take to auction. He's $1800.00."

Aw, shit. I nearly bite my lip. Okay, I've had this happen before. I drive five or six hours to pick up an antique lamp or chair and the guy selling it figures he'll raise the price.

He assumes if I've driven that far, I'm not going to deny him the extra fifty or hundred bucks.

"Yeah, well, when we messaged last night, you told me it was $1200.00. Firm."

"You want the horse or not?"

Okay, here's where it gets a little dicey. I usually walk away if they renege or back out. I've learned that before I get into the car, I've got to promise myself that at anytime during the deal, I could lose it. It comes with the blonde hair, wide blue eyes and the way people perceive me because some idiot decided to stereotype women with the same traits as me. Well, and as Bella pointed out, I sometimes use them to my advantage. So I've learned to just keep saying in my mind, I didn't want or need it anyway. Besides, it is insulting. I simply shrug and walk away. There's a fifty-fifty chance they'll suddenly remember the price they quoted me, figure out I'm not as ditzy as they thought.

With Brody's horse, it's a little different. While I reach out and touch the muzzle, it sniffs me and I'm wondering if horses are like dogs and Jack can smell Brody on me. I don't know, but he leans into me and rubs his muzzle on my fingers like he's on Jolanna's side and enticing me to buy him. And all's I can see is Brody Wells with a smile on his face riding through the fields yesterday. I see him at the fair, flirting with the judges and tipping his hat. I think this is probably the very first time I feel hard-pressed enough to just hand over the money and leave.

"I'll tell you what," I say. "My fiancé doesn't need a horse so bad that I can't afford our wedding. I thought it would be a nice gift. But I've got to back down. I get it, though. I understand. You want the horse. It reminds you of your ex-boyfriend."

She stands there looking at me. I can see a bit of irritation creeping up her face. I can see she doesn't think Brody's as much a shit as she would like everybody to believe. And she certainly doesn't want anybody thinking she's keeping the horse around because she misses him. I am pretty sure, too, her pack outside can hear what we are talking about in the barn. I hear a bit of snickering outside and she looks up quickly like she is a bit worried they hear what I am saying.

I think she is sizing up the situation. I'm not sure how much horses are, but at any auction, it is hit or miss if you're going to get a really good price out of something you're selling or a really, really horrible deal. Most of the time, you don't get lucky especially if you have a lot of something. Or it is old and a little worn down.

"I've got other horses that are cheaper, sweetie, if you can't afford this one."

"Naw, that's okay," I say. My stomach is rumbling scared right then. There's a certain amount of open door space I can give before I walk away. Why do I feel like I will lose something if I walk away now and not get the horse? If I do walk, chances are she's not going to come running after me if her friends are out there accessing if their alpha-female pack leader is going to yield to someone like me half her size.

"I'll still take the ring," I say. "I don't want to leave empty-handed."

She looks at me, then kind of leans back against the side of the stall with a sly smile pursing her lips. I notice how deep pink they are. I watch as she reaches into her pocket, tugs out a diamond ring and holds it out flat in the palm of her hand. "No horse, no ring, sweetie."

It is hot and I'm starting to sweat in the dank, dark barn. I get a little woozy mad when she calls me "sweetie" again. The image of her laying naked on a couch and her finger wiggling toward Brody crosses my mind. No *sex, no paycheck, sweetie,* I imagine her saying. Ug.

I blink to get rid of the thought, lean in, pluck the ring from her palm. I look at it closely. *To Grace, my love,* it says.

"Okay, it's like this," I utter while I'm holding the ring. "You got me. I've driven five hours to get here. You know I don't want to go back empty-handed. But a deal is a deal whether it was made online or not. But I'm willing to give you a little extra. I'll give you $1500.00 for both."

"I won't take less than $1800.00."

She starts to walk away, reaches down to grab the ring from my fingers. I snap my hand shut. "Then I will pay you $1800.00."

She stops and I reach into my purse, snatch out the money and count it out in her hands. $1800.00 was a lot of waitressing at Hobie's Bar and Grille, Great Escapes Family Restaurant, and thirteen wedding gigs. Jolanna Petigo waves one of her wolf pack over, tells her to walk the horse out to the trailer. I stand back, let her tug Jack from his stall. He ambles out like he knows Brody is waiting for him in the cab of the truck. And me, I watch while Bella gets out of the driver's seat and opens the back end to the trailer. Without too much fuss, Jack walks right into the trailer and Bella and Jolanna's lackey shoves the door close behind him.

It should have gone smoothly from there. It probably no more than forty steps from where I stand just on the outside of the barn door to the passenger door of Bella Johnson's truck. There is nothing but air between us. I could have been there in less than forty seconds.

Well, there was nothing between the truck and me except Jolanna Petigo and one minor flaw in the plan I never devised in the first place. With an evil twist of her lips, Jolanna whips out her cell phone, takes a picture of the horse's butt in the back of the trailer and punches a few numbers in her phone.

And here lies the flaw. It rings to the cell phone she is calling. It must have occurred to Jolanna the exact moment she sent the picture of Brody Wells's horse to him and decided to call his cell phone to rub it in, that the person she is calling is just about thirty-seven steps away. And he has a cell phone ringing in exact correspondence to the phone in the truck.

I am just getting ready to put the ring in my purse for safe keeping when I look up to see her eyeing her phone, then walking her gaze along the path I should have taken two minutes earlier. It stops at the truck. Jolanna's eyes narrow. She stands there still for less than twenty seconds while the realization seeps in slowly and building along with it, a certain anger. She disconnects the call, then waits for the count of ten, then dials once more. Again, Brody's cell phone rings. I watch helplessly as she pivots on her feet so she is less than an arms-length away from me.

"You bitch."

Chapter −14

Note to Self: 1) Don't be late for show

2) Pick up ice for black eye

"Go!" I can hardly take in air, my breaths are coming in puffs. "Go, go, go!."

I am running next to the passenger side of the truck as I spit that out, my hands flailing in front of me trying to grasp anything I can to latch on to the door. Brody is halfway out the window reaching for me, but Bella has her foot to the accelerator, the tires are churning gravel at my shins and although Robert quite often tells me my legs are my best feature when I have them wrapped around him during sex, they aren't as fast as a truck. I'm having a hard time trying to keep up.

My hand is on my right cheek just below my eye. Jolanna Petigo hit me so hard and so fast, I didn't have time to duck. I just took three long strides backward and fell on my butt in the dirt. My purse went flying left, Gayle's ring went right and other than hearing some the gasps from the layer of girls on the fence, I don't remember much but a moment of black and dust when I skidded to a halt against the barn door.

Of course, Jolanna cursed and she booted me in the side. I think she tried to pull me up by my hair while I squealed like a newborn pig. It wasn't a flattering moment for me. I only know I felt her fist hit my temple and my ribs before I used my right boot to kick her in the knee. The only thing I could think of was the feel of the ring that had been clasped in my palm before it was sent flying into the air, lost in a misty halo of dust.

She didn't even cringe when I kicked her. I rolled to my belly, crawled like a spider on the ground thinking I must surely be crazy that a ring is more important than getting murdered.

I see a glint of gold, pat the ground, bring up a handful of sand and say a short and heartfelt prayer to God—*Dear God,* I pray silently, *Please let me have the ring and please don't let this woman kill me.*

But if God is listening, I'm not sure. While Jolanna Petigo lets out a scream of oaths, I feel her hand reach out, snatch me up by the sleeve of my t-shirt and toss me like a baby doll on the ground. I roll right to my belly and push myself to a crawl and then an outright run. Just as she is about to step on my heels, I come to a complete stop and shove my skinny arm straight out. Jolanna's neck runs smack into my bony fist. I hear her gag, then scream: "GET HER!"

Two weeks earlier, I had been driving down the road. For some reason, a little squirrel came running out right in front of my car with a nut in his mouth. He saw my car, tucked his butt and took off in a run with his tail between his legs. The squirrel barely missed my front tire before it bounded off the road. For a millisecond, the image popped up in my mind while I did the same running from Jolanna's outstretched arm. I dip but once to snag my purse. When I come up, I am only one step away from the girls still lounging on the fence. I don't know what gets into me, but I think I see them start to dismount and I kind of freak. I cannot take on Jolanna, much less her rabid pack of wolves. They will kill me dead.

I push both my arms out in front of me, palms outward and hit that fence on my way through. All seven of the girls are toppling down backward and forward in a jumbled mass while I stumble over them toward the truck.

I can see it and I can barely make out Brody's head leaning out the window waving his arms toward me while I am screaming: "Go, go, go!" And Bella takes that moment to hit the accelerator with her foot and take off.

So this is where I am huffing and puffing while Brody leans out the window and grabs me by the arms. It isn't so graceful climbing into the passenger side window of a truck while it is moving thirty miles an hour and gaining speed down the road. And it hurts. I latch on to Brody's neck and he tugs me through the window. I can feel every inch of my body from ribs to hips dragging across the tip of window still sticking up. Then I'm nearly flopped on Brody's lap and the floor. I wallow there trying to right myself while Bella takes a hard right on the driveway out into the gravel road at a speed better suited for a Nascar race.

By the time I right myself, Brody is patting the dashboard with one hand and looking through the back window. He is absently latching on to my upper arm to help me to the truck seat. I don't think any of us are comfortable that Jolanna Petigo and her pack aren't following us until we hit the highway and are snugly packed between a couple semi-trucks and a convertible.

There was a smothering quiet in the cab. I slip between Bella and Brody and buckle my seatbelt. My heart is pounding, my head is aching and I can't get my hands to stop shaking.

When I finally catch my breath, I turn to Brody and grit my teeth. "Alright, Cowboy," I say. "Yes, she has a hard right swing and it's a little slow at first. Thanks for the heads up on that. But you could have, at some point, informed me that after that swing, your ex-girlfriend drops to the right and then she comes up with her fist on the left really fast."

Both Brody and Bella burst into hysterical laugher. It is so hard, tears are spilling down Bella's face and she is weaving on and off the road. I'm not sure if they are laughing at me or at what I said.

Andrea and Robert make fun of me all the time, laughing like they have some inside joke when I say something they think is stupid. It is humiliating. I have learned to laugh along so I don't feel like the butt-end of a joke. And so I do the same with Brody and Bella, but my feelings are hurt. Even worse, I get to listen to the two rehashing the story for the next hour and a half between fits of laughter. I just smile wanly. Bella's favorite part, I can tell, is when I bowled over Jolanna's wolf pack. Bella thinks this is especially funny and nudges me hard with her elbow.

I'm sore all over and a little humbled already for letting Jolanna swindle me out of six-hundred bucks. I just wish I could nurse my wounds. I am wondering if I will be one big bruise tomorrow morning so I tug up my shirt in the back and tell Brody to look at it, see if I have any welts. His gaze makes a roll toward Bella before he gets a funny lop-sided grin to his lips. "Yeah," he says, poking his forefinger on my back, then my side. Then he works over to my ribs in front where Jolanna kicked me hard. "You've got a boot print here."

"Crap, what am I going to tell Robert?" I rub my hand over my eyes, lean against the seat and tug my shirt back down.

At four o'clock, we stop at a gas station off the highway. Bella uses a wallet and tugs it out of the back of her jeans. I walk around the truck, snatch the last of my money from my purse. "I got $200.00 bucks left," I say, handing her the last of my money. "I don't know how much it is to fill up your truck."

She takes the money at first and looks at me funny. Maybe she wonders if I am lying to her about the amount I still have or maybe she knows the deal went kind of south. She just shakes her head back and forth and shoves the money back at me.

"Naw, I got it." Then turns her back to me and pumps the gas.

"Bella, what time do you think we'll get back?" I ask her back. I would have asked Brody, but he jumped out as soon as we stopped and went into the little shop connected to the gas station. I'm starting to worry again about making it on time for Drew. She just shrugs.

"Probably about 6:00 or 7:00. You in a hurry or something?"

"Yeah, kind of," I mutter. My stomach is already starting to get the little jumpy-queasy feeling I get right before I sing in front of an audience. I am hoping I don't get car sick. "I've got to work tonight at 7:00." She just ignores me. "I mean I *have to* work tonight somewhere. If I don't, I'll get fired." I stand there awkwardly for a second, then look around for an excuse to be anywhere but standing next to her.

"I thought you had that little shop in town." Bella barely turns.

"I work a couple jobs to pay the rent there."

She doesn't answer at all. I stand there and wait. I see a picnic table under a wooden shelter and set my eyes on it. Robert has been trying to get ahold of me for an hour and I've been ignoring him. I know it will be a fight on the phone if I call him so try to get some distance between me and the truck. But first, I need to text Drew who is also messaging me every half hour.

I don't get to do either. As soon as I sit down on the top of the picnic table and pull my phone from my purse, I see a shadow cross over my bare knees.

"Here." It is Brody and he is thrusting a can of soda towards me. My tummy is too woozy, so I shake my head. "I'm not that thirsty," I tell him.

"It's for your eye." He reaches out a finger from around the soda and points to my right eye. "You're going to get a shiner. It's already turning black and blue."

Yeah, that's all I need for Drew's big show tonight. A black eye. I look up at Brody. He's kind of smiling down at me or at least trying to force a smile while he pushes up his cowboy hat and peers at me. It's really sexy when he does that. I see a splash of freckles on his nose and I nod and take the pop. Gingerly, I push it above my cheek. It feels cool and moist and takes away the ache.

"So were you able to get Jack for a good price?" he asks and shrugs his shoulders. "I guess I'm just wondering what I'm going to need to pay you back."

"Oh, you shouldn't ask," I groan while he pivots on his feet and sits down next to me. Close. So close, I can feel the warmth of his arm against mine. "Jolanna raised the price to $1800.00 and I folded like a little girl who trades in her little brother for a kitten."

"That sounds like Jolanna," he sits back, bumps up my hand with his knuckle. "You probably think I'm nuts for dating her."

"Well, no, beyond the anger and control issues, she is pretty beautiful—she's got the doe eyes thing going and a nice butt. I can see how certain other things might get overlooked." I look at Brody and laugh. "I'd date her if I was into that."

Brody is staring at me strangely, then chuckles before he sighs. "It might take a couple months or so to get it back to you. I applied for a job at the feed store. They said they'd call. I know it's a lot, but—"

"I'll let you in on a little secret," I interrupt. "It's part of the money I've been saving to buy the Knick-Knack Shop.

"I thought you owned that."

"Nope," I say. "Like my car and my house, it is owned by Robert's family and Big Bob's bank. You probably understand this. Like a farm, when you have a little business, it isn't easy getting loans. So Robert makes the payment on my car and I kind of rent my house from his dad. I've been working three jobs for the last four or five years to make enough money to buy the building the shop is in."

"I'm sorry, I'll pay you back as soon as possible."

I sniff a laugh. "It doesn't matter, Cowboy. I'm kind of in the same boat you are with your farm. I heard from your mom that Big Bob is selling the entire building the Knick-Knack Shop is in and all the buildings attached to it, tearing it down. There's no way I can buy the whole block." Then I stop and point a finger at him.

"Oops, I do have good news, though. I almost forgot." I peer over to where Bella is finishing at the gas pump, her eyes seeming to focus on the gas lid. Standing, I reach into my pocket of the jeans shorts, delve inside and wiggle out his mom's ring along with a scattering of dust. Then I hold it aloft. "Ta da!" I say.

"No shit." His eyes widen and he cracks a huge grin while he gently takes the ring from my fingers. Damn, it was one nice smile. "I don't know how to thank you enough. You saved my life, Journey." Then he laughs and adjusts his hat. "I would kiss you again if Bella wasn't here."

I know I blush. I can feel my cheeks turning hot red. All of a sudden, I see his cheeks turn red too.

"I shouldn't have said that. Wow, that was way out of line."

"We shouldn't have kissed," I reply, while I sit back down. "But we did. And it is too late. I say we just put it behind us and move on. I'm not telling Robert. Nobody has to know."

"Yeah, except Zach," he agrees, but now he is not looking at me and his smile has dropped.

"Regardless, you can return a favor," I tell him. I push my hand on his arm for effect. "I've got to get to work by 7:00. Can you see if Bella can put her foot to the accelerator? Please, Brody."

Brody's eyes jumped up when I say the last two words. I can't describe his expression then. I had only asked him nicely. Then he looks down, drops his gaze to my hand resting on his skin. I simply pull it away, turn my attention to the ground.

"I can try, but you know Bella. She might go slower if I ask her," he says as he gets up. He stands there while I rise, pats his hands on his jeans. "So can I ask what was wrong with the kiss?"

What was wrong with the kiss? There wasn't a damn thing wrong with the kiss. Well, maybe there was. I stand there and stare at him. I know I can feel myself blush again. I don't know why I can talk to a million men and not feel my face burn, but when I am looking at Brody, I flush crimson. My eyes go back and forth between his. They are so blue, so beautiful.

"What was wrong with the kiss?" I repeat back to him almost a little too softly. I think he might not hear it because it is carried away in the wind.

But he's standing there staring at me waiting for me to finish.

"Okay, well, what was wrong was that it was just—too right." I say. Then I wait for him to snicker a laugh like everyone else does when I say something that makes sense to me, but not to anyone else. But he doesn't. "It was perfect," I go on. "I'm the one that didn't want it to stop."

So he looks over my shoulder really quick, leans in and then smacks his lips right on mine. It is fast and soft and makes my heart flip-flop again while he stands back and eyes me curiously.

"That wasn't an open invitation," I huff like I'm mad, but it is really difficult to come off angry when I know I've got a little smile playing on my lips.

"Yeah, but now we can count this as two dates," he says smugly. Oh, I remember Brody Wells's old arrogance and it appears to be back. Yep, dead broke, he was not.

"The first one with 'Satan' wasn't bad enough for you?" I sniffed. "You had to add this one as a double-header in hell?"

"I didn't think the first one was so bad," he counters. "In fact, it was probably the best date I've ever been on." He waves me toward the truck with his hand. "I got to do one of the things I like the most which is riding a horse and I got a steak dinner out of it." He reaches up and tugs on his chin, then looks at me slyly while we walk. "Hell, I didn't even have to sleep with you for the steak dinner."

"Is that what you expect when you take a girl out for steak?" I ask him. "I thought the usual criteria was three dates before you sleep with someone." I think he believes I am serious because he stops, puts a hand out and tugs me to a halt.

"No, I am just kidding," he says, looking wide eyed and serious. "I'm just saying that, you know. I'm not working on a third date." Then Brody's face turns a bright crimson. "Shit, you're just playing with me, aren't you?"

"I am," I tell him just as my phone makes its funny ting-ting with a text message. I grin up at him before I grapple with the phone and follow Brody's shadow toward the truck. Absently, I scroll down to see Andrea has sent me an image. I've been avoiding her all day. But decide to read the last one she's sent:

What's this? She writes and I poke at the image so it comes up in the screen. It looks like a newspaper article so I squint into the phone and try to make it bigger.

Journey Dawn Bacon., and Broderick Delbert Wells both of Bacon Valley, Ohio were married Thursday, June 6th, eleven o'clock in the morning at the Bacon Valley Municipal Courthouse, Zachary Metzler officiated.

The bride is the daughter of Ms. Delilah Bacon.

The bridegroom is the son of Mr. and Mrs. John Wells of Bacon Valley, Ohio.

I come to a complete halt, blinking. Quickly, I text her back. *Ha ha. Is this your idea of a joke?*

There was a lapse of about ten seconds before she sends me another text with an image of the Bacon Valley Chronicle with her chubby finger pointing under a heading that screams COMMUNITY ANNOUNCMENTS.

Brody has stopped, turning to wait for me with a concerned look on his face. "Everything okay?"

Instead of answering at first, I simply hold up my phone so he can see the announcement. "This is in the newspaper today." I watch him read it from afar.

I narrow my eyes, try to read his expression and figure out if he is a part of this joke. His brow is furrowed, Brody moves up until he is holding my hand and the phone closer to his face.

"Wh—at?" he draws out the word, stepping back. He twists his head to one side and is staring at me hard like he is waiting for a punch line to a joke.

"Andrea just sent this. She said it was in today's newspaper," I feel a bit of irritation creep up on my shoulders. "I am assuming Andrea wouldn't do this because Robert would kill me. So it has to be one of your friends or cousins who did the write-up."

Bella gives us a shout, but Brody just looks at me and looks at the phone. "I don't think any of my friends would do this either, Journey. They don't hate you that much."

"Yeah, Cowboy, they do," I tell him with a straight face. "You have no idea."

I snap my hand away. I am already about to throw up because I am terrified of performing tonight and terrified I'm going to be late. Now I am going to have to contend with the town, my mother, and Robert too. I stomp past Brody, sure it was one of his friends and sit down hard in the truck.

Chapter −15

Note to Self: 1) Don't forget to go to Robert's Parent's house for dinner 5:00

2) Tell Brody not to tell anybody I sing at the bar

It occurred to me at about 6:00 that I was never going to have time to get to my house, change clothes, grab my car and be at Hobie's Bar and Grille by 7:00 o'clock. I finally give in and ask Bella if she could please, please, please drop me off there instead of my house. I did not tell her the reason for going there. She complies without a word. There is only a roll of her eyes at Brody who has gone back to being his distant self, more interested in what is on his phone than talking to anyone else.

Drew is freaking out when I text him and tell him to get one of his friends to get my guitar and clothes out of my car and take it to Hobie's. Bella is driving an even-tempered 55 miles per hour when I ask her to drop me off at the bar. I had hoped to keep this aspect of my life a secret from Brody and his family. I had miraculously managed to do so from Robert, Andrea, and my own mother for nearly five years. I can't understand why it isn't so easy with these people.

"Can you do me a huge favor and not tell anyone you are dropping me off at Hobie's Bar and Grille?" I mutter to Bella and Brody while my eyes skip from one to the other. I am tucked between the two in the center of the seat. "I'm begging you." We are only five minutes away. I can't wait to get out of the truck. Still, I feel woozy and dizzy and scared about singing. I hate getting up on stage.

"Because your boyfriend would kill you if he knew you were meeting some guy there?" Bella offers amicably.

"No, because I work there," I correct her politely. "And my mother and Robert do not know this." Why did that almost sound worse? Then I smile sarcastically. "Well, it appears from the Bacon Valley Chronicle, I'm married to Brody. So we're family now. You have to be nice to me."

"Yeah, I'm never going to be family with you, Bacon," Bella grunts. "And even if I was family with you, I'd still want to beat the shit out of you every time you walk in the room."

"What the heck, Bella!" I gasp. "Do you always have to be so caustic?" I turn to Brody and shake my head. "Can you call off your guard dog, Cowboy?"

Brody turns and gives me a half smile and one of his classic shrugs. "I'm just glad you two are warming up to each other."

"So that guy you have been texting all day is not some boyfriend on the side, huh?" Bella interrupts, looks over my head at Brody. Bella rolls her eyes. I have a good idea she has been eavesdropping on my conversations with Drew.

"No, he is not," I tell her honestly. "He works in the kitchen. I serve drinks."

"At a bar," Bella sniffs a loud laugh. "I find that unbelievable, *church girl*."

"Well, it is true. Besides, Drew doesn't like girls like me," I say.

"That's not difficult to imagine. I don't know many guys are into girls like you for anything else than a good laugh and a —"

"Enough," Brody interrupts just in time. He holds his hand up and Bella's mouth clamps shut. I'm not sure what she was going to say. I didn't want to know.

"Yeah, I'll shut up *Cotton Candy and Coke*," Bella says, sliding the last words in like she is giving Brody a name. "That's what I'm going to call you now."

"Shut up, Bella." Now Brody looks uncomfortable. I can't help wonder what inside joke this could be between the two cousins. I hope Brody doesn't have a drug problem.

It doesn't matter. We are pulling into Hobie's lot and it is completely packed. I feel butterflies in my tummy so bad, I am almost ready to open the truck window in case I get sick. Bella pulls to one side and off in the grass while I struggle to get out from between them. Brody swings open the door, steps out easily.

"You know what?" I say hotly. "It's not worth it. I am sick of arguing with you, Bella. And I don't really care if you believe me or not. I honestly don't care. You and this town laugh at me like I'm a ditz and dumb and shallow. But you and half the people in Bacon Valley are nothing but a bunch of shallow idiots for thinking that. You don't know me. You don't even bother to get to know me. As much as I appreciate you trailering Brody's horse, every bit of this ride has been hell and you are a bitch. That is clear. I can see it. Everybody can see it," I groan loudly, waving my hand in the air. "But I haven't done anything to show that I'm the slut and dumbass you make me out to be. And just remember who took a punch for your cousin here in that barn while you sat on your fat ass in the truck." I pause there because I am scooting across the vinyl seat and getting ready to slide out of the truck. Brody reaches out and takes my arm, helping me make the step down. It is nice, his gesture.

It reminds me of Delbert opening the door for me with a gentlemanly sweep of his hand when we left the store at night.

Brody is just staring at me and then looks over my shoulder to Bella like he is waiting for her to say something. I see her staring hard at the windshield, fidgeting in the seat and wonder if she is going to get out and punch me. She just looks angry, really angry.

"Either say it now or don't ever give me crap again, Bella." I finally say. "Because since we were in kindergarten, you have done nothing but bully me and I'm tired of it. This is your last chance."

"Oh, come on. You and your friends were just as bad, Bacon. And my last chance or what? You going to carry a baseball bat with you?" Bella mutters. She is tugging on her lip, still staring out the windshield. "I'll do whatever I want and stop picking on you whenever I want."

"Like I said, it isn't worth it, Bella," I mutter. Really quickly, she snaps her head toward me like she is going to say something. But she doesn't. I just shake my head, turn to Brody. "I'm assuming you'll find out about the newspaper announcement from Zach as soon as you can," I say softly.

"Yeah, of course," He looks over top my head toward the parking lot. You can hear the music inside the bar and there are people milling around outside. "Do you want me to walk you up to the door or something?" he asks. I can see his gaze narrow like he's taking in a dark city street full of shady looking characters. "It looks kind of rough. Let me walk you up."

"I'm fine," I tell him, brushing him away. It is 7:06 and I have to get inside quickly. I skirt him a second to look into the rearview mirror of the truck. Crap. My eye is a mild shade of blood red and deep blue.

"You got a ride home?" Brody asks.

"No, but I'll figure something out," I back away and smile, then reach out and tug his hat off his head. "Hey, Cowboy, let me borrow your hat tonight, cover up my eye."

He just rolls his hands through his hair and looks kind of sheepish before shoving his hands into his pockets.

"Yeah, alright."

I have to push my way through the crowd to get to the rickety stage. It isn't much more than old boards from a barn that used to be out back and a microphone plopped in the front. You can't hardly move in front of it for all the worn tables and chairs filled with patrons. Halfway through my singing, I usually have them pull back a few tables so the local Coalville line dancing club, The Posse, can get out and kick up their boots while I sing. There's usually enough room; it isn't always so crowded in the summer when the Midwest College of Rendville is on its summer term.

I'm scooting through the front tables, trying to wedge myself between full chairs when Drew sees me. He has just started to pluck his guitar and I see him draw a huge sigh of relief. He extends his hand and tows me up to the stage. His eyes scan over my jean shorts, cowboy hat, and t-shirt, then to my cowboy boots. It isn't my usual stage wear.

I am surprised to see some lights and huge cameras set up in front of and behind the stage. It looks like an entire production crew and I lean into Drew, "I thought you just invited your family."

He just shakes his head as if he is just as surprised as me. Then he waves someone up who hands me my guitar and I take in a deep breath, let it out again. *Please God, don't let me throw up on the stage—*

"You are fine, Journey," Drew says softly. "I'm right here." He knows I hate this part, the getting started.

He tells me my eyes get wide and I look like a five year-old who just had a clown jump out at her in a dark room. He tucks his knuckle under my chin, makes me look into his eyes. "Just sing," he tells me. Then he throws on a big smile and turns toward the audience.

"And not a moment too late, the other half of Drew's Journey, I'd like to introduce you to Journey, yeah that's her real name—" then he turns to me and tips his head to the side. "I hope you're ready for this," he looks a little stage struck himself. But I nod my head, "Drew's Journey? Where did that come from?" He just laughs and I turn, give the crowd a big smile and we start to sing.

Most of the time when Drew and I sing, we do a few duets, then we take turns with our solos. After we sing, I do my usual and wait on tables so the waitresses can get a break. He heads back to the kitchen and washes dishes and makes burgers and fries if folks order then. But that's when we have about thirty minutes, and we're singing to mosquitos and drunks because everybody else is still getting home from work or paying a babysitter so they can get out for the night. Tonight, we've got forty-five minutes and we had practiced mostly his songs, with me playing my guitar in the background. Like a well-tuned piano, we belt out our tunes like we usually do. Drew croons to the girls, I flirt with the single guys in front. The crowd is into it; I can tell they are Drew's family because a few even scream. I can see Drew looking anxiously at a certain corner of the room and I get a good feeling that's where the music scout must be.

And too quickly, it is over. We take our half-bows. I bow out the back door of the kitchen and throw up for six minutes by the dumpster. My jumpy stomach is gone and it is replaced with a good tired feeling so I beg a ride home from somebody, Drew walks out to the crowd and sits with his friends.

"What do you think you are doing?" It is Hobie and he is wearing his good jeans and a button up shirt. I have just waved down Martha Bean who is filling up her tray with beers. She tells me she can take me home, but it might be 2:30 in the morning before she can. She has to clean up after closing.

"I'm trying to get a ride home, Hobie," I tell him but his hand goes out in front of him.

"No, Bread and Butter, you're not done yet. Get your ass out there."

I groan and complain that I've got to get home. I can hear Billy Gentry's band warming up and I want to get out of there before it gets too crowded. But he won't listen and pokes a finger outside the kitchen.

I wait for him to turn and I snatch up an apron to put over my shorts. I grab a tray and head out to the floor and hit the first table that flags me down.

"What the hell are you doing, Journey?"

I hear Hobie's voice over the mic. My hands are full of used beer bottles while I plop them on the sticky tray. I look up and realize he is talking to me.

"You told me to get my ass out here!" I yell back. "I've got my ass back out here. What the hell?"

"I told you to get your ass back up here!" he growls, his finger jabbing downward to the stage. Everybody thinks this is funny and I stand there red-faced with the bottles dangling in my fingers. "Well, you could have clarified that." I mumble to myself. I snatch up the bottles and take them back to the garbage can in the kitchen, griping to no one in particular while my stomach's getting queasy again. I feel drained and don't think I can get back up there again. My nerves can only stand so much.

When I finally get up on stage, I see Billy Gentry wagging his finger and I look down to see my apron still dangling from my waist. I quickly snatch it off and toss it to him. "You sing. We'll play." he says.

I must have looked at him skeptically because he holds his hand aloft at his band. "We've been doing this for a forty years. We know your songs. Just sing."

And so I do, forgetting about the crowd and the smell of stale beer on lips and the way the guitars sound like they are banging around in a barrel against the walls. I figure everybody is going to leave after Drew sings. But even those that were headed for the door, turn around and come back in. That feels good like they really want to hear me sing. I look out in the darkness and ignore the cameras that keep slipping up behind me and in front of me. Old Bill Williams, who I call Drunk Will, sitting in the back gives me a hearty whoop and asks me out loud about how I got that 'ol' shiner.' Everybody is looking at him, then the eyes all come back up to me. I know right then why I like singing here. It is like singing at a family meal.

"Well, it entails a horse, a cowboy and the cowboy's ex-girlfriend," I tell him back. "And I'm not saying if I got the worst end of the deal or not." Drunk Will thinks this is funny as hell. His brother gives me a "aw, baby, sing it." I make them move tables for the line dancers and everybody moves because nobody wants to fight with the person holding the mic. It feels alright for another forty-five minutes.

This time, when it is over, I call Drew up to sing our last slow song together. It is an old country song that I always sing when I see Smalltalk coming in the door. It is strangely quiet when we are done. I think that maybe something is wrong before they start to clap, something I don't usually hear when it is only drunks in the audience.

Then Billy Gentry comes up and slaps me on the back. Tells me: "Be a good girl, Ditzy, get me a damn beer and be quick about it."

"Drew, can you give me a ride home?" I grab his sleeve after I get Billy's beer. But Drew's not looking at me. Instead, I see one of the girls from the crowd giving him a little wave. She has raven black hair and is Drew's type—a little chubby, lots of makeup and boobs to die for. He looks torn. "Yeah, yeah, whatever," he says. He's excited. He says the scout told him he would give him a call. "Tomorrow. I went back and talked to him." I didn't remind him, they always told him that. His eyes are dead set on a teeny-weeny tank top and a whole lot of cleavage.

"You mind riding on the back of my motorcycle without a helmet?" he asks me. As if I would.

"No, are you nuts?" I swipe my hand over my face. "That thing is a deathtrap."

"I bet she doesn't think so," he says nodding to the brunette. She nods back coolly and I can only think I wish I could be that with-it.

"Listen, I can find you a ride." He is looking around wildly. My back is sweaty and I don't want to take off the cowboy hat because I know my hair is flat underneath.

"I can see if I can borrow my uncle's car. Hang on —" Drew starts to walk into the crowd, but I feel a tug on my shoulder and turn to see Brody Wells standing behind me. He is looking at me differently. I'm not sure how to describe his expression. Perhaps I would compare it to the look Robert has when he is eyeing a new car at a sales lot. His eyes are staring at my own like Robert's eyes examine a set of tires to see if they are in good shape or not. I wonder if my makeup is messed up. I don't know why I'm suddenly worried about what I look like.

"Me and Bella can give you a ride," he says. "We waited. I wasn't sure if you had a lift home or not. I just didn't feel right leaving you."

"Are you sure that's a good idea?" I ask him. "I'm not sure Bella wants to give me a ride."

"It's okay," he starts. Drew had stopped mid-step, turning slightly. I can see him eyeing Brody slowly and suspiciously and then looking at me.

"You know this guy?" he asks. Then he steps forward, points at his eye and then at Brody. "He didn't do that, right?" Drew has a straight face, his eyes narrowed.

"No, Drew," I answer. "His ex-girlfriend did." Drew chews on this a moment, then stares at me to the count of five.

"It sounds like a foundation to a good country song, Journey," Drew tells me. I can see he is gnawing on the idea already. "You're telling me the truth, right?"

"Yes."

Then all of a sudden, Drew sticks out his hand toward Brody. Brody reaches out a little slowly, unsure, but shakes it.

"Yeah, I'm Drew. Ha ha, good luck with that."

I am looking at Drew, thinking I want to kill him then while Brody acknowledges him and returns the shake with a nod and his own name. I close my eyes for just a moment, then give Drew the most scathing glare I can conjure up. He just steps away then, wraps his arm around the brunette and leans in close to her.

"What'd he mean by that?" Brody asks while I duck down to avoid Hobie's glance my way. Hobie is raising his hand like he is trying to catch my attention.

"I dunno. He's got big boobs on the brain." Brody kind of smiles, looks at the girl, then back at me.

"Hey!" I hear Hobie's voice and look across three tables. He is standing there with a couple guys in button up shirts and khaki pants. It isn't the typical clothing of the bar on Saturday night, at least not Hobie's. He is trying to catch my attention. I figure he wants that damn birth certificate. I groan and duck down. Then I reach out, snatch up Brody's arm and drag him out the back door.

It isn't until we pull into the little road where my house is that we even speak again. Bella and Brody are quiet during the ride back. I'm so tired, I almost fall to sleep against the door.

"So—how long have you been singing at the bar?" Brody asks. His voice is soft and husky in the silence.

"Four years," I answer while I cup a yawn. "Almost five."

"I didn't know," he mutters.

"Most people from Bacon Valley don't," I answer. "Not even Robert and Delilah have a clue. The type of people they hang out with are not the kind who go to the bar."

"No, that's not what I mean. I didn't know how good you sing."

I look up long enough to catch his face. He looks serious, but I can't help but wait for the punchline. Nothing comes as I slowly pull his hat off my head and give it back to him.

As we round Oak Street to Maple Court, I can see a few cars in my driveway. One is Delilah's, the other is Robert's and the third is the Bacon Valley police cruiser.

"Oh, holy hell," I mumble. All eyes in the truck are on my driveway. "Bella, stop here before you get to the drive," I tell her as I point a block down from my house. She stops the truck and the trailer makes a grinding halt behind it.

I watch in horror as I see Delilah and Smalltalk coming from my porch and staring down the street. My mother is dabbing her eyes with a tissue.

Slowly, I ease out of the truck. I wait until Bella starts to pull away in the darkness before I walk toward home. I can feel my heart pounding a scared beat in my chest like when I was seven years-old and I broke one of Delilah's hand-painted lamps.

Delilah meets me at the driveway, looks me up and down. I can tell she does not approve of my jean shorts, worn boots and sweaty t-shirt because I can see a certain "do I know you?" on her face.

"Oh, Journey," she nearly sighs my name. Her eyes are wide like she is scared, but her teeth are grinding inside her jaws. "What did you do to your eye?"

"I bumped it, Delilah," I mutter. "It really isn't that bad." It wasn't a lie. I bumped it on Jolanna's fist.

"Oh, dear." Now her eyes are closed, one hand reaching out to snag my forearm and the other covering her lips. "Where have you been?" she asks me, her eyes over my shoulder and to the tail lights of the trailer driving away. "We were so worried about you." She herds me into my tiny foyer and looks me up and down. Her head shakes back and forth. "Are you going to answer me?"

"Worried is an understatement," Robert's face is angry. He is staring hard at my face. His head shakes back and forth suspiciously. "It looks like more than a bump. What did you hit it on?" He doesn't let me answer. Instead, he holds out both hands. "What is wrong with you lately? You can't just take off and not let anyone know where you are. We thought you had gotten kidnapped or murdered." He turns and waves a hand at my living room. I take it in, blink at the drawers of my desk that had been pulled from their station.

"Oh, my gosh," I can hardly breathe.

"I drove by your shop at about four in the afternoon and the front door was wide open."

It looked like someone had trashed my house. I walk around in a daze, trying to take it all in.

"My shop?'

"Yes, it is trashed too."

Chapter –16

I'm starting out by saying I'm breaking up with you with a song. Yeah, I know it's wrong. But think about it, baby, everything about us has been long gone, gone, gone—

I am standing just inside the Knick-Knack Shop. It is dark and quiet except for the sound of the bare boards beneath my feet creaking with each step. I am too anxious about my shop to worry if Smalltalk is going to grab me from behind and drag me into the alley. He seems to be the only one at home concerned about how I feel about my house and shop getting broken into.

"Journey, let me go first. I want to make sure no one is in here."

I turn slightly to the sound of Smalltalk's voice. My phone is ringing in my purse and I nod absently, then open the latch and pull out my cell phone. It is Hobie and I groan softly before I answer it. I turn, step out on to the dark sidewalk.

"I did not get my birth certificate, but I am working on it," I tell him before he asks.

"Birth certificate?" he tosses out the word as a question and as if he has no clue what I am talking about. "Oh, yeah, that would be nice. But that ain't why I called, Bread and Butter. You ducked out too quickly. There's a couple friends of mine who want to sit down and talk out some kind of singing deal. What do you say about that?"

"Um, I guess I say I'm not interested," I tell him honestly. I'm not sure how I feel right then. I'm kind of happy somebody thinks I sing pretty good. But there's no way I'm doing it for a living.

I don't think my stomach can stand all the puking up. "I'm kind of busy now, Hobie. My shop got broken into tonight. Just tell them I appreciate the thought, but I've already got a job. Did they call Drew yet?"

Hobie hesitates on the other end. "Sweetie, these chances don't come up but once in a lifetime. "

"I know," I tell him honestly. "I know." What I can't tell him is that there were so many reasons I can't. It isn't just stage fright. It isn't that Robert and my mother would find out I have been singing in a bar for five years. That they would not approve. I just like living in Bacon Valley. I didn't want to leave like Delilah did and when the songs stop coming, return and be sad and alone for the rest of my life.

"Hobie, I have to go." I don't let him answer, just hang up the phone feeling guilty like it is my only chance and I've blown it even if it isn't something I ever wanted.

Smalltalk has a high beam flashlight in one hand and it lights up the room well, but leaves scary shadows dancing on the walls from our own bodies and the bookshelves. He pauses once on the tiny receipts with songs words written on them. "They really trashed this place. Get back, please."

He is in full police attire complete with Smoky Bear hat. He has a wary glint to his eyes I have not seen before. His other hand is settled on the gun at his belt. I can see his fingers firmly planted on the handle.

"Okay, Officer McGee," I say softly. Although my legs are firmly fixed just one step within the doorway, my mind is running across the room to the small square hole in the floor that was once used as the makeshift safe. It is here that I keep the silver purse and dance card, tucked away safe along with my nightly deposits. I am praying it is still there. It seems so important right now considering everything else went to hell after Bella dropped me off in my cul-de-sac tonight.

I watch while Smalltalk weaves around the rooms. When he has peered into each one, he turns on the old lights. They flicker and leave a yellow pasty color across the floor. Antiques are scattered around. I can see a couple broken glasses.

"I'm so sorry about what happened tonight," Smalltalk comes up beside me while I lean over to right the deep green metal garbage can that had been toppled sideways on the ground.

"Robert and I have been avoiding some issues we disagree on for a long time," I reply. "The fight had to happen. I am sorry you had to listen to it."

The fight. It started when I mentioned the dance purse to Officer McGee. "I really don't know why someone would break into my home and my shop. Everything in the shop is affordable. But there is one thing that I've gotten recently that has stirred up a few phone calls. Before Delbert died he gave me a silver dance card purse," I had said. "Dance card purses aren't that uncommon. However, when I listed this particular one online, I started getting calls immediately. Freddy Johnson tried to buy it at Delbert's funeral, for heaven's sakes. Then I had two men show up and were angry when I didn't sell it. It was probably the only item in the store really worth stealing. At least as far as the two men in the black car were concerned."

"Freddy Johnson," Robert lapped it up like a starving cat licks up a bowl of sour milk. "Officer McGee, I would check that boy first. He's shady as hell. I could see him doing this." He took it in, but with pursed lips like it was giving him a belly ache. I looked up to see Robert standing in the middle of my living room, arms crossed while his eyes were scanning the walls like he didn't approve of something. "Why didn't you simply sell the purse, Journey Dawn?" he asked with a deep exhalation of air.

"Isn't that what you are supposed to do?"

"I didn't sell the purse, Robert," I said softly. "Because Delbert gave it to me. It was a gift."

"Then why did you list the purse?" he asked with a smug lift of his lips. "If you place it online, it only seems reasonable you would want to sell it. I can see where someone would get upset about it." Then, while I stared at him not sure how to answer him, he shook his head. "Do you realize you completely forgot about my family's big dinner tonight?" Robert was furrowing his brow, gritting his teeth. "I told you it was important and you simply did not show. Everyone was there. You weren't."

"You didn't tell me anything about a dinner," I protested.

"Dear, he did." Delilah reached out and touched my arm with her fingers. "It was right before the funeral. It was a big deal tonight."

"You were there?" I asked. It was strange. My mother never went to dinner with the Ironwoods. They both looked at each other and then back at me.

"Where were you?" Robert asked. "I think that's the big question." he said. Then he stopped, held up his index finger into the air. "No, I think the biggest question is —" he reached into the pocket of his button up shirt and pulls out a piece of paper. I could see it from where I stood even with my glasses off. It was the newspaper clipping with the announcement of Brody and my own wedding. "—this!"

I groaned, waved a hand. "I don't know how that happened," I bit my lip, tried to look everywhere but at my boyfriend and my mom. Of course, I didn't want to tell them about my walk to the courthouse to get my birth certificate. They would ask why I needed it. A flood of lies would follow and I'm not so good at tying lies together.

"Robert, it was obviously a mistake. Andrea sent me a copy. I'll give them a call in the morning. But I was working tonight. I was helping a customer find something," I said.

"With a horse trailer?" Delilah shook her head. "Journey, what is going on—the newspaper announcement, coming and going at all hours of the day and night?"

"Nothing is going on." I was tired, irritable and felt goosebumps roll up my arms then. "And yes, with a horse trailer," I returned. "I find stuff, Delilah, and it isn't always little things or antiques. Sometimes it is—other stuff. Big stuff."

"You spend way too much time finding *stuff*."

"You worked all day, Robert," I retorted angrily. "Why is your work more important than mine?"

"Because I have a job and you have a junk yard!" he blew up. "Do we have to rehash this over and over again? Oh my God, Journey, when will you get it into your head that your old shop is worthless?" he said. He looked to Delilah who nodded her head up down. "And now it is just dangerous. I won't have it, Journey," he told me. "It is stopping right here. What if you would have been at home or at the shop? You could have been killed."

"Oh, great, now you've got another excuse to get rid of my shop," I retorted. "Robert, I'm not giving up the shop just because somebody broke into my house. You need to get that into your head."

"He's right," Delilah had agreed. My eyes shot hard and hot at her. She just shivered and closed her eyes. "Oh, to think what horrors they could have done."

"He's not right, Delilah," I spat. "Quit siding with him. I like my store. Please excuse yourself so I can discuss this with Robert alone. I don't like to be ganged up on."

I glared at her until she whisked herself off to the bathroom. Smalltalk pretended to take a phone call and set his sights for my front porch.

"You know, sometimes you can be so unfeeling, you know that? I mean, do you have a heart inside you? Do you like the shop more than me?" Robert asked quickly. "Because at some point you are going to have to choose between the shop or me."

He just picked the wrong time to say those words. Because a rumble of anger had settled in my belly and a shiver of irritation slipped up my spine. It ended with my hands clenched into fists. "Okay, thanks for making it so damn easy!" I screamed at him. "I'll save us both the agony of continuing this stupid relationship. We're done. I am breaking up with you. I choose the shop!"

"Well, good, then I'm glad I didn't waste the next fifty years of my life with someone who would choose junk over me!" That was when Robert slapped the pretty little black velvet ring box on the table. It had a beautiful red bow tied on top. He pointed to it with his finger, tossed his hands in the air. "That's why we had the supper tonight. My entire family was there to celebrate our damn engagement. And what do you do? You manage to make me look like an idiot. You know what? I would rather live my next fifty years by myself than be with you." Then I saw his eyes narrow suspiciously. He looked left, then right, then directly at me. "Does this have to do with what happened between Andrea and me?" he asked gruffly and softly. "What did she tell you?"

I nearly choked. My facial expression must have explained it all while I sat there chewing on his words.

"No," I answered. "Is there something you need to tell me?"

"Just forget about it!" Robert growled. He left with a slam of the door and Delilah went right after. Smalltalk and I stood there awkwardly. My face felt like it had drained of color. I started to cry and he came over and stood in front of me.

"Let's go check your shop, how about we do that?"

And so we are here at the Knick-Knack Shop.

"Well," Officer McGee comes up beside me picks up a couple pieces of stray paper laying on the floor, "I didn't mean I was sorry about the fight between you and Robert." He stops and kind of pushes out a half-smile. "Or the fight with your mother. I meant this—" He waved a hand around the room. "Nobody should have to deal with something like this. Can you tell if anything is missing?"

"Can you keep a secret?" I ask him. He is keeping his distance while I stand there above the rug hiding the little safety deposit box.

"Of course," he nods. The he gives me a fatherly tip to his chin while he wags a finger at me. "As long as it is within the bounds of the law."

"It is," I say and drop to my knees. I push away the rug, unlock the box with shaking hands, tug out the shoebox and open the lid to reveal the contents inside. I make a great sigh in relief and hug the box to my chest. Smalltalk comes over and hovers just above me. I put the box down and lift the lid, expose the contents inside.

"I think this is what they wanted, those two men in the black car I was telling you about," I divulge while I take out the silver purse and hold it aloft. "Delbert Johnson gave me this before he died. Told me a story about how he won it in a car race on Goose Creek Road."

I stand and hand Smalltalk the purse. He rolls it around his hands, opens it up and peers inside.

"This is the purse you're talking about?" he asks me. "The one you think someone is looking for?"

"Yes."

I watch him. I know I have a cautious look to my narrowed eyes—chin tipped downward while I stare at Smalltalk through my lashes. He stops for a moment, looks up at me and chuckles.

"You look like your mom when you do that," he says with a half-smile. He must have seen my face drop to a glare because he went on quickly: "I suppose that's not what a daughter wants to hear, huh?"

"Um," I mutter. He is always comparing me to Delilah. He rubs his chin, turns the purse over in his hands. Like everyone else who takes a look at the purse, he rolls his finger over the initials M.L.

"M.L.," he says softly. Smalltalk lets the letters roll across his lips like he is licking a sweet sucker, his brow furrowing. "M.L. You say Delbert won this at a race on Goose Creek Road?" He looks up and I nod. Then he goes on, "They were still racing that road when I was a kid. If I remember correctly, there was a wreck out there while some kids were racing. A car rolled off with a couple teens in it and the girl in the passenger seat got thrown out and killed." He shakes his head, hands the purse back to me. "It was a little before my time," he says. "I just remember my mom talking about it. Whenever I took off in my car when I was in high school, she always warned me about driving too fast. Then she mentioned the wreck on Goose Creek." I take back the purse and replace it gently in the shoebox.

"You might want to put that in a lockbox at the bank," Smalltalk suggests. I nod amicably, but I'm not sure what to do with it. I just want to hold it now. It reminds me of Delbert.

"You definitely need to get some better locks for the doors and a security system if you have expensive things in here."

"I don't know." I look around the shop, think about the mess and hope nothing is broken. "Maybe it isn't the purse at all," I say. "I looked these up online and they run less than a hundred dollars. I'd rather keep it close, you know?"

"Maybe it isn't the worth monetarily, then, but the sentimental value," Smalltalk throws out. He leans against my counter. "People get murdered over pets in a divorce nowadays. I can help you change locks and maybe put in a new door, add some curtains to the front and stuff like that, Journey."

Oh and here we go again. I push the wood back on the floor, stand up and then use my foot to cover it with the rug. "That isn't necessary. I really don't think I need a man around for a bit, if you understand. I need some time to myself."

"Yes, of course," he waves a hand and bobs his head up and down like he understands where I stand. "Your mom did a good job of making you independent. But don't ever hesitate to ask me for help—" Smalltalk pushes his rear from the counter and gives me a subtle grin before he reaches up and rubs his forefinger just above his eye. It is a nervous gesture. I do the exact same thing when Delilah pushes out her palm and stops me from finishing a sentence to defend something I have done.

"By the way, Journey Dawn," he tells me without expression. "I did get to see you sing for about an hour tonight before I got the 911 call from your mother. She wanted to file a missing person report. I talked her out of it.

I said you were probably stuck in traffic someplace they didn't have cell phone service. I figured I wasn't lying. The cars were backed up nearly to the highway for the show tonight. She was rather insistent and said she would go over my head if she needed to do it."

"And who would that be?" I ask with a laugh. "It would have to be your mother because I know it isn't the mayor. He is scared to death of her and won't answer her calls if he sees it on caller ID."

He seems to think this is hilarious and laughs really hard. "Regardless," Smalltalk says, "you blew the crowd away tonight. But at some point, you're going to have to tell your mother where you go on the weekends. Or at least call her once in a while so she can keep tabs on you."

"What are you my daddy now?" I ask him, eyes rolling. I should not have said such a caustic thing, but I was tired, irritable. I close my eyes, take in a breath. It is calming. "I'm sorry, Officer McGee. It was really nice of you to come here with me. I shouldn't have said that."

But for one second, I see his eyes widen. Had it been anyone else, I would have mistaken his expression for surprise at my insulting remark. Not Officer McGee. He turns abruptly, saunters toward the back room and pauses at the door. After a moment, he nods toward the blue, flounced dress in one corner. "Is that real?" he asks. "I mean, if you don't mind me asking. I do the Civil War reenactments down at the park. I've never seen any of the women dress in one as nice as this one."

"Yes, it is authentic," I say with a yawn. "I purchased it for a museum. I didn't know you were in the battle thingies. But I haven't been to one in a long time. I suppose you and Eddy Walters from EMS are on the same team in these?"

Smalltalk grabs another soda crate and starts helping me pick up. I remember I had saved, in my purse, the pop can Brody gave me today to put on my eye. I plop it inside the lockbox with my other keepsakes including the receipt from Cayce's horse and doll from Great Escapes Restaurant.

"They aren't necessarily teams," he says. "We prefer to call them reenactments." Then he smiles. "You know, Eddy's been talking about asking you out." Smalltalk grabs a crate and tosses a couple glasses into it. "For your sake and Delbert's."

"Delbert used to call him EMS Eddy."

"Well, EMS Eddy's not a bad guy. Maybe since you and Robert broke up, you could go on a date with him."

"We broke up an hour ago," I groan. "Really? Are you trying to fix me up too?" I am half-bent, picking up an old wooden soda crate. I stop long enough to roll my eyes.

"Too early, huh?"

"Yes. Way too early," I say. "He'll probably send me flowers tomorrow and we'll be back together."

I laugh. Smalltalk doesn't. I look up absently and he is staring at me hard. "I don't see that in your eyes." His brow is furrowed.

It is quiet between us before Smalltalk sighs. "It is late. I'm supposed to be off tonight. How about we call it a night, huh? I can come back tomorrow and help you clean up. Nonetheless, there is a reenactment on Friday—or as you call it, a battle thingie. If you're interested, it would be one more date out of the way." Then Smalltalk stops. "You're okay, right?" He points a forefinger at his eye and wiggles it in a circle. "Your eye. Somebody didn't do that do you, right? I mean, I know whose truck and trailer that was who brought you home. I know you two don't get along."

My hands reach down to snatch up the cigar box.

"I probably shouldn't lie to a police officer," I say. "Somebody did do it to me. But it wasn't Bella Johnson. It is a long story, but in the short, I found Brody Wells's horse and his ex-girlfriend was trying to sell it. I tried to buy it without her knowing that I knew Brody. She figured it out after the sale and punched me."

"Did you get the horse?"

"I did."

"Bravo, then," he tells me. "Then wear it like a medal of honor." I think this is funny and laugh hard. It feels good. Today was stressful. Our laughter blends together and we both cackle at the same time.

But I only knew the half of it. Smalltalk takes me home. It is nearly noiseless in the cruiser. Only the blare of the police radio breaks the silence once in a while. It is not Smalltalk's usual demeanor. Most of the time I have ever been with him, he chatters aimlessly about something or other. Then, when he drops me off at my house, he rolls down the window as I start to walk up the sidewalk.

"Hey, do you find stuff that's stolen?" He has a half-kilter, sheepish grin on his lips like he is going to laugh.

"I guess. I mean, I can try." I stop and face the police cruiser. "But isn't that your job?"

He bobs his head side to side like he knows I'm making a little joke. Then he takes in a long breath and gives me a gaze that is something short of cautious. "Okay, Journey, so if you are good at finding things. Do me a favor. Your mama took my heart a long time ago. Stole it right from my chest. I've never gotten it back. I was wondering if you could help her find it."

I just stand there staring at him, so flustered I don't say a word at first. It was shocking in a way and so it lays like a stinky pair of socks between us for a moment. Then I start to thinking and then thinking a little harder. Smalltalk. Delilah. Smalltalk and Delilah. I see him teaching me how to fish, think about him walking me to my car at Hobie's every night I work there. Heck, his family sends me a check for twenty dollars every Christmas. He always sits behind Delilah and me at church.

"How—how long ago was this—that Delilah stole your heart?" I stutter. I think his face pales somewhat in the car. I think he knows that I know the secret they have kept from me. He just shrugs. "Can't say how long. Maybe a bit before you were born. Just as long as I can remember."

My belly does a flip-flop. I almost feel a little dizzy. I stare at him for a moment. He stares at me. "Are you telling me something that I don't know?" I muster.

"I'm not sure," Smalltalk mumbles. He scrubs his face with his hand. Then we both force the same polite and uncomfortable smile that drops abruptly.

"Holy shit," is all I say and walk numbly to the door. It is one-thirty in the morning and suddenly, I am woozy and wide awake. I knew why Delilah wouldn't let me have my birth certificate. She didn't want me to know who the idiot was who slept with her that hot night she got pregnant with me. I'm thinking it just might be Smalltalk.

Chapter –17

Note to Self: Break up with best friend

Robert sends me flowers every day for four days. He doesn't bother to come over and help me clean up my shop and house. Instead, he keeps texting me sweet messages and gives Andrea a few hours a day off work to help me. He always spends a couple hundred dollars in gifts after one of our big fights.

Today there are two dozen red roses on my front porch, a huge stuffed panda bear with a pink bow that sits as big as a person on one of three wooden rocking chairs on my porch, and twelve 'I'm sorry' messages on my phone. They are tucked between Drew whining about not hearing from the music scout and six voicemails from Hobie that I don't want to hear. I know he is either calling me to waitress at the bar another day off my schedule, bugging me about my birth certificate, or ready to call me an idiot for not calling up his buddies who will probably promise to make me a star, then tell me I have to sleep with them to do it. Either way, I just don't feel like going into the bar and I'm not into being verbally abused by Zach again at the city offices.

I'm sitting here staring at all of this. The only thing I can think of is Brody Wells's perfect blue-jeaned butt when he turned to open Bella's truck door for me the other night. I am trying to shove it out of my mind. It is difficult because I keep getting cards of congratulations for getting married from everyone in town. Then when I open the mailbox and see the cards, I also see his pale yellow tight t-shirt on muscled shoulders and his eyes. *Why,* I ask myself. *Why, why, why?* Because of all the people I could be thinking about now, it has to be Brody Wells?

But, oh my gosh, his image has inundated my every thought for the last week and it isn't coming to a stop. I'm not sure if it is simply because I thought he was such a shit and he kind of turns out to be pretty nice or simply because he knows how to kiss a girl. The kiss. Now, my tummy is jumping around.

"He's so sweet," Andrea interrupts my thoughts while we rock in the two chairs on either side of the bear. She isn't talking about Brody. She is speaking of Robert. "You know, if you simply told him you love him. He would give you the world. It isn't that hard to say." Andrea has spent more time chatting to me than picking up broken glass and books in my living room today. "You're so lucky you have him." She has brought over a milkshake from the ice cream place in town. I called and told her about my shop and house getting broken into and she told me that chocolate cures everything. So my shake is double chocolate and hers is peanut butter. We slurp them up while the scent of roses fills the air. They kind of make my stomach turn because I associate the smell of roses with fighting now. But the early morning sun is shining and it feels good on my skin. It warms me, makes me relaxed while I stare at the bear that stares stupidly out toward the street. Then I turn to Andrea.

"But I don't have him," I say firmly. "We broke up."

"Oh, you're so funny," she answers with a giggle. "You always fight and break up. That's almost your *thing*. Everybody knows you two fight, you break up, and then you make up. Just so you know, though, everybody is saying he is the one who hit you in the eye."

I ignore the rumors. Still, strangely, I realize it is our *thing*. It isn't normal. People who love each other don't habitually fight and break up.

I gnaw on this a moment like a puppy chews on a stale piece of shoe leather instead of a fresh steak bone. What if Robert is the only one who will ever love me like Delilah always tells me? My hand reaches over to delicately lay on my little handbag, and I pat the brown leather gently. It has become a habit over the past few days, touching the handbag. Inside is the silver purse and dance card. It feels safe there. Somehow, it reminds me of Delbert and I feel safe. Then I think about the promise I made to him. I think about the awkward date I had with Brody and wonder if, even with a kiss, Delbert would consider it a date at all. We really didn't hold hands. Then I think about Brody's little girl and I remember that it is a two for one package with them. I would feel like I was imposing on something special they have. I'd probably feel left out.

I sigh and try to push Brody out of my head. Instead, I stare at Andrea, I see the same faraway gaze Robert has when we talk about her. She is so pretty with her dark brown eyes and perfect hair. When I tell Robert that, he usually tells me she is a bit too pudgy for guys like him. He doesn't like short hair. He also always makes a point to tell me she talks too much and sometimes when she laughs she snorts. He hates when girls do that. But there is something he must like about Andrea. Because when he talks about Andrea, he gets a funny look in his eyes like he's remembering something about her. I've never thought much about it. We've all been friends for what seems a thousand years.

"Why are you looking at me like that?" she suddenly asks. I jerk my gaze away. I hadn't realized my eyes have closed to tiny slits and I am nibbling on my bottom lip. Andrea knows me like the back of her hand, knows my reactions to certain circumstances like suspicion and doubt.

"So what happened between you and Robert?" I say flatly while I turn the same direction the panda bear is staring and take on his same expression. She nearly chokes on her milkshake. I don't turn, but I know she is nervously pulling her straw in and out of the lid of the milkshake cup because it is making a squeaky squeal over and over. As Andrea knows me. I know her. She is nervous, cagey.

"What?" she finally asks in one long word that she draws out to at least the count of five. "Nothing happened. What did he tell you?"

I don't answer. I simply keep rocking slowly back and forth in my chair, over and over to the creak and groan of the porch beneath the rockers. I wonder if she is telling the truth and Robert is just lashing out in anger at me. I suddenly feel alone in the world and doubt if I can really break up with Robert, really let him go this time. I don't want to be alone. It scares me. I realize that weakness in myself. Like twenty times before, I bet we'll get back together. The thought feels like a crutch and I hang on to it. Then I feel angry at myself for being so scared to be single and taking care of myself. So I think of Delbert and I nibble on my lip again.

"I don't know what he told you, Journey, but it was when you two broke up. It was never when you were together," she says softly and almost as if she has to vomit the words between us. "It only happened a few times, I swear."

"*What* only happened a few times?" I ask her suddenly feeling like I have been collecting photographs for the last three years, but I haven't bothered to look closely at them. Like—oh, there's the picture where Andrea and Robert are always going out to eat together and here's the one where I call and Andrea is watching late movies with him after we fight.

"I don't know. We didn't go all the way. It was just me doing stuff for him."

"Stuff *for* him?"

"I told you that it wasn't when you were dating," she stumbles over her words like they are, possibly, what Robert and she had hashed out together ahead of time. The pitch in her voice changes. I can tell she is starting to cry.

"We have really never stopped dating until four days ago," I say blandly. "Robert has threatened to break up. We have never said those words until this week."

"I know. I know." she starts sobbing. Her hands are waving in front of her, shaking wildly. "I didn't think it was wrong, Journey. Please don't hate me. He just needs somebody when you don't—respond to him. I don't know why I did it. I just didn't think—"

"*Respond* to him?" I grunt. "You've got to be kidding me. I hope to God you are not equating *responding* with *sleeping* with Robert. Because I respond to him in that way more often than I really want." I don't know if I am insulted that she defends Robert or I realize that perhaps I am not responsive to his touch because I really don't like or dislike being with him.

"Can you please leave?" I say, standing up. I know the blood has drained from my face. She bobs her head up and down really quickly. Tears are streaming down her face, her nose is pink and her thick mascara is running rivers along her cheeks. She isn't so pretty right now.

"Oh, Journey, I'm so sorry."

"Well, be sorry somewhere else," I huff. Then I pick up the flowers and shove them at her. She absently takes them. Then I pick up the teddy bear and toss it on the dried brown grass of my lawn. "And take all this crap with you."

I hear her say those words, but I don't really feel a lump in my throat. I wonder if I am really as unfeeling as Roberts tells me all the time when I would rather work at my shop than sit at home watching TV with him. I am thinking that maybe I wasn't as blind to that photo collection in my mind as I thought. Maybe I just don't want to look at them, don't want to think my best friend and my boyfriend are screwing around behind my back. Or maybe Robert is right, I just don't care about anything.

I am angry when I lock my front door and head off to the shop. I am thinking about Robert and a picture of him flashes in my mind when I enter the building. I see him always telling me I don't think ideas out before I act upon them. He is right and I am irritated so I act upon his words. After I turn the lights on in the Knick-Knack Shop, I call the police station in town. I think Delbert is right about Robert right now and I feel like I have to prove it to myself.

The dispatch picks up and sends the call over to Smalltalk. "You said that EMS Eddy might go out with me," I say to Smalltalk. "Will you ask him if I can go to the Civil War reenactment this weekend?"

"You and your mother have got to quit dialing 9-1-1 to contact me for non-emergency purposes," he tells me after a long lull. He says nothing about the other night or our talk. In fact, I had passed him the other day on the street and he simply gave me a neighborly wave. I think we both are eager to avoid it. I wonder if maybe he just thinks I might be his daughter, because I can't imagine small town Smalltalk with big city Delilah. The very idea seems ludicrous.

"I guess I'm just not sure what constitutes an emergency," I tell him. "I am having a crisis. I am angry at Robert because I found out that he and Andrea have been hooking up. Doesn't that count?"

I think I am being funny in a sarcastic kind of way. Smalltalk does not.

"No," he states firmly. "You are not in any danger. If you were in danger, that is an emergency. Because you are out having a good time and forget to call your mother at 11:00 to let her know you are safely home is not an emergency as she seems to believe. Asking me to set you up on a date because you are mad at your ex-boyfriend is not an emergency as you appear to think." Then he does one of his classic sighs like he is giving in to my request. "Yeah, I'll talk to him."

I only have to wait seven minutes and Smalltalk calls me back. "Please note that I am calling you on my cell phone, Journey Dawn," he tells me bluntly. "I am not calling you on the emergency line. But I have three things to discuss with you. I've got them written down so I didn't forget to call you today."

I groan inwardly, but not aloud. I wished I had not called him earlier. I had a feeling he was going to bring up our conversation from the other night. I hear him rooting around on his desk like he is looking for his notes.

"Ah, found the note. Okay, here goes. Yes, EMS Eddy will take you to the reenactment on Friday," Smalltalk leans back in his chair. I can tell because the chair makes a creaking sound. "He says to be ready at nine in the morning. He will pick you up. He says don't be late. He hates being late. The second thing is that Hobie is trying to reach you from the bar. He says it is very important."

"He called you to call me?" I ask with a whine eased between.

"Yes, he did. He said exactly this: 'Tell Bread and Butter to call me. It is important.' Now, the other thing is this. I looked up the police report on the wreck that occurred on Goose Creek Road on March 23rd of 1940.

It happened   on the same week as the big flood that hit the Ohio valley." He clears his throat. "I think you might want to hear this. You ready?"

"Yes," I answer. I forget about Hobie. I am suddenly alert, my fingers reaching down to my purse and patting it gently.

"Okay, here goes," Smalltalk says. "Just so you know, Bacon Valley and this quarter of Ohio were hit with a couple big storms and the region was nearly under water for about three days that March. Peter Barker was the Bacon Valley police officer that arrived on the scene of the wreck. I didn't really know about it, but he notes the flood at the top of the page. I think he was working that night and had nine or ten call outs that because of high water. Then there was a robbery. I almost couldn't find this report because it was tucked in with the rest. There was a thick file about the rescue of a couple with kids who drove into Goose Creek five or six miles away on that same night. But I'm going to read you the report."

Smalltalk swishes the papers, the chair creaks again. "It goes like this: *Officer arrived on scene at 10:14 p.m. A 1926 Chrysler Imperial owned by E.B. Dodge was laying upturned in Goose Creek. Torrential rain had forced the creek over the bank on to Goose Creek Road. This vehicle along with a 1922 Ford farm truck were competing in a race. The Chrysler ran into water that had surpassed the creek bank and was along the roadway. It skidded approximately twelve feet, then hit a submerged log on the road and turned over. Parties stated two males were in the car and two females were in the rumble seat. The truck had two males. All parties in the truck were uninjured. Two males: Edward Benjamin Dodge and Harry Franco and one female: Mary Young from the car were taken to Grandy Hospital where they are listed in stable condition.*

17 year-old female, Molly Lender of Winford, Ohio, has not been found at the scene. She was ejected from the rumble seat into Goose Creek when the Chrysler Imperial overturned. It is believed that she was swept downstream. A search party was started at 11:19 p.m. No body was found. The deceased's family has been informed."

"Molly Lender," I say quietly. "That's her initials on the purse—M.L."

"Yeah," Smalltalk says on the other end. His voice echoes my own, quiet and hoarse. "I kept thinking about those initials for the last three days. I kept racking my brain trying to remember where I had seen those initials. Then it hit me. When I first came on to the police force here, Peter Barker was always pulling out that file on the wreck and staring at it. You know, they never found her body. Probably got caught up in a tree and ended up in some deep pocket of the Ohio River. It was the only missing person case this town has ever had. You may have heard Delbert or your mama say: 'the river never gave her up.'"

"I have. Delilah says it all the time when I don't finish something. She'll say: 'the river never gave her up. It won't give you up either if you don't clean your living room.'"

"That's where the saying came from and the ghost story. You've heard it. A woman that walks out of the creek if you call her name. They never found her body in that river so nobody ever got to know exactly how that story ended. It was also the first car death in Bacon Valley. And it was also the same night that Fenton and Son Hardware Store was robbed. In fact, there was a list of folks on the scene that were interviewed. I didn't see Delbert among them. However, I saw Andrew Fenton—they called him Junior then. I couldn't recall any of the other names. That was the first robbery in the region." Smalltalk clears his throat.

"There were always rumors that Junior Fenton was the one who stole the money. It put a rift in the family back then. Andrew Fenton Senior nearly ripped 'And Son' off the front of the store. It was a bad night for the Fentons and a bad night for Peter Barker." Smalltalk takes a breath. "He was just a kid out of high school then and got the job at the police station. Everybody tried to tell him that he couldn't be everywhere that night. It was impossible. He saved so many folks from the flood. But he didn't see it that way. Still doesn't. I saw him up at the senior center the other day. He asked me if I ever solved the only two unsolvable crimes in Bacon Valley—the robbery and Molly's body never being found. Said it was the worst day of his life."

I was quiet on the other end of the phone. It was sad. "Delbert told me the girl who owned the silver purse and the dance card gave it to him after a race," I finally whisper. "He said she told him if he showed up at her school's formal dance, she would save all the dances on the card just for him. I suppose she never got to dance with anyone."

"Well," Smalltalk replies. "I suppose that's why he held on to it so long."

"You know, he told me he never got to meet her at the dance," I murmur. "I just assumed he just couldn't go or didn't want to go to it." Then I look up to the ceiling, think about the two men who came into my shop. "Do you think it is somebody in her family trying to find the purse?"

"I don't know, Journey, I really don't know."

I can hear the radio blare in the background of the police station. Smalltalk sighs and tells me he has to answer a dispatch call. I wish I had someone to call and share this news. I don't. So I pull out my guitar and start to strum something. It relaxes me until I see a shadow cross the door.

Chapter –18

Note to Self: Buy a wedding ring

I know I'm jumpy now. For good reason. I feel my heart take on a quickened beat. Yet when the door opens wide, it is Brody Wells and he is tugging along his little girl. She has her princess doll clasped hard to her chest and she stops just as I reach out and catch the bookshelves before the door slams hard behind them. The glass shakes and I see Brody cringe.

"It's okay," I tell them, releasing the bookshelf slowly and watching to make sure it still doesn't topple over. It does not, and I lay my guitar down on the counter. Cayce cups her palm and waves her little fingers at me beauty pageant-style. I do the same in return.

"Hey, you got a minute to talk?" Brody gives his daughter a little push forward and they both take a couple steps toward where I am leaning with my elbows on the top of the counter.

"Of course."

I watch while he looks around and sets his eyes on a crate with baseballs inside. He picks it up, sets it down in front of Cayce. Then he points to it and tells her to take a look and see which one is the biggest. She nods, but she keeps smiling a wide-mouthed smile at me. I see Brody eyeing her with a furrowed brow.

"I don't know why she acts like this when you're around." He looks a little confused, distressed. "Really, Cayce isn't always —"

"Parade smile," I interrupt him. But I'm looking at Cayce who nods knowingly. "Come on, Brody, you haven't been to a Fourth of July parade? You know, like the pageant princesses sitting on the cars. That's the wave."

"Grandma Gayle showed me some of her old movies," Cayce says while she drops to her knees at the crate. She still hasn't unlatched from the doll. "I saw *her* sitting on a car doing that." *Her* was referring to me, I think. "Grandma says she was the Bacon Valley fair princess. You had on a blue dress."

"I did," I answer. Brody walks up to the counter, his tennis shoes making a creaking sound on the old wooden floors with each step.

"I like her daddy," she tells Brody while she leans hard into the crate and picks up a worn baseball. "She's a princess just like in my book, right? But real."

"Sure, honey." But he is hardly listening. Brody is flustered and takes a glance over his shoulder toward the door as he leans hard into the counter. "I just have a minute. Ashley's waiting in the car." His eyes are wavering and not exactly catching mine. His fingers are nervously tapping out a beat on the counter. I just stand there, a nervous prickle easing up my arms.

"I wanted to thank you again for finding my horse and mom's ring. And the steak dinner was really nice when we got locked out of your car."

"No big deal," I tell him. "Thanks for letting me use you to cross another guy off your grandpa's dance card list." He works up a sly smile, then lets it fall. Brody bobs his head up and down like he wants to say more. For the count of ten, he just wavers there.

"Yeah, well, and another thing. I have some strange news for you," he finally says. Then he holds up one hand palm out as if stopping me from answering right away. "And before you completely freak out, I'm taking care of it. I just kind of found out yesterday and I just didn't know how to approach you about it."

"Spit it out, Cowboy," I say slowly. Surely it couldn't be that horrible. I didn't understand why he was drawing it out; it was excruciating. He stands back a moment, looks to the door, pats his hand hard on the counter. Then he scrubs his hand over his head.

"Okay, here goes. We're really married." He comes to a standstill completely and stares hard at me like he is waiting for some remarkable reaction. His eyes dart back and forth between mine.

"Say something, please," Brody says, swallowing hard. I can only see his blue eyes. I forget what he is saying.

And I don't know what to say. I think he is surely joking so I laugh and roll my eyes. "Why are you telling me this, Cowboy?" I ask him. "What's the punchline." He does not laugh with me. In fact, he looks a little pale.

"There isn't a punchline, Journey," he tells me. "When Zach went through that whole fake wedding thing at the courthouse, the papers we signed were legitimate. He's an actual officiant for the courthouse. He marries people all the time. He was going to shred the papers we signed. But it was lunch time and he accidently left them on the desk in the main office. You know how Zach is. I swear, if he can screw something up, he will. He forgets crap all the time. The interns in the office just figured he had forgotten to file them and really thought we were getting married. One of them took the papers down to whatever office records the information and had them filed. That's why we were in the newspaper. Oh, my God do not look at me like that. What are you thinking?"

I'm not thinking. I am just staring at him. Seldom can I make a good comeback with a clever remark. Still, I have done enough pageants that I have learned how to fool most folks with at least something intelligible to cover for a moment of being purely dumbstruck.

This time, I cannot. I am wordless as the blood drains from my face and I waver there staring at him. Brody pats the counter, then turns and rubs his hand on his face.

"Listen, I promise I'll take care of it. Just give me a couple days. Zach said we can probably get it annulled and nobody will ever know."

"Probably?"

"No, I mean," Brody stutters. "We will definitely get a divorce or whatever—"

"Divorce?" I feel my heart flutter in a panic. "I don't want a divorce! I don't want that on whatever permanent record the county keeps. My mom can't know this!"

"No, not that," Brody takes in a deep breath, shakes his head back and forth. His face is flushed. Behind him, Cayce has started singing while she lines the balls up in a row. She looks up and gives me the pageant wave again. I wave back. "It really isn't a big deal. I just don't want Zach to get fired from his job. He meant well when he did it. Sometimes, he's just misguided."

"Misguided," I repeat. There, that did it. The words started pouring out of my mouth then. "At what point has Zach ever meant *well*, Brody Wells, when it comes to me? He should be fired. Normal people don't do the things he does. And in the courthouse, they have to hire normal people. In second grade, he told our teacher I was copying off his test paper. In fourth grade, he pushed me off the slide every day. In high school, he spray painted my car purple. Did he mean well then? No. Nothing has changed. Don't tell me he meant well. He refuses to find my birth certificate. He forced me to ask you out in front of everyone at the restaurant. I would just as soon march right over to the courthouse now and turn him in —no, better yet,"

I say and turn. I pick up my purse, rifle through it and pull out my phone. "I am going to call the Bacon Valley police and report him right now. That butthole has picked on me one time too many."

I start to put in the old 9-1-1, then my finger wobbles over the last number. "Crap, I don't know the police station phone number and Officer McGee has banned me from calling 9-1-1 unless it is an emergency. I consider this an emergency . Wouldn't you?"

At first, Brody looks like he has just taken a lick of a pickle when I say that. Then he tips his head to one side and gazes at me with his eyes narrowed like he is the one waiting for the punchline to a joke this time. I realize how stupid I just sounded while I slowly lower my hand with the phone.

I see this look on Robert all the time. It is kind of like my words come out like a puzzle and he has to piece each one together to make sense of it. I wait for Brody to point this out with some witty, mean remark. But he doesn't. He just breaks out into a laugh. "You're so funny," he says. The color has come back to his face and I know he really thinks I am kidding. And it is kind of difficult to be mad when somebody is smiling because they think you are being kind to them, even when you're not.

"So does that mean you'll give us a couple days to figure this out?" Brody asks before he adds, "sweetie." and chuckles like it is funny. He doesn't realize that as soon as my initial shock has melted away, I am trying to both digest the information and forcing away a certain wondering of what it would be like to be married to him.

I don't get to answer. The door bursts open and Kylee Thurston sticks her head inside, one hand on the door knob and the other on the door frame. I reach up, catch the bookshelf.

"Did you call your mom or what?" she asks Brody. "Does she have a phone in here? If not, we'll just stop by the house and drop her on our way. Your dad or somebody is at home that can watch her, right?"

Brody is looking at me guardedly. Kylee doesn't even bother to greet me. Instead, she just taps her foot on the floor. "Hello—" she says sarcastically when Brody doesn't answer.

I am sitting there still holding my phone and I bring it out, hand it over to Brody. "Here it is," I say as if that was the plan all along. "Why don't you try to call again." He takes it and I can see by his bland expression, he doesn't want to do something. But he takes the phone and dials anyway, waits a moment, then hands it back to me.

"Nobody's home, Kylee," he says. "You guys just go on without me."

He turns and even I can see Kylee is livid. "I thought your mom was meeting us after work? You told me she was going to meet us." Her jaws have clamped shut and she is glaring hard at Cayce who has stopped singing and is now giving Kylee a wide-eyed stare. "I don't want to go without you. Once again, I'll be the only one who doesn't have her boyfriend with her. We can't go to an R-rated movie if—" she looks down at Cayce and wags her head back and forth, "you have to drag your kid with you."

I can see Cayce's eyes dance from Kylee to Brody. I remember that look. I remember what it feels like, wondering if Delilah was going to be disappointed if she had to stay with me instead of going out with her friends.

"I'll watch her," I pop up. As soon as I do, I regret it. I'm supposed to practice with Drew tonight. But I also don't want to see the look on Cayce's face that represented what I felt back when I was her age.

"That'll work, right?" Kylee says and I can't read Brody's face while he looks to Cayce and then at me.

"I really don't mind," I lie. "We'll have fun. Stay out as long as you want. We'll have a sleepover."

Cayce pokes at the crate, doesn't say anything. "We'll dress up like princesses," I say. "How's that sound?"

She looks up, not entirely convinced. But she nods her head up and down. I think Brody is even less excited than she is.

Chapter −19

Date Three

Smalltalk does a drive around my cul-de-sac every two hours. Until 11:00 p.m., he honks softly to let me know he has stepped up his surveillance of the area. I think he believes it makes me feel safer. I can't decide if it makes me feel safe or if he is just reminding me of our conversation the other night. Tonight, Cayce and I are dressed in fluffy dresses when he passes at 10:00. We stand at the window and wave while he goes past.

Smalltalk waves back, but I see him slow a bit like he notes the motorcycle in the driveway and the extra kid at the window. I wonder if he runs the tags on the bike. It belongs to Drew. Usually Drew and I meet at his mobile home out on his dad's old gravel farm road and practice. Since Robert wasn't around, he can come to my house. It is the first time he has ever been here. It is kind of nice.

For a few hours, we sit on the couch with Cayce on my lap and go over our newer songs. I can tell, though, Drew is a little down that the music scout never called back. He seems a little withdrawn until we build a fort in the kitchen. I drag out a couple old boxes of pageant clothes and Cayce finds a pink flouncy dress she likes. I choose lime green. Drew tells me I look like a skinny pickle and puts on a suit Robert left in the closet. It drapes over him like a tent. He plays the prince for a while in our games until he gets bored and turns on the TV. At 10:15, Cayce starts to cry for her daddy, then I make up a silly little lullaby I sing to her and she falls asleep in her dress on my chest while we sit on my old brown couch.

"Put your arm around me and I can call this date number three," I yawn in the cup of my hand and tell Drew.

He is texting one of his big-boobed girlfriends, but nods lazily and tosses an arm over my shoulders.

"As long as we don't have to sleep together," he tells me.

I curl my lip. "I find that insulting considering you told me the other night you'd slept with the bartender, Bailey, at Hobie's. She's like three times your age."

"Come on, Journey. I thought you liked Bailey," He rolls his eyes, leans away and acts like I am distracting him from whoever he was texting. "You said you liked it when you looked out and saw her singing your songs with you while she worked." I wiggle around and play with Cayce's hair while she sleeps. She makes a cute cooing sound and cuddles in closer. "What is up with you? You're the only one that doesn't bug me about this stuff. Lay off." He takes a moment to glare at me. It is kind of hard to take him seriously in Robert's old suit. Besides, his eyes are brilliant beneath the dark bangs.

"I'm just worried that I'll never find somebody that likes me like I like them or that I like as much as they like me," I start to say. I watch as Drew's eyes get wider and wider like he's going to explode. "What if —"

"What if you just watch the TV, Journey. Write another song," he says. "I can't concentrate. And it isn't just because it smells like a funeral in here with all the flowers."

Drew waves a finger in the air toward the latest three dozen roses Robert has sent. "I won't sleep with you because it would ruin the way we react to each other on stage. And women like you are too much work." My feelings are hurt and I tell him so. "See that's what I mean, too much work. I have to worry about saying stupid stuff around you when you're acting girlie and stuff."

Then he holds his phone out like he is handing it to me. "Hobie just had one of the waitresses text me again. Says he is trying to get ahold of you. He's called me twenty times this week. Tell me you didn't lose your phone again."

"I didn't," I say and push away the phone. "I just don't want to call him. He'll make me come into work."

Brody knocks on the door at about 11:15. Drew answers it and lets him inside. Then Drew mumbles something about getting the hell out of here. He says it is boring.

"Like you have anything better to do," I whine at him. "Who else our age is going to make a fort to play in, huh? Next time, you're going to be the evil witch. I get to be the prince."

Brody is standing at the doorway facing the couch, looking uncomfortable while he shifts left to right. He turns his gaze back and forth between Drew, then Cayce and finally, me. Drew is dragging off Robert's old suitcoat and shrugs at Brody. He plops the coat on the chair and looks himself up and down.

He ignores me and says to Brody: "The shit we don't do to keep women happy, huh?" Then Drew stops and extends his hand to Brody. "I remember you from the other night at the bar, don't I? You were the one that gave Journey a ride. Your girlfriend beat her up."

"Ex-girlfriend, yeah," Brody laughs and looks over at me. He's got a nice laugh, not too soft and not too loud. "She's my hero." He lifts his voice a little and gives it a twang like a woman's voice. He isn't wearing his hat and keeps scrubbing his hand through his hair.

"Some hero," I mumble. "I got one hit in the face. It hurt. I wasn't sticking around and ran like hell."

Brody kind of shrugs in agreement, then tosses out a hand. "I'm thinking you got off better than her." Brody looks up at Drew. "Did she tell you after she got hit, she knocked down a fence full of my exes' friends. It looked like a crime scene for a minute."

Drew turns and walks back over to me. He grabs up his guitar on the couch, then leans over and gives me a quick peck on the forehead. "Listen. Don't be upset with me. It isn't you," Drew says quietly. "I like you because you don't like me in that way. I think it is the same way with you. I like Bailey because I don't have to be anybody else when I'm around her. You of all people ought to understand that. See you Saturday, right?"

"Of course."

"And you'll call Hobie."

"No," I tell him while I watch him walk out the door. "I won't." I didn't tell him why Hobie was bothering me. I'm not quite sure how to handle the situation if they don't want Drew. He is the only reason I sing up there. If I was by myself, I would be too scared. It just wouldn't happen.

Just as he closes the door, Brody walks over and hovers above me and Cayce. He looks like he is going to reach out and snatch Cayce up. I push out a hand and stop him.

"I get five more minutes," I tell him. "It's like holding a little, warm kitten."

So he sits down at the end of the couch. My dress is splayed all over and it puffs into the air when he sits down. "I've got to be honest," I say. "I really didn't understand why Delilah made me go to all those pageant things and dress up until tonight. But Cayce wanted to be a princess and so I dug out the dresses. I got one on her and she was so cute, I curled her hair and added makeup. I kind of didn't want to stop because she just—sparkled.

I think she liked it much more than I did at her age."

"I thought you lived for the pageants and the parades."

"Oh, no." I close my eyes, shake my head. "I have anxiety, stage fright. I throw up, feel like I'm going to faint. I can't stand to be in front of people. Delilah got me started to help me stop stuttering. I know, what was she thinking?"

Brody furrows his brow, plucks at the knees of his pants. He barely looks at me. "You wouldn't know it. You're always so calm. And you looked pretty happy singing with Drew at the bar the other night."

"After I threw up by the dumpster," I tell him. "I wouldn't be doing it if it wasn't for Drew. You know, if you watch, you'll see him reaching out and nudging me once in a while with his fingers. He just seems to know five seconds before I start to panic. He gives me a poke and I know he's got my back if anything happens."

"Thanks for not turning in Zach to the cops," he says and he has a funny twist to his lips like he is teasing me. I ignore it. "His family is just plain mental sometimes. If it got out that he did that to us, I think his dad would beat the crap out of him."

"Still?" I ask.

"Yeah, his dad shoves him around all the time, gets mad over nothing. As soon as Zach's dad gets home from work, he starts grabbing the beers. The more beer he drinks, the meaner he gets. Zach still lives at home. I know it is to watch over his mom."

It is silent then between us. I still have a hard time feeling sorry for Zach. However, I feel bad Brody has to feel like he needs to protect him.

"Thanks for taking her tonight," Brody tells me. "You know, Cayce thinks you're a real princess. She has this whole story concocted in her head that you are being held by some evil king."

"Who is the evil king?"

Brody looks up, casts me a strange stare. I suppose he doesn't want to say it is Robert.

"Dunno." He pulls out his wallet, takes out a twenty dollar bill and hands it to me. "Here."

"You don't have to pay me." I can hardly see anything but Cayce's face between all the puff in our dresses.

"Take it, please. You don't know what it is like to come back and see her—like this." He takes the twenty dollars back, drops it on the end table. "It's been a long ride. When her mama decided she didn't want her, she left her on my front porch. She bit and kicked other kids. I couldn't find a sitter."

"Well, she didn't bite or kick me. She danced with Drew and had tea with me." I wave a hand around the room. It is a mess. There are a couple blanket forts and pillows from my bed we used as a moat. "The important thing is she was happy. Were you?"

"Was I—happy?" he asked as if nobody ever inquired this of him.

"Did you have fun on your date?"

"Oh," he says, wavers there. "Well, yes and no. You know, Bella's right about some things. She says I go from one bad relationship to the next. And if the new one isn't crappy enough, I go back for more abuse from the last." He is quiet for a moment, puts his elbows on his knees, clasps his hands between. Then Brody looks at my little table in front of the couch. It has three piles of torn pieces of lined paper on it, each with words to songs that just sound stupid.

I had ripped them up, tossed them to the closest place I could reach.

"Songs," I say. "I write songs. Sometimes it gets frustrating. I get these sudden inspirations rushing at me and I grab anything I can find to write on." I feel like I should get up and toss them in the trash, but my eyes work over to the trash can and it is full of more little pieces of paper. I turn, note that Brody's eyes have followed my own.

"I know. Everybody says I'm obsessive compulsive."

"For writing songs?" He asks a bit indifferently, shrugging. For just a moment, I think he might think I'm crazy because I say anything at all. Then, Brody turns to me. "I dunno. I'm not very good at writing stuff. I think it's kind of cool you do it." He pushes a hand out as if waving the thought away. "But—here's what happened tonight. There were eight of us hanging out. We all went to the movies and then like we used to do in high school, we went down to the park in town. I just kept worrying about leaving Cayce."

"She was fine. I wouldn't hurt her."

"Yeah, I know that. I wasn't worried about you," he says. "Well, I guess I was a little worried. She usually won't let me leave her. I figured she would drive you crazy crying and stuff."

"She cried a little before she fell to sleep. I just cuddled her and played with her hair. I sang her a lullaby while Drew played his guitar. It lasted twenty minutes. I know how she felt. She misses her daddy. I was like that with Delilah," I tell him. "I used to worry about her even when I was Cayce's age. She didn't have anybody else."

"Yeah, that's Cayce, I think." He looks at her and acts like he wants to reach out and pick her up. But he doesn't. He leans back on the couch and he is quiet again.

"So what did you guys do at the park?"

"You mean like me and Kylee?"

"Sure."

"I don't know. We just hung out." He heaves out a breathe. "Okay, let me tell you something."

"Okay—" I sound apprehensive because Brody is kind of rocking forward, tapping his knee. I feel like he has some big secret and I'm not sure I want to know it.

"Kylee and I are walking, she is like clinging to my hand, you know hard like she's trying to pull me a little closer to her. I'm thinking that maybe I should call you, make sure everything's okay. We stop by this tree and she asks if I remember what we did there in tenth grade. It was our first kiss." He shrugs. "I remembered. I know what she wants. She wants me to kiss her. And I know this sounds crazy, but I'm thinking that yeah, okay, I'll kiss her and then all of a sudden, I—can't kiss her. I don't— want to kiss her."

"I get it." I tell him. "Because your mind was focused on Cayce. She was fine."

"No, because I'm married to you."

My eyes shoot upward, catch Brody Wells's eyes in my own. His have this puppy-eyed gaze like he thinks I'm going to laugh at him or maybe he doesn't know how I'll react at all. I don't even say anything. I just feel a little smile coming up on my lips.

"Please don't laugh. I know we're really not married."

But the smile is a mixed emotion I can't quite define. It is a strange kind of sensation. I'm not sure if I'm on the verge of laughing or crying. I think that what Brody divulges to me is as gallant as any prince in any book his daughter might own. Then it hits me. He's right. We are husband and wife.

"Well, yeah, we kind of are—really married." I shift and Cayce slides along the slippery flounces of the dress.

I haven't really thought about it. He is right. For the last few days, I have been looking at our wedding situation in the same way I look at the check I sign for my electric bill each month. It is there and it will be gone.

I feel a little sick to my stomach and dizzy to my head. I let Cayce slide from my arms on to the couch, and I squeeze from beneath her until I can stand up. I tug a little blanket over her and then stand there in the flounced lime dress and hug my temples between my finger and thumb.

"Can you excuse me a minute," I mumble. "I need—a moment."

"Yeah, sure," Brody answers. "Maybe we should get going. It is late. Are you alright?"

"I don't know," I tell him honestly. "I really don't know. I need some time. "

"Okay," Brody is flustered. "I'm sorry. I shouldn't have said anything. I'll get it fixed. I'll call Zach and hurry it up. I need to. Mom has gotten a hundred calls from people in town wishing us well. I haven't said anything to Mom and Dad about it actually happening. They think it was just a misprint. They would completely freak out."

I am flustered. We both stand there staring at each other until he rubs his palms together, looks toward the door. "I can stay or I can go," he tells me. "I'm sorry I brought this up. You're right. It really doesn't mean anything."

"I didn't say it didn't mean anything, did I?" I answer sharply. "I mean, I'm not seeing it as just a piece of paper anymore that should have gotten tossed in the trash. It's like the promise I made to your grandpa about dating other guys. It was a pact, an agreement. I didn't want to do it, but there's something of an obligation involved, right?"

"I obviously think so or I would have stayed with Kylee."

"Can you leave now?" I ask him, hands coming up in front of me. "Because I am going to lose it, freak out." I think I am feeling sick to my tummy, sick to my heart. Losing Delbert and breaking up with Robert. Finding out that Robert and Andrea were going out on me. My house and shop getting broken into. And then the whole marriage thing with a guy I thought was a complete shit up until a week ago. It is just too much.

I make this tiny little peep. It sounds like the baby chicks Smalltalk used to take me to pet at the hardware store around Easter. Then I feel my lips start to pucker, feel my eyes start to well up with tears.

"Holy crap, please don't cry."

If a full-grown cow would have come through the roof of my house right then and landed on the floor between the two of us, Brody would have no less than the same traumatized expression he has on his face right now. His eyes are wide, his jaws are working their way up and down. His head is shaking back and forth when his hands come up in front of him like he is trying to figure out how to put the brakes on the crazy getting ready to come out of me.

He jumps up and wavers about three steps from me. But I'm good at holding them back. Robert hates it when I cry. He says it isn't fair that I use it to win a fight. So I bite down hard on my lip and tell Brody that I won't cry. I'm pretty sure all guys must feel the same way. My eyes are wide, I hold my breath. "Okay. I think I can do this," I tell Brody with a soft voice. I don't want to wake up Cayce. I bob my head up and down. "But you should probably leave if you don't want to see it. Because I'm going to—cry and it isn't going to be pretty."

I wave a finger toward the front door as if Brody doesn't know the right direction to go. His eyes follow it, but his legs just stand right there. Then he takes one step forward and then another. I can't help think he is coming toward me like I've seen rangers approaching an injured grizzly bear on the nature channel. He brings out one arm, lets it fall so it barely grazes my arm so softly, it tickles.

"You know, whatever it is, it's going to be okay."

I probably would have run to the bathroom, locked myself inside, and sobbed quietly to myself had he not leaned in and used his hand to pull me toward him. I do not have the option of sparing my humility. I just press my head to his shoulder and feel the tears start sliding down my cheeks.

He pats my back for ten minutes while I snivel like a two year old. Then while I snuffle back the hiccup breaths that come after a good cry, we sit down on the couch. He puts his arm around me and pats my shoulder like a father pats a daughter. I sniffle into a pink tissue and sponge my eyes with the hem of the lime green dress. Then I tell Brody all about my crappy couple weeks. I tell him about Robert and me fighting and all the roses he sends makes my house smell like funeral. I tell him that makes me think of his grandpa all the time and I'm afraid I'll never be able to fulfill my promise to him. Then I fill him in on what Smalltalk had found out about the little silver purse and to whom it belonged.

"Molly Lender. They never found her body—and I think those guys in the black car that followed us while we were heading to the pawn shop in Midland were the ones that broke into my house and the shop. I think there's something more to the purse."

"Why don't you just sell it to them? Wouldn't that solve the problem?" Brody asks softly. I shift and he asks if I want him to move his arm. I tell him no, not really.

"I don't want to sell it," I tell him. "As crazy as it sounds, I keep thinking that there is some message your grandpa was trying to give to me before he died."

"Wouldn't he just come out and say it?" Brody asks. "Grandpa Del wasn't one to hold back. Especially when he got older."

"Well, he kind of told me. He wanted me to fill out the dance card. He didn't like Robert much. There was just something more, something I can't quite put my finger on. And it's just strange. He told me that he won it in a car race. The guy backed out of giving him his car papers when Delbert won. He said the loser of the race gave him the silver purse of the girl who was in the car with him. And later, she gave him the dance card and told him she'd save all the dances for him if he brought it and met her at the formal at her school." I lean in a little to Brody. I'm not sure why. It just felt right. He didn't push me away. "But Smalltalk told me on the phone that during the race, the car went off the road and she was ejected into Goose Creek. I don't understand why Delbert would have—lied to me."

"Maybe he raced him twice," Brody suggests. "Or maybe Grandpa Del had forgotten. He was pretty old."

"Brody, I know he was old. But it was his heart that gave out, not his mind," I say. "Maybe it doesn't mean anything at all. Maybe he —"

Cayce's dress rustles next to Brody. I watch as she pushes herself up on skinny arms, her sleepy-eyed head with hair sticking up peers around her daddy. In one smooth snap, he pulls his arm from around my shoulders. Then she crawls on his lap.

"I should get her back to Mom and Dad's." Brody says while Cayce crawls up and puts her arms around his shoulders. "I got an early morning tomorrow. I've got to get up early and help box more stuff. Then Zach and I are going to ride ATVs one last time before it rains."

She is half-asleep and tucks her head into his neck. "Are you okay now? I wouldn't worry too much about stuff. I'll have Mom drop off the dress Cayce's wearing when she goes into work tomorrow."

"Yes, of course," I answer. But I wasn't. Now I had one more thing to add to my plate. I have a super-huge crush coming on Brody Wells. And it isn't going away soon.

Chapter −20

Note to Self: Date with EMS Eddy 9:00

I am always late. But I am barely halfway through stuffing myself into the blue satin Civil War era dress when EMS Eddy begins banging his fist to my front door. Not once, not twice, but three times before I scuttle out with a hooped cage-like crinoline barely covering the cotton chemise.

"Will you give me a damn break, Eddy?" I hiss through a small crack I make between door and frame. The only contraption of this dress I have figured out is the sexy little whalebone corset overtop the lace bodice. This is only because I had worn a corset once for Robert after he got hooked on a History TV show based in Victorian England.

The wooden cage is supposed to drape around my waist, over these holy-hell scratchy garments, and beneath the dress. Its ultimate goal is to push the dress out like a full -bloomed flower. But at every angle, I cannot get the contraption to work. "I don't know how to put on this damn corset, much less the wooden thing that's supposed to go under the dress!"

"It is almost nine o'clock. The reenactment starts in thirty minutes. If we are late, we cannot participate." EMS Eddy is livid when he comes in the door. He is dressed in full military uniform, freshly ironed by his mother. He is donning a reproduction sword near his waist. He pushes through the door and snatches up my outfit. Like a well-honed machine building a doll, he puts me together.

"There!" he exclaims, looking me up and down in the same way a car mechanic stands back and scrutinizes the well-purring engine of the car he has just fixed. He does not note my hair. I am feeling a little insulted since I got up at four in the morning to scan the internet on 1860s hair fashions, and I put my hair up real pretty Victorian-style.

Had I known that the dressing disaster was a precursor for the rest of the day, I would have stopped right there. Gallant as EMS Eddy appeared in his unstained Union soldier attire, he did not seem to notice all the work I put into the hairstyle.

Once we get to the improvised battlefield, I find myself standing uncomfortably near the parking lot. I am out of the way of the two sides of soldiers and in the company of Wednesday Farmer, the Bacon Valley Public Library librarian. She arrives in a pioneer costume and keeps talking with a British accent to whoever will listen or can't duck away. There are three fat women in bustled dresses and showing a lot of cleavage from Winford who keep whispering stuff to each other behind their fans and then peering snobbishly at me. I see Smalltalk out among the soldiers in a rebel outfit. He gives me a thumbs up before a rebel soldier shoots him fake-dead in the chest. I wave back while he gracefully falls to the ground.

There is a pretty big crowd that turns up to watch considering it looks like it is going to rain. I just want to leave. The corset is digging into my ribs. I can't duck out to the parking lot and take off because EMS Eddy has driven me here. It is at least three miles for me to walk home. I knew this was a mistake. The thought of getting the dress muddy if it rains and losing out on a thousand dollars is sneaking up on me. I am bored out of my mind.

It would have been nothing more than mere boredom and later kicking myself in the butt for wanting to please Delbert Johnson if two things did not happen consecutively less than one minute apart and after the second of two battles was to begin. One, Brody shows up. Two, I shoot EMS Eddy in the leg.

It should never have happened. However, I hear a couple loud engines at the far end of the parking lot near a sign that clearly states: NO ATVS IN PARK. They are followed, not long after, by a whole round of catcalls, hisses, and whistles.

I would not have turned at all had Wednesday Farmer not jabbed me in the shoulder to tell me that whoever was yelling was trying to get my attention. I do not know why I turn because it occurs to me I already know who it is because I have spent most of my life being heckled by the three idiots stopped on their ATVs just outside the park. I can see Brody Wells is back to being an jerk while he sits there looking all smug beside Bella Johnson and Zach Metzler who are both laughing so hard they are bent over in their seats.

"Journey, I've got to go."

That is when EMS Eddy arrives so I can shoot him. "I got an emergency callout message from the fire department." He comes loping over and shoves his gun into my hands. "I've got to go. I need to drive the ambulance," he tells me.

"Oh, please don't leave me here," is all I say. I try to use my arms to plead for him to get someone else to pick up the old lady who has gotten her arm caught in her stairway ride chair. The gun is a little heavier than I expect. It flips sideways on the fingers of my right hand. Impulsively, I reach down to grab it in the center where the trigger is located. How was I to know it is loaded with a patch and gunpowder, ready to fire?

There is just one loud BOOM. I yelp, EMS Eddy yowls like a cat who has its tail stepped upon as the blast of gunpowder crashes out of the barrel and the butt of the gun slips through my fingers and rams into his left knee.

"You could have shot my damn head off!" And that is what EMS Eddy is screaming at me while the Bacon Valley ambulance is making a U-turn in the fire department parking lot and heading toward the park at full speed to save Eddy.

"Why did you give me a loaded gun?" I scream back at him. I'm sure my voice is louder than it needs to be because the sound of the gun is now making my ears ring. Everyone is staring at us while he sits down and rubs his leg. He's not bleeding, but he is whining like a big baby while he rocks a little back and forth cradling his leg. Smalltalk comes up, pushes the crowd back with his waving hands. But I hardly notice while I see EMS Eddy staring up at me, his lips contorted in a growl and his fist waving in the air.

"Because any idiot would have simply held it! But not you. You have to stand there staring at me with that same stupid, idiot look on your face as you had when somebody asked you a simple question in school like what is one plus one? And you would answer six." He does this little dance with his head and starts saying "duh" to me. Then he curses into the air to the sound of the sirens. "You're a frigging train wreck waiting to happen!"

"That's enough, Eddy." That's Brody who says those words. He isn't laughing anymore, just has a deadpan stare at Eddy. He pushes a hand on Eddy's shoulder to get him to stop wiggling. I can hear the ambulance making the beeping sound as it backs up and I fade into the crowd. I just want to be invisible right then, to run and hide and have people quit staring at me like I tried to murder someone.

I work my way to the railroad tracks outside town. I know if I take them, it is a shortcut toward town. I don't want to call Delilah, but I am thinking I might not have a choice.

She'll probably tell me something like 'you reap what you sow' or 'you shouldn't have placed all your eggs in one basket' or some other saying I can't quite figure out how it relates to what is going on.

The sky is a deep gray and the kind of puffy clouds that come before a summer storm. I hear the thunder and I figure I've got twenty minutes to find somewhere underneath the trees before I watch a thousand dollars in genuine Civil War attire get ruined. I dig my phone from my purse, get ready to poke in Delilah's phone number when I hear what I really, really didn't want to hear and it is the sound of ATVs coming up behind me.

One comes up beside me and I have to take three steps back to keep it from throwing dirt on the dress.

"Hey, you need a ride?"

I hold my hands out as if to display the dress I am wearing and furrow my brow. "In this dress on an ATV?" I ask with sarcasm tinging my tone. "Are you crazy? Brody, it is worth a thousand bucks. I can't get it dirty. If I do, the museum I bought it for isn't going to buy it from me."

"I'll go slow. We can get to Grandpa's old house on the back side of the farm before it rains. It is just a few miles away," he tells me. "I'll drop you off and then go get my truck. I can come pick you up in it."

"You don't understand," I tell him. I am yelling over the ATV. "The underskirt has a wooden cage and it doesn't bend—much."

Well, it did bend enough to sit backwards on the ATV. If it had not been humiliating enough shooting EMS Eddy, it was far worse seeing cars slow down to figure out why a huge blue flower was bumping along on the tail end of an ATV.

"What were you doing with that asshole Eddy?" Brody asks, turning his head and yelling over the engine.

"Trying to get in another date to ease my conscience." I answer. When I say it, it sounds really stupid. "Your grandpa suggested it. Smalltalk said he was nice."

"Well, of course he would be nice to a cop. Everybody's nice to a cop," Brody says. "Why didn't you just ask me?"

"Well, for starters, with our history, it didn't even occur to me you would go. Besides your grandpa told me to fill up the card," I say honestly. "He said I needed to dance with more than just one guy. I already danced with you, Brody. I mean, really, doesn't it scare you a bit? I shot the last guy I went on a date with." He seems to find this hilarious and I can feel his back bobbing up and down while he laughs hard and loud. And despite the muck flipping up from his tires, I laugh a little too.

It starts to drizzle, then rain. We ride for a few more minutes, me bumping around and holding on desperately. Then all hell seems to break loose from the clouds above us. When Brody finally pulls into the gravel drive beneath a long line of old maple trees, he jumps off and takes my hand to help me from catching the dress on the vehicle and we make a mad dash to the porch.

It was only six months ago that John Wells brought Delbert over from his old two-story farm house on Goose Creek Road to live with them in the larger second home on the property. It still looks lived-in, the exterior has a fresh coat of white paint and the grass is recently mowed. Flowers are blooming in the little concrete pots in front of the porch. I can almost imagine Delbert sitting there in a white chair on the porch, sneaking a smoke from one of the cigars I ordered for him online.

"Oh-my-God," I say while I look down at the rain spattered, mud-flecked hemline. I'm not sure I can dab the stains off. "It's ruined. This is a real Civil War dress."

"It's just water and mud," Brody advises. "We can wipe it off. Easy-peasy. That's what Grandpa would say, right?"

"Easy-peasy," I repeat. But I don't think it is going to be that simple. He slips his hand underneath a ratty rug in front of the door and pulls out a house key, which he uses to unlock the door.

It is only the carpeted inside that has the faint hint of not being lived in. It is warm and the air is stale because the windows have been closed. After we slip inside, he runs to get some washrags while I awkwardly clamber up steps to a walk-in bathroom upstairs.

Buttons. The dress looks like it has fifty of them running from my belly button to my chin. I don't have much room to move between the sink along the wall and the toilet on the other end of the room. The buttons are tiny, made for wee servant fingers to manipulate, not slightly calloused fingers from playing guitar. I can't wiggle them. They are teeny-weeny and I try to be careful not to pull them too hard. I can hear Brody's banging footsteps coming up the stairway and he stops just short of the door, peers inside. In both hands, he has damp rags and he hovers there before I give him a glare.

"Well, don't just stand there, Cowboy." I wave my hand in front of my dress. "I'm drying fast and I got a million buttons to—unbutton. It took EMS Eddy and me twenty minutes to get me dressed. I would think a healthy man like you could get me out of it in ten. Help."

He opens his mouth to say something. Nothing comes out, but he is stifling a grin beneath pinched lips.

"What?"

"Please don't make me say what I want to say right now."

"Is it mean because I said something stupid?"

"Well," he seems to ponder the question, then plops the dishrags on the porcelain sink. "It wasn't stupid, just easy to manipulate to my advantage. I was just thinking if I wasn't a gentleman, and I am, I could get you out of this dress in four minutes flat."

It was kind of funny. I laugh, softly and a little self-consciously, while he takes two steps, then reaches out and starts to help me unbutton. Close. Brody is so close I can smell the outdoors on his clothes. He has the scent of the forest and wind. I can feel his warmth and the tickle of his fingers while he pops off one button and then another.

"It isn't like anyone can disapprove," Brody says, his eyes coming up for just a moment to lock on mine. "We are married." I roll my eyes. "Well, this is kind of sexy," he informs me, looking up long enough so that I can see he's a little shy about the whole thing too. He smiles sheepishly. "I'm sorry. I'm joking."

I just look at him, roll my eyes. "I get that. This is awkward for me too."

"You know, I'm going to keep saying dumbass things, Journey. I am apologizing before I say them."

"Just don't say them," I tell Brody. He's doing a better job of unbuttoning, so I hold my hands to the side. He won't look up, just works his way down in the silence until he reaches my waist. I have to say it is much easier to step out of the hoop skirt and dress than getting into it. I am able to walk right out while Brody holds on to the bodice, kneels down so it is lower than me and lays it gently on the floor.

"Voila!" I announce and take a giant step forward in the small room where I end up right in front of Brody. I use his shoulder to keep upright while I make a short turn so I don't walk on the hem. He is kneeling and his face has blanched to a creamy white while he looks up at me. I look down at the corset and little pantaloons wondering why he is looking at me with something short of horror. Nothing. I can see nothing amiss.

"What's wrong, Cowboy?" I hiss, waiting for some nasty retort. "Just say it. Spit it out."

"I'm not sure I can. I suppose—Holy-mother-of-God." He just mutters that and stands up quickly which places him so close to me that my eyes nearly cross when I look up at him. He tips forward, uses my shoulders to right himself and just dangles there with his fingers barely grazing my skin.

"If it is the dress," I say hotly, my face burning. "I was trying to look the part today. This is the underwear they wore back in the olden days."

"No, it isn't the underwear," he says a little too loudly, then drops his voice. His hand comes out, touches my arm like I've seen him do when he talks to people. Then he snaps it away quickly. "No, you're so frigging beautiful right now I'm dizzy and I think my lips just turned numb." I guess I would describe his soft laugh as a chuckle. "I'm sorry. I said too much."

Maybe. I was completely silent for a moment. I don't know. Then, I am kind of giggling along with him, the kind of bantering laughter between two people who are experiencing an attraction, awkward as it might be, and not expecting it.

"Oh." It is all that stumbles out of my mouth. Now I am blushing and wishing I could cover it up. I can't. And we are close and I lean into him, just a little.

Brody Wells picks up on it; he leans in too. His fingers slip along my elbow, up my arm. I'm looking up and he's looking down and we just kiss. At first, we almost miss. More quiet laughter. Then our lips hit spot on and my stomach makes this wild bumpety-jerk. It is clumsy and discomfiting and—really sexy. Then he nudges me backward, kissing my neck and my shoulders and we're doing this walk toward the door, down the hallway and I'm assuming, to one of the bedrooms.

It's kind of like a dance, our feet walking in perfect synchronization, our bodies barely touching, rolling along one wall. He whispers something in my ear and it tickles.

"Do you like this?" he asks.

"Yeah." I whisper. He's kissing me, I'm kissing him and neither of us can stop laughing. My bottom hits the end of a bed and I sit down slowly because Brody is holding me, keeping me from falling. Still he almost tumbles on top of me, misses and for some reason, we think this is funny. And we're laughing and kissing, touching and trying to figure out what each other likes. For just a moment, our eyes meet and it is like we both know where this is going. There is a lull, but it isn't as if either of us are thinking if we should do this or not do this because it seems like it is all about the moment. We both want it, need it. I want it, need it. And so we don't stop.

We end up under a crochet quilt afterwards. I have my head on Brody's shoulder, tucked into his arm. His fingers are stroking the crook of my arm, my fingers are playing on the skin of his chest. I can hear his heartbeat against my temple. I think we are both waiting for the other to say something. It is quiet except the rain pelting against the window and a tree limb tapping on the tin roof. Oh and there is a bit of thunder crackling across the sky.

"I didn't see that coming." I finally say. I peer up at Brody who is looking down at me. His eyes are so blue right then, it reminds me of a clear summer sky.

"Me either," Brody says.

"It was nice," I say.

"Yeah, it was—really nice."

"I'm not sure where we go from here," I tell him. "Or do I even need to ask that? Maybe people don't discuss it. I don't know. I've only been with one person. Maybe this happens all the time with other people. Should I shut up and just get up and go?" I suddenly feel like a freak. I've never told anybody but Robert I've only slept with him. Now Brody probably thinks I'm such a loser, no other guy would want to sleep with me.

I think Brody is going to answer. The sound of a truck door slamming shut forces my eyes to open wide. Then there is the kind of ting-ting that comes from leaving car lights on.

"Oh, no," Brody mumbles. "I'd know that sound anywhere. That's my dad. He was checking the electric fences in the back pastures this morning. He probably saw my four wheeler in the drive on his way back."

He has not even ended his sentence before I hop out of the bed. Brody slides to the side, grabs his pants and t-shirt and shoves himself into both. "I'll go down and see if I can just get him to go home, alright? Stay here. Get dressed. I'll figure something out."

Chapter —21

Note to Self: Sing your heart out

Drew doesn't show up at Hobie's on Friday night. Another cook who looks about a hundred years-old is flipping hamburgers over the greasy grill instead. I look at him; he doesn't look up from his spatula. He flips a burger, then he squishes it down with the spatula and the oil makes a sizzling sound crackling in the air.

Something is terribly wrong. A man by the name of Ducky Baker greets me with an outstretched hand when I slide in the back door twenty minutes late for my waitressing shift. The only thing I can think is: *Ducky. Who has a name like Ducky?*

"So who do we have here?" he asks. Ducky is tall and pudgy and has thinning gray hair and a bulbous nose. He is wearing a wrinkled gray suit and smiles a toothy grin while he pushes his silver-rimmed glasses up on his nose.

"Journey," I answer. I give him a polite smile, but my eyes are scanning the kitchen. I lean to the right to peek out the kitchen doors to the stage. I can see the drummer from Billy Gentry's band lugging out some of his equipment. It is too early for them to be setting up. I feel a pang of doubt while a lump starts creeping into my throat. I wonder if maybe Hobie doesn't want Drew and me to sing there anymore. But the camera crew is there again setting up. I feel my heart drop. I realize I'm back to waitressing full time instead of singing. It's not like I'm out much financially. I was only getting $50.00 a night for singing.

"Hey, Hobie, where's Drew?" I see Hobie just outside the door. I snatch up a white apron and flip it in half while I walk out to see where he is. Then I tie up the waist and stop just short of Hobie.

"He doesn't work here anymore."

I just stand there thinking that this is just the icing on the cake for today. It isn't enough that Drew quit. Brody's dad had come upstairs this afternoon while I was trying to toss a sheet around myself. He abruptly escorted me out, sheet and all. He and Brody and I left in his truck with the $1000.00 dress flapping in the wind in the truck bed behind us.

It was the longest, most silent ride I have ever taken. It was only made worse by the comment I overheard John Wells saying downstairs between whispers right before his footsteps thumped up the stairway. It went something like: *You can't just keep dropping off your daughter with your mom. You can't just take off when you promise her you'll help drive the boxes to your aunt's. Son, at some point in your life you are going to have to quit making dumbass mistakes and meeting these dumbass women. What were you thinking? Or what were you thinking with? Do you want a bunch of stupid babies as silly-headed as their mama running around your house? Find a nice girl with actual brains in her head that you can make conversation with over the table and settle it down. I'm telling you, you'll be happier.*

Now, while that patters around my head like marbles on a tin roof, I stand there thinking that maybe John Wells is right. I am pretty stupid. I didn't see it coming with Drew. I should have known it was coming someday when he finally got a contract or maybe decided to take the chance and head to California for a music career. He is way to good to be stuck here in Hobie's bar.

The only think I can say to Hobie is: "Oh." I start to turn and Ducky Baker must have been two inches behind me because I almost slam right into him with one step.

"Excuse me," I mutter, dropping my head and try to walk around.

Hobie latches on to my upper arm and forces me to a stop.

"I'm fired too," I say. Then it hits me that if Drew isn't here, Hobie doesn't need me screeching in the air up on the stage as Robert would describe my singing. And he certainly doesn't need me to wait tables.

"No, you're not fired, Journey," Ducky says to me. He keeps pushing his glasses up on along the bridge of his nose with his wrinkle-knuckled forefinger. "We are interested in setting you up with a contract to sing. You are quite good. You've obviously had experience with this. Where else have you performed?"

"Great Escapes Restaurants, weddings, church. I used to sing at fairs when I was in high school," I answer absently while I use the forefinger of one hand on the fingers of my other hand to count them. "In college, I did a few gigs on street corners and bars. Please don't be offended, but I don't want to do it all the time. I have another job, a shop. That's why I sing. To pay for it. And I don't want to leave Bacon Valley," I reiterate. "I just like to sing with Drew. Were you the agent who was here listening to him on Friday?"

"No, that wasn't me." Ducky says. "Well, you won't have to leave," he tells me. He wraps an arm around my shoulder and herds me toward Hobie's office. For twenty minutes, he yaks about this great idea he and Hobie have about setting up a performance venue right here at Hobie's with big names. He wants me to host it. "We'll bring in all sorts of music performers to play here. You'll open up for them and do the introductions. We've got backers. We think this is going to work."

I laugh a bit sarcastically: "Out here in the middle of nowhere? At this place?"

Ducky looks like I am dashing his dreams. Hobie looks mad. "This isn't nowhere anymore. Not with internet and TV. I'll tell you what," Ducky says. His frown turns back to a big smile. He keeps pressing down his suit jacket with his fingers like he is trying to iron out the wrinkles with them. "Those songs of yours, most of them you write yourself?" he asks. I nod skeptically. "Let me record a couple tonight right here while you're doing your usual, get them on the radio. If they pop to listeners, you'll think about it?"

If they pop? I doubt they would, but if I was going to sing anyway, I didn't really care. "You'll have to sign a paper that says I can set it up. For royalties and stuff."

I look at Hobie for reassurance and he nods. My heart is making a little patter in my chest and my tummy is starting its usual soppy rolling around. I feel like I'm going to get sick. "I don't know, Hobie, you know I'm not so good without Drew," I say. "He kind of helps me through when I get scared."

"Drew is out, Bread and Butter. He's not coming back." Hobie is looking at me with an expression I have never seen on him—serious and with the same eager, beseeching gaze of Delilah's cat when she forgets to put his food out for him.

"But why?" I ask. "He didn't say anything to me, not a word. I just talked to him two days ago. I—"

"Baby, I'm sure he's on his motorcycle halfway to Nashville," Hobie interrupts me. "But let's not worry about him tonight. Boys like that are a dime a dozen—"

"No, Drew is different," I start, my head shaking back and forth. "Let me call him. I bet he'd come back."

"Journey, you're getting yourself upset. There is nothing we can do tonight. The band is warming up.

They know your songs. It is just like any Friday night, no different. You've been up there by yourself plenty of times. How about giving us a chance. We'll all be in this together, a team. You've got nothing to lose. I'll be right there for you. Front row."

"The initial contract is only two months," Ducky says and I turn my head to him. "Two months. Me and a few others are footing the bill, investing the cash in this venture. You've just got to sing."

"Ducky here is my attorney," Hobie says. "He can be yours too. If it doesn't work, you go back to singing and waitressing just like you've always done. If it does, maybe you can pay cash for that little shop of yours."

"Hey, where's that cute little cowboy hat you had on the other night?" Ducky pats his head.

"On the cowboy's head I borrowed it from, I guess," I answer.

"Can you get it back, at least for tonight?"

"I— I can try," I stutter. I can only see the last image I have of Brody Wells ingrained in my head and it is the horrified expression he gave me after he had come upstairs behind his father, knowing I heard what John Wells had said.

"Call the cowboy," Ducky says. "You got the jean shorts and t-shirt. That's cute. But get the hat. Pronto."

The hat. Ducky says I need the hat. *Pronto*, whatever that means. Brody's cowboy hat. So I stand in the parking lot leaning against my car for five minutes, thinking if I call him and ask him to use his hat, he's going to think I'm crazy. Or he'll believe I'm looking for an excuse to talk to him. Hells bells, I didn't even have his phone number. I only have Bella's. So five times, I dial Bella's number and hang up before it rings.

Then while I'm banging my cowboy-booted foot against my front end tire thinking it would just be easier to tell Ducky I can't get the hat but still trying to work up enough guts to do it, the phone rings.

"Why the hell do you keep dialing me and hanging up?"

I about double over with embarrassment. It's Bella screaming at me on the other end. I wish I could crawl underneath my car. "I'm looking for Brody's number," I stutter and she actually makes fun of me for this. "Well— well," she mocks me. "Why would I give you Brody's number, huh? The last time I saw you, you were trying to kill that poor guy at the park. You got a gun with you?"

"Bella, please just give me his number."

"He's sitting right here next to me, Piece of Bacon, but maybe I don't want to give you his number. Why don't you leave him alone—"

I hear a rustling and have a good feeling Brody is grabbing the phone from her hand. I'm right.

"Hey," he says on the other end.

"Hey," I return. Then I blurt out: "Can I ask a favor of you?"

"Yeah," he answers, but draws out the word like he isn't certain he wants to give me a favor at all.

"I'm down here at Hobie's bar and we're setting up for tonight and I need to —I need to borrow your hat again," I tell him, wincing. "The guy who is setting it up wants me to match last week so he can piece together both shows."

"Yeah, we can do that. We were just going to pick up some milk at the store for Bella's dad. We've got Cayce with us," he says. "Can you meet us out front?"

I stand outside for thirty-two minutes. I swear, Bella probably drives the speed limit all the way to the bar. I know for a fact she never drives less than 5 miles over the speed limit. Twice, she has tried to hit me when she rolls through stop signs. But they pull up in her black truck and Bella honks her horn real loud when she slides by making me jump.

"Making a few extra bucks tonight picking up guys out here?" Bella yells after she rolls the passenger side window down. She thinks this is hilarious and laughs. I just roll my eyes. I don't feel confident enough to do anything else. I still have the fringes of brown and yellow around my eye from the last girl who hit me. My cocky has dwindled down a bit too. Brody smiles politely at me and maybe a little apologetically, takes off his hat and hands it to me. I am waving at Cayce sitting between them. She reaches out like she wants me to grab her hand. I'm not sure what to do, so I hold up my fingers for a high five. She punches my palm with her fingers.

"Hey, long time, no see." he says. He's got kind of a smug smile while he stares at me.

I just grin at him like an idiot until Bella points it out with one of her classic crappy remarks. "Brody, just give her the five bucks and get your business done before some other guy comes along and offers seven for her." My smile drops. I push the hat on my head. The parking lot is full. I'm getting stares standing there next to the truck.

"I'll bring it back to you," I tell him, then shy back a little. "Or maybe it would be better if you stopped in at the shop." I sniff. "I don't think your dad likes me much."

"You heard him. Oh, I was afraid of that," Brody looks uncomfortable, scrubs a hand to his face. "He is really stressed out with losing the farm, you know? I'm sorry, I'm really sorry about that."

"You used to say that kind of stuff to me all the time, Cowboy," I tell him. He is patting his leg nervously. I look behind me, catch the image of Ducky waving at me to come inside. I don't like to watch Brody squirm now like I used to enjoy it.

"I did."

"We can't control what everybody else says, right?" I ask him. "You agree with him?"

"No. I was just teasing when I did it in school, Journey," he says, looking me right in the eyes. Bella is taking all this in, but she is looking out the driver's side window. I see her forefinger tapping out a death march on the steering wheel. I know she wants to tell Brody to shut up and move on. I don't know why she hates me so much.

"I got to go," I say.

"Can I go with you?" Cayce looks like she is going to climb out of her car seat, but Brody stops her.

"No, Journey's got to work, baby. Tell her to sing her heart out and we'll go get ice cream."

"Sing your heart out," Cayce says and gives me a thumbs up.

"Sing your heart out," I repeat it. "I'll do just that." I liked the sound of those words. Then I step back so they can leave. "Are you at least going to call me, Cowboy?" I ask.

"I might," he says as Bella hits the gas.

Sing your heart out. It sounds like a bad ending to some country music song.

"Come on, come on, come on!" Hobie is waving his arm toward the door. My head is spinning.

"Got your hat?" Ducky asks and he pops me a knuckle on the head.

"She's good to go." Hobie points to the stage. I feel like a ping-pong ball and Hobie and Ducky are the paddles.

I keep getting banged back and forth between the two.

"Can you excuse me for a minute?" I ask. However, I don't wait for them to answer before I burst through the kitchen door and out into the dark back lot behind the bar and throw up next to the dumpster. But this time, Drew isn't there to pat my back.

When I am done behind the kitchen, I sing my heart out anyway for the usual crowd and do my usual things. I give Billy Gentry a list of my songs and his band does just fine. No, we do better than fine. It is like we meld together and sound like a real band, a really good band. Then right toward the end, I take in a deep breath. I do what I usually do and I try out a new song. Well, a new old song. It is one I have tucked into the lockbox in the Knick-Knack Shop and never quite felt like it was done. Because it is the same old crowd that would listen no matter what, that would cheer whether I forgot the words or the beat.

"Thanks for coming out and listening tonight," I say softly. "You know I always show my heart on the stage. You've listened to my daddy issues, been there for me when I sang about the fights I had with my boyfriend. But tonight, I'm going to do a new old song that's sat on my shelf for seven years. It's about a boy I had a crush on back in the day. Back a long time ago. I spent a lot of time dreaming about him, never got up the guts to ask him out. Now I'm falling back in love with him—maybe this time, he'll see the light— Or maybe it's just a crazy, silly kind o f love—"

Found myself outside your bedroom window last Friday after school.

Thinking about those crazy, silly little things we used to do. The time you stood up in front of everybody at the county fair, You said I was yours. Your friends gave you crap. You said you didn't care.

There was the time we stood on the train tracks
screamed at the train,
Riding your horse into the sunset. Dancing in the rain.
Jumping on your bed. There were a hundred other things
before I realized it was all in my head.
All in my head, all in my head, all in my head, head, head.
Those crazy silly little things that never happened, all in
my head.
Now I wonder if I'm in your head too. Maybe you stood
outside my window after school.
Like two ships that never pass in the night. Did you ever
think about those crazy, silly little things we used to do.
Like the time you passed me the note in class.
I took it and instead of tossing it back,
I kept it close to my heart. I stood up, told them all to kiss
my ass
Riding your horse into the sunset. Dancing in the rain.
Jumping on your bed.
There are a hundred other things before you realized it
was all in your head.
All in your head, all in your head, all in your head, head,
head.
And you wish I didn't stop doing those crazy little silly
things with you.

I think I popped. I sang my heart out just like Cayce told me to do. Then as I start to give my usual wave to the crowd to leave, Billy Gentry starts plucking a few notes from the duet Drew and I always sing together at the end.

I hover there, one foot leaving the stage and the other planted firmly by the mic. Then he starts singing the part Drew starts out with. I've got no choice but to sing my end when it comes to my turn, then we join together at the end.

Old Drunk Will gives me his usual whoop and his brother gives me his standard "Aw, baby, sing it." Then right over the mic, Billy Gentry gives a hearty laugh and says: "Be a good girl, Ditzy, get me a damn beer and be quick about it."

I can't look at Billy Gentry the entire time we are singing that last song, but my eyes spark and look up at him. I am so insulted, I can not speak. But when it is all said and done and I walk off the stage, Hobie is donning a genuine smile.

"Are you in?" he asks. I blink at him. It feels so good to hear my song onstage. "I'll try it out, Hobie," I tell him. "For a couple months. But you got to talk to Gentry about being so rude. I don't like it."

Chapter –22

Note to Self: Return Brody's Hat and find out he didn't like me after all

Delbert always told me summer days in Bacon Valley go by slower than a slug crawls along on a cold highway. He is right. I find myself wiling away the long, hot hours, poking around the internet and searching for more information on the dance card purse. I pull up six historical newspapers from the 1930s with reports about the car wreck where Molly Lender died.

The Winford Press has a short memorial section where it states: *Molly Lender, Winford High School, drowned early morning last Saturday. The driver of the vehicle, Edward Benjamin Dodge, was injured. The two were to be married March 30. Funeral services were held at Winford Holy Hands Church—* A picture that looks like the ones they take for high school yearbooks is placed below the obituary. Molly is staring at me through the paper, dark, shoulder-length hair and big, sad eyes Delilah would describe as doe-like. She was beautiful.

I find a picture of the grave on a website they put up for her at their family plot in a little cemetery in Winford. I wondered what it was like for her family to see it there and know she wasn't seven feet down below her headstone. Could it be that someone in her family was still living that remembered the purse? On a whim, I search up the Lender family in Winford. A Della Lender is listed in the phone book. I jot down her address and phone number.

An entire two weeks grind by and not a word from Brody. It doesn't surprise me. I made a clumsy attempt at getting his attention by taking back his hat two days later.

I parked in his driveway, followed the sound of voices to this huge old barn they have. Somebody was singing. It was Brody. He was belting out an off-key version of my *Crazy, Silly Love Song* he'd heard at the bar the other night. I find it a bit amusing. The song was about him. He didn't know it even though he stopped dead still in mid-note when I walked in. Brody and his dad were throwing bales of hay from their trailer to an upper room in the barn.

Brody stopped long enough to swipe a hand through his hair, give his dad a sideways glance with the same expression I would expect out of a pup who was getting ready to be spanked. "I brought back your hat." I stand there holding it out. "Thanks for letting me borrow it."

Brody is standing by one of about twelve stalls. He waves a hand, tells me to keep it. I kind of let my hand waver there in the air, then quickly hold the hat at my waist. Both of the men are staring at me like they are waiting for me to make some big statement. "That's all I needed."

"Thank you for bringing the hat, Journey," John Wells says. "But Brody needs to get back to work. We've got a lot to do before the sale."

I thought Brody liked me. I stole a quick glance at Brody's eyes. I felt my heart sink. There wasn't anything in there but the same tiresome gaze Robert gets when there's nothing on TV and he has to watch the same game again. I guess he got what he wanted. And I was damn quick, like an idiot, to give it out to him. I nodded and waved away the dust wafting in the air. I wanted to flip him my middle finger and tell him that Smalltalk had warned me just the other day that there'd be more men knocking on my door because Hobie's Bar and Grille was filling up every weekend night. Lots of them weren't looking for a relationship, just a one night stand. Guess he was right. But I didn't say anything about that.

"See you around," I said instead. But I didn't.

I did see Drew, though. It had surprised me. It was on the third week I sang with Billy Gentry's band. Hobie had told me Drew had taken off somewhere. He had his paycheck sitting on his desk, but had not picked it up. I figured he was right. I drove my car past his trailer five times, knocked on the door twice. The grass hadn't been mowed. Nobody was home. Or at least, nobody answered.

Hobie doesn't have me waiting tables much anymore. I go in on Tuesdays and Wednesdays now for a few hours to practice with the band. It is difficult because Billy Gentry is always making insulting sexist wisecracks about me. He thinks it is funny and everybody laughs. Sometimes I laugh politely too. I am doing just that Thursday afternoon when I see Drew coming in the front door. Hobie meets him with an envelope, but I see Drew looking up at me. I'm still a little mad at him for never saying goodbye and just not showing up. Hobie is pushing on Drew with his hand, kind of patting him back toward the door. I give him a little wave, sweep off my guitar and start down from the stage.

There's only a few people lounging in the bar. It is dark and stinks like old stale cigarettes and beer long ago spilled on the floor. I even hear the bottom of my tennis shoes sticking to the old floor.

"Hey, Hobie, let me talk to him. Drew!" I scurry up to give him a hug, but his cool face stops me short. If it wasn't so dark, I really would think his lip twitched when my feet came to a stop. I refuse to let my smile drop. Hobie is standing there, shaking his head.

"Journey, don't," Hobie tells me. "He's already been escorted off the premises once. He is getting his check and leaving."

I furrow my brow, asking Drew with my eyes what happened.

"Hey, I missed you," I say. Hobie is pointing a finger at the door. Two of his bouncers are making their way toward Drew.

"Yeah, it looks like it," Drew grunts. He nods to the stage, his eyes hot and angry. "Glad it worked out for you, Journey. It's nice to be used as somebody else's stepping stone. Never thought I'd have to watch my back with you. Never occurred to me."

The bouncers cut him short. One uses his hand to push Drew's shoulder so he is facing the door. Drew throws up his hands. "I'm out of here. You don't need to be a prick about it."

"He's bad news," Hobie huffs. He waves a hand at really nobody sitting at the bar and tables. "Shows over." Then he leans over to me, wiggles a finger. "Some money came up missing. Drew was the only one in the kitchen the other night. I laid down the receipts. Billy saw Drew go in and when he came out, the money was gone."

"I don't believe that," I tell Hobie. I look him in the eyes and he nods his head up and down. I don't say anything. I go back up to the stage. I just don't feel like singing, though. After a while, we call it a day.

On the way home, I decide to drive past Drew's trailer. He isn't there. A girl with long, brown hair and an angry sneer imprinted hard on her face answers the door and tells me he is working with his uncle installing roofs. "Tell him I stopped by. I need to talk to him," I tell her. "I'm Journey Bacon."

"I know who you are," she says with a sassy shake to her shoulders. She's dressed in an old t-shirt and raggedy shorts. "I'll tell him. But he ain't gonna call you back.

I guarantee it."

"He's got no right being mad at me, if that's what you are implying," I tell her. "Hobie said he took some money."

"Took some money?" she snickers, crosses her arms. "That's what they told you? Or did you make that up yourself. Bullshit. That's bullshit. You stole it from him and you know it. He worked hard to get as far as he did and you come in and slut around with your boss and get him fired. Drew's good and you know it. Better than your voice that sounds like a cat yowling. You know, I told him I'd watch out for you. I heard about you in high school. Yeah, don't remember me?"

I didn't. I thought I knew everybody. Bacon Valley High School wasn't that big.

"My dad owned the hardware store before your dumbass boyfriend's family stole it from us," she tells me. "Fenton and Son Hardware. Andrew Fenton Senior was my grandpa, Andrew Junior was my dad. Big Bob decided he wanted to buy the block and foreclosed on our store. That store had been in my family for seventy-years. My dad was never late on a bill. Then Big Bob talked him into some stupid investment. Because he wanted the store. The day Big Bob locked the doors, my dad died a little. Now he works at a gas station. I had to quit college to help out. *Now* you remember me?"

Jenna Fenton. I wouldn't have recognized her now. In school, she was always perky and smiled a lot. Now not so much. I stand there staring at her, wishing I had a witty comeback or some reply to tell her it was all a lie. All's I can come up with is a nod of my head. "Just tell Drew I stopped by."

Robert is standing in my living room when I get home tonight. He looks worried, his brow furrowed when I unlock the door, step inside. He had been drinking a beer.

I can see the bottle sitting on the table. There is also a white bag from a carryout pizza place and the meatball sub wrapping is laying partly crumbled next to the beer.

"How long have you been here?" I ask him, slowly easing in the doorway.

"Just enough time to eat and watch a game," Robert says. "Not long."

"Well—" I start. Then my words just lounge there behind my tongue. They won't come out. I'm not sure how to approach this situation. I don't like that he is in my house and we're not dating anymore. I know he doesn't see it this way. I am scared to cross those bounds where I kick him out.

"Baby, come back to me, I'm sorry," he says. I stand there for a moment with my keys dangling in my hand, focusing on this invisible line between us. I try to sort through the feelings running through my head. I feel a bit of anger there that he let himself inside without asking.

I'm not sure if this is strange so I settle on my belly because that's where the funny, happy, tickling feeling is when I'm around Brody. I let my hand rest just above my belly button, wait for something to stir inside. Nothing. I realize it just isn't there and never has been. I don't love Robert Ironwood and I know this now. Loving isn't hanging around someone because people tell you that you aren't going to get anybody better than that boy. Or just because your mama approves of him. I'm thinking that love comes within me and it just isn't there.

Still I'm not so good at confrontations. I think if I was a superhero and I had a certain weakness that my enemies could use to bring me down, it would be that I don't want anyone to hate me.

All's they would have to do is give me the stink-eye and I would crumple like a wet noodle to the ground. The very thought that Robert would narrow his eyes, grit his teeth and frown at me left me powerless, vulnerable.

The idea he would be on the phone with Delilah the moment he would stomp out the door drained my strength. It would kill me if everybody in town thought I was mean to him and that I was bad.

So as usual, I flounder there. I can't tell him. I just stand there knowing I can't because every time I've broken up with him before, we end up here. I force a smile, take whatever gift he offers, both wondering and fearing what he would do if I deny him. I think we have been through this two-hundred times. I'm terrified to take the step. What will Delilah think of me? What will Robert's family do if I break up with him. What? What? What?

"Is that a yes?" he asks, a half smile playing on his lips. They are puffy, pale, and pursed like a kitten getting ready to lap up milk. It is one more thing on the list of reasons I don't like him. And so he leans forward and I can see his lips part like he is going to kiss me as if this would fix everything. I make a little gasp, a tiny explosion of air that seeps through my lips.

I feel like my head could explode then. I imagine spending the rest of my life never knowing what love could be, being stuck with Robert. I don't love him. And so for some reason, I just say it. My cheeks are numb, my lips are moving and I stand there with my hand out as he comes walking up to me with his hands outstretched expecting me to take him in like those two-hundred times before. But I can't lie anymore. I just can't.

My hand shoots out and lands gently on his chest, stops him dead. "No, Robert, I'm not getting back with you." I say it and can't believe I do.

I wait for just a moment for my life to start crumbling before my eyes, for my head to pop off or something horrible to happen because I decide to end it here. Nothing happens. He just narrows his eyes to tiny slits and lifts one corner of his puffy lips.

"Who is it? Who else is there? You'll be sorry. When they realize what you're really like, they'll be out that door."

"There is nobody else," I say. But really? Does he not realize that I am thinking? It would be better to be with nobody at all than being with him. Because that is how I feel.

"You've got to be kidding me," he says. "I know you're lying. Okay, I'll give you more time. But you'll come back to me. I guarantee it."

He calls me a bitch and slams the door so hard that the house shakes. I flinch. It is almost like the air in the room clears when he is gone. I breathe in. I breathe out. A weight is lifted off my chest. I feel emancipated. I feel so good I scan the contract Ducky gave me, sign it and take a picture. Then I send it to his cell phone. I get out my guitar, pluck on it a while, and text Drew to see how he is doing. Then I cry into my hands.

Chapter −23

Note to Self: Have a One night stand with Cute guy in front row

There's a guy who has been sitting at the front table near the stage on Friday and Saturday nights for the last couple weeks. He's cute and muscular with chocolate brown hair and deep auburn eyes. He sits with a bunch of his friends, tossing back beers and stuffing requests for songs in a little box on the stage with huge tips.

Once in a while, when I sing I see him smiling up at me like he's got a secret. He reminds me of Brody. He used to sit out in the stands and eat his lunch at the Bacon Valley Fair and listen to me sing even when hardly anybody else was around, stuffing French Fries drenched with catsup into his mouth. I always wondered why he didn't weigh four-hundred pounds, the amount of food he ate at the fair.

Drew would warn me about guys like him, the ones that just want to be with me because I'm up on the stage singing. *They just want a little piece of it. One night stands.* he would say. But Drew is gone and I'm stuck with Billy Gentry whose only advice to me is wear something that shows more cleavage and *come on over and sit on papa's lap for a minute.* I don't. Nor do I listen to the twenty other belittling remarks he makes after each song I sing. Instead of Drew and I playing around on the stage, encouraging the crowd to join in, Billy Gentry jumps in with a stupid remark, then starts playing a song that Hobie and I have on the little cheat sheets I keep.

Regardless, the boy in the front row, his name is Ben. I know because he held up a napkin last Friday with his name written on it. It had his number. I didn't call him. I just imagined Delilah standing over my body in the morgue saying: *I always told her to never meet up with strangers.*

This is what she gets for never heeding my advice.
Saturday, Ben leaves some lavender roses on the stage.
They are tied with a little red bow and a note that has his
phone number. They are sitting on the side of the stage with
a couple teddy bears, two red roses and a half-used dirty
white napkin someone has fashioned into a flower.

"What do lavender roses mean?" I ask Bailey the
Bartender while she stuffs her foot into the garbage can to
push down the trash, leaving room for more. She looks it up
on her phone and tells me it means 'love at first sight.'

It is romantic so the next Friday when he leaves me a
dozen more, I belt one out and flirt a little with him. After
I'm finished at 11:00 p.m., I talk to him a bit. I'm new at
this. Still, it doesn't feel so awkward even when Smalltalk
steps in beside me and tells me he'll walk me to my car. Ben
seems okay with this. "I would expect you'd have an escort
from the local police." he tells me. "You've got my number."

"Really?" I say flat out to Smalltalk while he stands
there looking like he just broke up an orgy. "Can I not have
a social life? He's cute. He's nice. How much does Hobie
pay you to do this?"

"He pays me nothing. I am doing this because I feel
like it is my obligation to do so. Those kinds of young men
are a dime a dozen," Smalltalk tells me with a firm purse of
his lips. "There's six more waiting in line behind him." He
throws out a hand and I follow it to a couple tables. They
are all staring at me with goofy smiles on their faces.
"Troubling, isn't it?" Smalltalk says. His chin is sideways,
his gaze wary. I stick my nose into the flowers. They smell
sweet and that's what I am thinking. Flowers. Love at first
sight. Brown eyes. "Journey, you need to listen to me. You
really need to be careful. You should see the way the men in
the audience look at you. I bet if I ran their license plates,
half of them would have warrants for their arrest.

You do not know where this young man came from, what kind of family he came from. He could be a serial killer for all you know."

"Did you run his license plates?" I ask, floored. I think that maybe this is what daddies do. Maybe I am right. He is the idiot Delilah slept with.

"Maybe, maybe not." He gives me a guilty smile. Then he delves into the little pocket he has on his police shirt. He has two pieces of paper in his hand. The first one has an image on it that looks like Smalltalk had made a copy on the police station printer. It is vague, but I see one man leaning against his car and another pumping gas. "These the guys who stopped into your shop?"

"Yeah," I look at the black and white images of the two men closely. The image is vague, hazy. I don't want to pull my glasses out of my pocket. Andrea tells me I look like a geek in them. "The short one had a bald head and his eyes were really beady like an ant." I poke at the man leaning against the car, his feet crossed. "I call him Beady Eyes." I roll my finger to the man pumping gas and I can see his thick head of hair. "That's Bushy Hair."

"Because he has bushy hair," Smalltalk finishes for me. He takes the picture and replaces it with the second piece of paper. It is creased a few times to make a small square. "Well here's the good news for you. I ran a partial plate that we got off the security camera at the Pump and Dump." He wiggles the paper in his fingers as if he wants me to take it. "The owners have a camera near the license plates for people who take off without paying for gas. Here is what Bushy Hair and Beady Eyes are all about—"

I do and open it up. It is a newspaper clipping with an advertisement that reads: WIFE CHEATING? HUSBAND LEFT YOU? ONE STOP PRIVATE INVESTIGATORS. WE GET IT DONE.

A phone number is circled in red. "The plates came back to a company name. The company is this one—" he pokes a finger at the advisement. "The company is owned by a man by the name of RJ Milford, a private investigator. But Rodney Johnson Milford, the owner, died six years ago. I'm assuming the business is being run illegally. So that means if they do something illegal, they are not worried about getting caught. Do you get where I'm going, Journey Dawn?"

I think about this a moment, slowly bob my head up and down. "Like breaking into my house."

"Anybody in here could be paid by them or be them," he tells me. "I don't know what is up with this little purse you have, but I'm willing to buy it from you for whatever you want if money is the reason you are holding on to it." He sees me shake my head back and forth, must recognize the concern on my face, because Smalltalk holds out a hand. "I get it. Delbert was your friend. But I just don't think Delbert would want you getting killed over the purse. Promise me you'll think about just selling it to those men. I'm going to do my best to try to catch them, but they may have forty people working for them. Something is up with that purse if they had the guts to break into your house, break into your shop. Promise me you'll be careful, lock your doors. Have someone escort you from car to house, work to car."

"I will," I say to him. Smalltalk breathes in deeply, holds out his arm as if guiding me toward the door. "On another note: you do know that the more people who come, the more likely it is your mama is going to find out you work here."

"This hole in the wall?" I ask him while I hand him back the advertisement. We start walking toward the back door, around the tables, and through the crowd.

Some stop to pat me on the back. Smalltalk gives them wary gazes, whispers something about going out the back door next time. I laugh. He just holds out his hands to his sides and gives me a knowing smile. "You laugh now, Journey, but I'm telling you. It isn't going to be a hole in the wall much longer when word gets out about your singing."

"I've been here five years. Nobody has claimed me yet." I take it as a complement and sigh. Just then, Smalltalk nudges me. I turn my attention to his face, follow his gaze to the table by the door. "There's your friend—he's John Wells's boy, right?"

I look up and see Brody looking at me. He smiles faintly at me, wiggles around uncomfortably. He is sitting across from Bella and with a few people I can't see against the oozy darkness. He still manages to give me a partial nod. It is the same type of reserved gesture I have seen pro wrestlers give each other after a fight. I am breathing in the flowers but for some reason, they don't smell so sweet now.

"Yeah," I reply to Smalltalk with a flat laugh. "But I'm not so sure he is my friend. I did him a couple favors and he acts like he doesn't even know me."

"Favors?" Smalltalk is acting like a daddy again. His eyes are narrowed, his head tipping slightly before he gives Brody a wary gaze.

"Yeah, I helped him find his horse, remember?"

"Oh," Smalltalk loses the suspicious expression. "We are from different generations, I'm going to have to read up on slang."

"Yeah," I say, remembering when he said he wanted to hook up with me. "His dad doesn't like me and he looks kind of embarrassed that I waved at him."

"That's the way nice boys look at a pretty girl, Journey Dawn," Smalltalk shakes his head. "The same way I see you looking at him. I imagine he's just shy. His dad's had some rough times recently with the farm and losing his father-in-law. I saw the oil company getting ready to set up their equipment. It has to be difficult to watch."

"Oil company?" I ask Smalltalk. Yet, my eyes are still on Brody who has decided to ignore me completely.

"Yeah, I guess the reason Big Bob let the Wells family hold on to the property for the last five years was because Delbert made a deal with Big Bob. He knew about the oil that was under the farm. Said he'd give him the rights if he didn't take the farm until he died. I think Delbert Johnson thought he had enough life insurance to cover the debt. He only had enough for the funeral and some taxes. At least Big Bob waited until he was dead."

I hate Big Bob right then. I hate his son for not telling me what they were doing to that farm. Most of all, I feel like an idiot because everybody thinks I am so stupid, they don't bother to tell me the truth most of the time.

"Maybe Delbert thought the purse was worth more than it is," I say. "But I should probably stay out of it," I tell Smalltalk. "It sounds like a mess. Maybe being friends with Brody Wells right now isn't such a good idea. People talk so much in this damn town."

"Yes, but it would be pretty boring without all the drama the Bacon women dole out." Smalltalk laughs into his fist like he has said something really funny. "But your mama, in her day, made you look tame, just so you know."

"You are kidding me." I shoot him a glare then do what I wanted to do all along. "Is that a dare?"

"Oh, my God, no," he laughs. But I'm thinking it might be a challenge. I lift my forefinger.

"I'm up for that challenge."

Just then, Bailey the Bartender snags my arm, waves an apron and a tray in front of me. "Can you wait some tables? I can't do the bar and help the girls. It's too crowded tonight."

"Okay, is it alright with Hobie?" I take the apron, nod my head. "Because he yelled at me so hard the last time I wanted to stay late that he made me cry."

"You really need to grow some balls, little girl," she tells me. "Yell at him back. He's not going to fire you."

"Oh my God!" I wave my hands. "Why does everybody tell me that?" I say. Then I shake my head, drop my arms. "I'm a girl. I'm not growing balls. And you are implying that I have to be a man to stick up for myself."

"That's not the point. It is a saying. If you think you can stick up for yourself in your girly-girl shoes, then do it. But you're not."

"Yeah, that's not going to happen." I shake my head. "I'll wait tables if you'll send out a free order of fries with a bowl of catsup to that table over there and the guy sitting right in the middle." I point to Brody. "He used to watch me sing at the fair with a super order of fries and catsup. I want to see if he remembers."

Bailey the Bartender wags her head up and down.

"Got to work," I say to Smalltalk. He nods his head, tosses a finger at me. "Call me when you are done. If I'm not out on a call, I will walk you to your car. If I have to leave, make sure somebody walks you to your car. Text me or something to let me know you got home safely." Smalltalk calls out. I watch him out of the corner of my eyes. I see him wave down a bouncer, point to me and the bouncer nods. I'm sure he is the backup for taking me to my car.

"Okay, daddy," I mouth to him when he looks back up at me. I stick out my tongue.

He gets a stern expression to his eyes. Then, he turns real quickly like he's trying to hide a smile. I need to get up the nerve to ask him straight out if he really is my father. Strangely, I waver there really wondering if he is or not.

I am so happy Bella has my cell phone number. Not really. I was being sarcastic about that thought. As soon as I am dropping eight beers at one table, I get a text from her that nobody has come to their table in forty-five minutes. Can I get my skinny ass over there? She gives me a list of drinks they need, an order of barbecue wings, and a burger.

Twelve minutes later, I have to skirt around Bella who is almost at the end of the table to drop down the napkins and their order.

"Here's your tip," she says. She hands me a quarter. "And here's another: be nice to my cousin or I'll murder you in your sleep." I suppose I have known this all along. The reason Brody always got my wrath is because of Bella. Everyone has their weakness. Brody is Bella's. He has always been the only thing I could use to take out my revenge. And so I did, but to my advantage.

"Hey, Brody, I bought you an order of catsup and some fries," I say, plopping it in front of him. I see Bella look up, eyes rolling when I lean a little into Brody and rub against him to set it down. "Remember these? The fair? Seats in the shade in the back?"

He looks at the fries, looks at me. Then he gets a funny little lop-sided grin. "Uh, yeah." We chitchat a few seconds about, of all things, the weather and farming. Now I know it is going to be hot tomorrow. There is no chance of rain. And he has one more day to get in the first cutting of hay, for whatever that means. There is a lull. It seems Brody Wells is more interested in texting on his phone. So I make polite conversation and think about leaving. It is a stupid mistake to try to talk.

It is stagnant for a moment while I wait a few more tables. Then I snatch up my phone and swoop back through to pick up a table beside Brody's table. I shove my phone under his nose and ask Brody for his cell phone number. Such, he pokes it into my contacts, then goes back to whoever he is texting.

"I don't know why you want it," he says without looking up from his phone. I think about this when I get back up to the bar. Then I text him a message that says: *Because you owe me money.*

Which he texts me back: *Yeah. Okay. I'm working on it. Got a job. I get it.*

No you don't get it. I like you.

Like me or like-like me?

Like-like.

You can't possibly pick a worse person to like-like right now. I just got a job at Dixon's Feed and Seed. No benefits. Part time. I can't buy you roses. I can't even afford to take you out right now. We got nothing in common. Minimum wage Job. Old truck. Kid. Dad. Nowhere to live. When I was at your house, you had more roses in your living room from guys than I saw at Grandpa's funeral.

I look up from my phone. I can see him across the small expanse between the bar and his table, but Brody is looking at me with a thin-lipped smile. He shrugs.

"Sorry," he mouths. My heart drops. Bailey is right. I need to grow a set of balls. I am about to cry.

Nothing in common. Is it because I don't know what you mean by hay cutting?

By the time I get over to the table, sit down on the long-planked seat, Brody is texting somebody on the phone. I don't care if everybody else is staring at me funny.

I reach out and push my hand on the phone, force him to snap his eyes away. "Brody, guys like you don't need roses or big fancy trucks to impress a girl." I tell him. "You don't need to prove to me what you're all about. I know that strange little date we went on was horrible for you, but it wasn't for me. You opened the door for me, you listened to what I had to say and acted like you were interested. You tried to hold my hand. You kissed me and made my stomach jump. You stuck around for your kid when her mama didn't care. To go out with you again, I'd split the gas with you and find out how far we could go on whatever we had. A buck and fifty cents each would get us out of Bacon Valley for a couple hours, away from all this shit and everybody else." I wave a hand in the hair above my head. "I'm really not the kind of girl who likes flowers. Maybe it might be fun finding out what I really like. Maybe you can explain to me what a hay cutting is." I stand up because he's not giving me any expression. "Or maybe you can just get on one of those farming dating sites I see on TV. That might be fun for you." I have to assume he just doesn't want to embarrass me in front of everybody there.

"Are you begging my cousin for a date?"

I open my mouth, wishing I had a comeback while I turn my head to glare at Bella. Everybody at the table is staring at us and my face suddenly is burning hot. Brody looks like I just shot him. His eyes are kind of wide, but he has that hardass stance around him again. I must have still been a little drunk from the show. I felt like the idiot Robert always tells me I am. *Journey, they don't want to hear all that—*

"Okay, I see where this is going." I say, leaning in to Brody so his ears are all that hear my words. "I guess I'm just not good at one night stands."

I really thought maybe I should work on it, though. Ben catches me by the bar around closing. It isn't so busy, so we talk over beers. He's funny and he's working as a waiter in a restaurant in Columbus while he puts himself through college. Pleasant conversation, real close and I'm kind of getting caught up in his eyes while he leans a little toward me on the barstool and tickles my arm with his hand. He has thick eyelashes and laughs at everything that comes out of my mouth. Everything. It is kind of cute and annoying at the same time, but I know he's nervous. I'm nervous.

"You know, I don't live that far from here," he says. "We could grab a six pack, watch a movie."

So I know it's coming. I saw it in his eyes two weeks ago. Ben likes me. He likes the way I look. I like him. I like the way he looks. I'm thinking that wrestling around with him on his bed or his couch or even the carpet sounds kind of good. Isn't this what happens now?

"Walk me to my car," I lean forward, whisper in his ear. "It's too crowded in here."

So we slip through the kitchen, out the back door of the bar. It is kind of misting, hardly even a sprinkle. I'm kind of holding his hand when we stop at my car. Another five minutes of chit-chat and I can feel him moving in, getting ready for the kiss. I hear crickets behind me and the bang of music inside the bar.

"Hey, Journey," I hear behind Ben. "We need to talk."

Ben just kind of takes a step back. I'm not sure he knows what to do. So he just says: "You know this guy?"

"Yeah," I don't know what else to say. I'm once again in a love-hate relationship in my mind with Brody Wells. "It's fine." I tell Ben, then turn my attention to Brody.

"What do you want?" I ask flatly.

"I was just checking to make sure you were—okay."

I close my eyes for a second, grit my teeth. "I am fine. Funny thing. You didn't seem to care two hours ago. Can you give us five minutes?"

Ben knows even before Brody shuffles his feet a little in the darkness with only a misty pattering on my windshield behind us that it isn't going to happen. I'm not going to his house. We're not having sex on his couch or his bed or the washer and dryer.

"You two are —?" he offers up while we stand now just face to face a good arms-length apart.

"We are— I don't know," I reply. "Complicated."

"How about married?" Brody just says it. I know my eyes are wide when I look over to where he is standing.

Ben curses beneath his breath and takes a step back. He eyes me like he's ready to be shot. "Is that true?"

"Well, yes and no," I say and it sounds really stupid. "I mean on paper, but not—" I don't know how to finish it. Instead, I snap my head to Brody. "Of all the times you could have used that card in whatever game you're playing you're tossing that in now?"

"I guess I did."

"Well, call me if it gets less married or complicated or whatever it is between you two," he says it just like that and just walks off. I know I could have followed him, just left Brody Wells in the darkness alone.

I don't. We wait until Ben's shadow fades away. Brody just steps up, stops right in front of me, looking down at me.

"What the hell? It's okay to use me, then reject me in front of your friends, then come out here and break up what could be a beautiful thing by telling Ben we're married?"

"A beautiful thing, yeah, okay." He sniffs. "Officer McGee asked me to check on you. There was a fight in the parking lot. He couldn't walk you to your car right now. That guy looked like he might hurt you."

"Quit being a jerk, Brody. Your job is done. You can tell Officer McGee when you check in with him that I am old enough to make certain choices. I am not a frigging two year old."

"Do you like that guy?"

"Yeah," I nod, my eyes glaring up at Brody. "I think I did. Even if it was just for —one night."

"I thought you weren't good at one night stands." Brody shakes his head of the sprinkles coming down, swipes his hand through his hair. "Didn't you just tell me that?"

"Uh huh," I mutter. "But it seems like everybody else is, including you, so maybe I should try it too. I got to go. I'm tired. Tell Officer McGee he should hire you at the police station," I say, "for a job well-done."

I start to snatch up my keys in my purse, start to push myself from the car. Then I look up and Brody's taking a step toward me. He doesn't say a word, just softly reaches around my neck and pulls me over to him. I would like to kick myself for taking the steps. My tummy is always weak to the tickling sensation I get when Brody is around. It gives my restrained mind (at least for the moment) a little elbow nudge telling my head that it is fine, baby, go ahead. I am precariously hanging in the balance between stupidly falling for Brody Wells's tricks again and—no, I am not suspended at all. I'm in. Shit.

The fingers of his other hand tip my head and he gives me a gentle kiss on the lips. Then he pushes me back against my car and his kisses aren't so gentle anymore. I know what he is thinking. That if I'm so damn horny and want a one night stand, I should make it with him.

He knows I'm vulnerable. He is using me. Why can't I use him? I can't. But I'm not sure I can explain it to him. Maybe I could try. "Listen, Brody—"

"You want me to stop?" he asks and there is such a long pause there, I'm thinking he probably thinks I'm drunk.

"Well, yes and no," I say. "I don't know if I can do this."

"You were going to do it with him."

"It wouldn't have been—the same," I tell him.

"I take it he had an apartment, right?" Brody whispers. "A soft couch, maybe a bear rug?"

I giggle. It sounds so funny. He doesn't understand I'm not talking about appliances or furniture right now. I meant the affection I felt for him. "I don't know so much about that." I blink up at him. It is raining harder. I'm wet, he's soaked. I can see his hair with little dribbles on the ends.

"Your car or my truck?" he asks, nodding to my car.

"You're not kidding, are you?" I ask. I know he's not because he's leaning forward, kissing my cheeks, feeling me up. He doesn't say anything, just reaches around me, opens up my back door. Brody looks a little to the right and left before we slip inside. I'm not nervous, unsure when we almost fall into the car, tripping over each other.

We both bumble around way too much for that. We can't get the damn door shut, can't stop kissing. I'm trying to get his shirt off, I can't because we're afraid if we sit up, somebody will see us even through the foggy windows with rain coming down on the windshield. He's too big in the car to get on top. I'm too little to get on the bottom.

We improvise the best we can, working around it. It's funny and sexy both at once even with heads banging against the door and Brody holding us both up with one hand on my floor.

We can't lay there after. It's too cramped. I'm alright with that and so is he. We just sit in the quiet, listening to the rain. I try putting my hair up in a tie, he keeps tugging it off. I could have fallen to sleep right there if I didn't catch the glare of a flashlight beaming out across the expanse from kitchen door to windshield.

"Journey Dawn, are you out there?"

It is Smalltalk who taps on the window. I groan, slip out with Brody not far behind.

"Yeah, Brody was just walking me to my car."

Brody laughs then. Right out loud, he just cracks up and I can't help but giggle too while Smalltalk gets that wary gaze to his eyes. "Okay, son, you probably should head out. I have to make sure Journey Dawn makes it home safely."

"We aren't thirteen years-old, Officer McGee," I tell him. He narrows his eyes, shakes his head.

"Yeah, that's what I'm afraid of."

Chapter −24
Note to Self: Become a Nun

"I've got four dollars in bills, three dollars and twenty-five cents in quarters, and a pocketful of nickels." Brody slaps down the four dollar bills in front of me. "Oh, and a kid that's probably worth ten cents." He steps back, lifts Cayce up on the counter so she is sitting with her back to me. Cayce giggles. "How far can we get out of town?"

I'm really surprised Brody is standing in front of me. I thought it would surely be another two weeks and another one night stand. It is Monday morning and I have just gotten off the phone with 89 year-old Della Lender. She was a younger sister of Molly. When I told her about the purse, she wanted to see it herself.

"Well," I start while I reach out and tickle Cayce's neck. "How about Winford?" I pick up the silver dance card purse and the little dance card and hold it up. "There's a lady in a nursing home there that may be able to tell me if this was her sister's purse."

"There's a mystery to this?" Brody asks, leaning in close with his elbows on the counter to look at it. He's wearing blue jeans, a blue button up shirt, and cologne. The scent is amazing and I can't help but smile. He takes the purse in his fingers and opens it up, peers inside.

"Well, it belonged to a girl that was killed in a car wreck," I tell him. "Your grandpa somehow ended up with her purse." Brody drops his chin warily and I hold up my hand. "She gave it to him. I put an ad online to get a quote and since then, I've had my house and shop broken into. You remember the guys who were following us? Officer McGee ran their plates and they are private investigators, we think. But I think there's more to the story."

"What would that be?" He looks up at me. Is there a twinkle of excitement hidden in there?

"I don't know," I answer.

"You know, there's still time to back out of the date," he says. His eyes roll to Cayce who is counting the fingers of her hand. "Most guys don't have—extra baggage. I bet —" he pauses there. I get what he's looking for.

"Ben."

"I suppose Ben doesn't."

"I don't know if he does or not," I say. "I didn't ask. It isn't something I use as a tool to rate a would-be one night stand. Besides, I prefer to call it a package deal," I tell him.

"You're being really nice about this," he says.

"You forget that I was a part of a package deal, Cowboy," I tell him. "I understand. I'm willing to give you two a chance. Not many guys gave Delilah the opportunity to do the same. Cayce made the cut. You want to try out too?"

Now he has a really serious look on his face as he stands up straight, stuffs his hands in his blue jeans pockets. "You're being nice about everything, even Zach's major screw up on the marriage thing. By the way, he is working on it. I don't know if I'm quite ready for anything."

"Anything more than a one night stand," I say. "Is this something that Zach and Bella have come up with for some sort of revenge?

"Well, they have mentioned it if you want the truth." He pats the counter, looks at the door like he's going to bolt. "She's pretty. Just do it, add her to your list and move on. When we were at Grandpa's house, I thought that's what we were doing. Because I figure a pretty girl like you does it all the time."

"Nice," I hiss. Suddenly, I'm feeling like a dirty slut.

"Then you start talking about me being the only one other than Robert and it kind of freaked me out. I'm not looking for a wife, you know?"

"Ha ha." I reach out, push his money back across the counter at him. "Funny thing, isn't it." I say flatly. "Because you got one."

I shoo him with my hand. "But for somebody who isn't looking for more than a one night stand, you're going about it the wrong way." I am suddenly taken aback while I snatch up my purse, dig out my keys. "You go out with me on a date from hell and kiss me like there's no tomorrow. I couldn't sleep for a week after that damn kiss. You saved me from that stupid reenactment and the idiot EMS Eddy. Then you and me, we—" I don't say the word I want to use in front of Cayce and instead, hold out my hands. "We do stuff. After that, I've got another sleepless week. You know what? Men do nothing more than give me grief. I'm going to become a nun—"

I'm standing at the door, opening it wide for him when he picks up Cayce, slides her off the counter. My back is to the door and I see Brody shoot a cautious gaze over my shoulder. The first thought going through my head is that it is Robert's shadow crossing over the little wooden wedge by the doorway. My heart starts to thump-thump-thump.

"Well, hello Miss Bacon." It isn't Robert at all. Instead, I turn slightly to see two cheap black suitcoats and Bushy Hair and Beady Eyes walking toward me and through the door.

I make a funny heave of breath and turn to Brody. "I bet you thought a date with me couldn't get worse," I mumble to him as I take one step back and nearly trip over his feet. "Well, I think it is."

Bushy Hair has a gun. Now honestly, he doesn't have it drawn. He is just making a big deal of it and teasing me with it. The pistol is just beneath his suitcoat and he has the cloth pushed back to expose the black handle. His fingers are tickling along the little snap holding it to the holster.

I see it and step back, push Brody with my body. I know Brody sees it too because just when Cayce squirms to see who is at the door, he doesn't fight me taking a couple steps back toward the counter again. We stop when we have no further to go.

"We—we were just getting ready to leave," I stutter. I'm trying not to fidget. Beady Eyes isn't quite in the door, he is grappling with something in his pocket, an asthma inhaler which he promptly pulls out and holds near his mouth. Bushy Hair has just passed the threshold and steps to his left side.

"Closing early today, huh?" Bushy Hair asks. He seems to be a bit surprised we are both staring at his gun and laughs aloud. "Oh, my gun. I do play with it a lot."

"The store is closed," I tell him. "You can come back tomorrow."

"Well, no we can't," Bushy Hair informs me. He stifles a yawn, looks back behind him to Beady Eyes and the door and nods as if he wants his partner to close it. "We are under a bit of pressure here to get the dance card purse. Come on, Blondie, you know what we want. I'm willing to give you five-hundred bucks for it. But this is the last offer."

Blondie? I feel like I am in a 1920s movie right then.

"Dude, Blondie here says she isn't selling it," Brody suddenly says, and I turn a bit shocked that he tells him that. "I think she told you that. You can just leave now—"

"YES, SHE IS!" Bushy Hair screams it and waves two fingers at Beady Eyes to close the door.

The loud yell startles Cayce and she lets out a yelp, then starts immediately crying. Beady Eyes reaches out with his free hand, then gives the old door a hard shove.

I count to three. But I don't reach out and grab the heavy, hardwood bookshelves like I usually do when someone slams the door. Instead, I lean to my right and shove the first of the bulky, unstable bookshelves as hard as I can with my shoulder. Between the slamming door and my weight, the bookshelves start falling like Dominoes, one after the other in perfect synchronization until they collapse hard and loudly directly on the two men whose hands are fending them off at the door.

They didn't expect it. I know that because they are sandwiched like peanut butter and jelly between two pieces of bread. I see Bushy Hair's head peering at me beneath the weight of the shelves, Beady Eye's arm, one inhaler and the gun spinning in circles before it comes to a halt three feet away.

Both Brody and I are staring at the gun. I can see Bushy Hair swatting the ground with his palm so close to the gun's handle that his fingertips nearly touch it. I also hear Beady Eyes taking in gasping breaths. Brody kneels and leans in to get the gun. Cayce squeals as Bushy Hair nearly snatches Brody's fingers. I make a quick kick of the inhaler toward Beady Hair's hand and reach down and snatch up the gun with my fingers.

So I'm standing here holding the pistol in my hands. I vaguely remember at the tender age of thirteen, Smalltalk taking me behind his house and showing me how dangerous guns were by letting me shoot some aluminum soda cans off his mother's fence. I remember feeling the power when the bullet burst from the gun. I got chills as it exploded into the cans, making a loud crackling. A long time has passed since then, but I still hold it like Smalltalk showed me.

I push my legs out for a good solid stance, flick the pistol off safety, and let the barrel fall to where the two men are smooshed between floor and bookshelf.

"I suggest you don't move except for the inhaler," I say. "Because I used to shoot cans off fences when I was a little girl. After three tries, I never, ever missed once. I liked the sound of the bullet hitting the can." I can hear Beady Eyes pushing on the inhaler while I lower the gun to his head. "I wonder what it would sound like on—flesh." I see Bushy Hair hold up the only arm sticking out. I narrow my right eye to hone in on his left eye.

"Are you crazy?" Bushy Hair asks. "Jesus, call the cops!"

"Okay, I think we can just call the cops, right?" I feel Brody banging my arm. I look down, don't take one eye off Bushy Hair. He is trying to give me his phone. "Journey? Am I right?"

His eyes are big like he really thinks I will shoot them. I wonder for a moment if I could. But I breathe out, take the phone from his fingers and still hold the barrel toward the men. I actually think if one clambers out, I will just shoot a warning shot and then, only if he doesn't stop, give him a bullet in the leg.

But Brody tugs me toward the counter. "Honestly, Journey, are you really willing to shoot one of them?" he hisses back. "Because I can't hold Cayce and take on two men and I think they are going to try to get out."

Did I have to tell him the last time I held a gun in my hands I shot EMS Eddy? But I sigh. I didn't want to bring that fiasco up again. And he is right. I pick the worms off the sidewalk after it rains to put them safely in the grass before someone steps on them. I can't imagine really pulling the trigger and hitting one of the two men across the room.

"I need to get my phone, Brody," I say. "I've got Officer McGee on contacts. You know, 9-1-1."

Brody has this new expression. It began about the time he started issuing somewhat of a restraint from making fun of me when I say something ridiculous like the time I told him I might be dumb, but I'm not stupid.

He narrows his eyes, gives me a good hard stare and slowly turns his head slightly sideways. It is almost like he is trying to mentally squeeze my head to shock my brain into working. I'm strangely intrigued at what I said that he would define as ridiculous. So I look at him and scratch my head with a free thumb. "What?"

"Do you really need to get 9-1-1 from your contacts?"

"Maybe," I say. But I take the phone from his fingers and tap in the numbers.

It is lunch time in Bacon Valley and I can hear Jane Little who works dispatch chewing on something while I tell her that I need someone to come to the shop.

"Journey, is this you?" she asks. "Is this the usual 9-1-1 call or a real emergency? McGee's in the kitchen. I hear the microwave running. He told me to tell you if it isn't an emergency, to call him on his cell phone."

"My definition of emergency is never the same as Officer McGee's—" I start, but Brody snatches the phone from my hand.

"Jane, this is an emergency. This is Brody Wells and there are two guys at Journey's shop with a gun."

Smalltalk gets to the Knick-Knack Shop in less than three minutes. He promptly calls the fire department to extricate Bushy Hair and Beady Eyes. The old oak bookshelves have pinned both the men's legs to the floor and Bushy Hair is screaming that he is going to sue me if he loses his foot.

"I never used the gun!" he kept saying to Smalltalk who was running their driver's licenses. "The girl is crazy. She's just stupid crazy. She tried to kill us with the bookshelves."

"You were going to shoot us!" I say in exasperation with my hands to my sides. "Can bookshelves be considered a weapon?" I ask Smalltalk with an antsy feeling in my belly. My reputation has preceded me again. I can see EMS Eddy, who is still dragging himself around on crutches, give me a knowing glare while he stuffs an oxygen mask on Beady Eyes.

"Who handed her the gun this time?" EMS Eddy grunts to Smalltalk. Smalltalk gives him a warning gaze.

"Anything can be considered a weapon if it is used to try to kill someone."

"I was protecting us. Smalltalk, I know it was these two who broke into my house. I know it!"

"In her defense," Brody is saying. "He did scream at her and hold his hand on the gun."

"Did he pull the gun out of the holster and aim it in your direction?" Smalltalk asks. "Did he imply that he was going to shoot you by saying something like: 'Stay there or I will kill you'?"

"No," I answer. "But he insinuated that he was going to shoot us. He played with it like the bad cowboys do in the old westerns right before they kill the good cowboy." I reach down, hold my hand at my side and wiggle my fingers. No one is following my hand. They are staring at me with The Look. I cringe.

"I cannot arrest them without proof they broke into your house and your shop," Smalltalk tells me after he pulls me aside. "They have no outstanding warrants, nothing other than traffic violations and minor offenses.

I can't even detain them if they have no priors or didn't really threaten you."

Cayce is getting restless. Everyone is staring at me like I have been my usual silly self and misunderstood the situation. "Did you ask them why they want the purse so badly?"

"They told me there were client confidentiality issues. They would have to check to see what they could tell me. But they did say their client was sick and possibly dying. I wouldn't trust that. They said if I wanted more information, I would have to get a warrant for their arrest. That isn't happening right now." Smalltalk looks from me to Brody. He smiles, nods to the door. "Why don't you and Brody get on out of here," Smalltalk tells me. "Go have fun. I'll do some more digging. Any problems, I'll let you know."

Chapter −25

Note to Self: Meet with Della Lender

Della Lender is living in what Delilah would politely call a small retirement village outside Winford. It is a nursing home. She is sitting in a wheelchair on the front porch waiting for me when we pull into the lot. She is bent in her chair, gray hair a bit uncombed like she has just gotten up out of bed. Her eyes are clear, though, and she smiles when I sit down beside her. Brody finds a grassy area to let Cayce run around. I lean in, hand her the purse.

"Um," she mumbles while her gnarled forefinger plays on the spirals etched into the purse. "M.L. Yes, this was Molly's purse. I remember this, I do. She slept with it under her pillow. My father got her this when she turned eighteen. Mother didn't approve. It was the first time daddy ignored mother. He picked the purse out for her special, had it wrapped in pink tissue paper. Mother didn't know about the gift until he gave it to Molly that day. I was about twelve. Molly let me hold it. I still remember that day." Della smiles and flicks open the top. She scans the inside. "So how did you come upon it?" she asks. "I don't remember what happened to all her things. After she died, Daddy closed off her room. I don't think anything ever changed even after I left for nursing school. Daddy died years later. I never went home."

"A friend of mine gave it to me," I say. "He was probably your sister's age. He said he won the purse in a car race."

Della sighs deeply. She looks up, her eyes a little less light. "That's how Molly died, you know," she says in a whisper like it is a dark secret better left unsaid. "I was so young. I remember it like it was yesterday when they came to the door, said Molly had gone in the creek with the car.

I was standing on the stairway. I remember my daddy just staring at the police officer at the door. The funeral was a haze. After that, we never spoke of Molly again. I'm just surprised she gave it away." It is warm out and Della fans a hand in front of her face. "That little purse was her pride and joy. I just don't think she would ever part with it. Did I tell you she kept it under her pillow?"

I smile. "You did."

Then Della does something I never expected. She slips a fingernail between the cover and inside of the purse and pops it open like a tiny book. I lean forward and within, I see two gold bands and a faded picture of a little girl with freckles on her nose and short, light hair. "Ah, there are things in her secret hiding place," she says. "Molly showed me this once." She pokes a finger at the bands so they scoot across the tarnished innards. Then she looks hard at the picture. "I don't know this little girl. It must have been one of her friend's little sisters." She turns it over. It says: *Our little Tina* on the back in pretty handwriting.

"Was she married?" I ask. "I mean, they look like wedding bands."

"Molly met a man the summer of 1939. Ben was his name." Della pushes herself up in her chair. "He wasn't much older than her, maybe nineteen. But he was a rich boy, a spoiled boy. I remember her sneaking out the back door at night. I watched her walking down Maple Street, saw his headlights fade away toward town. The next spring, she found out she was pregnant with his child. You know, that happens often now, having children out of wedlock. Not so much then. It was talked about that Molly would be sent away to a Catholic girls home and the baby given up for adoption. But we weren't Catholic and Daddy couldn't afford it. Mother was so afraid our reputation would be tarnished, that daddy would be fired from his job," she says.

"So mother decided that Molly would marry Ben. I don't think it went over big with his family or the man. My sister cried a lot into her pillow at night. I heard her. She told mother at the table one night that Ben hit her. I don't think mother believed her. Daddy never had much say with mother. Just after Molly died, I remember him standing at her grave saying she was much better off. It was a strange thing to say, I think, even if she was." Della breathed in deeply then, closed the purse and handed it back to me. There were tears in her eyes. "I don't want to see this. It brings back bad memories. I'm sorry, child. You don't want to hear an old woman drudge up old memories. I just wish it would have been different. I wish I could have stopped her from getting in the truck that night."

"I'm sorry," I tell her. But I'm thinking, did she say *truck*? I fished a tissue out of my purse and handed it to her to wipe her eyes. "If she is anything like every girl I know, you couldn't have stopped her from seeing her boyfriend—did you say it was a truck picking her up?"

"Uh huh. She wasn't with Ben that night. When he came along, she had already left."

"With whom did she leave?" I ask, puzzled. Did it really matter? I didn't know. Molly Lender's story had suddenly gotten a different middle, a strange little twist in the plot, leading to its horrible finish of a pretty young woman with her whole life ahead of her ending up drowned in a creek. The storyline was simple. A girl hops in the back of her boyfriend's car and as they race down the roadway, they get in a wreck and she dies. End of story. But now what was sandwiched between the beginning and middle, wasn't so simple. She isn't with the guy who was her boyfriend, she is pregnant, and there are wedding bands.

Della doesn't speak for a moment. She stares at me long and hard, her eyes a bright sky blue from the pools of tears puddling beneath. "I don't know, honey," she finally tells me. "I really don't know. It doesn't matter anyway. Everyone we knew is long dead and gone."

"I don't understand," I say. "The police report said she was in the car with Benjamin Dodge. The newspaper article I pulled up from the Winford Press stated she was in the car with her fiancé—his name was Benjamin Dodge."

"Oh, sweetie, just let it go," she says to me, waving a hand in the air like I am being silly. "Some things just don't have meaning." I nod and rub my fingers on my lips, thinking perhaps she is right. It didn't make a difference at all. I had the purse and I could sell it for a bit of money and get out alive.

So I look over to Brody who is swinging Cayce around in the grass. He puts her down and waves. I wave back.

"You have such a pretty family," Della tells me. "Your little girl looks like you."

I start to tell her Cayce isn't mine. I don't. Instead, I thank her for meeting with me. She hands me back the purse and I start to stand. I reach into my own purse and pull out one of my business cards with my information on the front: Journey Dawn Bacon. Bacon Valley Knick-Knack Shop. *If you can't find it, I can. Try me.* I almost hesitate each time I pass one out. Robert told me it sounds like I'm selling sexual favors. I got THE LOOK from him when I showed him one. I hand it to Della.

"If you have any more information, please let me know. Since I got this, I have had several people try to buy it from me. Two private investigators have threatened me if I didn't sell it to them." I admit to her softly and with a smile.

"Someone broke into my house," I tell her. "It just seems like there is more to its story, something I don't know."

Della dabs her eyes. She stares at the purse. "I don't know," she says. "Daddy didn't have a whole lot of money. I don't think the purse, itself, is that valuable." I nod and turn, thank her again. And then she wags a hand at me. "You know. It is strange the wedding bands were in the purse. Only Molly knew you could pull out the cover and place something there. She said it was our little secret. But she only ever kept loose change in there. I—I think the Dodge's ordered the rings several weeks before Molly and Ben were supposed to wed. It was a week before the wedding that Molly was killed. I don't know why Molly would have them in the purse. Usually the men hold the rings."

"Maybe I will check with the Dodge family." I realize, perhaps, someone in Ben Dodge's family might want the purse. Maybe they wanted the rings returned to the family like Gayle Wells did.

"Oh, sweetie, some things are just better left alone." Della smiles at me sweetly. I recognize a bit of warning in her tone. "Whatever secrets Molly had went with her down that creek. No use digging up old bones for that family or my own."

"You've outdone yourself again, Not only did you almost get us shot this morning, you've reduced an old lady to tears. I'm impressed," Brody teases me while we climb into his truck. "Most people associate fate with good things. I think ours is destined to go down with a fiery explosion. What new strategy do you have to bring our date to a catastrophic ending? I am intrigued."

"Who was the one who picked up the pistol and stopped the bad guys from killing us? Was it you? Nope."

I give him a sarcastic wiggle of my neck. "Oh, that's right. It was me."

I glare at him, but I'm not really angry. I am looking up the Ben Dodge family of Winford on my phone. "It is amazing what you can find online," I tell Brody, staring at the address. "You mind going past one more place? I promise, we don't need to stop. I found the address of the family of the man who was going to marry Molly."

"What good will that do you?"

"Us." I say, waving my finger back and forth between us. "You're in on this too, right? It was your grandpa's. But I'm not quite sure," I say. "I'm just trying to get the whole picture, you know?"

"It sounds to me like you know the whole story. Or is this something you do with all your antiques?" Brody is smiling, his eyes are twinkling deep blue. "Because it must take a year to collect each one if you go about it like this with every toothpick and baseball in your shop."

I think about this a moment while we pull out. "I suppose that's why I like finding stuff. I like the stories that come with them. Everything we own has a story with it, even if it is only a couple paragraphs. We hold it. We cherish it. Maybe we get rid of it. But up until the point it isn't ours anymore, it holds a little piece of our soul in it." I finally divulge to Brody while I hold up my hand, then clasp it closed quickly into a fist. "And I think it is strange that your grandpa had the purse. Officer McGee mentioned a truck being there, but your grandpa's name wasn't among those interviewed. It's like there's something more that I'm not getting. Something your grandpa was trying to tell me but I just didn't listen."

"You're the definition of oxymoron, you know that, right?" he tells me.

"I hope to God you aren't back to calling me stupid again," I mutter. "I don't know what oxymoron means. I slept thought most of my English classes in college."

"No, not at all. It is two opposites side by side." Brody situates himself in the seat. "Awfully pretty, clearly mysterious, clearly confused. I just can't figure you out. We have *two* one night stands. Do people do that? When I think I've got you summed up in one word, you do the opposite."

"Still confused," I tell him. "But you got a problem with me being an oxymoron? Because I think it bothered Robert. He was always calling me a ditz too."

"You're not a ditz. You are out of my comfort zone."

"Is that good or not?" I sneak a quick look up at him, catch him staring hard at me before I turn away. He doesn't answer.

I am delving into my purse looking for scrap paper to write down a bit of a song. It is a nervous habit. I find myself doing this more and more lately. I have nightmares some nights of drowning in tiny balls of shredded songs.

"There's a pen in the glove compartment," Brody says. "And there might be a map or napkin to write on. You can write on Kentucky. Try not to mess up the Ohio one too bad." It scares me a little that he recognizes what I am doing. Maybe it startles him too. We both get quiet until I finally can't stand it any longer and flip open the little door to the glove compartment and tug out a tissue inside. Brody laughs really hard at me. "I bet myself it wouldn't be five minutes before you couldn't stand it any longer." I flip him my middle finger above Cayce's head so she doesn't see it.

Thirty minutes later, we are driving down Bonaparte Lane outside Winford. Cayce is playing I-spy with me and giggling between us. It is one of those areas out past the towns, past the middle-class suburbs and in the country with huge houses, winding asphalt driveways and big yards.

Just as we slow for a winding turn, I see Brody narrow his eyes. He shoves his foot on the brakes and we come to a grinding standstill.

"Is that the address?" he asks, pointing out the windshield. I look at the GPS on my phone. It is. "Look who is turning into the drive. Black car. Is that the same car that followed us? Isn't it the same one those two suits had?"

He points right before he backs up the truck and starts to turn it around.

"Yeah," I mutter. I reach out my hand, point to the back bumper of the black car. "It has a little green and white sticker on the back bumper that says: *when guns are outlawed, only outlaws have guns.*"

"Okay, well, that is the end of this trip," Brody says and wheels the car around. "Does that answer your question? It's obviously the family of the guy who the dead woman was going to marry. He probably wants the rings like my mom wanted hers. My suggestion would be to sell the purse back to them. I mean, you're not out anything, right? The purse was free. Grandpa wouldn't want you in danger. Maybe he wanted it to go back to the family."

I'm not so convinced. "Are guns still legal to carry?" I ask Brody thinking about the bumper sticker. "Because that might mean they are bad guys, right? Do you see what I'm saying?"

He obviously didn't. I get THE LOOK. Then it changes to the tipped head expression. He turns his head long enough to take me in and scrubs a hand across his face like he really, really wants to make fun of me. He does not. Brody just nibbles on his bottom lip. "Guns that have been legally obtained are lawful," he says. "That's what the bumper sticker is implying. You know, if you make it illegal to have guns, then only people who break the law are going to have them."

"Oh," I say, letting the idea sink into my brain. I don't understand how he can make me feel so good and so bad at the same time. I feel like an idiot around him sometimes. Love-hate. Oh. Now I get the oxymoron thing.

It was quiet in the car for a good ten minutes, except for the sound of Cayce tapping on a game on my phone. She's comfortable between us, keeps leaning to the right and resting her head and hands on my arm. Her touch is soft and sweet and I tickle her in return. I could get used to this, being with Brody and Cayce. I look out the window, watch the trees go by, sing with the radio. The entire time, I'm thinking that Brody must be thinking how much an idiot I am and wishing for an excuse to drop me off at home.

"I hope you're not mad that I suggested you get rid of the silver purse," Brody finally breaks the silence. "I'm not telling you what to do at all."

"You're probably right." I shrug. "There is just something in my gut telling me I shouldn't." I look over at Brody, wait for him to snatch a glance at me. "Then again, I don't have the best track record for making decisions. Ask Robert or Andrea or Delilah. They have a whole list of things I don't do right, or shouldn't do, or could have done. You and Bella spent most of our childhood making fun of me for it. I don't care. I miss your grandpa because he didn't care either. He was all in on whatever stupid thing I suggested. I think he'd help me rob a bank if I came up with a plan."

"I just think people have responsibilities, Journey," Brody says carefully. "Robert has to worry about how people perceive him at the bank, your mother worries about how people see her at church. I've got a kid. We all can't just fly by the seat of our pants because our mamas will fix everything when we fall. There's no way most people could end up singing in a dirty old bar." He stares at me, shrugs.

"I mean, How many people can open a little shop in the middle of nowhere, own a nice house and an expensive car and still be able to get by without somebody feeding them cash from their grandparent's savings funds?"

I am floored he says this. I turn slowly, stare at him so hard, I swear he can feel my mind peeling away the first two layers of his flesh. "Take me home," I tell him. "Better yet, take me to Hobie's. I'd rather be with mean old Billy Gentry telling me I'm a stupid ditz than hearing you say it. I thought you were different. I thought you liked me for who I am. But you are nothing but the same old hardass, redneck jerk you ever were. I just got out of a relationship with a judgmental bastard. I'm never doing that again. Never. God, Brody, why did you even bother to ask me out today if you think these things of me?"

"Why do you think, Journey?" he says flatly. "Use your head." He looks straight ahead. It hits me like a load of bricks then, the reason. Because I slept with him. And he wanted an easy screw again.

"Well, here's a an oxymoron or two to sum up whatever *this* is while we sit for the rest of the ride in *deafening silence*, Butt Head," I wave my hand between us, unable to even describe this stupid relationship. "Bitter sweet and pretty ugly."

"Are you mad at me too?" I hear Cayce say to me. She is staring up at me, looks like she is getting ready to cry. I put on my beauty pageant smile, hide the tears that want to spurt out. What an idiot I am.

"Of course not, sweetie," I tell her and give her a kiss on her head. "I had fun riding around with you today." I push back the tears I want to cry and put my arm around her shoulders. I feel dirty and used, but it isn't her fault. "How about we play a game before your daddy drops me off at the *dirty old bar*?"

Chapter −26

Note to Self: Don't tell the guys you write songs about them. It kind of freaks them out.

There's a massive old oak tree on a hill overlooking John Wells's farm. It is sitting on what most people in town call The Old Sledding Hill or simply just The Hill. Everybody goes there in winter with their plastic sleds and wooden toboggans and slide down the hill. Close to Christmas, John builds big bonfires for people to warm up around. Gayle sets out a table with hot chocolate to drink and marshmallows to roast over the fire.

Most of the hill is barren except for this tree. When I was in high school, I used to park along Goose Creek Road and hike up an old trail to sit in the branches of the old oak when nobody was on the hill. I watched everyone milling around down below. I couldn't make out what they said most of the time, but I got to see them interact. I saw them share picnics together in summer, clean the yard of leaves in fall. There were the Christmas parties in the winter and the dragging out of the farm stuff in spring.

The Wells embodied everything I thought a normal family would be. It was so different and so magical compared to the quiet breakfasts at the table with Delilah and the rigid, structured life I experienced when my grandparents lived with us. I wished I was part of this big, happy, noisy clan. Sometimes, I would bring a book and read or play my guitar. Most of the time, I just sat there wishing the tree was mine, wishing I was anybody but Delilah Bacon's scatterbrained, beauty queen daughter. Who would have known someone had been watching me?

"They are planning on cutting down the tree at the top of The Hill."

Bella Johnson is leaning against her truck with her arms folded and a smug purse to her lips. Her truck is in the parking lot of Hobie's Bar and behind the kitchen, smooshed between my car and the back door. How does she know I park there? I can only suppose Brody told her about our meeting there.

The parking lot is too crowded since Hobie has started bringing in some old, popular bands. I have to park right out back now next to the vans or buses or whatever contraption the groups have to drive. Besides, I can't get out the front door anymore without being approached by a small mob who want to buy me a beer or tell me how they couldn't believe they never knew about this bar before or how I sing like an angel. If they only knew how badly I just wanted to be home in my comfy old bed reading a book under the dim lamplight instead of feeling my stomach jump and lurch while I stare out into the murky darkness beyond the stage trying desperately not to get eye contact with anyone. I always wish Drew would be there with me to poke me in the side, let me know I wasn't going to completely screw up and puke all over the front row. I don't think they would be so excited for me if they knew all that.

It is so crowded tonight, Hobie is worried the fire department is going to come out and close him down for being over capacity. He has opened up the front so people can bring chairs and sit outside. He doesn't like the idea Smalltalk is here walking me to my car, especially because I have still not found my birth certificate. He follows us out and tells Smalltalk that he can have Billy Gentry start escorting me to my car after the show.

"Are you kidding me?" I turn around, shake my head back and forth. "You're going to have that old pervert walk me to my car? Do you not see the way he treats me up on the stage?"

"That's a part of his act from the old days," Hobie tells me. "People expect it. It is his *thing*." His thing.

"You're in the wrong century, Hobie," I tell him. I know he won't listen. "It is degrading. Women actually vote now, you know. Make it not his *thing*."

It was right about then, I see Bella leaning against her truck and she makes the announcement about the tree.

"What's your point?" Is all I can come up with because I am almost struck dumb she is there at all. My only thought is she is coming through on her threats for the last ten years and was here to beat me up.

"I don't know," she tips her head up at a cocky angle. "You just spend a lot of time up there. I thought you'd want to know."

"How— ?"

"My house is right down the hill, dipshit," she says. She does this funny walk with her forefinger and middle finger in the air. "I have watched your skinny ass taking the trail since you were like fourteen."

"It hasn't been that long," I mumble. Smalltalk has stopped, says a quick hello to Bella and wavers there. I have paused by the hood of my car and fumble for the keys in my purse.

"I don't know what to tell you," I say. My gut hurts though. The image of a stump where the old tree is now standing hovers around my head. "I've got no control over what they do with the old Johnson land."

"They are signing the papers over this week."

"What's your point, Bella?" I ask. "I don't own the tree or the land."

"I'm just saying," she says. I think she wants me to feel her pain. And I do. But there's no way I am admitting it to her.

"You made a trip all the way from Bacon Valley to Winford to tell me this news." She doesn't answer, just looks over my shoulder at Smalltalk who promptly sighs as if he has gotten the hint that I do not.

"Oh, you want to talk," he says. Again, Bella doesn't say anything while Smalltalk fusses with his keys. "Ladies, you alright if I get on out of here?" Smalltalk says between us. "I am on my late lunch break. I've got to do some rounds." He is smiling. I feel little assurance that he thinks I am in danger. I think I am. However, I watch him go and he turns to smile at me. I wonder if he'll remember the strained face I'm giving him after Bella murders me and he finds me cut up in a black plastic garbage bag under the billboard signs out front.

So I am standing there behind the kitchen with only the lopsided flood light over the dumpster sending a yellowish glow across our vehicles. I am fiddling with my own keys. She stares at me. I stare at her. "What?" I finally say, ducking my head and tossing out my hands.

"You need to give Brody another chance."

"A chance at what?" I ask. "Another round of being mean to me? Of using me and having the balls to just say it out loud? What are you talking about?"

"He screwed up. He knows it. Bacon, he likes you. I don't know why the hell he likes you—you're like this little beady-eyed, scrawny, Barbie Doll thing on meth."

"I think your usual description of personalities like that are cotton candy and crack." I wiggle my keys, a futile attempt to hint I needed to get out of here. "Which is mean and hateful. I don't like it."

"No," she laughs out loud. "That's Brody when he's around you. He gets crazy stupid."

"He can be crazy stupid somewhere else," I work my way around the hood of my car. "I'd rather be alone than being with somebody who has nothing better to say to me than I live off my mother's purse strings. I work my ass off." I open my car door and stand there staring at Bella over the door. "I'm not dating another bully. I'm not."

"Brody isn't a bully."

"Yes," I say slapping the hood of my car for expression. "He is. He told me I didn't have morals and I was irresponsible for working in a dirty bar, Bella. I have to work. I don't particularly like it any more than he likes working at Dixon's Feed and Seed in town."

"That's being an asshole, not a bully," Bella stands up straight. "You just tell assholes to go take a walk." She jabs a thumb behind her. "They either do or don't. I can tell you right now, Brody's not going to go take a walk. Not away from you. He'll hear you out, maybe you'll convince him he's worth more than he thinks he's worth. Maybe he'll figure out you're not like the other ones and he doesn't have to throw the first verbal punch before his ego is massacred."

I stop, take Bella in. Did she just admit he was wrong? Maybe she is just telling me to grow a pair of balls like everybody else. Or maybe she doesn't want to lose her cousin, her best friend again.

"Why are you telling me this, Bella?" I think she is lying. Maybe she is trying to get closer to corner me and hit me over the head with a baseball bat.

"Because you won't get into my truck if I don't."

"Get— into—your—truck?" I look at Bella. She is wearing a tank top and jeans. She is me times three. She has more muscle on her arms than I have on my legs. I shoot a gaze right to left and wonder if anybody would hear me if I scream. I want to ask her if she is planning on murdering me whether I get into her truck or not.

"Yeah. Because I want you to see something."

"The barrel of your rifle?" I ask, my finger pointing to the back window of her truck. She keeps a hunting rifle mounted there. "I can see it from here."

She laughs and stabs a finger in my direction. "You know, you are funny sometimes."

"Am I?" I ask. Didn't she understand I was serious?

"Will you just get your scrawny ass into my truck?" she barks. I jump and against my better judgement, I slowly make my way to Bella Johnson's truck and get inside, close the door. It is dark inside and silent before she shoves the key into the ignition and starts the truck up. "Wow, I can't believe you actually got inside," she says with a smile. "You need to grow a pair of balls, Bacon."

I think she is trying to be funny. I am also sure she knows everybody else tells me the same thing. It is like she can scent out my weaknesses, use them to her advantage.

The radio is playing country music low and soft. I sit back in silence as she drives out of Winford and toward Bacon Valley. Up and down dark roads, past places I know. I realize if she doesn't take me to some dark corner of the woods and shoot me, I didn't think to ask her if she was going to take me back to my car or if I am going to have to walk.

I know when we pull along old Goose Creek Road and past Delbert's old place, her own house is less than a quarter mile away. It would be easy to bury my body there. But she stops before she gets there, puts the truck in park on a gravel pull-off.

"You know, if you stab or shoot me there's going to be lots of blood." I tell Bella. "I'm a bleeder. They'll find me eventually and trace the murder back to you. I hit my nose on a stage prop a couple weeks ago and there was more blood—"

"Oh, my God, shut up, Piece of Bacon," she tells me sliding out of the truck. "Yeah, I saw it. You were turning cartwheels on the stage. It's all over Facebook."

She thinks I am kidding. I'm not. She waves a hand for me to follow and I know exactly where we are because it is the same place I park to get to the big old tree on The Hill. I can smell the sweet scent of trees and old leaves and a bit of fog rolling in. For the moment, it feels safe like the feeling I would get when I would hike there and sit in the tree. So we hike along the trail in the dark with the crickets chirping and the frogs in Goose Creek drowning out the sound of our footsteps until we crest the hilltop.

I see lights, little tiki torches illuminating a path in a V-shape all the way to the big tree. It is pretty like little dancing fireflies. I take it in, see Brody walking toward us. He stops just short, no expression on his face. Maybe a small wince is hiding behind his lips.

"Hey," he says to me.

"I didn't even have to hit her once," Bella tells him with one of her hearty guffaws. Then she drops the laugh, nods to Brody. "I'll get Cayce and take her back to the house and leave you two alone."

"She's sound asleep in the truck. I pulled it up to the top of the hill."

We just stand there looking at each other while Bella gets Cayce, then leaves down the trail. I am waiting for Brody to say something. He just keeps running his hand through his hair, stands there like he's working up to something, then cracks a faint smile. "Did she have to use her gun to get you here?" he finally asks me. "I mean, because I told her after the crappy things I said, you wouldn't even bother to throw a stick at me."

"It was mean," I said. "But I'm here." I extend a hand toward the lights. "What's all this?"

"Well, it is romantic lighting," Brody is peering at me, wriggling nervously in his blue jeans and t-shirt like a fifteen year old vying for his first kiss. He reaches out his hand, wiggles his fingers until I warily take them in my own. Does it feel awkward? No, it just feels warm and right and makes my stomach do those funny little jumps. "And supper," he tells me while he tugs me along between the tiki lamps. The flames dance in the bit of wind and leave shadows at our feet. "Late supper, I know."

"Real late supper," I say. "It's midnight."

"But you were working and you told me you can't eat before you sing because it makes you sick to your stomach, so I thought it would be a good way to—start."

"Start what?"

"Whatever this is—between us. Just don't laugh at me. I've never done this before. I never wanted to do this girly-girl stuff before." He tugs me forward, waves his hand at the ground. "I'm scared shitless I'm going to do something wrong and—"

He stops there. I let him wrestle with whatever words he wants to shove out there. His jaws are working, but nothing is coming out. Then I shrug. "Screw things up between you and me? You have already done that. Look, I'm here." I point to the ground. "I think it is funny that when you put my suitcases back in the trunk of my car after the funeral, you asked me when I was taking off. You're more of a flight risk than me, Brody, you know that, right?"

"I just don't get what you see in me," he says. "Especially when you've got guys knocking themselves out to get to you on that stage."

"Yes, you texted me the list of things you aren't," I sigh. "Add one more to the list: someone who doesn't like girly-girl stuff."

There is a quilt laying there with a bunch of tiny candles. Between, there are little sandwiches and potato chips and two cans of sodas with little straws sticking out of each.

"That didn't sound right, what I just said, " Brody corrects himself. "I meant, I never had anyone I wanted to do this for—someone special and girly-girl who likes this stuff. Sit. Please."

"I'm girly-girl?" I ask him while I plop down on the quilt. Our hands are still connected and he comes along with me. His eyes get big and he does the running his free hand through his hair a hundred times again while he sits down right next to me.

"Is that a bad thing to say?" he tells me. "I just mean you dress nicely, wear makeup and stuff." He shifts a little so his shoulders are touching my own. Brody reaches down, takes a sandwich and hands it to me.

"Then, no, I don't think so," I answer, taking the sandwich in my fingers. "Saying I work in a dirty bar and I'm not responsible. That's pretty crappy, though." I take a bite, wait for his answer. Brody rubs a hand on his face.

"I know I can say I'm sorry for that a million times. I am sorry. It was a stupid thing to say. But it will still be there between us. Am I right?"

He reaches over, snatches up something from the blanket. It is a couple of small tablets of lined paper and two pens tied with a bow on top. "Bella said to get you flowers. I figured you'd like this better. Song stuff—I mean, stuff to write your songs with."

Song stuff. My heart jumps while I press it to my chest. "Brody, you're scaring me. This is perfect." It kind of scares me that he understands me. And the sandwich is good. I haven't had a peanut butter and jelly in a long time.

It is creamy and sweet and has way too much grape jelly and a little bit of butter. "I don't have a friend left in the world, Brody," I divulge to him. "I could use a few. And those guys sitting in the bar, they don't know me, know how weird I am. So—it's your lucky day. I'm pretty forgiving right now. You are officially forgiven." I bump him with my shoulder. "Just don't do it again."

"What happened to Andrea?" he asks. "I thought you two were inseparable—nearly interchangeable."

"Funny, that's what Robert seemed to believe too."

Brody eyes me curiously so I elaborate. "I guess every time we got into a fight, she was there to comfort him—and not with tissues, old sappy movies, and a big bowl of chocolate ice cream like I was stuck with all alone in my living room."

"No way."

"Yes, way," I reply. I grab up the chips and start munching. I'm hungry. "Stupid me," I say between bites. "After four years, I never figured out why I couldn't get ahold of Andrea to cry on her shoulder for the first thirty minutes after a fight with Robert. He was always telling me how he thought she was too chubby, he didn't like brunettes. Her laugh annoyed him, she was too loud, too smart-mouthed, too straight-laced, too boring. She was everything he didn't like except, I suppose, one thing."

"Do I ask what that was?" Brody smiles cautiously.

I hesitate. "Well, from what I understand, she was really great at blowjobs. Because he was happy to be around her when she was doing that to him. Evidently, blowjobs are the key to Robert's heart."

"Blowjobs are the key to every man's heart, Journey." Brody says. When I groan, give him a playful shove, he just laughs and says I fell right into that one. "You're too easy."

"Again, not easy enough," I point out. "And in saying that, apparently at certain levels of a relationship it is okay for someone to give a blowjob to someone else's boyfriend. It isn't as bad as going all the way. I was unaware of this particular bit of etiquette. Then again, it isn't something I ever learned at any of my beauty queen classes. "

"She couldn't be that good if it only lasted thirty minutes," Brody offers. Then he nibbles on his lip, pokes me in the leg. "And from what I have experienced with you, he is one complete and huge idiot. You are amazing in that department and quite skilled in a few others."

"Oh, please, let's not go there," I tell him. I know I am blushing ten shades of red. So is Brody. It is quiet for a minute.

"Did I say too much?" he asks softly.

"Not at all," I answer. "I'm the one who brought up the blowjobs." The wind is taking away my words, a couple strong gusts playing havoc with the flames on the tiki torches.

"I was hoping it didn't. You're easy to talk to, Journey. I don't think I could discuss blowjobs with any other woman I know. I like that you tell me how you feel. I suppose I would say you are an open book."

"What's that mean?"

"It doesn't bother you to say anything about yourself."

He's right. "I've spent the last four years writing songs about what I know best and its me. I sing them for anybody who'll listen." It is warm outside and the wind feels good against my cheeks. "Daddy issues. Boyfriend fights. Bills not getting paid. I shove my bare, beating heart out every weekend for folks to see. I've learned if I feel it, somebody else out there does too. I've skinned my knees. They've skinned their knees. It hurts." I take a breath.

"I'm kind of putting a band aid on all our skinned knees of life by letting them know they aren't alone. Whether it is hurting or embarrassing or just feeling love for the first time. After a while, I just get used to it."

"Well, please don't ever sing a song about me." Brody leans in a bit. I feel him next to me. My heart starts pumping hard like it does when he touches me.

"And a song about my best friend giving my boyfriend a blowjob would be better?"

"No." Brody sighs, then tips his head. "Maybe if it was reworded a little differently."

I try to improvise a quick song about Robert and Andrea and every time I get to those little naughty words, I just stop. Brody thinks this is really funny and he laughs so hard, he has tears in his eyes.

When he swipes them away, I poke him with a knuckle in the ribs.

"Alright. I'm going to confess something. I already have songs about you," I say softly. I can't look at him and instead tickle my fingers on his wrist. "The song you were singing the other day in the barn when I came in— *All In My Head*. I wrote that in high school for you." I sing a little bit of it for him: *Riding your horse into the sunset. Dancing in the rain. Jumping on your bed. There were a hundred other things before I realized it was all in my head. All in my head, all in my head, all in my head, head, head. Those crazy silly little things that never happened, all in my head.* I didn't dig it out and sing it until two years ago when I thought you were long gone. *And For Mine Own Heartbeat be True.* That one was yours too. When we were in Missus Ritchie's math class and you sat down in front of me, I was always terrified that you'd hear my heart beating because it did that when you came close to me. If you ask me what one plus one is now, I will probably say ten.

I couldn't hear a damn thing in her class because of you."

Brody Wells doesn't say anything, just feels rigid against my side. I know I've said too much. An open book. He was right. Robert was right. Nobody wants to hear this kind of stuff. "Does it help I didn't think it was anything more than being scared shitless you were going to come up with something else to torment me?"

"Are you kidding me?" he asks. I want to laugh and say that I am, but I'm not. I just shrug.

"Listen, I'll tell you what you want to hear." I adjust my character, try to play the game Robert always played. I got good at reading his expressions and telling him what he wanted to hear and not necessarily what I wanted to say. Life is easier that way.

"I don't know what that means."

"It means, I can't tell if you're mad at me for saying that," I tell him with honesty. "If you are, I'll say what you want to hear. Then we get along. I call it Robert's Rule."

"Robert's Rule." He narrows his eyes, looks to the right like he can't quite figure out this puzzle. THE LOOK. "Just tell me what you want to say, Journey," he says. "Not what you think I want to hear."

I start to open my mouth. Then I realize that for my entire life, I've done nothing more than tell people what they want to hear. If I say something they don't agree with, I manipulated my words around and let them be right. That is, except for Brody and Bella and their friends because I didn't give a rat's ass what they thought until right now.

"You know what?" I ask, but I don't wait for Brody to answer. I sit back, contemplate the thought. I've got nothing. "I don't think I know how to do that. I don't know what to do if you don't like what I say."

"Just say what you feel. I'm not going to dislike you for that."

"Okay," I say. "I wrote those songs for you because I had a huge crush on you since high school. I didn't care if you were a jackass to me or not, I just thought in my tiny mind that at some point, you were going to change, *see* something in me too."

"I do," he said. He leans up, kneels down in front of me and takes my head in his hands.

"I see it too." Then he kisses me in the way that makes my heart do that funny thumping, eyes looking hard into mine. "I saw it back then. That's why I sat there eating those nasty French fries next to the garbage can with flies all around. But, like you, the timing just wasn't right. We weren't quite—there."

I'm thinking I could stay married to this guy in front of me, whether it is only on a stupid piece of paper that should have gotten tossed or not. Then, there is just the tiniest spattering of raindrop on my cheek and a crackle of thunder. Another summer storm. And we run to his truck.

So we're stuck in the truck while it pours down rain on the peanut butter and jelly sandwiches and his mom's old quilt. My hair is wet, his shirt is wet. I'm on one side of the truck, he's on the other. "I guess it is another screwed up date," I say. I lean over and tug his shirt where it has raindrop splashes on it. "We're jinxed."

He grabs my hand, gives me a tug and pulls me over so my back is to his chest. Then Brody wraps his arms around my waist and rests his chin on my head. "You know, I wasn't thinking that at all," Brody says. "I was thinking I am the damn luckiest guy in the entire world right now with Journey Dawn Bacon sitting next to me in my truck."

"Actually, it is Journey Wells, right?" I say.

It is quiet between us. Desperate to break the lull, I start chanting *Rain, rain go away, come again another day.* And Brody doesn't even miss a beat. He starts singing it with me. He's off key and soft, but I turn to him and he smiles an embarrassed half-grin. "Sorry, it probably scares you. I'm not a singer like you. Even my mom tells me to tone it down when we sing hymns in church. But you used to always look so happy singing with Drew. I know you like it. I know you miss him, huh?"

I do and I find it incredibly comforting that Brody even noticed I miss him and understands. I'm blinking my too-big eyes, swiping away the tears there. I'm wanting to tell him how I really feel. I love him. I can't. It is too soon. I don't want him to feel like he has to say it back. I know he just completely freaked out when I called myself Journey Wells.

"What happened here?" he asks me softly, concerned eyes wavering back and forth to my own. "My singing is that bad?"

"Not at all," I whisper.

Chapter −27
Note to Self: Love sucks

Hobie has no clue what love is or how people react to it.

"It isn't that difficult to say the words: *'Hey, I'm Journey and I'm going to sing a song just for you.'* Point to the crowd. Sing your song." He is standing in front of the stage with his arms crossed and shaking his head watching me poke a message into my phone.

"Two more seconds," I tell him. The stage is real wood and shiny now. There isn't anybody else there but Billy Gentry, his band and the camera guys who are filming a couple songs for Ducky so he can show them to some investors in Kentucky. He is building an entire sound room behind Hobie's office to record the songs. I can't imagine how much he has invested.

"You've done this a thousand times without stuttering or dropping the mic or texting somebody, all of which you have done in the last four minutes. *Four* minutes, mind you. Why are you so goofy this week?"

"She's always goofy," Billy growls behind me. "We're just good at cleaning up after her whenever she starts singing the wrong song or screws her lines up." He is grumpier than usual today because he had to get up before noon. He already has two empty beer bottles lined up next to his right boot. I am trying to maintain my composure. It is difficult. I honestly think Billy Gentry gets off on trying to suck the happiness out of me.

"I am not always goofy," I say in my defense. Although I admit I'm looking like an idiot with a smile I can't wipe off my face. "And just because."

"Because you banged your head on something hard?" Hobie asks. "I don't get it."

"Because I can't get this guy out of my head," I tell him knocking the top of my head with my knuckles. I can't. I eat, drink and dream of Brody when I go to sleep. Every second of the day we are both free, which isn't much, we find a way to talk on the phone, text or meet. "He's all I think about. I'm in love. And it isn't the stupid kind of love that people get. It is real."

"Real love." Hobie's eyes roll. "Well, be in *real love* after you work. Not now. I want to get lunch before midnight."

I am texting my mother. She is still angry with me. Joy Littleton volunteers with Delilah at the food pantry. Her husband takes meals to seniors in Winford. He saw my empty car parked behind Hobie's last week in the morning where I left it to ride with Bella. He calls Delilah who is sure I have gotten kidnapped or worse, I am dead in some ditch somewhere. I tell her I ran out of gas and someone towed me to the closest place I could leave it. It sounds lame when it comes out of my mouth. I'm not sure she believes it.

She gives me one of her old sayings: *Birds of a feather flock together.* I ask her what that means and she just sighs. *Just be careful who you hang out with.* She cuts her lesson short then. Delilah has other things on her mind. Robert has stopped in to talk to her. I tell her I don't want to see him. So she sets up lunch for all of us today. She is probably getting the text message right now that I won't make it. My phone is turned off. I won't get her scathing reply while she sits alone with Robert at some little diner off the highway.

I feel a twinge of guilt. It's the kind lingering in the belly and the back of the mind and pops up once in a while. Robert and I have been friends for seven years. It seems to feed on the little lulls we have during the taping session while Billy Gentry whines and gets drunker and drunker.

I had hoped the bad feeling would die off by afternoon. Brody and I are hanging out today, meeting at a gas station parking lot at three o'clock between Winford and Bacon Valley. He says he wants to show me something. He won't tell me exactly what that *something* is. I am intrigued. What could possibly be at a gas station and important to me? I hope he is not going to try to show me how to change a tire like Smalltalk tried to do last week.

We finally finish at two in the afternoon. I get to the gas station a half hour early. By four o'clock, I've texted Brody five times, try to call him on the phone. I call and Brody doesn't pick up. His voice mailbox is full. I'm thinking maybe I'm at the wrong place. It is a gas station with a car repair garage—Dan Keyes Gas and Used Car Sales. There are a bunch of run-down cars in a side parking lot with prices sprayed on in white paint on their windshields. I can hear the grinding of the electric wrenches they use to loosen lug nuts on tires in the shop. Did he tell me the name? Were there two gas stations and I'm at the wrong one? I doubted it. The next closest town is twenty-five miles away.

I sit on the hood for another half hour, then hunker down in the driver's seat until six o'clock. I'm beginning to understand why Robert likes me so much. I am like a stupid hound dog tied out behind the house with a rope. I'll sit there all day waiting for my master to come home. I'm not even mad. Okay, maybe a little.

A *little* meant I figure I will make a stop at Brody's house and hope his dad isn't home. I'm just not one to pop in on folks when they don't know I'm coming. However, I didn't want to go home and find Delilah and Robert sitting in my driveway.

"Oh, crap, I completely forgot." That's what Brody tells me when I come to a stop and roll down my window.

"Two minutes ago, I picked up my phone and got your texts." He is standing an arms-length away from my driver's side window. He looks like he just got up out of bed, his hair is askew, his shirt half-tucked and half hanging out. I'm thinking that it is half past six o'clock in the evening. It is odd. I reluctantly get out of the car, hover there with the door open in the round gravel turnaround five feet from his front porch.

"I'm so sorry." Brody rubs his head, looks back at his front porch like he's worried someone will see us here. "Oh, no, how long were you sitting there?"

"I didn't wait that long. It isn't a big deal," I lie. Surely, he knows I'm lying. If he got my texts, he knows I was there by three o'clock. And it is six-thirty now. Now I'm thinking that he just frigging slept the day away and didn't care at all. Maybe I'm just thinking he likes me and he doesn't. "No big deal." I wiggle my car keys, start to get back in the car. "Maybe we can do it another time."

"Journey, I really didn't mean to stand you up." His face is pale. I can see it when he comes around the door and holds it for me. "We just got things going on, okay? I'll call you."

"It's fine," I say since he won't elaborate on whatever it is. I force my beauty queen smile and vow to myself that I won't be that old hound dog sitting out back tied up, waiting day and night loyally there for him to come pet me. I spent far too long doing that for Robert. Who am I kidding? I would like to think our relationship just isn't that far along. We are just a few weeks in. Probably for him. For me, it dates back to the beginnings of the crush in junior high school so maybe in my mind, I've skipped a few steps and we've been married six years.

"God, I am so stupid," I say aloud. I bang my head with my hand and close the door behind me. Stupid, stupid.

Of course, Brody is giving me THE LOOK.

"Did I miss something?" he asks, his hands on the open window, looking down at me.

"No, I did," I push my key into the car and start it. "About ten or twelve years."

"Journey, you are not making any sense," he tells me. "Please don't leave mad. You look mad."

I didn't think I looked mad. I had on my biggest fake smile. I guess it could fool the judges, fool Robert and Andrea and Delilah, but it doesn't fool Brody.

"I know you're lying. I know that smile. You wore it in the pig barn passing out ribbons during the fair when it was one-hundred and ten degrees out. Nobody is that happy in a stinking pig barn at one-hundred and ten degrees with Bella making snorting noses behind your back."

"You don't know that," I say. "Maybe I like the smell of pigs."

"Yeah," Brody scratches his head, leans back. "I don't think so." He breathes in, tries to force a smile himself. "Alright, it is just that Dad had chest pains last night. He got into a yelling fight with the lumber crew yesterday. They were coming out to take down the tree on the hill. They aren't supposed to do it until next week. But it —"

"Is he okay?" I wonder if there are different levels of feeling stupid. Because now I'm thinking there has to be a stupid that comes along with being self-centered and it is really high up on the ladder. Could it not occur to me he really had a reason?

"He's alright, just not feeling good. We thought it was a heart attack. It wasn't. The doctor at the hospital just said it was stress related," he sighs, looks back at the house.

I can see Gayle squeezing out the wooden screen door. Brody cringes and leans in a little and his voice drops.

"Mom's freaking out. We were supposed to sign the papers over today to the bank. We obviously couldn't even do that. We were out all night while they ran tests. I did all the farm work this morning, then fell asleep about noon when we got back. I really set my alarm on the phone to at least call you. It went dead. I just wasn't thinking."

"Why didn't you call me last night? I could have watched Cayce or helped." My eyes work around Brody. Gayle is making her way down from the porch, a beeline toward my car, her tennis shoes make a tap-tap-tap on the wooden steps.

"I don't know, Journey," he says. "It wouldn't have been a good idea. I don't know if you want me to be brutally honest or not, but I guess I have to be if you and I want to keep going out. It isn't going to be easy for us. Our family is going to stay at my aunt's for a while. She doesn't have enough room for us all. My sisters are going to my uncle's and my brothers are staying with Bella— I could keep going. They are mad and fight and—we're just kind of falling apart as he sees it. I see it. And for some reason, Dad's got to blame someone. He kind of pins our whole family falling apart on the Ironwoods and the Bacons. He thinks everybody is ripping him off, taking the farm. And you —are an easy target."

I think he wants to say more. Gayle stops behind him and Brody moves over, halts his words. I only have something hard settling into my stomach.

"Hi, Journey," she says amid pursed lips. She sounds tired, looks rigid. It is a side of Gayle I have never seen. She is always so relaxed and always smiling.

I think maybe she hates me too. So I push up another smile for politeness, "I am leaving," I say. "Sorry to bother you." I start to push the car in gear, but Gayle holds up a hand.

"Hang on, honey," she says. "I know this sounds like a lot to ask of you. But anything can help right now. I don't know if Brody told you about what is going on with his father—"

"I have a couple thousand in the bank, Gayle, I can give it to you." It was the wrong thing to say. It was rude and presumptuous. I was living up to my scatterbrained image, say-something-stupid-and-stick-your-foot-into-your -mouth-later. "Is—is that enough?" I see Brody's eyes get wide, see Gayle grit her teeth. It is another thing I have never seen her do.

"No, we don't want your money, honey," she says. "That was not what I wanted to ask at all. Perhaps another time."

"Of course," I answer. My face was its usual shade of what I am now going to label as Stupid Red. I can't even look at Brody. Gayle is still standing there, though, and I know she must think I am too witless to ask a question.

She finally chews on her bottom lip, reaches out and pats Brody's back. "I wouldn't ask you if I knew of any other option. I mean, maybe you can talk to Robert and his dad. See if they can hold off another couple weeks on the tree and the paperwork. We'll be out of the house by then. It won't be right in John's face."

I look at Brody out of the corner of my eyes. I realize he hasn't even told his family we have been seeing each other this last month. Then again, it isn't like I've discussed it with Delilah either.

"Mom, I don't know if that's a good idea," Brody looks like he has eaten a sour pickle. "Journey and Robert aren't—"

Dating anymore. I could finish that myself, but didn't let Brody. "No, I'll see what I can do," I say to Gayle.

I don't even look at Brody.

"Thank you, honey." She looks relieved as if I can actually do anything. I feel smaller than a tiny ant by smiling the old beauty queen smile. Brody just looks away with an expression that I think might be annoyed. He waits for his mom to leave, then shoves his hands into his pockets.

"I am so sorry," I start to mutter an apology, but he rolls back and forth on his heels and waves it away.

"Yeah, you don't have to talk to Robert," he says. "Just say you did."

"Okay." I'm clinging to my steering wheel, getting ready to put my foot on the gas. I can't get out of there quick enough in my mind.

"The thing I wanted to show you at the gas station, did you see it?" he asks.

"See what?" I ask.

"I stopped in there for gas yesterday," he says. "I had to fill up some cans for the tractor. I went inside to pay for it and nobody was at the register. So I went to the garage to find somebody. The guy was under a car. He said he was changing the oil, he'd be right out. It was Drew Billings."

"*My* Drew Billings?" I ask. Brody bobs his head up and down. "Hobie said he picked up his paycheck and he went to Nashville or California or something."

"He's not in Nashville and he's not in California," Brody tells me. "He's right between Winford and Bacon Valley. I think he's staying in a room there. I hope you don't mind. I told him you'd stopped by his house a bunch of times, tried to call him. He just laughed, said he should have figured this was going to happen from the start. He'd get left in the dust. He said he thought you were different."

"I am different," I say.

"I know. I told him that." Brody reaches out and flicks my arm with his finger. "Journey, he knows that too. He's just hurt and dealing it in the only way he knows how. Kind of like my dad. Eventually, he'll come around too. So maybe go talk to Drew. Prove it to him. Figure it out."

Chapter −28

Note to Self: Just Stay Away from Drew

I am kneeling on my hands and knees on the gritty garage floor of Dan Keyes Gas and Used Car Sales. My elbows are bent and my butt is kind of up in the air while I try to peer into the darkness underneath the car. I know the fat guy with glasses, grubby coveralls, and greasy hair who is ringing up a customer in the next room is staring at my butt. He makes a low whistle. I will at least give him credit for waiting until the bell on the door makes a twinkling sound after the lady leaves to make this impolite gesture.

"I know that you think I wanted to go on without you. I didn't. " I am telling the darkness and the black and dirty pants legs sticking out. "Jenna Fenton told me I stole the contract from you. It isn't true. Hobie told me you stole money and left town."

He doesn't answer. I just hear him tightening or loosening something underneath. A shadow slips across my arms and I know it is the creepy guy at the register. I don't want to look up. It isn't that I just don't want to make eye contact with him again, I know he was going to tell me to leave. He tells me ten minutes ago, I only have five minutes of Drew's time. Five minutes and he has to get back to work.

"Please, please, please forgive me."

"No."

I realize the answer is coming from above me. I scoot up and see Drew towering over me. Confused, I look from the legs under the car to him.

"He told me you were under the car."

"That's Matt under the car. And why do you think Cal told you that, Journey?" Drew says blandly. I look over at the guy at the register. He is grinning deviously.

I call him Creepy Cal in my mind.

I look back to Drew, take him in. He is wearing the same kind of coveralls, once tan and now a hazy gray with streaks of black and rips along the legs.

"You need to leave," he tells me. His face is dirty, smudges of black on his cheeks. He is holding a red cloth and a tool in his hands, working it like he is cleaning it off. His fingers look like he dunked them in black ink. He catches me looking at them and nods to the door. "Just leave, Journey, nothing you can say to me will change my mind. Don't bother me. I know what you're all about. You have your little show now. Isn't that what you wanted all along? Whether I stole something or not, does not matter. I'm not going back to that shithole."

"If you stole money, I can pay it back for you. Then Hobie will let you come back to work." I realize my mistake the moment it comes from my mouth. I see a storm brewing in Drew's eyes and I've seen him get angry before.

"You bitch. So you're calling me a thief, too," He sniffs a hard laugh. "I am a lot of things, city girl, but I'm not a thief. If you knew me at all, you'd know that. That dumbass Billy took the money and blamed it on me. But you, you are the one who jumped up on the stage after we sang together. You stood up there and took all the shine out of my show. You knew what you were doing. Get out." He raises his arm, points to the open garage door. It is hot inside the garage and I can see the breeze outside blowing the raggedy bushes in front of the gas pumps.

"No, I didn't know. Hobie made me get up there. I'm sorry. I didn't mean it. I told Hobie I wanted to sing with you. I — "

"GET OUT!"

I jump, startled at his shout. He pushes a foot forward like he is going to come after me and I take a step back. He just shakes his head back and forth, holds his hands up. His face is angry, his lips pull back into a sneer. "Journey, I'm giving you to the count of five. If you're not out of here—"

I didn't want to hear the end of his threat. I drive off as fast as I can, spewing gravel at the pumps. I stop about ten miles away at a little park and sit on the hood of my car feeling sorry for myself and for Drew and feeling a stomach ache coming on. I feel like I have just lost my best friend. I really can't imagine singing forever without Drew.

I call Brody, thinking he might make me feel better.

"Not you again," he teases me. Just hearing his voice on the other end makes me feel a little better.

"I went to see Drew and he made me leave," I whine. I don't want to cry, but I feel like it. So I imagine step-daddy and the tears just faded away into a lump in my throat.

"Give it time."

"I don't want to give it time. I want to sing with him again."

"Tell Hobie that."

"I have a thousand times. He said he stole money. Drew wouldn't do that. Drew said Billy Gentry took it."

Brody sighs. "Can I be honest?" he asks me. "Here's how I am seeing it. This whole thing with Drew stealing money didn't come up until you got that contract to sing at the bar. Maybe Hobie is just making it up so he doesn't have Drew there. Maybe he doesn't have enough to pay a band and you and Drew."

"I don't know."

"Just a thought," he tells me. "And here's another. Zach just called. He wants a bonfire tonight —"

Chapter -29

Note to Self: Screw up Telling Brody I love you

"Alright, tell us everything about this dance card Grandpa Del gave you. Tell everybody the story. It's really cool." Brody Wells says. "This is where the ghost story started."

I'm not sure I want to tell anyone the story. For one thing, Zach Metzler has just gotten done relating the story of Andrea peeing her pants the night he and Brody scared us down here looking for the ghost. There was a lot of laughter after. However, Brody's eyes are lit up like lights on a tree on Christmas eve. I am beginning to think he is more excited about the mysterious purse than me.

I don't have much of a choice. I am sitting on a rotting, cold log on a sandy section of bank along Goose Creek, using Cayce as my shield while she perches daintily there on my lap. There is a campfire and mostly people I don't know very well, but remember vaguely around town. And of the people I do know, Zach Metzler is among them along with Ashley Walters and her boyfriend, Luke Jackson. To make matters even more uncomfortable, Kylee Thurston is stone-faced sitting across from me. Well, her lips look like she has eaten a sour pickle. They are staring at me with stone-cold stares, these friends of Brody Wells who have always disliked me, made fun of me behind my back. I just want to fade into the blackness behind me along with the laughter after Zach's retelling of the horrible event.

I knew this place existed. For lack of anyplace else to hang out, Brody and his friends spent a lot of time here growing up. I remember hearing them talk about it, remember wishing I had someplace other than my own room to spend my evenings. Once in a while, Andrea and I would come down here during the day to loll in the sunshine in our bathing suits.

The town of Bacon Valley doesn't have a swimming pool and it is the closest thing to a beach we have. Not long after Brody and his gang would show up, we would leave.

There was always a fire ring made of stones there, burnt wood in the middle. Sometimes, the flood waters would knock it out, but the ghostly hands of those who came at night seemed to rebuild it again the next time we were there. It is the same fire pit we sit around now. I feel like I should have left before dark because I have always been a visitor of the day. Brody and his friends own the night here. I am the outsider who got pulled into the dark. I don't belong here now.

"I don't think they want to hear about it," I say, feeling uncomfortable and like a little kid in a room full of big adults. I'm just not used to one on one conversations with people. I suppose Robert has always jumped right in, pushing himself in front of me and taking control. I am to blame. I let him. It was easier than fighting him, easier just to sit back and not have to work at a conversation or worry if people like me after I say something stupid. I'm used to fading away into the nothingness behind him, laughing at his stupid jokes like everybody else and simply daydreaming away until it is time to leave.

With Brody, I am learning it isn't so easy to fade into the background. He wants to shove me out in front of people and it is about as comfortable as having ants crawling in my pants. They don't like me, his friends. I can see it in their blank, bored stares.

"Just tell them." Brody leans into me, reaches out and holds my hand. "You're better at it than me." I could have fainted then wondering what Kylee is thinking, wondering if he is just using me to make her jealous.

There is a whole new kind of stare at me now. It is less bored and more irritated. Except, of course, Kylee who looks like she could lunge across the fire and rip my eyes out.

"Well, Brody's grandpa used to come into my store a lot and hang out," I tell them. It isn't so easy with everybody staring at me. "But you probably all know that." In Hobie's, it is a bit darker and I can stare into the oozy mist of nothingness. Here, I got nothing but eyes blinking at me, waiting for a story. Brody's hand is warm to my cool fingers and it feels good, comfortable and reassuring when he gives my own hand a couple squeezes. "One day he gave me a little silver purse and a dance card in a cigar box. I— I have them with me." I reach down, grab up my purse. Then I delve around until I find both sitting at the bottom. I take them out and hand them to Brody who passes them to Zach sitting next to him.

"So this is how the rumor got started about the promise," Ashley Walters is taking the little dance card from Zach. She carefully opens it and looks inside.

"Well, it wasn't a rumor," I say. "Brody's grandpa kept telling me I needed to date around before I got married. I never listened." I shuffle Cayce to my left, lean around Brody and Zach and point to the little lines beneath the dances. "Look. See all those lines? The girls used to carry these and the boys would sign up for different dances that would happen all night. There were slow dances and fast ones."

"Why is this one all blank?" Zach asked. "Must have been a fat girl with pimples."

A few groan while I shake my head. "No. Brody's grandpa said she gave the dance card to him and said if he showed up, she would save all the dances for him.

But she died before he could."

"Oh, that's tragically romantic." Ashley whispers. She looks at Brody with wide, sad eyes. "Did your grandpa ever tell you about her?"

"No."

"Here's what's even cooler," I say. "The girl's name was Molly Lender and Officer McGee told me she got killed right here." I point just beyond the trail we walked to get here. "She drowned while some kids were out racing their cars on Goose Creek Road. She was in the back seat. It really happened. He read me the report."

"She's the ghost, Kylee," Brody says. "You remember coming out here and scaring the shit out of ourselves looking for her? They never found her body. Maybe she was trying to show somebody where it was."

"We didn't spend a whole lot of time looking for her in your truck," Kylee returns crossly, her eyes on me. I know what she is insinuating. Brody just waves a hand and I lean back next to him. I hear him mumble a *sorry*. I just shrug and tell him it's okay.

"So the ghost story has some truth to it," I tell them all, ignoring Kylee's stare. "There really could have been a girl wearing white and walking along the creek. And you're holding her dance card and purse."

"Oh, that's creepy. It's like a horror story," Ashley laughs anxiously. "Maybe they'll find us all slashed up out here and there's nothing left but body parts and—this book."

"If anybody gets murdered in this story, it would be Brody and Journey," Zach tells everybody. "I don't think she's looking for her body at all. I think ol' Molly Lender is looking for the purse and that dance card. They are the ones who have it. They'll die first."

"Actually," Brody says with a sly smile. "Ashley is the one who is holding it right now."

Ashley waves it in the air, then quickly passes the book on, has a funny nervous look on her face. "Get this thing away from me!"

It isn't long before the entire conversation centers around who will die and in what sequence. Then another girl pipes up: "So you didn't finish about the promise and everybody wants to know. How many dates did Mister Johnson make you promise you'd go on?"

"Oh," I groan, leaning back. "Count them. There are nineteen."

"You've gone on nineteen dates?" someone asks.

"She's only gone out with two guys," Brody says. "One where she almost killed me running off the road in the middle of nowhere. And the second was the one where she almost shot Eddy Walter's leg off. Maybe that would be a quarter of a date since she left him with only two arms and one leg." I shove him playfully with my shoulder for reminding everybody of my faux paus. He still thinks he is funny and chuckles under his breath.

"You have seventeen more guys to go out with?" Ashley asks me. "There aren't that many guys in this entire county."

"You better run, Luke," Zach says to Ashley's boyfriend and he points to another guy lounging on the ground who has a short beard and is holding his hands out as if to ward me off. "Journey's on the prowl for dates."

"No, I'm done," I say, shaking my head. "And that's all I'm going to say." I look over at Brody who hasn't said anything. He's just looking at me, eyes going back and forth between my own, reading my gaze, maybe reading my mind.

"Really." It isn't a question he asks. It is more like an observation.

"Yeah, really," I reply, trying not to smile, but feeling a baby smile playing on my lips. "I don't think your grandpa was talking about the numbers, he was talking about the journey and I'm there." We have a moment while I stare at Brody staring at me. It is just like the two of us are the only ones in a hundred mile radius. We connect right then, really connect. We don't care that everybody is staring at us for lack of anything better to do. He reaches out and swipes my bangs from my eyes. I smell the fire, hear the crackle of wood burning within the small circle of stones. I feel a bit of warm summer air on my cheeks and it pushes my hair over so it covers my eyes. Yet, the only thing I still see is Brody looking directly into my own gaze. It is like we can see each other's souls, like we can feel each other's souls.

It feels like a millions years pass by. It is only about thirty seconds. The fire pops really loud and I jump instinctively. I wish I had never pulled my eyes away from Brody's right then. I could have stared at him an eternity.

"Okay, I hear your songs on the radio," I hear Ashley say. I blink and turn my head toward her. Still, Brody is holding my hand so tight it almost hurts and I catch a glance of Cayce slipping down so her head is on Brody's lap. Her eyes are on me, however, and she is smiling. "What are the odds you've got your guitar and you can sing something now?"

Songs? I guess I need to listen to the radio more often. I just didn't have the time. The guitar, however, is in my car. Zach goes to get it and returns, lugging the dilapidated case and all. "My contract with Hobie and his attorney says I can't do a public performance anymore except at Hobie's, so this is just between us," I let them know.

I play a few notes, then start to sing one of my old songs I wrote and sing at the bar. I think it is a little odd, they all know the words and start quietly singing along. Then, I sing three more and each time, they sing along like they've heard them enough to know the words.

"How the hell do you know the words?" I stop long enough to ask them. I think it might be some kind of joke. I have never seen any of the eight or nine people there at the bar.

"The radio," Zach says, he is giving me the kind of perplexed expression Reverend Wilson gave Delilah the other day at choir practice when her ancient flip phone kept making a ting-ting sound every time a text message came through. She held it aloft and asked if anyone knew what it meant. Was her battery low? Because she'd been plugging in the phone every time she heard that sound.

"They are all over the radio, Journey," Zach goes on in the same slow, soft tone Reverend Wilson used when he opened Delilah's phone and explained she had probably ten million texts on it that she never read. "And on every video sharing site there is. People take videos of you singing on their phones. You haven't heard them?"

"No," I say. "How did they get on the radio?"

They all think this is funny and laugh really hard. My face is red and Brody gives me a strange kind of smile. I just shrug it off. The worry starts to creep in, then. At some point, Delilah is going to hear someone say they heard them too. I'm not quite sure how I am going to tell her I sing at a bar. I think she would keel over and die.

The only one who isn't friendly with me now is Kylee who has gone from cantankerous to quiet and subdued. I should have known explosives, over time, have the same kind of reaction. They just sit there all quiet and getting stronger and stronger until they react and get ready to blow.

"Really? This is what you want?" I hear from across the fire. My eyes can barely see Kylee's lips moving while she starts to get up. "A thousand times, I have heard you call her retarded and weird and downright ugly, Brody. What the hell? What is wrong with you? Are you on drugs?"

She gets up, rounds the fire. I sit there, find myself looking up at her nervously when she pauses momentarily right in front of me. "It's the kind of thing you do, isn't it," Kylee says to me. "I remember your best friend Andrea was going out with Robert before you came in and stole him out from under her. But I guess you aren't such a good lay, huh? Seeings rumor has it he's been screwing her for the last four years and you were too stupid to know it, J—J—Journey."

Nobody has used the stutter in a long time. It was always like a gut punch when I least expected it back in grade school and once in a while, in high school. By then, I'd learned to work around it. Nothing changes, though. It still takes my breath away.

Nobody says anything. I don't think they know what they could say to make it right. Kylee starts to walk past me. I follow her steps with my eyes, craning my neck and she leans in hard to her right. Her right knee grazes my arm and part of my shoulder, sending me and my guitar wheeling sideways. I fall straight back off the log I am sitting on with Brody. My guitar goes bouncing to the dewy ground. Luckily, Cayce is mostly on Brody or she would have landed on the hard shore along with me.

I can see Brody trying desperately to catch me and at the same time, not toss Cayce off his lap. I make an embarrassing turn so my legs go whipping into the air, then I stop and right myself. I have no choice but to come to my feet.

"You want to take me on, bitch?" Kylee hisses. When I rise, I am standing face to face with her.

"No," I tell her. "I don't." It isn't that she is bigger than me. She really isn't. And it isn't that I am worried she will kick my butt from here to the creek. She would. I am still the outsider and I don't know how it will end whether she kicks my butt or not. I didn't want Cayce to see one person hit another.

"I get it, Kylee, I do." I say, holding her at bay with my hands out in front of me. "It was wrong of me to show up here tonight. I didn't know you were going to be here."

"Why wouldn't I be here?" she yowled at me. "This is *my* place. These are *my* friends. Brody was *my* boyfriend until you came slutting around again."

"I get what you're saying," I say. I look down at Brody. "I'll go."

"No, you don't need to go," Brody is rising now, lugging Cayce up in his arms. "Let Kylee leave. She's mad. She shouldn't have —"

"I am not coming between you and your friends," I finally say, softly and so I thought he was the only one who could hear. "Don't put me in that position. Brody, I can't. They are a part of you. This whole place is a part of you and them. She is right. These are her friends. They are your friends. I will leave now and we can hang out tomorrow."

I see Kylee smiling smugly. She is looking at Ashley and is nodding her head as if they are giving each other some kind of signal.

I think he sees the light. Brody is staring into my eyes again. He looks upset, maybe a bit angry at me like I have turned my back on him. I grab up my guitar from the ground, say a quick goodbye. I see Kylee, out of the corner of my eye, working her way back to the driftwood she had been sitting on.

I am sticking my guitar into my car when I hear the footsteps behind me. I feel a hand on my shoulder tap me, turn to see Brody standing there. "I'm making the choice. I'd rather be with you. I think they get it. If they don't, screw it—"

He never finishes. We both turn to see Zach and Ashley coming up from the creek. In fact, all of those sitting around the campfire minus one or two and Kylee were heading toward the cars. No, they were heading toward us.

"I was thinking we could find a restaurant open this late," Zach says to Brody. "I'm starving. You two in?"

Later, Brody drops Cayce off at home and tucks her into bed. She begs me to sing the little lullaby I made up for her and I do. She gets this sweet smile on her lips when I do and her eyes get all dreamy until they just simply close.

We go and find an out of the way place behind his grandpa's old house and sit in his truck. I can't help but notice there are a handful of my old pieces of song paper on the dash I have shoved between window and glass. It makes me feel good that he doesn't mind them there.

"You've always wanted to be a farmer, haven't you?" I ask just out of the blue. I am sitting with my back to the passenger side door and my legs on the dash just staring at Brody. His face is halfway lit by the moonlight. He is wearing a t-shirt and I can see his muscles through the thin material. I can't stop looking at him. I just can't get enough of him. It's almost like if I stare really, really hard at him, I can store up the feeling I get when I'm with him until the next time I see him.

He's wearing a ball cap. I'm thinking that even without his cowboy hat, he looks like a farm boy. Maybe everything I've ever seen him do had to do with farming.

I'm just thinking until I had the Knick-Knack Shop, I was floundering around like a little fish in big water looking for food but nothing seemed to look good. I wished I could be so determined to know what I wanted all the way back in high school.

He doesn't answer right away. "Why would you say that?" I can't see his eyes right now, they are in the shadows of the truck.

"I don't know," I answer. He sounds a bit offended. "I guess I just assumed that you did because you were into the farming clubs in school and now, you're working your family farm with your dad. Did I say something wrong?"

"I'm not so sure cultivating crops and raising cattle is much of a full-time job anymore. There's not much money in it. Sometimes, we barely live from paycheck to paycheck."

I reach up and play with the cracked window visor above me. "My shop doesn't make much money. I've got to work a couple jobs. But I think I would die without it. I'm not sure money is so important. Maybe I'm wrong."

"Do you like dating a guy who is so broke he can't even take you to the movies?" he asks me. "I mean, here we sit."

"I am getting sick of parking in your car to be together," I tell Brody. "But it isn't because there's something better to do that costs money. I'd rather be poor and happy than rich and unhappy like the Ironwoods. I think you want to be a farmer. I think if you want to be a farmer, you be a farmer. Do what you want to do."

"You think so?"

"I know so." The back of my neck is sweaty. I grab a hair tie from my purse, put my hair up into a pony tail. I feel like we have to sneak around. I don't know how long it is going to last, this charade. I am hoping until Robert stops sending me flowers and making Delilah check on me.

"Hanging out like this won't be forever," is his answer. "We just have to do it slow and easy and wait just a little while longer—"

"And some miracle to make your daddy like me," I finish for him. It is strange and uncomfortable and tricky all at once. It seems everyone who doesn't know me, knows Brody. Everyone who doesn't know Brody knows me.

"Cayce will start school in August. We'll have more time to be alone then."

"I like having Cayce around," I remind him.

"You don't want to be alone with me?"

"Not really." I play with a scowl on my lips. "Yuck. Kind of like me trashing your truck all the time." I say, pointing to the paper on the dash. "It's sick."

"Maybe I like your old songs there. They remind me of you." I lean into Brody's chest and start to unbutton his shirt.

"Yeah, of course, trash."

"Yeah, I'm thinking you like being with me too," he says. "Because you're acting like it right now."

"We're still married," I say. "I can do what I want."

"You could do what you want without us being married." Brody wiggles the hair tie back off my hair so it falls on his bare chest. I make it all the way to the bottom of his shirt, then start to twist the button on the jeans of his pants. I feel him playing with my hair. He likes to roll it around his finger and make little curls.

"Now what are you doing?"

"I'm trying to find the key to your heart, Cowboy," I say softly.

"Hey," he says. He reaches down, pushes a finger under my chin so I have to sit up a bit and look at him.

"You don't have to do that. You had it a long time ago. You know that right?"

"Um. I do now." I can feel my heart pattering in my chest when I look into his blue eyes, hear his words. I feel like a little bird he's caught in his hands. I want to run because putting my heart out in front of him is so damn scary. I have never done this before. I'm not sure if he has. Yet, his grasp is soft and sweet and gentle. I want to stay there forever.

"This is scary, Brody," I whisper while he's still looking at me and I'm looking at him. My hand is still playing absently with the button of his jeans.

"What's scary?" he looks concerned, his brow furrowing, his chin tipping a bit. He is so close, I can see the freckles dotting his nose, see the flecks of brown in his eyes.

"You and me and being this close. Maybe you don't feel it like I do. But—"

"Oh, yeah, I do," he tells me. "I'm terrified and ecstatic both at the same time. That I can tell you this and not feel like a complete idiot ought to tell you something."

"It used to scare me standing up on the stage baring my heart to everybody, telling them all my secrets," I say. "But I don't even know if I can write a song that can grasp what I'm feeling right now."

"Yeah, you could start by finding the key to my heart," he laughs softly. I know he's kidding, breaking the awkward that comes after baring the soul.

"Okay," I answer and start working my way with kisses on his chest, then his belly.

"I was just kidding, Journey." I feel him tugging lightly on my shirt to pull me up. "You don't have to do that." But I don't stop.

"Yeah, I want to."

Chapter −30

Love Leaves Softly. Summer bittersweet.
If I'd told you I loved you, would it have made a difference to you or me?

I used to stand up on the stage and sing. I looked like a rigid mannequin, belting out song after song without a bit of feeling. I remember Drew telling me that. He was right. Nobody listened. They just drank and yelled mean and naughty things. When bands came, I tried to copy their movements, their gestures, their mannerisms. I put on my fake smile.

It was when I first started working at Hobie's. Drew was still just cleaning dishes back then. I was waiting on tables. We didn't really cross paths except when I dropped off a food order. I didn't really like him. I thought he was skanky. He didn't like me. He thought I was conceited.

Then one day, I was singing softly to myself while I was mopping the floor in the bathroom. It was after closing and like two in the morning. I thought everybody but Hobie was gone. I saw a shadow melt across the bathroom floor, along the worn out, brow-flecked linoleum until it stopped just short of the wet and gray, dirty yarn strings of the mop. I looked up. He just stood there eyeing me, not saying a word.

"What?" I asked hotly. "Not good enough for you?"

"No," he returned. "I was just wondering why you don't sing like that on stage."

"Because no one could hear me," I told him.

"Maybe that would be better because you sound like a dying cat screaming into the mic now," he said flatly. "And you are so fakey. You paste on this phony smile and stand on the stage like one of those creepy store mannequins."

Drew had taken a moment to pose with his arms bent strangely just for show. "You aren't country. You've got no feeling because you're not feeling it. And you'll never feel it. So why don't you give all those guys out there a break. Just go home to your rich boyfriend and your sterile little house in that safe and secure environment where you will never get those feelings because you are living in a bubble without emotion. You didn't grow up with that music slinking under your bedroom door at night while you were going to sleep. Your grandma and grandpa didn't dance to it at the wedding anniversary on an old dirty kitchen floor with the music coming from an AM radio that's old and smudged and crackly. Your mama didn't even sing you a country lullaby to get you to sleep at night. You didn't grow up with country so you'll never be country and you're putting down everything that I live for by disrespecting it like you do."

Halfway through his agonizing appraisal of my singing, I had started to cry. Big, hot tears came down my cheeks and I had sobbing hiccups shaking me toward the end.

"Waa, Waa," Drew mocked me, used his fists to pretend-wipe his eyes. "Big pampered baby can't take a good spanking." I felt chills crawl up my spine and I went straight from blubbering to all-out, crazy angry as hell. I remember Drew turned his back to me to leave. I picked up the mop and slugged him so hard in the ribs with the handle, he fell flat on his face on the cruddy floor. I still remember how good it felt to feel the handle of that mop plunge into the soft skin of his underbelly until it came to an abrupt halt at bone. Then I spun the handle around and slapped him with the sloppy end of the mop while he crawled across the floor yelling cuss words at me.

He never apologized for his words. He just got up that night with a wild-wide look to his eyes. "Jesus-crap-and hell, I didn't expect that," he said backing up and wiping his hands on his pants. "Why don't you put a little of *that* emotion in your songs. Minus the crazy-ass shit."

"It was six months before I spoke to him again without wanting to scratch his eyes out," I finish telling Brody the same story. "But mean or not, he taught me how to feel the music, feel the crowd. He's mellowed out a bit since then."

"I guess so. He's scared crap-less of you. Now I am a little fearful too after you tell me about your crazies and just about killing him with a mop." Brody laughs low. We're inside his truck and parked behind Hobie's. It seems like it's about the only place we can meet. We're still at that fine line between wanting to let anybody know we like-like each other because we just don't give a shit anymore and worried it might all be over if we did because nobody understands.

He's leaning with his back to the door of his truck and his left arm resting on the steering wheel. I'm on the far end. "Are you ever going to give me back my hat?" he laughs, pointing at it, then wiggling his finger at me. "Give it back."

"No," I tell him. "It's mine. I have to wear it to work."

"No, it isn't yours," he tells me, laughing softly while he reaches out like he's going to grab the hat and instead, tips it over my face. I try to shove it back up; Brody tickles me in the ribs. "At least if you're going to steal my hat, wear it over here."

I slide over, still giggling and lay with my back to his chest like we like to lay. I take off the hat, stick it on the dashboard. It is quiet except for the crickets and the quiet isn't awkward anymore. Brody taps out a beat on my tummy with one hand, tickles my ear with the other.

He reaches above his visor, tugs an envelope out. He holds it in front of us. I can see my name on the front. "I don't know what you want to do with this," he says. "Zach gave it to me. He said you just need to sign the papers and then they can set up a court date."

"A court date?"

"Yeah, I know. We just have to stand in front of a judge and tell him it was —a mistake."

"A mistake," I repeat. It kind of tastes bad on my lips. "Won't it be in the newspapers?" Of course, I'm not really wallowing in that particular worry as much as the strange idea that we are really married and if we get the marriage annulled, where will our relationship stand?

"I suppose." Brody shifts a bit and wiggles a finger in my hair. "He hasn't said anything yet to anyone, just found out how its done. He says as soon as we're ready, he'll do it. He's scared he'll lose his job." Brody clears his throat at my silence. "You don't have a remark for that one?"

"Well, sure, but if it wasn't for Zach and his stupid pranks, I wouldn't be sitting here with you now. As far as you are concerned, he hasn't crapped on you like Andrea did to me." I take the envelope and toss it so plops on the dash. "So as far as friends stand on my scale right now, he's a seven. I'd give him an eight, but he did blackmail me so he loses a point."

"He's had his share of things."

"You remember in high school when he glued the books together on the shelf in the library and the whole shelf fell and pinned poor old Miss Brewster, the substitute librarian?"

"He got detention for two weeks with that one," Brody sniggers. "How about the time he tossed that big ball of firecrackers into the city parking lot and the cars all started honking."

"Oh, or the time he shut me in the show pen with a bull one year while the newspapers were trying to get pictures. I had that stupid, super puffy, red dress that year."

"Yeah, I don't know if I was more scared for the bull or you," Brody laughs. I elbow him in the ribs and he grunts. It is quiet again and he wraps his arms around my waist. I'm thinking about old fairs and sitting in the truck with Brody and how I wish we could just be here forever. I think that autumn and winter are only a stone's throw away. Will he want to park his truck in my driveway so we can meet where it is warm? Or will it end once summer is over? The thought makes me shiver.

"Are you cold?"

"No, I just wish summer wouldn't end."

But my summer will end only three days later even though it is a hot afternoon in early July. So far, I have managed to dodge Robert and Andrea. As far as Delilah, I am able to stay long enough in her presence that about the time she asks questions, I am almost to the door. I do, however, ask her over the phone if she will talk to the Ironwoods about extending the Wells's stay. I hear nothing from her until Tuesday when she asks me over for a cup of coffee.

Such, then, along comes the chill of my winter just as I sit down on one of the leather barstools settled along Delilah's breakfast nook in her kitchen. "I don't think I've ever seen you wear your dresses this short, dear, or a shirt showing so much cleavage." I reach down and self-consciously tug up the shirt.

I really don't have that much cleavage and it certainly isn't showing. I am wearing a black skirt and black tank top. She is eyeing me strangely while pouring me a cup of coffee.

As soon as I look up, she dons a fake smile.

"Sweetie, can I ask you something personal and you won't be angry?"

"Shoot." I say.

"What?" she asks. "What does that mean?"

"Just ask."

"Are you on drugs?" I am sitting here, my elbows on the expensive wooden table. It is eleven in the morning. Delilah had turned on the TV above us and we half-watch, half-talk about how good the coffee tastes. I can hear the newsman on the local TV station saying it is going to be a hot one today. Above are rows of wine glasses to my right a huge bay window overlooking the town of Bacon Valley below. The coffee smells good. She is strangely easygoing this day. I think, perhaps, while we sit there, maybe everything going on in my life is going to be okay.

"No, Delilah, I am not on drugs."

"Oh, that's good," she says, not looking any less relieved. "You asked me to talk to Robert Senior about extending the Wells's stay at the house and to delay the cutting of the big tree in their yard," she says quite softly.

"Uh huh," I answer. I follow her eyes over my head and out the bay window. My head turns in just enough time to see Robert Ironwood's car pull into the driveway. I freeze. My cheeks feel suddenly numb. As if in slow motion, I watch the car park in Delilah's driveway and out pours Robert, his father and then, his mother.

I am nearly stupefied. "Delilah, what is going on?" I start to rise, try to plan an escape out the back door. But my own vehicle is now parked-in by Robert's car.

"Sweetie, we're just having coffee together, the Ironwoods and the Bacons. That used to happen once in a while, didn't it?"

"No," I shake my head adamantly back and forth. "Never."

"Hmm, perhaps it should have."

I want to buck. I can't. I've got nowhere to go. I watch Delilah get up from the table, I hear her modest-heeled shoes clack across the stone floors into the foyer. My stomach hops and jumps. My mother answers the door. I hear footsteps come back into the kitchen as I start to rise, see shadows pour into the doorway.

"Oh, Journey, you look so skinny!"

That is Robert's mother, Peggy. She flows in with her long sweater blowing behind her and gives me the kind of shallow hug reserved for rich people. She always wears sweaters even in summer. She hates the outside and only goes from her air-conditioned car to her air-conditioned garage connected to her home, rarely stepping foot outside. She smells of liquor and yesterday's perfume still clinging to her sweater. I peer over her shoulder and cringe inwardly as I see Robert with another damn dozen of red roses in his hand.

"For you," he says as his mother steps back and away, fading into the place my mother is standing. I mumble something sounding like *this-isn't-necessary* and take one step away.

"I was actually getting ready—" To go. That was how I was going to finish the sentence. I don't take them.

Delilah intercedes and adds: "—head to the living room to talk." In a swoop of her arms, she gives me a rough, little push and herds reluctant me like a dumb sheep into the living room. I know I have no choice but to sit down on Delilah's sectional leather couch while Delilah and the Ironwoods crowd around me.

"I know this looks like an intervention," Delilah laughs a little too loudly while they plop down around me.

"Ha Ha!" Big Bob laughs heartily. He is exactly as described—big. He is six feet and nine inches and barrel-chested. When he sits, I can see the couch grind a little under the weight. Big Bob is wearing a camel brown suit, more appropriate for a business meeting. They all pick up his imitation laugh. I sit there looking left to right, the only one unsmiling while my hands work hard clasped at my knees.

"We're just worried about you, dear," Peggy Ironwood says. She reaches out a hand to pat my knee, stops and pulls it back like I have impetigo. "We know the breakup has been hard on both you and Robert. Oh, you're so, so skinny."

"It really—" I want to finish with *hasn't*. I don't get the luxury. Delilah interrupts with a cough and a hug to my shoulders. "Sweetie, don't be shy. We know how hard it is."

"Wow, she looks overwhelmed," Robert leans over thrusts the flowers at me. I take them. I don't have a choice. He holds them out two inches from my face and just stands there for the count of ten not moving. "How about you folks going in the kitchen for a cup of coffee while Journey and I talk alone."

I'm not sure if Delilah expects this. It is almost like the four of them have written up a well-practiced script and suddenly they change the lines when she isn't looking. She keeps her cool, however, stands and waves Big Bob and Peggy through the long hallway and to the kitchen where we started. So now I am stuck with Robert. He always makes me feel tiny like a child in his midst. He is wearing a suit, the same camel brown as his father. He has a fresh, too-short haircut and I realize how much his face looks like a pudgy, four year-old child.

"I was kind of hoping you'd stop being mad at me, baby," he says in his soft, gruff tone. "You don't know how bad I miss you. I made some mistakes. I get that. But I can't imagine marrying anybody but you."

I put out my hand to stop his words. He waves it away.

"Let me finish," he says, shifting on the couch. "I know you're not perfect either, alright?" He reaches into his suit jacket and pulls what appears to be pictures out. Then, he lays them out one by one in front of me. I stare with drawn breath as the last month of my life unfolds before me in images. Singing at Hobie's. Waiting tables at Great Escapes Restaurant. Muddled images of Brody and me in his truck in the parking lot. Me sitting with some of Hobie's customers, guys, that make me look like I am sitting on their laps and flirting. I wasn't. There were probably twenty of those. "At what point were you going to tell us about the bar?"

I just stare at the pictures, stunned and numb. "How—how did you get these—*why* did you take these?"

"I hired a guy, a private investigator. He was fairly cheap," Robert tells me. "And I did it because I can't stand to see you falling into the wrong crowd, falling so deep. I love you, baby, and I'll do whatever it takes to get you well."

"I'm not sick." I start to rise, feel Robert's hand on my shoulder. I hear Peggy laugh in the other room. I sit back down. "Does Delilah know about this?"

"Not yet, I haven't shown these to your mother or my own mom. Just my dad. He was pissed," Robert leans back. He holds his hands into the air and makes the sound I can only compare to fireworks going off. "My dad wanted to take back your house and your car right there on the spot, kick you out."

"My house? My car?" I ask. "You can't do that."

"Well, yes, we can. You remember, they are both in my name. Dad co-signed. We can't have you missing payments and hurting our credit. Besides, I told him we could work it out. It would kill Delilah to know you worked in a dump like that, just kill her. You can quit. That you have a drinking problem, drug addiction or some mental issue, we can deal with. There are so many medications out there to help with these kinds of issues. But we don't need to let her know right away."

"I don't have any issues," I say. "I don't drink, other than an occasional beer, and I don't do drugs." I reach out try to snatch up the pictures. Robert is quicker and gives me a gentle shove back. I have a mental image of a truck towing away my car, of my couch and loveseat tossed to the curb or sitting on the front lawn with me locked out. And, oh-crap, it isn't even my couch and loveseat, nor my oven or refrigerator. It is all in Robert's name.

"Baby, why are you doing this to everybody? Why the hell are you screwing around with that loser Brody—or all those dumbasses? Who are all these guys?"

"I don't have to explain anything to you," I mumble. It comes out soft and sweet and scared. My house. My car. He wants to take it away.

"Well, let's call in Delilah and you can explain it to her."

I look at Robert and his beady eyes with his knowing, controlling gaze. I can't think quickly enough. I'm not ready to confront Delilah about working at Hobie's.

She doesn't care that I'm saving up to buy the Knick-Knack Shop. She just doesn't get it. But I know Robert. And I know he is working up to something. Even stupid me can figure that one out.

"What is it you want, Robert?" I hiss flatly. I feel sick to the pit of my stomach. Why? Because when we were in high school, Robert's team never lost a basketball game, never lost a football game. The Ironwoods always got the prime property for sale in town, always won the biggest prize at the Christmas silent auction. They won the prettiest lawn award in town every spring and never paid a parking fine. Everyone went to their bank for loans or they were shunned by everyone the Ironwoods knew. And everyone knew the Ironwoods. What the Ironwoods wanted, the Ironwoods got.

"I want you, baby, you know that." And I was also included in that pot.

"No, you don't," I tell him. "There are a hundred other women out there for you. Maybe it just isn't me. Robert, I am —" *not getting back with you.*

Of course, he interrupts. I can see his cheeks reddening, see his shoulders tighten. I am getting ready to stare at the angry Robert, the temper tantrum Robert who always gets what he wants. I feel my hand begging to twist out, feign his emotional blows. Especially when it comes to the girl-who-has-no-balls. This is always the point that I start feeling like I'm going to throw up, have a panic attack. So I go into trauma mode, tuck my chin down and stare at my hands. Not this time, I stare him in the eyes, feel my ankle bouncing, feel my heart jumping.

"Before you say anything," he interrupts my trying-to -grow-some-balls behavior. "I want you to think about what I say. Don't answer right away. Okay, okay?"

I've got no choice while he chucks me under the chin. "Yeah, okay."

"Dad is getting a lot of flack at the bank about foreclosing on the old Johnson farm," he tells me softly.

"I have a sweet deal for you. Marry me and Dad will refinance their home at an affordable price. They keep the farm, the—tree. We get each other. What a deal, huh? It will be our secret. Nobody knows. Nobody."

"What? That's—" I am thinking the word I am looking for is preposterous. Delilah uses it a lot when she is describing the price of sky-rocketing gas. She uses it to label her dresses when she can't quite fit into them anymore because she's gained a couple extra pounds. And she once told me it was preposterous that her attorney slipped in a couple extra charges on her bill when she used his services to close the deal on her new house.

It won't come to my tongue, though. I just find myself tipping my head and staring at Robert with THE LOOK. It is the first time I had ever been able to use it. Is he joking?

"Journey, you need help. We can go to counseling."

"Counseling? For what? Just because I don't want to go out with you anymore?"

"Let's not be silly. You need help for whatever addictions you have, whatever mental issues you are dealing with right now." Robert looks over my shoulder, drops his voice. He actually thinks I am crazy for not wanting to be with him. "We can overcome this together. We've always known you've been a little slow. I've gotten used to it. In fact, it is a part of you and I—I—love that."

Love. Did he say love? Did he actually stutter?

"I am not crazy," I almost whine. "I am not slow. My mental acuity was tested in third and tenth grade. Both times, I tested higher than average. Delilah said it was probably higher than my teachers. I just say things —I just— can't think things out sometimes." Like now. I'm dizzy with confusion. God, Robert is right. I'm stupid. And God, Bailey the Bartender is right. I've got no balls.

"Okay, I get it. It is a lot to suck into that little head of yours." Robert sits back, holds his hands out in front of himself. "We'll give it two days. You think it out. When you drive your little car with the built-in GPS and the satellite radio and the leather seats, think about riding a ten speed bike instead. See if it is worth it to you. When you go home to that cute little house in the cul-de-sac with shutters and a white picket fence, imagine living in a frigging box along the highway." He starts to rise, pats me on the head like I'm a little girl. "You watch the Wells family disintegrate, watch them fall apart. Just remember, I gave you the chance to stop it and the only thing you have to do is marry me."

"I can keep the Knick-Knack Shop?" I ask. I don't know I already feel like I have to barter for it. There is no way I will marry Robert. I hated him right now, right?

"I don't know. We planned on you working at the bank. Oh, and one more thing you should know before you find out somewhere else," he says and I dumbly look up. "You need to be nice to your mom, give her some slack. She didn't want us to say anything. I told her you'd want to know."

Still I sit there with wide eyes staring at Robert, wanting to get up and walk out. Wanting to run far, far away. Where was Drew with his motorcycle right now? I can see me with my suitcase in my hand, riding off into the sunset—that suddenly turns into an old crappy gas station with me sharing a cot in the back with him. Back to back, that is.

"Your mom went in for some testing at the doctors," he whispers, his eyes looking up and over my shoulder. I feel his hand come out, lay atop mine. "She's going to be alright, but the doctor found some issues with her heart. Nothing pills won't help, but we have to be careful now. Be nice. Go to church once in a while."

Chapter –31

Note to Self: Break up with Brody

I'm standing in the Knick-Knack Shop. It is four in the afternoon. I know the time because someone dropped off a cardboard box of Christmas ornaments, old state fair souvenirs and a clock shaped like a cat. It meows four times, then stops. Sometimes I think I am more like purgatory for people's old treasures. They aren't pretty enough to still keep around. Their owners aren't quite ready to imagine them sitting at the garbage dump. Limbo.

I look around, try to see my shop through my customer's eyes. It is dark, except for a couple spikes of light seeping through the curtain on the front window. It is dusty and more than a little disorganized. I have comic books on the same shelf as baseball cards and little lead Civil War figurines. There are toys near the bottom and tools on top. A couple baseballs have rolled off their plastic bases and are laying on the floor. Two shelves are still broken because I haven't fixed them since I toppled them over on Bushy Hair and Beady Eyes.

I am watching Andrea slip in through the door. It seems like a long time since she has visited my shop. Still, she remembers not to slam the door.

"You said you wanted to talk?" she asks. "I just have a few minutes. I'm on a lunch break." She is stiff, guarded. She doesn't wear it well. I've seen her dress her personality this way at the bank. She's never like this around me.

"I only need a few minutes," I say and lean against my counter. "So you're aware of the deal Robert offered me?"

"Deal?" she repeats. She blinks, looks upward. Those brown eyes can never lie to me.

"I marry him and he refinances the old Johnson property so they won't lose it," I say.

"I—I didn't know that," she stutters. "I don't know what you're talking about."

"Okay," I say, the word flat like a cold, stale pancake laying between us.

"Is that all you needed?" she asks. She fidgets with her purse, pretends to check her cell phone. I am looking at Andrea and I realize I am staring at a stranger. I don't know her at all.

"What would you do?" I ask her. "If Robert told you he would take everything away from you and from those you love if you didn't marry him, would you do it?"

"I can't make that decision for you, Journey." Andrea puts her phone away and closes her purse. "What you are saying sounds downright silly. But what I do know is that both Robert and Bob Senior left work this morning to talk to you. So I think it sounds like something you are making up because you just aren't quite done getting back at Robert and me. Or you are mad at something they said because you don't agree with them. It is classic Journey Bacon. Everybody spoils you like an only child. And I can't tell by your stone face if you are just being mean to me or you really want my advice. I can only say that Robert would only be looking out for what is best for you. He loves you."

"That doesn't bother you?" I remain calm, simply eye her carefully. "That he *loves* me, but screws you on the side?"

"You make it sound like it happened often. It didn't."

"That it happened at all was wrong, Andrea," I say. "You know, I think the only reason you were ever friends with me was to be with Robert."

"Is that all you want?" she gives me a glassy stare.

"You got your say. You think it was wrong. I am sorry I slept with your boyfriend." She carried no remorse on her face, held no regret in her tone of voice.

I watch her leave. I wish I could reach out and grab her shirt, make her turn around so she tells me she really, really is sorry. Maybe Robert forced her to have sex with him or he would fire her or—some other logical excuse for betraying my trust.

"You know what the sad part of all this is?" I tell her back while she opens the door. "I still love you as my best friend. I miss you like hell. I wish it hadn't happened."

She only turns and sneers at me. "You—you have it all, Journey. You've got the looks and you've got the guy. Why can't you just take what you have and be happy, huh? Why does there always have to be drama with you?" She lifts up her phone and wags it at me. "By the way, the reason Robert found out was he heard your song on the radio last week when he was at a meeting in Detroit. Then he found downloads of your singles on the internet."

"My songs for sale online?"

"Don't act so stupid, Journey," she growls and slams the door.

It is like a countdown after Andrea leaves. I can't sit still. I can't even be happy when I find out what she says is true about my videos being online. The only thing that keeps churning through my mind is Andrea not acting like Andrea anymore. I have to assume Robert Senior paid her a hefty sum to remain neutral. Or perhaps he threatened to fire her. I call Hobie. I listen to the clock meow out the hours as they pass. Nobody comes to my store, nobody leaves. I go through the motions I usually go through on Tuesdays—waiting tables at Billy Wright's Bar and Grille from five to seven and then off to Hobie's to practice until ten.

Every hour that passes, I see myself digging a tiny hole that gets deeper and deeper. Two days. It passes quickly and I'm standing there on Thursday, thinking that maybe it was all a stupid nightmare and somebody is going to wake me up. But the only one who stops in the shop Thursday afternoon just as I'm getting ready to leave for Hobie's is a guy with a tow truck and an antsy pace to his steps.

"Can I help you?" I ask him when he comes in the door.

"Are you Journey Dawn Bacon of 516 Maple Court?"

"Yeah."

"I'm supposed to get you to sign some papers or get the keys to your car."

"Sign papers?" I ask, but I know. I pick up my phone, tap in Robert's number and ask him if he sent someone to tow my car.

"John Wells just came in the door. Dad's waiting for your decision. Just sign the papers. It's a prenuptial agreement. I'll have it notarized here at the bank."

I walk around the man standing there waiting for my signature, waiting for my keys and peek out the window. Yes, Robert was not lying. John Wells's truck is in front of the bank. So is Brody's. I can see Gayle lingering at the door. She has a tissue to her eyes. She is openly crying on the sidewalk while Brody leans in hard to talk to her.

"Shit!" I hiss. I have the phone in my hand and I stare at it. Five, four, three, two. That countdown is done.

"Make the call, baby." Robert says while I stare at the guy holding out the papers. "I'll send him off. Or I'll refinance the house so they can afford it. No one but the notary sees the papers. It is exactly as discussed. And if you say anything, the whole deal is off."

Baby made the call. I scan the document, barely understand the legal words. I put my chicken scratch signature on the paper. Two seconds later, the tow truck guy answers his phone. He promptly leaves. Then I get into my car and drive to the pull-off gravel area on Goose Creek. I climb up to the top of The Hill and wiggle up into the tree. I stay there an hour and forty minutes, staring out over the old Johnson farm. I wonder if Delbert had this grand scheme planned all along. Maybe he was really evil and that's why he suggested I date his grandson. That was why he gave me the dance card and purse. He knew I would be sitting here and his family would have the farm. My heart would be broken in pieces and laying bloody and beaten into a thousand pieces on the ground.

"Naw," I say to myself. I wait another ten minutes before I see the trucks pull into the drive. I watch them get out—John and Gayle and Brody and an uncle or two. Three or four kids come running from the house. It is the happiest I have seen anyone. They are laughing and cheering and dancing. Hell, I think one of the twelve year-olds even made a makeshift cake. All the while I watch, soaking it in, feeling myself smiling. Then I brace myself for my own future, climb down from the tree and head toward home.

Still, The hardest thing I've ever done is tell Brody Wells I couldn't see him anymore. It was on Friday morning. He came into my shop, Cayce in tow.

"I don't know what we did to deserve this, Journey, but did you hear the good news? Did you get my texts? The bank decided to refinance the house. We aren't going to lose it. And the payments aren't bad at all. It's a twenty year loan, but what the heck? It's only two hundred a month. I sent about a thousand texts telling you. You didn't answer. I figured you either lost your phone again or you got busy at the bar. I almost stopped in, but we went out for dinner."

I'm standing there rigid, holding on to the book case like I always do. "I need to fix that for you." he says. He looks at it from afar, sizes the case up. Brody reaches out a knuckle and knocks on the hard wood. "This is good wood. I could rebuild them, bolt them to the floor." I still haven't spoken. He doesn't seem to notice.

"Brody, you don't need to fix them, but thank you." I am wearing a black lace dress today and really high heels. It suits my mood, dark and angry and sad. Cayce walks over to where the baseballs are and starts picking them out one at a time.

"Can I have one of these?" she asks, beaming up.

"You can have any one you want, sweetie," I tell her. "Pick one out."

My voice is stale like the stagnant water collecting in an old red bucket underneath the leaky pipe in the shop bathroom sink. Brody releases the bookshelf, slowly turns his attention to me.

"Are you—alright?" He asks. His hair is freshly combed and he is wearing a nice blue button up shirt and jeans. I can tell he made an effort to dress up today. His eyes dart back and forth between my own. Maybe he saw the ghosts of yesterday's tears in them. Maybe it was simply the expression on my face.

"I can't see you anymore, Brody," the words come out of my mouth like a rotting mouse mummifying beneath the fridge. "I'm sorry." I had not practiced saying it. I would have sobbed and sobbed. He just stands there staring at me like he's waiting for the punch line. It is silent until a loud car drives past the shop out front.

"Is it because I didn't show up at the gas station that day?" He asks me. The smile is wiped off his face, I can't tell what has replaced it. "I mean, I can make it up to you. Did I say something wrong?"

"No," I say. I put on my beauty queen facade, minus the smile. "Robert apologized and we're getting back together. I—I just couldn't throw away all those years. We're giving it another try."

Brody just stands there. He goes from looking like he thinks this is a big joke to letting is soak in. Soak in with gasoline, I would guess. I think it would be better if he yelled at me. I was prepared for that. He doesn't. Brody Wells just looks hurt, while he stares at the floor between us for a moment.

"That's okay. I'm not that far in," he tells me. "I'm surprised, but I shoulda seen it coming. I didn't this time. I thought you were different. Come on, Cayce." He takes one of the balls out of her hands and carefully places it back into the bin. I see her look up, see a storm brewing in her eyes. She wants the ball. She doesn't want to leave. "I want to stay with Journey," she says, pointing at me. "Daddy, I want to stay with Journey."

"Not today." He snatches her up just as she starts to protest. Then I see her look at her daddy's face. She just gets this expression I can't quite describe. Her tiny eyes are blinking wide and hurt almost like she has gotten stung by a bee. She knows. Cayce wraps her arms around her daddy's neck and just stares at me. She just stares at me like I'm a stranger.

I wait until I hear the throaty rattle of his truck disappear down the street. Then I calmly walk to the door, lock it tight.

"Good girl." Robert comes from the back room. "You know, you did the right thing. I hate to see that family lose it all." He is adjusting his tie with both hands, wiggling his neck like it is too tight. "Fix this for me, baby. I can't get it right."

I swallow hard and turn. I reach up and tug a bit right to left so it is centered right down the middle. Then I imagine my hands slipping along his tie a little higher, stopping just above the collarbone. Then I can feel my fingers tightening the silk material around his neck. I imagine him just folding, his face turning blue—

"That's too tight." Robert swats my hands away. I blink and nod, loosen the tie a bit. "It's probably a good thing we both sowed our oats before we got married. Now we can move on."

I can't even talk. I feel like I'm sinking into some hole. My throat feels constricted, my heart is heavy and dark. I just cling to the picture in my mind of Brody's family pulling into their house and cheering.

Later, at Hobie's I try hard to belt out my usual songs. I can't. Robert comes along, sits in Hobie's office while I sing. He chats it up with Billy and Hobie like they are old buddies.

"He says you're going to be worth a lot, sweetheart," Robert tells me on the way home. "I'm thinking maybe we give it a few more weeks and then, when your contract is out, we just let it go. You hate big crowds, remember? You get your moment in the sunshine, then you can sing at church. Your mama would like that. Singing in a disgusting shithole, I'm not so crazed about that. How about we celebrate a bit tonight. I'll stay over at your place or you can come to mine."

I stare at him long and hard. "Robert, if we're going to do this marriage thing, I want to do it right. I want to do it the old-fashioned way. I want to wait until we get married to have sex again. A clean slate like you wanted."

"Then we better get it done fast, huh?"

Chapter −32

Note to Self: Ask Smalltalk if he's my daddy

Robert bought me a new car. It is a little cherry red Corvette. It does sixty miles per hour in a little over three seconds. It can get up to one-hundred and ninety miles per hour. I know it can go one-hundred and fifty-two because eight minutes ago, I was sitting at a little gravel pull off just outside town. I had stopped long enough to figure out who had called me on my cell phone, then hung up. It is the eighth time in the last two days. It is beginning to bug me. I don't recognize the phone number.

I look in my rearview mirror. I can see a little white four door car almost coming to a stop as if whoever is driving realizes I have pulled off the road. I pull out slowly and drive about twenty-five miles per hour for about fifteen minutes and until I see the white car hanging back a bit. Then, I push my one-hundred and twenty-five dollar high heels into the accelerator and kick it so hard, the car makes a funky weaving for about two seconds. One second later, I am doing sixty miles per hour. The rest, well, what matters is the white car is lost in my dust.

Okay, it would be assumed it was Bushy Hair and Beady Eyes. However, since the gun incident, I have not had a confrontation with the two men. I suppose Smalltalk has scared them enough that perhaps they have told their client it simply isn't worth going to jail. At least, I assume such. I tuck it into its little hiding place beside the dance card in the Knick-Knack Shop for the next three weeks, taking them out once in a while to run my fingers across the little spirals, turn the pages of the little book. Do I think of Delbert when I do this? Yes, a little. More often, though, my mind takes me back to the county fair and the skinny boy who used to sit back in the stands and eat his French fries while I sang.

The skinny boy is the reason I am being followed. I believe Robert is behind the white car long gone in my rearview mirror. He is having someone follow me, whether it is a person he's paid or one of his dumb cousins or nephews, I'm not sure. However, the one thing I am sure of is that it is just one more thing among many others I simply do not like.

For example, I do not like working at the bank. I am there now from eight in the morning until five in the afternoon, Monday through Friday. Those are the days Robert can babysit me. On Tuesday and Thursday afternoons during practice and Friday and Saturday nights when I sing, he has a gentleman's agreement with Hobie that I won't come or go without making sure someone isn't given a call. I do not like the idea I am being passed off like a child from one person to another.

I go out to the table where Brody and his friends used to sit. Now, there are people I don't recognize who wave me over and herd me in. They all want me to sit with them, buy me a drink.

"I just want a soda," I tell a guy who introduces himself as Sam one night. The next, it is a man named Frank. Some of them are members of the newer bands Hobie invites in that appear before I sing. They stick around and listen to my songs. I'm just not like them. I want to go home. But Robert might be there, so I stay as long as I can.

I have a good idea Robert looks at all my texts and phone calls and he knows when I come, when I leave. He has become my warden. So when I hit the gas and dust the little white car shadowing me, I feel like I am escaping my prison, even if it is only for a brief moment in time. What I don't realize is there is a police car parked behind Grandview Grocery Mart whose driver sees the little blaze of red Corvette speeding past.

I hear the siren behind me before I see the flash of police lights bouncing red and blue in my rearview mirror. I feel a ball in the pit of my stomach, those little prickles of doubt. I wasn't going over the speed limit at least for the last ten miles.

Slowly, I ease to the side of the gravel road, my car cloaked in a shroud of dust. I don't know if it is one of the rigid state officers with unsmiling faces and clean-shaven heads that look like hard-boiled eggs or one of our county sheriffs. Then I see the swaggering walk and recognize the hat.

"Journey, do you realize you were doing one-hundred and twenty-eight miles per hour when you passed me on South Main outside town?" Smalltalk is standing outside my driver's side window, legs splayed to either side and arms folded across his chest.

Well, it was probably closer to 148 to 150 miles an hour. I don't divulge this. Delilah told me to never contradict an officer on the roadway. Not all of them are good and decent people. And they carry guns. She says to simply smile, accept the ticket and if needed, fight the damn thing in court.

So I just smile and hold my hand out, waiting for the ticket.

"I'm not giving you a ticket this time," he tells me, relaxing his arms. "I am assuming you were having difficulty handling the car. Just don't go so fast next time. Maybe I can take you down to the old race track outside town. We can go over some of those things you learned in driver's education—"

"Do you do this with every driver with a speeding ticket violation?" I ask him.

I don't know why it comes out of my lips so angrily.

No, I do. I have been smothered in nothing but Robert and his family for three weeks and the last fourteen minutes were the only freedom I have seen. I suppose Smalltalk is just one more person paid by the Ironwoods to spy on me.

"So this is what happens to nice little girls when they start to get famous," he says dully. "They get rude and hurt people and drive their fast cars, not caring if they kill somebody else."

"Can I leave?" I ask him. "One song played on our local news station does not make me famous. This is Robert's car. I am on Goose Creek Road where nobody ever goes anymore. The only one I am hurting is myself."

"And that's so much better," Smalltalk takes in a deep breath. "I am about four seconds away from having you park this car, impounding it for a few weeks and driving you back to town."

I stare at him, long and hard. I know I am giving him the same bored expression Delilah used to give me in junior high when I asked to wear jeans over and over again. He is right. I am driving dangerously. I imagine myself flying out of the car into the creek just like Molly Lender did the night her boyfriend wrecked. I cringe. I really don't want to die. I just want to get away from Robert. I just want to get away from Billy Gentry and run away off somewhere I can have my shop and be who I am and smile again. I don't want to sit around Bacon Valley and watch Brody find some beautiful girl and have ten kids with her. Every one of them would be like a nail in my coffin. It would kill me to see him this way.

I laugh to myself and imagine the only way I could do that would be to drive my damn car off the old rusty bridge over the creek and run like hell off into the sunset. I see myself then, doing just that, taking my car to the edge, letting it slip into the water.

I stand on the edge, looking toward someplace else. Then I walk away, just walk—away.

"Oh," I say aloud. "What if Molly didn't die at all?" I realize Smalltalk is giving me THE LOOK. I know I have a faraway look to my eyes before I blink, see him staring at me.

"What do you mean?" he asks.

"Nothing," I say. "I was—I'm sorry I was driving fast." I want to reach for the phone, call Brody and share my strange little thought. I stop. I know Robert checks my calls, my texts.

"Officer McGee, could you get a note to Brody Wells for me?" I ask. "I mean, without anybody knowing. Just between you and me."

He looks me up and down, nods his head. "As long as it is legal." I scrabble around in my purse, but the only thing I can find to write on is a clean tissue that nearly falls apart while I write: *What if Molly isn't dead. What if she just wanted to go away?* I fold it in half and hand it to Smalltalk.

He takes it in his hand, stares at the folded note. Then Officer McGee scrubs a hand over his face. "I'm going to bare my soul, step out of my uniform right now and talk to you like a man."

I suppose I am looking at him with horror. Two years ago, I was invited to a bachelorette party and during the course of the evening, a male stripper showed up dressed as a policeman. He gyrated and pranced about, stripping off everything down to a tiny pair of navy blue underwear with red and white stripes and SPANK ME written on the rear.

As soon as I hear Smalltalk saying *bare*, I imagine him undressing right there in front of me with a sequence of twists and swivels straight down to his underpants.

I'm confused because somewhere in the back of my mind, I have replaced that blank image of a father with his own face over the last couple months. I am obviously wrong.

"I mean—I mean," he stutters because surely he sees my wide eyes. "I meant that figuratively. I am going to talk to you like someone who has known you since the day you were born."

"Oh," I breathe out the word, realizing I have been holding my breath thinking he is going to extort me for some kind of sexual favor in return for not issuing me a ticket.

"I thought you were asking me for something else," I mumble. Am I giving him THE LOOK?

"No, of course not, sweetie," he tells me. He holds up the tissue and shakes his head back and forth. "I just want to give you some advice. You can take it or not." His face gets a faraway glaze and he sighs deep in his chest. "I see that boy out at the bar every weekend, standing in the back in the shadows with his hands in his pockets and a look on his face like I remember having way back in the day. Maybe you remember when I used to take you fishing, huh? I used to stick a worm on the hook at the end of your pole and you'd cast it out, catch one of those little bluegill at my mom's little pond."

"I remember."

"Well, sometimes you didn't just reel it in. You played with the bluegill, let it go out a bit and reel it, then let it go again. I always asked you why you did this and you said—"

"I liked the way it felt," I interrupt him. I remembered feeling like I was in control. I had the little bugger on the hook and he was mine. And I wanted to keep it that way for a while. I was in control and I liked it a lot.

"I liked to keep it on the line and know it was there. It was mine, that little bluegill. I wanted to play with it for as long as I could."

"Yeah, well, I used to have to take the pole out of your hands or you'd play with it until you killed the little fish. You just didn't want to stop, didn't think that it could hurt it." Smalltalk rocks back and forth on his feet. He gives me a hard stare. "I can't stop you now. I can only tell you. Don't do that with the boy," he says, "If you plan on marrying Robert Ironwood, let the boy off the hook or he'll just be hard and bitter and angry."

"Like my mama did to you?"

Smalltalk's head snaps upward. There is such a long lull, I think I am mistaken. Then Smalltalk's head swings out. He looks up to the sky. "Did she tell you something?"

"No," I say. It feels good to not lie right then. All's I do is lie now. "So are you my father, Officer McGee?"

He sniffs a laugh, looks to the ground. "I would be honored to be your father. But I'm not. I just kind of took that position when you were a kid, thinking I could encourage your mom to like me. Then you kind of grew on me."

I felt like a balloon and Smalltalk had just stuck a pin in me. POP! I'm not sure why. Perhaps I held on to some hope he was my father because he was there and he was nice to me when I was a little girl.

"I figured that was why nobody could find my birth certificate," I say. "I've been trying forever to get it. I assumed it had my father's name on it. You were the only one who has kind of been there for me— I mean, when I thought you weren't trying to *hook up* with me."

He stifles a smile, but I see it. But then he looks up. "I'm sorry," he tells me.

His eyes are concerned, his face a bit pale. "Maybe you need to discuss this with your mother, huh?"

"I can't right now, she's having heart problems," I mutter. "Robert said she went to the doctor and I have to be careful what I tell her. She might have a heart attack."

"Heart problems?" Smalltalk tips his head, looks a bit skeptical and surprised both at once. "A heart attack, your mother? She seemed pretty spry when I saw her working out at the country club the other day."

"She was working out at the country club gym?"

"Uh huh." Smalltalk starts pumping his arms up and down, marching on his feet. "She was on some kind of a stair-stepper with arm things that go back and forth."

"An elliptical? Really?" I am the one looking skeptical now. "But Robert said—" I clamp my lips shut tight.

"Maybe you should go straight to your mom and ask her what is going on."

"Officer McGee—" *I don't know what to do. I'm being held hostage by Robert so the Wells family doesn't lose their home. I love Brody. And I want to sing at the bar. I don't want it to all go away. I love my little store. Please help me, please—! If I marry Robert, I think I will just shrivel up and die.* I start to open my mouth to say something, but the words just won't come out. "You can give me back the note. You're right. I've got to let him go."

He has the note in his hand, looks down at it dangling there. "Are you sure he's the one you want to let go, sweetie?"

"I have obligations," I say, squinting against the sun. But he turns, doesn't give the note back to me.

"Slow down." That's all Smalltalk says. Slow down.

Chapter −33

Note to Self: Tell Brody I love you
Note to Journey: I love you too

Delilah is so proud I am working a full-time job at the bank, she comes in and opens a Christmas savings account. On a Tuesday and on the third week working there, she waltzes in and makes a big show of *signing up with Journey Bacon who has the big desk by the front window.*

I take it all in stride. I flash my beauty queen smile while Andrea hovers over me like a robot guiding me in the intricacies of every boring aspect of customer accounts. She doesn't smile, doesn't chitchat. Everything is done by the books where I am concerned. I look up long enough to see Andrea's face. It is puffy and her cheeks have broken out. I know she is stressed, hates being around me now. She has gained three pounds since I saw her last and she is moody. But she does smile at Delilah who is beaming up at me. Robert gives me a thumbs up through the doors of his big office. Then he sends me into the kitchen to make her a cup of coffee.

I see Andrea peering at Robert while I walk out the door. He gives her a wave toward the front of the office. "Hey, close the curtains, can you?" he calls out from his desk. She walks over and shuts the front curtains on the big bay windows in the front of the bank, something I have seen Robert do when the light glares hard during the day.

I am surprised when I return and before I sit down, she pulls me aside. "Just giving you a heads-up." Andrea says in almost a whisper. Her face is deadpan. "John and Gayle Wells are coming in to sign the loan papers to refinance their home loan. I overheard Robert talking to them on the phone a few minutes ago."

I don't really know what to say. My heart makes a pitter-patter because it is too stupid to know if Brody is with them, I won't be able to lay against his chest, smell the sweet, musky scent of his skin.

"Maybe I'll leave for a half hour or so." I say to her. "I mean, if that's okay with you. You are my supervisor. I'll take an early lunch."

"Journey, I don't think that is a good idea."

She is so poker-faced and so much a stranger right then, I stand there trying to decipher why she is saying this to me. Does she just want to watch me suffer through seeing Brody walk in and watch my face while I feel my heart ripping out?

"Robert doesn't think all the other workers would think it is fair if you just leave when you want. He wants you to stay at your desk." She looks around warily. "Do you want me to get you a pill or something? I have some nerve pills in my purse."

"No." Still, I see her looking toward the front windows. I sit down at my desk and pull out some papers. I ignore everyone who comes in and comes out. I appear to stay focused on my work, but my mind is churning. Why did they close the curtains. Why won't they let me leave for a while?

I don't wait too long before I rise. I walk across the expanse of the bank, a death march, seeing heads go up and catch the restrained look on the other staff faces while I go to the curtain and gently pull it back.

"Baby, come back and sit down."

I hear Robert's voice behind me. The only thing I can see in front of me through the tiny part of curtains is the dented dumpster container parked outside the Knick-Knack Shop. I stare at it. I can't move.

My eyes make a long, slow turn toward Robert's office. The door is closed.

"Journey, you need to come back and sit down." Andrea says softly behind me.

"I need to leave for a moment," I say in a croaky tone that she could well recognize as the point I am going to cry.

"I'm telling you to go sit down."

I think my entire heart just died a little the moment I see the dumpster, watch them rip off the Knick-Knack Shop sign in front. Robert Ironwood has finally been victorious in taking the last thing that I worked for, that I love. It is the final straw, the last thing I have that is my own.

I really think I can go sit down. I start to turn, but I feel the hard rock in my throat settle in and nearly choke on the sob. Andrea's hand is on my arm, clenched hard and tight. I simply peel each finger off, walk the twelve long steps across the ugly brown bank carpet and open the door to walk outside.

I can't do anything more than walk to the side of the bank building, a brick wall in a small alley. I put my head in my hands and cry in the dim light. I feel dead inside while I watch a crew of men chuck the basket of baseballs into the dumpster. Then there is the old school desk, the oak book cases and a hundred other trinkets I have collected over the last few years.

"I'm sorry." It is Andrea who is standing there next to me when I feel the softness of a tissue whisk across my arm.

"No, you're not," I hiss back, snatching the tissue from her hand. "You never liked me. I'm not stupid. You like Robert. You hung around me to be with him."

"I used to think that too until —" she stops. "Until you weren't there anymore and it was just me and him. Then I realized, it wasn't the same."

"Well, now we're all together again," I tell her. "What's the new arrangement? You on the weekends and me on the weekdays?"

"Don't say that. I have no choice. I need the insurance. He hasn't touched me since you two got back together."

I know she is lying. "And how long will it be before he needs us both again," I spit at her. I heave a sob with the sound of my little souvenirs and hard-earned antiques banging against the bin.

"I'm pregnant." Andrea says it just like that. My eyes peel away from the shop and the dumpster and the hard-hat men ripping it to pieces like a Band-Aid coarsely and ruthlessly ripped from soft flesh. "He wants me to get an abortion this weekend. He is going to drive me to some medical office that does it cheap. No one will know."

"I know now," I say and waver there staring at Andrea, letting her words sink in. "It's Robert's."

"Yes," she says. "I don't want to get an abortion. I —I don't know why. I just don't. I don't want it to be his, but it is and it is alive in me and I can feel it. But I can't lose my job and I know if I don't go with him this weekend, I will lose it and I won't have insurance and I can't raise a baby. My mother and father will send me packing if I am pregnant without a husband."

"You don't need to get an abortion. We can fix this, make it right," I say without even knowing what I could possibly do to make anything right now. My whole life is a freaking mess, how can I fix hers?

Andrea seems to recognize this. She hands me another tissue so I can wipe my eyes. "Clean it up. Put your chin up high. Here comes Robert. He is walking John Wells to his car." she says. "I think they are going for coffee at the restaurant. He knows Brody is waiting in the car.

I honestly believe he is doing it on purpose. Isn't he a shit?"

"At least you don't have to marry him," I swipe my nose with the tissue and sniff. I don't even realize until Andrea reaches up and fixes my hair with her fingers that Bella's truck is in the parking spot across the street. I suppose she is gloating; she can see me crying like a baby.

"After Robert leaves, I have a couple little things I want to get from the shop," I tell Andrea. I don't know if they'll rip up the floor. I'm scared they'll find my little hiding place, the old Fenton safe.

"I'll cover for you."

It is cool in the Knick-Knack Shop and bare by the time I get inside. I leave the door open just a little to let the light in. The men have left. There are a couple marbles on the floor the workmen didn't bother to pick up. I pluck them up, hold them tightly in my fist. The dust is still settling. It is dark and naked inside, like a dead body without a soul anymore. I guess I didn't have as many treasures as I thought. However, I feel empty now inside too. It is like the building that held all my antique mirrors how I feel—soulless, empty, dead.

The tears come again while I kneel down on the floor and open the old wooden piece of floor. I unlock the safe and dredge out my treasures—the teddy bear, the cigar box now filled with everything that has to do with Molly Lender, news clippings and obituary and the little things too good for me to part with. There is $357.67 of play money I keep in a little purse for buying stuff and for register cash. It occurs to me when I pull it out, I have always felt I had to hide this money from Robert. He says I shouldn't waste so much money on my little trinkets. I snatch up a ripped, yellow plastic grocery bag from the dumpster on the way into the shop. It is this I use to place all my stuff, all that is left of my heart.

I dab the tears away with my tissue and try to stop. If Robert sees them, he'll be mad. He hates my puffy lips and red nose when I cry. Just as I rise, I hear the back door close. The hinges are squeaky and it makes me jump. I don't know who I expect to come in, but I know my eyes are wide. I am a bit daunted. It is Bella Johnson and she takes up most of the doorway.

"I suppose you are here to rub it in or beat me up," I say, trying to take Andrea's advice and push up my chin. "Have at it."

"Nope, it isn't as much fun when somebody else makes you cry, Bacon," she says without any expression on her face. She runs a hand through her hair, takes the forefinger of her right hand and pushes a bit of extra behind her ear. Then she thrusts an envelope at me. "Brody just wants me to give you this. You left it on the dash of his truck. You need to sign it. They'll set up a court date."

"Okay." I take the envelope and start to put it in the plastic bag.

"No, now." Bella is holding her hand out, wiggling her fingers. "Don't leave him hanging."

I don't want to do it. I just stare at her for the longest four seconds of my life. Then, I take the pen she pulls from her pocket, open the envelope and sign my name—backwards. Right after, I put a little O and X. I don't know why I do this. I don't even think he'll remember what it means. Or if it will do more harm than good. It just happens.

I am starting to put the paper back into the envelope when I hear Robert's distinctive trudging steps. I hear him sniff, hear him stop a cough with his fist.

"Oh, please leave before he gets here!" I whisper scream at Bella.

I don't think I have ever seen a frightened look to her face. However, at that moment and just before she narrows her eyes to irritated slits, they widen. I give her a push with my fingers, kind of step with her toward the back room and toss my yellow plastic bag around the corner. With one swoop of my hand, I swing the door between the rooms closed, hoping quicker would leave a less loud squeak of hinges. It is the back door, though, I am worried about when I turn and hear Robert kick his shoes at the front door.

"I was trying to slip this by without you knowing," Robert stops in the middle of the room, pulls out his suit jacket with his fingers and tugs at it a couple times. He always does this. He tells me it helps dry the sweat on his shirt inside. "You could have gone into the back room and cried instead of making a big deal right out on the sidewalk. I'd rather not look like a ruthless bastard."

He is a rather ruthless bastard. I didn't say that at all. No sense in making him mad. I may not seem like I have nothing left, but if Robert can find some way to control me through something, he will. "So what is done, is done," he says. "We'll call it a clean slate. I never slept with Andrea. You never —"

"Robert, I don't really want to discuss this now," I say. What I really didn't want was Bella hearing anything she can use against me. I have yet to hear the door close. If she has slipped outside, it was quick and quiet.

"But I think we need to discuss it," he tells me. "I don't want you bellyaching about any of this in the future. If we lay it all to rest right now, we're like starting all over again. You ought to be happy. You got out far better than dad and me. Your little screw got his family farm back.

Oh, don't look at me like that. I had you followed. I know you were meeting with him all over the place. You saw the pictures. You've got no ground to walk on. We, on the other hand, lost a hell of a lot of money in oil rights and that tree was worth a couple thousand dollars in wood. We could have sold the farm in ten minutes flat even without the land and made enough money, you and I could have gone to any island you want for our honeymoon. The only thing you have to worry about now is me. And, of course, not telling anybody."

"Oh, Robert," I say. I could die right then. If Bella is there, she can hear the whole thing. If she says one word to anyone, I know in the blink of an eye Robert will find a way to take the farm again. "Okay, clean slate. Whatever you want." I try to smile but the puffy crying lips make my expression more a pout. My legs are a little wobbly. I can only pray Bella is not in the back room now, taking in all that was said.

"Aw, c'mon, give me one of those beauty queen smiles," he says. Ah, that I can do. Fake smiles are my thing now. "You can come have some coffee with me and Gayle and John to celebrate.

"You know," I twiddle my thumbs. "I don't really want anyone to see me like this, Robert. I look like a clown with red eyes and a big red nose. Can you give me about a fifteen minute leeway. I just want to stand in here a few more minutes by myself. I'll use the bathroom, get the mascara gunk from under my eyes."

"I'll wait."

"No, please," I say. "Give me that. Just a few minutes to —kind of close out this chapter of my life."

He bobs his head up and down, straightens his tie. "Alright. Fifteen minutes. If you aren't back at work in fifteen minutes, I'm coming back down here, got it?"

I wait until his shadow is long gone. Then I count to ten. I pray to God over and over that Bella isn't back there and with each step I'll take to the doorway between the rooms. For some reason, God isn't listening. Of course, maybe I should have started pleading my case a few minutes earlier.

It is a new expression I have never seen on Bella when I scoot the door open and peer inside. She is standing in the shadows, the bulk of her frame hidden within the corner of the room. Only the toes of her size 8 shoes poke out past the light that dapples the floor with blotches of gray and yellow from the slightly open door.

"Bella, you have to promise me you won't tell Brody." I am standing there with my hands crossed in front of me at my waist. "You can't. You won't tell your Uncle John or Aunt Gayle. You can't tell anybody. If Robert finds out that you even know, he'll find some way to take away the house or hurt someone. That's why he refinanced with the bank."

"So he's got you held hostage for what, forty years?"

"Not that long. It's like twenty." I breathe in, breathe out. "I don't know. The payments are really low." I look up, shrug. "I get a Corvette out of it."

"Yeah, I suppose. It was last year's model, you know that right? Anyways, how does someone get into a mess like this?" she asks me.

Strangely, I realize I have never had a civil conversation with her before. "You fall in love so hard you'll do anything for someone." It sounds sappy and sits there between us like a plate of warm milk I know any cat with a mean tongue like Bella would lap right up. "Please don't make fun of me."

"I actually wasn't," she says. "I thought it was weird when you dumped him. The way you two looked at each other, hung out together—it seemed —real."

"It was. So don't let anybody find out because I can almost bet your house or your car or your cows and tractor are financed in some way by the Ironwoods and the bank." I reach down, pick up the bag. I can see her eyes dart to the contents, then back to me. "If Robert knows you know, he'll use it against you."

She ignores me, nods to the little red bear. "Still got that bear Brody got you in high school, huh?"

"I still have the stupid little valentine he gave me in grade school." I reach into the bag, shuffle around until I pull it out.

"The one with the red velvet lion on it." Bella shifts, straightens her shoulders and stares at the car. "I helped him pick that out." There is a stifling silence. I keep turning to see if Robert is coming back. I am desperately trying to stuff everything from the bag into my purse.

"Well, I have to get back to work," I tell her, nibbling my lip. "You won't tell anybody. Promise?"

"Naw," she says and starts to turn. "You know, I was never going to beat you up, Bacon, just so you know."

"That's reassuring."

"I actually like you. You're the only one who doesn't look at me like I'm a freak."

"You know, you have a strange way of showing it. But I don't understand what you mean. Why would I think you're a freak."

She holds out her arms as if to display something to me. "Look at me. Do I look like any other woman you know?"

"Do I look like any woman you know?" I ask her in return, holding out my hands. "I don't know any other girl my age who feels like she has to please her mother by wearing three-hundred dollar dresses. Who is afraid she'll let her down if her lipstick isn't perfect and her heels aren't high enough. And then, to make matters worse, enjoys wearing the dresses and heels too."

Bella laughs aloud. "You're a mess, Bacon."

"I am."

"It doesn't mean I won't beat the crap out of you some time in the future."

Bella leaves out the back door. But she does beat the crap out of me after all, emotionally and not physically though. On my counter I find a little Post-it note that I had crumpled up. I must have accidently left it somewhere where Brody found it. *Note to Self: Tell Brody I love you*

Underneath it is a baby blue Post-it. It is crisp and new and in Brody's handwriting. *Note to Journey: I love you too*

I can do no more than sob into my hands. Then, I leave out the front. I don't look back, don't want to look back. My heart feels like it is melting hot caramel dropped on a stovetop all the way back to the bank. I go to my desk and pull up my checking account. I have $32,371.00 in it. I look at it. I don't need it anymore. My shop is gone. There is no more collecting pennies in the couch to help pay for it, working extra hours at Great Expectations to fund my dream. I don't want Robert using it on a stupid honeymoon to Cancun. I can't run away. So I empty my entire savings account. I deposit it into Andrea's. Then I write it down on a piece of paper and drop it on her desk.

"What is this?"

I am halfway out the door and swing around with my hand on the frame. "It is how much you have in your bank account should you decide you would rather get fired than do what you don't want to do this weekend. I'll be there for you whatever you want to do."

"I can't take this." She starts to rise, her fingers on her lips. She looks at the paper, then back to me.

"Andrea, it is already there."

Chapter −34

Sometimes you got to step
away from the dance.
Take a look around
Give life a chance.

"Here. We only have a couple days to get this done." Andrea tells me and plops a white, plastic file container on my desk. "Since you are the newest employee, you get stuck with it."

I look up at her face, brown hair bobbing at her shoulders. Andrea's expression is unreadable. The container she sets before me hovers there atop a stack of papers I should have finished two days ago. Everyone is irritated with me because I am so slow. They don't say anything because they fear the wrath of Big Bob or Robert.

Instead, I get what Delilah calls *stink eye,* a scathing glare that as far as this office is concerned, is reserved expressly for the inept future wife of the bank owner's son. I have heard them whisper my new nickname, Slow-Mo. I don't care. I don't want to be here. I want to be out on the highway with my window rolled down, my arm resting on the door and my hair blowing in the wind searching for the perfect antique. I had three calls this week to search for hard to find items. I had to turn them down.

"Oh, please," I groan. "No, no, no." I start to rise in protest. I see a few gazes turn from stink eye to something I can almost describe as sadistic pleasure at my complaint. "I am so far behind as it is. This is quite possibly the only thing I hated doing at my shop. Paperwork sucks."

"Then you need to catch up and your paperwork will be done." Andrea says louder, straightening up. Was she nuts? That's all my job is now, paperwork.

I move one piece of paper from one file to another, plop the information on the computer, monotonous day after day, colorless hour after hour.

"Take it home with you if you have to." Andrea has a glower to her eyes. "But get your work done. Do it." I see the container start to squirm its way down the stack of papers and I reach out to steady it. It is heavy.

"Do what?" I ask her while she walks away. She doesn't answer just then. Instead, she closes her door and calls me on the phone.

"Those are the Johnson's house payments for the last God-knows-how-many years. Run through them and see if they really missed any mortgage payments. Maybe we can find something missing. If you find something wrong, we can prove Big Bob has been swindling people. Then there is no reason Robert can take that farm again. You're free. It is easy to falsify accounts in the computer. Checks disappear or don't show up or the system shuts down and information is lost. Big Bob does it all the time."

"When you said we just have a couple days, does this mean I get to do those weird Lamaze classes with you?" I whisper.

"Maybe. Hush, or someone will hear you."

Freddy Johnson is waiting for me at my front door that same evening. He is scrubbing the top of his curly black head nervously. I see his car, catch him pacing back and forth when I drive up to the end of my cul-de-sac. There is no exit for me. He sees me, gives me a big wave and looks relieved. I pull into the driveway and lug the plastic crate with a blanket overtop up my sidewalk.

"What's up, Freddy?" I ask him, balancing the container on my tiny porch gate so I can get my keys.

He is always dancing around when I talk to him like he is six years-old and has to go to the bathroom.

"I was sent here by Benjamin Dodge." he starts. "He wants to know if you're ready to sell the purse."

"Benjamin Dodge," I repeat. "Is this the same Benjamin Dodge who was in the car wreck on Goose Creek years ago? Molly Lender's fiancé?" And the same man who had me followed by Bushy Hair and Beady Eyes.

"I don't know anything about that. I just know he has hired me to get the purse. Journey, you and I both know I had it first. Grandpa Delbert was going to give it to me. I can probably take you to court over this stupid purse. Grandpa was senile and you took advantage of him when you got it from him." Freddy takes out his wallet. "Nobody else has called about it, have they?"

"Senile?" I laugh out loud. "Your grandpa was in no way senile. And no, nobody else wants the purse." I lie. I had a few calls. "What made him decide to call in his hound dogs and send you out?"

"I don't know what you're talking about."

"Yes, you do," I reply, opening the door and backing inside with the box. I set it down and Freddy starts coming in. I promptly wave my hand at the door. "Out. You're not coming inside. You're like a bloodsucking vampire. If I invite you in, you'll be here all the time."

"Aw, come on, Journey," he whines, but still backs out. He lets the screen door close between us and then presses his face close to it.

"If you tell me why he wants the purse so badly he would send two guys out with guns, I might not chase you down the driveway with my broom."

"Oh, Journey, he just wants the purse, that's all."

"You can tell Mister Dodge that I am not selling the purse." I close the front door with my foot. I can hear Freddy out on the porch moving around for a long time.

"If you don't leave," I finally say. "I'm calling the cops."

I wait until I hear his car pull away. I should have known Freddy was the link between Benjamin Dodge and the purse. He had been trying to get it even when Delbert was still alive. It made me wonder just how he had known someone was looking for it. And how he has found out Delbert gave it to me.

I go over to my desk, open my laptop and type in a search for SILVER DANCE PURSE M.L. I am six pages in before something catches my eye. It is an advertisement in a local online newspaper around Winford: *Dance Card Purse. Silver. Collector searching for old dance card purse with M.L. engraved on the front.* I freeze. Beneath it is a phone number. I quickly jot it down. Then I look it up online too to see if it comes back to Benjamin Dodge. It does not. The name assigned to the phone number is a Tina Lavelle.

"Tina Lavelle," I say to myself. "Tina." The name is familiar. I open up the purse, wiggle my thumb into the secret latch and open it to expose the picture of the little girl inside. *Tina*, it said. *Our little girl.* Gingerly, I pick up my cell phone and poke the numbers into the pad. It rings once, then twice. I almost hang up wondering if it is another of Benjamin Dodge's ploys to get the purse. No one answers and it automatically goes to a robotic sounding voicemail. I hang up. It would have to wait. I have three days to run through the file before Andrea's future with the bank would become tediously hanging by a thread between Robert's chubby fingers. I write down the phone number, stuff it in my purse to try later at work.

By two in the morning, I have files covering half my bedroom. Andrea had meticulously collated computer reports year by year. Each month with a non-payment was marked with an X-Default. I just needed to find each X-Default and then, sort through the box and try find a check that was actually cashed for the payment.

So every cashed check and money order mailed to the bank are in the piles laying on my bed, across my nightstand and on to the floor sorted by year. I have checked the first ten years. Not a darn thing seems out of place. There are no non-payments. And yet, it just seems my life depends upon finding just one miscalculation to show the Ironwoods have falsely stated the Johnsons and the Wells have not paid their mortgage.

I fall to sleep around four in the morning. In another hour, I have to get up for work at the bank. I don't bother to clean up the room. I decide to simply lock the door to my bedroom behind me. I have twelve more years to check. Tomorrow, I work at the bank until five and then, I only have an hour between working at the bank and practicing at Hobie's to run through some more files.

I just don't realize the extent Robert is going through to control every aspect of my life. Nor do I understand how much Andrea is willing to do to get me out of their lives so she can have Robert for her self.

At no point, do I have a clue Robert has been leaving work long enough to come into my home and examine it to make sure Brody Wells or any other man has not been visiting me when he isn't around. Nevertheless, I would find this out at one in the afternoon of the next day when I am eating lunch in the breakroom.

I am just sitting there at the table with Lillian Thomas and Carol Smith, munching on my salad when Robert comes into the room.

He has a manila folder clutched to his chest. "Could you ladies please leave us a moment," Robert tells them. I see Lillian look up from her deli sandwich, a piece of meat slipping from her lips. "Today, we are going to try a little tough love. I'm going to show you what it will be like without me around, without your mother around. And before you give me that pouty look, I have already talked to her. This is something we feel we need to do to get you a little scared straight. You are to go home this afternoon and you may take whatever you want from your house. Then I am changing the locks to the door at four in the afternoon. Give me the keys to your car."

I am sitting there in mid-chew, staring at Robert. My heart is pounding and I can see through the glass windows that everyone is staring at me.

"You can't do this," I say. "It is my house, my car. Robert, please, why are you being so hard on me?"

"Because I love you. And I can do it to you. It is my car. I make the payments. It is my father's house. He makes the payments." Robert holds out his right hand, palm up. "The keys."

"I haven't done anything to deserve this." I am digging in my purse in shock. I can't help but think Robert is crazy right then. Why hadn't I ever noticed it before? Because I was just along for the ride like Delbert said. Crap, he was right all along. I never *didn't* do anything Robert asked me to do.

I hand him the keys. That's when Robert slips the manila folder on the table in front of me and opens it wide with his fingers. "What the hell were you thinking?" he asks, poking a forefinger at the collated copy of the file Andrea had printed for me. My eyes snap out to the bank office area. I see Andrea. She looks at me. I see her gaze. And I realize, she has set me up.

Robert scoots the packet away to show a small section of the cancelled checks I have been sorting through. "Are you trying to screw me? Yeah, baby, you are. So get the hell out of here."

"You were sneaking around my house?"

"Actually, it is my house. You are just living in it."

He is wagging his thumb to the door. "Do not call your mother. She is sick."

I get up, push the chair beneath the table. I see my food sitting there. Oddly, I wonder if I should take it. Did he stop all my bank accounts so I can't access them?

"You're not going to take away the Johnson farm again, are you?"

"We'll just see how well you do out in the real world without Mommy and Robert to take care of you. Let's just see how you do. And when you come crawling back to me, hell, yes, I might take away the farm again. Or maybe I won't. Now, get out."

Robert won't let me talk to anyone and escorts me to my desk to get my purse and then to the front door. "You don't have to do this," I tell him. "Robert, this is crazy."

"No, you're the one with the crazies. What is it with all those little pieces of paper at your desk and in the trash can, huh? You write down words that don't make sense. I think you'll see a different light once you're out in the world alone, baby," he tells me. I see the office staff staring at me. They shake their heads, let their eyes roll. I know they think Robert and I are just having another one of our fights. He has one of his office clerks ride with us to my house. I am mildly panicking, possibly in shock. It keeps churning over and over in my mind how Andrea tricked me so easily and I fell for it. I can almost bet there isn't anything in that office that would have entangled the Ironwoods in any scandal.

My face is numb while I lug out a backpack and fill it with enough clothes I can fit inside. I take a black plastic bag and toss in my dresses, my jeans, my shampoo and bathrooms supplies. I grab the silver purse, my guitar, the dance card, the plastic bag from the shop. When I step outside, Robert takes my keys. I am afraid to fight him, talk back. I realize I am scared of everything.

I'm scared to stand on stage, frightened of relationships, scared Delilah will disapprove of everything I do or say. *I'm just terrified of being me.* Everyone is right. I need to grow a set of balls. It isn't happening now, though, while I walk down the sidewalk looking like a homeless person with a black trash bag full of clothes swinging across my shoulder.

"Oh," I say aloud. "I am a homeless person."

I call Delilah. She doesn't answer. I am thinking I have nobody left in the world who doesn't think I'm either crazy, stupid or a bitch. Or they are friends with Robert. And if they are friends with me, they end up being collateral damage in whatever mess I happen to be in, whenever Robert needs someone or something to take away from me.

I wonder why Robert left me my phone, then I realize he knew I had no one to call. And maybe, just maybe he has a way of knowing where I am when I have it, tracking my steps. It is another way for him to squirt lemon in my eye.

I try to call Drew. He doesn't answer, but Creepy Cal who stared at my butt the entire time picks up the phone.

"Drew's not in today."

"Can you give me his home phone or his cell phone?"

"He don't got no phone."

I think the tears are about to fall while I press the phone to my ear and head off along the main road from my subdivision.

"Okay, let me ask you this. Do you have any used cars for a couple hundred bucks?" Just two minutes after I finish the call, I take the phone and toss it into the grass by the side of the road.

Chapter –35

Note to Self: When all else goes to shit, watch the Sun rise

I am sitting in my car, admiring the sun rise. It is orange and green and a deep red. Up to that moment while I was laying in the backseat of my new and very used kind-of-lime -green Ford Pinto with black doors, I am trying to pinpoint the exact moment my life started to spiral downward.

It was a muddy sky then, I could just see above the dashboard and it was still dark. I was cuddled in the faded pink princess comforter I bought for two dollars at Goodwill. Then the glint of light catches my eye just above the silver duct tape holding up the sagging rearview mirror that keeps falling off when I turn on the car. That is, when the car turns on.

I sit up and peer outside to the dawn of a new day, leaning against the back of the driver's side seat—and the seat flips forward, spilling me into the steering wheel. My right foot wheels around and gets tossed into the air. If that isn't enough, the cardboard box of CDs Ducky gave me to pass out and that are planted on the passenger side front seat crashes to the floor. There are two hundred in the box, minus one I mailed to Cayce because I sang her lullaby on it.

On the cover, they have a browned, vintage image of Hobie's Bar and Grille in the background and me standing in the parking lot in ripped-jeans, a tank top, big red sunglasses and holding my guitar. I'm kind of off-color except the sunglasses some really red lipstick the makeup artist slopped on me and my blue eyes. *Exes and Beaus* is written in red cursive across the front.

On the back is: Rebel Child. There are X's and O's underneath it. I am staring face to face with me on a CD. I think if look like a twelve year old who got into her mom's makeup. I shove it away.

"Shit," I groan.

Still, I can't complain. I got the car for a hundred and fifty bucks. Creepy Cal told me there were some issues with the fuel tank back in the 1970s. He showed me how the back seat pulls downs so there is extra room to store things. *Or make a bed,* he told me and wiggled his eyebrows. This certain model was hard to get rid of still. "That's all that is wrong with this baby. Don't worry, just don't stop real fast in front of somebody." He told me. *Just don't stop fast in front of anybody. Got it.*

"And don't drive it at night. The lights in the rear ain't working." *The lights in the rear ain't working. Got it.*

"And—and one more thing. The other reason I couldn't sell this puppy was because there's this smell sometimes. Nobody died in it or anything. I don't think." *It's got a smell. Got it.*

"It's dangerous and it stinks," I repeat. "And the lime green color doesn't discourage people from buying it too?" I had asked. "Maybe you can knock off another ten bucks for the black doors?" He didn't. He said it cost him ten bucks in gas to come pick me up off the highway where I had called him. He leered at my boobs the entire drive to Dan Keyes Gas and Used Car Sales. Then I drove off into the sunset.

Now it is eight sunsets and nine sunrises later I have managed to survive on my own. Of course, my bedroom is the back seat of the Pinto, my dining room table is the cracked dashboard and my backyard is a lonely stretch of abandoned gravel parking lot at Hobie's Bar and Grille.

There are fourteen miscellaneous-shaped car fresheners dangling like wind chimes at various locations of the interior. The strange scent of death still hovers nearby. I try to be optimistic. Nobody knows it is my car. I haven't looked over my shoulder for Robert or Beady Eyes and Bushy Hair since I got it.

Hobie knows I park here. He doesn't know I am taking up residence. I asked him for a key to the bar so I can come in and practice when no one is there. I am actually washing off in the kitchen sinks before anybody gets there because the truck stop that has showers in it on the highway takes me a half hour to drive to and I can only afford it twice a week. Plus some of the early morning, close-to-the-highway clientele unnerve me when they follow me in to the restrooms. Three days ago, I found a guy sleeping against my passenger side door.

As far as being able to hide the car. I tell Hobie I am getting a ride home every night from a guy named Chase Smith. No, he doesn't exist. It is just the names of two different companies who have parallel billboard advertisements on the road in front of Hobie's. Sweet Chase drops me off in the morning. I tell Hobie I wanted to keep my old car parked out there just in case something doesn't work out with him. They just assume I don't want to add on the extra mileage on my Corvette so I'm driving a banged-up thing and I don't want Robert to see it parked in another man's driveway.

My back aches, my head hurts, and my legs are asleep from being tucked into my chest most of the night. I can't sleep because the rear window takes up a quarter of the car and the security lights Hobie installed recently shine in the windows all night. Added to this, Billy Gentry plays poker until four or five in the morning. His crew of idiots whoop it up all the way to their cars and wake me up.

It is fodder for four more songs written in the front seat of my car with my back to the passenger side door and my feet propped up on the steering wheel.

Then there is the issue that I think Creepy Cal might own the second set of keys to the car. I have vivid nightmares of waking up and seeing him smiling his toothy, bearded grin over top of me and wiggling the extra set of keys in his dirty, pudgy fingers. I keep Smalltalk's bear repellent in my purse and my purse tucked against my side.

I've got this little ache that won't go away in my chest. It's been festering there for a while. Then it just kind of opens up like a brand new wound four days ago. Ducky set me up with a little table and I was signing CDs in a new music shop inside a mall an hour and a half away. I finished writing my name on one and I looked up and Brody Wells was standing in front of me.

"Listen," he says to me. His word sounded angry, his usually laughing eyes are deadpan. He has leaned down a little so nobody else could hear. His voice is soft, hoarse. "Here's a couple hundred of the money I owe you." He pokes the white envelope with his finger. "I would have paid you sooner but I don't know where you're living now and I'm not about to ask around for your address. I saw you were here in a newspaper so I decided to track you down. Send a text with your address to Bella. I'll write you a check next time and mail it." He taps the table, then bites a little on his lip. "And —and don't send my kid stuff. Don't send her your music. Your songs have cuss words and I don't want her listening to that kind of stuff."

I look up, feel my face redden while he plops the CD I sent Cayce on the table in front of me. "You're cold and heartless, Journey, it's like you think it is okay to use people like stepping stones along the way to get where you want to go. Well, I'm not one of those stones and Cayce isn't either."

I wiggle in my seat, knowing there were a few people who can hear his words, even whispered. All's I could think to say is: "And she's never heard you cuss?"

I try not to think about the moment and my stupid remark. The teenage girl behind him is dragging her dad. When it is their turn, her daddy leans over, pokes at the cover and then nods toward Brody who is sauntering with an angry swagger out the door. "That must be the ex, huh?"

"Believe it or not, no," I say and everybody in the line laughs.

For now, though, I am watching the sun rise and feeling the warmth on my face. This is usually the day I sit around in my pajamas just a couple hours extra before I go into the Knick-Knack Shop. Without the shop, I find myself with a lot of time to spare in a stale car. I pop open my newly purchased $25.00 pay-as-you-go flip phone and check for any messages. Of course, there are none.

Around eight in the morning, I realize it is getting time for me to leave. Ducky wants me to sign and sell my music CDS at some music festival two hours away. It is the fourth one in the last two weeks. I just have to sing for forty-five minutes, then sit at a table for a few hours with the monotonous job of staring at a mall parking lot or signing cover after cover with X and O HUGS AND KISSES JOURNEY DAWN.

I am praying my little mobile home will get me there. It takes four tries before I can get my car started. Finally the engine makes a guttural cry of grief, then grumbles louder than the roar of a sick lion. Four loud firebombs blast a gray cloud into the air where the muffler used to be located.

A spire of smoke follows me out of the parking lot as I drive into the sunrise. I am thinking of the sunrise while I sit at the festival seven hours and forty-two CD sales later.

I just had to sing three songs up on what I call *the little kid's stage*. It is small compared to the real stage across the grassy meadow where the big names are playing today. It is settled back just as far from the event as possible, the stands are a little rickety because of the swampy layer of mud they are settled on. Just to my right is a long line of port-a-potties and their smell wafts over once in a while. There's a lady making announcements about a raffle while the crowd oozes toward the next show on the *big kids stage* where all of those around me dream they will be one day. Not me, of course. I'm hoping my car starts so I can get back to my little gravel nightly landing pad and that somewhere along the way, it doesn't explode. It is late in the afternoon. Everybody seems more interested in the little tents with food and some singer way off and so far away, I can barely hear him.

Now, I just have to ask their names, sign my CDs, and listen while they tell me they heard my songs on the radio. Every person seems to think it is important I know this. I haven't even heard them on the radio because my car radio doesn't work. And my cell phone doesn't have internet access. At least this show is country music themed. It is busier than the last one that was some sort of a historical festival where people dressed up like they just stepped out of a medieval castle. Every person that came up to talk to me wanted to know if I played a fife on the disc.

Ducky sent a girl named Courtney to sit with me and collect money. She has black hair and a tattoo on her neck that she says runs all the way from her jaw to her left knee. She keeps pulling up her shirt to expose the big yellow sun surrounding her belly button and half her left breast to the cute guys that come up.

When there is a lull, she is more interested in tapping messages on her cell phone than talking to me.

My eyes are aching. They set my table facing the sun along a long line of wannabe artists who are aspiring to be stars, but have yet to get that hit. I even feel out of place here. I don't want to be a superstar or some country music legend. I just want to sing. I just want my shop.

"Hey, you're Journey Dawn, right?" It is pretty obvious. I look up into the sunshine, squint my eyes and try to wiggle back and forth so that the man whose voice is attached to the shadow will block the sun long enough I can get eye contact. I have two huge poster boards on either side of my table with my CD cover on them and my name.

"Uh, yeah," I say, leaning over to eye the sign and pointing a finger at it. The guy kind of stands back, looks embarrassed. He's really pretty for a guy. He's got dark hair like Drew's, but it is cut super short. His complexion is so flawless I want to reach out and touch it and see if it is real.

I didn't mean to hurt his self-esteem, so I laugh and try for a quick recovery. "I guess really, it's just Journey Dawn Bacon. My boss doesn't think that sounds sexy though, so—" I drop my voice to what I would call a sexy whisper, give it a little twang and say, "it is Journey Dawn." He doesn't look local. He's wearing designer jeans, a cowboy hat and an expensive shirt. His stance is a bit more professional than the guys lined up in front of him. And he laughs without holding back right then instead of looking at me like he has no clue I am trying to be funny.

"Yeah, we've actually met before." He crosses his arms over his chest. "I sat down at your table after you sang at a bar in Ohio. We just talked for a minute. Next thing I know, I'm hearing your songs on the radio."

Courtney holds out her hand to take money. She looks up from her phone, stops and then peers at me from the corner of her eyes.

"I just listened to you sing now. You're good. I mean really good." He hasn't even reached in his back pocket for his wallet yet. He eyes Courtney's outstretched hand, shakes his head. "Well, no, I didn't come over here to buy a CD."

"You don't have to buy anything," I tell him. God knows I couldn't afford to buy the sugar-crusted elephant ear at the little food trailer next to me. "Your smile is enough. Thank you anyway. Maybe I'll see you at Hobie's again." I kind of sit there, smile, wait for him to say what he wants and leave. He doesn't. I see everybody staring at him, kind of eyeing him like they know him.

"Well, Journey Bacon, I'm Sam Littleton."

I stretch out my hand to shake his and he pumps it up and down. "Hi, Sam."

"Well, I'm a part of a band and we're here just stopping in and we thought maybe we could play backup for you when you sing again—today."

"Oh, you must be at the big kids stage," I say.

"Big kids stage?" He tips his head to the side. A classic THE LOOK imprinted on his face.

"Yeah, I'm sorry. Surely you had the big kids table at Thanksgiving in the front of the dining room for the adults and kids over fourteen with China and good silverware. Then, there is the little kids table at the back with the plastic spoons and paper plates. Well, over there with the huge stands and carefully placed in the cool pines is the big kids stage—" I click my tongue and point like a gun at the big venue stage. Then, I turn and point to the smaller one in the swamp. "Over here and three steps from getting eaten by an alligator in the swamp and four steps from the very bowels of hell because there aren't any trees, is the little kids stage. If you can't find it, just follow the waft of the outhouses and it will lead you there. And I appreciate it. But I think—"

I look to the little stage I sang on earlier. "I think I only get one song in on this stage. And my wallet can't afford the other. I don't know if my boss paid for more than one show."

The guy laughs. His eyes light up and make me smile along. He doesn't make fun of whatever I said that was probably stupid and instead, nods behind him. "How about if I can get you on the big kids stage."

"If you can get me on any stage, I will sing," I tell him. "But there has to be a garbage can nearby." Ah, I manage to get a second The Look out of him.

"I get nervous and throw up after every show."

He laughs again, then stops because I'm not laughing. "You're not kidding, are you?"

"No."

I don't know anybody who can just jump in with a singer and play like they've known them all their life. Sam and his band do just that, however, with just a few minor glitches because my timing is off. When I was in college, I had a group of friends who sat around in an old dank bar and we just played whatever we wanted. We were always just a little off, a little off-tune or something that just didn't work. With Billy Gentry, I had to practice three days a week and he still screwed up all the time even when he wasn't drunk.

Maybe I'm just not used to a real, professional band. It was like those little mistakes I make, they just work around them. Sam doesn't seem to care. The whole band just laughs it off right there on the stage without even missing a beat.

"You going to live?" It is their drummer who says that. He has a thick, southern drawl. It sounds like they called him Stoner.

His face is flushed when we are done. He is leaning against a big pole behind the stage, texting somebody on his phone while I vomit into a black trash bin crusted with food.

"Stage fright." Stoner looks up long enough to comment. "That's topophobia, right?"

"Maybe. Mine is glossophobia," I tell him, my words sounding like a drum coming up from the barrel. "I stuttered when I was little. My mother put me in beauty pageants to help me get over it. Man, those judges ground me into the dirt about my appearance, my singing, my speech. After the dust settled, I figured nothing could be worse. Getting up there a few minutes ago isn't so bad. I still get sick, though."

"Yeah, well, that *was* intense."

"Me throwing up or the music?" I mumble. He reaches around, hands me a paper towel and I swipe it across my mouth. *No awkward moment here*, I think sarcastically to myself.

"Your singing. Damn, you didn't even take a breath. And our band with you. It was pretty good." he says. "By the way, it isn't a big deal."

"Pretty good?" I retort. He smiles and bobs his head up and down.

"Okay, we kind of connected, you think?"

"Yeah, it was cool." I have to admit, I enjoyed the cheers. I did not, however, appreciate that they added two more songs. I know my eyes were wide when they started to play them. I sang them a couple times at wedding receptions, so it didn't throw me off too bad. I turned my head slowly around, gave them the same stink-eye the staff would give me in Robert's office.

"It wouldn't be so intense, if you didn't surprise me with the other two songs," I grumble, but with a smile.

"I think Sam was funning with you," he draws in a breath, blows it out. He has brown hair and lots of freckles. When he puffs out his cheeks, he looks like a six year-old boy.

"You mind trying out another song?" he asks me. "I mean, back there at the picnic tables with your guitar? I'll bring mine." He points to a little scrubby area with a rickety, gray picnic table. "I wrote it. Well, I'm writing it. It is a work in progress. I was thinking it might work for your voice. We could play a little, tweak it, and see what comes out."

"Sure." I look at the sky. I suppose I have a few hours before it gets dark. "I just have to leave so I can get home before dark."

"Is your mama waiting up for you, or are we going to have to look for a glass slipper?"

"Huh?" I ask, then catch what Stoner is saying. "No, my ride doesn't even come close to a pumpkin carriage. It looks more like a half-eaten pickle. But I can't stay out past dark because my back lights don't work and Creepy Cal who sold me the car for a hundred and fifty bucks said if I get hit from behind, I'll blow up the better part of Ohio." I bring up my hand and make fireworks with my fingers. "Boom."

"Oh, okay. That's cool."

If I have to choose between laying with my head on Brody Wells's chest in his truck on a hot afternoon or picking guitars on an old table while about eighty people come up and sit down around us, I'd still pick lounging with Brody. Settled in there on the bench with Stoner sitting across from me, our heads bent together and our fingers playing on the strings is a close second. I have always just plucked around until I work up a song. I never had anyone bang back and forth with me, letting me fine-tune the words or wiggle around the musical notes.

"Sorry about the notepaper." He's got it written on a tiny pad of lined paper.

"I usually grab a napkin when an idea pops in my mind," I tell him. "I wrote Exes and Beaus with a felt tip marker on the back of two grocery receipts and a past-due electric bill. This looks like something Beethoven would have written on a tablet compared to mine." We laugh.

Moonlight escapes through the blinds
Falls on images left behind.
Faded pictures from the past
Old memories that didn't last.
Damn the moonlight. Send it away.
I don't, don't, don't want to see our life fade.
Away, Away, Away.
Cross the sky another day.
Chase it away
Away, away, away. Chase the moon away.

"It's called *Chasing the Moon.* I wrote this —I wrote this one night when I came home and found all our old pictures sitting on the kitchen counter, my wife and me," Stoner says. "I'd been gone two weeks on a short tour. The house was dark. The suitcases were gone. I thought my wife had left me. I really, really thought she was gone. We'd had so many stupid fights because I was gone all the time, never home. I really was ready to break down then. I stood there staring at the pictures, those beautiful pictures of us. Then I saw she had placed one picture at a time, from the first minute we met until the most recent all the way to the bedroom. I'm like picking them up one at a time and as I get closer to the bedroom, I think I hear the satin covers shift. And I'm like, there's either a burglar in there or I've got a second chance. And she was there just waiting for me. She said she wanted to leave and couldn't."

The song is insanely haunting. Every note that he plays on his guitar settles into the air. I am terrified I can't do it justice even after we are there three hours. "No, your voice needs to go up, up, up three times, then just let it fade away," he says and I adjust the rhythm, adjust the depth.

Then Stoner just sits back and says: "Okay, just sing it." He gets someone to hold out the tablet of paper in front of me so I can echo what he is playing on his own guitar, a little softer, a few notes behind. It is difficult because I have to mimic his notes and still sing at the same time. His voice joins my own, echoing the words and abruptly, he raises his hand to point me to go stronger, higher, ride the notes upward while he keeps singing the words. I'm pushing myself, trying to please him because I can see in his eyes this song means the world to him. And it is nearly perfect, even the end when we just let it fade away to nothing except the sound of clapping around us.

We knock fists and I am just sitting there with a little smile on my face, not saying anything.

"So what'd you think?" It is Sam sitting behind me, his head bobbing up and down like he likes it too. "You're awfully quiet."

"Oh," I laugh a little, a smile playing on my lips. "I guess I was just thinking. I got up this morning and I thought the world had gone to shit, you know. It's been a rough week. Then I look out my window and I see this beautiful, beautiful sunrise all reds, golds and oranges. I just breathe it in with my eyes. And I'm smiling. And while I'm sitting there staring at it, taking it all in, I realize I'm not thinking anymore that I've got one more crappy day ahead of me. I'm thinking that God must have set up this whole sunrise thing this morning maybe just to get me to smile for the first time in a while. And if I can smile, maybe I can put a bit of sunrise in somebody else's life—

I can change the world one smile at a time. And when I looked out at everybody just now, I saw people smiling. And it did turn out to be a good day, you know?" I sigh because there's just one thing missing in my sunrise. "I just miss my cowboy."

Everybody is real quiet then. I'm used to opening my heart to a crowd. I'm not so sure everyone else was used to it outside of Hobie's and Great Escape Restaurants. So I just shrug. I can't change myself. My eyes turn to the sky and I realize it is nearly seven o'clock. "Listen, this has been fun, but I've got to go." I jump up a little quickly. "Maybe I'll see you guys at another show, we can do this again."

"Yeah," Stoner says. "That'd be great."

Courtney cleans up my table and she follows me out to my car to help me load everything inside. She stuffs in the boxes and one falls to the side and an envelope is exposed on the top.

"Oh, yeah, some guy stopped by," she says real laid back while she snatches up the envelope, hands it to me. "Cowboy hat. Blonde hair. Walked with a swagger. Hotter than holy hell. He was with some guy—or maybe it was a girl. Whatever. He said he'd wait to talk to you, but you looked busy. He left this for you." She kind of looks around, shrugs. "I thought there were two. Maybe not."

It was just another envelope with money inside. Another $100.00.

"He said something about catching up with you so he could get a receipt. I told him I could write him one, but he said he'd get it from you," Courtney tells me. She tugs on an earlobe full of earrings. "He bought one of your CDs."

I would like to say I got out of there at that point. It wasn't that easy. My car wouldn't start and I had to get Sam and his friends to give me a push to get me out of the lot.

They tease me about my lime green chariot with black doors and get a big laugh out of the smoke pouring out of it. I see them fanning their faces until I lose sight of them in my rearview mirror.

Chapter –36

Note to Self: Grow a Set of balls

The cat was out of the bag. At least, those would be the words Delilah uses to describe my situation while standing in front of Hobie's Bar and Grille on Saturday at six in the evening. She is dressed in a prudent skirt, button-up blouse, and white pumps with dust on them from the gravel parking lot. She is twisting a little with her foot behind her, trying to wipe the tiny flecks off with a baby blue Kleenex.

She won't come inside and there is a long and meandering line of people getting their driver's licenses checked at the front door by cute thirty-something cowboys and handing Courtney the cover charges. Delilah's Bacon Valley United Church roots will not allow her to set one foot within the doorway of what I have personally heard Reverend Wilson call the front door of the very bowels of Hell.

Delilah's practical clothing is in stark contrast to the boots and jeans and tank tops of the girls staring at us in line. They keep taking pictures and I can imagine how this is going to go over on their social networks. To make matters worse, Smalltalk is standing with her in full police uniform, arms crossed and legs splayed like he's getting ready to break up a fight. He hasn't said a word.

"What? You've never disagreed with your mama?" I ask two girls who had moved up to hear the conversation. "Can you give us a moment?" One girl nods her head knowingly. I give her a geeky thumbs up.

"Well, Journey Dawn, the cat is now out of the bag. What are you going to do?" Delilah says ignoring the crowd.

"I don't know what that means." I just say it. Because I really have no clue.

"It means that your secret it out," she says. Then I get the historical account. "They used to put kittens in bags and sell them as piglets. When the buyer opened the bag, let the cat out—"

"I got it," I interrupt her. "I didn't want you to know I was working at a bar. Who told you?"

"Singing at a bar," she counters, waving a hand at the building. "This is different. I raised you better than —this."

"Who told you?"

"Robert. If you really want to know. He is worried about you like we all are, disappearing without a trace." I peer behind her at Smalltalk and he has the tiniest of back and forth shake to his head. Obviously, the entire cat has not been let out of the bag. He never told her he knew where I was. *Great*, I think sarcastically, *even the cops are afraid of my mom.*

I sigh. "You raised me to be independent, Delilah," I tell her. I don't have time to fight. I have to get my makeup on. I have to check to make sure my guitar's tuned. "You taught me how to sing and try not to be scared in front of people. I haven't been able to accomplish any of this my whole life because Robert was always around. Now he's not and I'm taking baby steps."

"Who are you?" she says and she isn't listening one bit. She is just staring at my jean shorts and tank top, my cowboy boots and my hair all laying down instead of plopped up on top.

"I don't know *me* either," I say. I see Ducky pushing himself through a bunch of people clustered at the door staring at us. He waves his hand at me. "I'm getting there. You can either figure it out with me or go stick with Robert. I've got to go."

"We'll discuss it before early service at church tomorrow morning." I hear her say. The 1980s retro band that is playing before me is about halfway through their program. I listened to them play this afternoon and remembered the sequence of songs.

"No, I don't want to get up that early—"

"Journey Dawn, promise me you'll be there tomorrow morning."

I see Delilah's eyes. I can't tell them no, so I bob my head up and down. "I promise."

Ducky swoops me up and herds me away from my mother like a baying calf through a barn door. My tummy is already jumpy. But he makes a remark, "You haven't been discussing contracts with other music labels, have you?"

"I don't even know what that is, Ducky. I just show up and sing or sign CDs. The rest of the stuff, I leave to you."

He is walking behind me, looking irritated and I'm not sure why. "You need to run everything through me, you hear me? You can't just fly with any bands that walk your way. You know how many have contacted us? We've got to take things slowly. You're stuck with Gentry for a while, stuck with us. We're all in head deep. You leave now and—"

"I'm not going anywhere. But you know how I feel about singing with Gentry. He's a shit."

"Well, you should care. We'll discuss the issue after you sing. Just remember, I got a lot of money invested in your career right now and in this joint. I've got contracts with other bands coming here for the next two years expecting the cameras and the promotion. Don't make me lose your trust if you're getting courted by other agencies."

I almost laugh. The idea that other bands would want a shithole in the wall waitress/singer like me is ludicrous. I stop myself because Ducky has the same expression on his face I've seen on John Wells when I came to visit Brody at the barn that day.

"You got about twenty minutes. Remember, we are taping *Exes and Beaus* and your last song, *Mama's Little Rebel.*"

"I got it."

"You know what?" he says to me. "I know you do. I've got no doubt you won't ever let me down if I don't let you down, right?"

"I just might kill Billy. That doesn't count, right?" I kid him. He rolls his eyes.

"Wait until you're off stage. I might be an attorney, but if you murder him on camera, there's not much I can do."

Just as I am about to get on stage, I get my first call on my new phone. I almost don't pick it up; I had just started to get up from a chair in Hobie's office. It is a woman's voice, familiar and she asks who this is as if she thought she was calling somebody and didn't recognize my voice.

"Is this Gayle?" I ask. "You dialed me. This is Journey. How'd you get my number?"

"I'm not Gayle."

I pause. The voices are almost the same. I tell her: "I'm sorry, I just got this new number. I think you're trying to reach someone else."

There is a long, thick silence, then the woman takes a breath. "I saw that someone with your number called a few times, didn't leave a message. Before you hang up. Are you the one with the silver purse?"

I pause, take a deep breath. Tina Lavelle. She had written a classified ad in the Winford newspaper. "Is this Tina Lavelle?" I ask cautiously.

"I am."

"I suppose you would like to see it. May I ask how you heard about the purse?"

"I think it belonged to my mom. I just found out she was from Winford, Ohio before she came here."

"Oh," I say. "From the information I got, I don't think the girl that owned this purse had any kids. She was only seventeen when she was killed in a car wreck. Maybe it isn't the one you are looking for," I say. "I just don't want to waste your time."

There was silence again. "Can we meet somewhere?"

I jot down the address to a little roadside restaurant off the highway in northern West Virginia. It is only an hour and a half away. My mind is churning with the vagueness of the conversation. Could this be a trick by Benjamin Dodge? Maybe he wants to get me out in the middle of an old strip mine, murder me, and dump me down an old well.

I don't have a lot of time to consider the different possibilities. I can hear Hobie introducing me and I've got to get up there and announce Billy Gentry's band. I go up on stage and force myself to lock eyes with the crowd once in a while. I make Hobie promise to set aside a small dance floor for the Coalville line dancers. He keeps true to his word and builds a small real wood floor so folks can get up and dance if they want. Lots of folks do because the cameras are always skimming out over them and they get to be on our local cable station.

Tonight isn't any different. I sing my songs and smile even though Billy Gentry is out of sequence and forgets two songs.

He makes a remark about my ass being too small twice and insinuates I am off-key three times.

And I don't like it when he forces me to sing the duets that Drew and I used to sing. But I put on a stiff upper lip and grin my way through the words, even when he forgets his and I have to prompt him. I excuse the "oh, baby" that he keeps doing to me with a creepy wink and implying that I sleep with him and call him Big Daddy.

Then at the end, I sit down on the stage so I'm almost down with the crowd sitting at the tables and standing in the back. I pull the mic down and lay it on the floor gently next to me and plop my guitar on my lap.

I've got one foot on some guy's seat and I can see he's grinning because the camera scans across him. "Tonight, we're taping this last song. I thought you all might want to be a part of it, hear yourselves on TV and maybe the radio. Do most of you know the words to Exes and Beaus?" I can hear them cheer. "So here's what we're going to do—"

I sang my heart out and at the end, I had them sing my part and I work my way up on a couple notes while they do just like Stoner and I did when we sang the other day. I can tell Billy doesn't like this. He wasn't expecting me to sit down with the crowd, sing just to them. He has no clue what to do with his drums and he is pissed.

It is magical, though, and the crowd goes wild at the end. I stand up and take my bow, hold my hand out and stand back to show off the band. I turn just in time to see Billy Gentry standing up with his arms held aloft in the air, his body gyrating like he is humping the air. I don't know what the hell he is doing while he walks up next to me and in the microphone makes a snort and says: "Be a good girl, Ditzy, get Big Daddy a damn beer and be quick about it."

Living in a car for two weeks has been quite humbling. It makes my back hurt, I don't slept well.

It is only one thing among many the last two months that I have succumbed to because of a half-witted man and people telling me I didn't stick up for myself. I can usually remain quite calm. However, I hit my limit. I close my eyes, count to ten like Delilah relates will help calm the temper. It doesn't work.

I simply draw in a breath and turn to Billy with my mic still on loud and clear. "Listen, I stand up here tonight and I sing my heart out for an hour and a half. The entire time, you sit behind me and bang that stupid-ass set of drums like a four year-old and as the night goes on and you get closer to your ninth or tenth bottle of beer, you start treating me like an ex-wife. But I'm not your ex-wife. And I don't have to put up with your snorts and your mean remarks so I get my monthly alimony check. I've put up with your shitty remarks for four years. I'm not going to do it anymore. Because between you and me—and this crowd behind us that's going to hear what I have to say whether they like it or not, you need this job more than I do, you realize that don't you? I could walk away right now and my life wouldn't be any worse for the wear than it is right now. Hell, it would be better because I wouldn't have to listen to you call me ditz and tits and dumb blonde. You aren't my Big Daddy. I have never slept with you and never will. Ever." Then Billy quite possibly makes the worst mistake of his life. He calls me "baby" for the last time.

"Oh, baby, I love it when you talk dirty to me."

"Dirty? You want dirty? Dirty is what you did to Drew. Dirty is stealing five-hundred dollars cash out of the box and blaming it on him. You think I don't know this? Here's more dirty for you. For the last two damn weeks, I've been living in a Pinto because my ex-boyfriend kicked me out of my house and took away my car keys." I take in a breath, heave it back out and narrow my eyes to slits.

I've lost my store, my mom thinks I'm going to hell for singing in a bar, and the guy I wrote every love song from the time I was six dumped me. Honestly, I can put my thumb out and hitch a ride out of this town in three seconds and I've got the world ahead of me. You, on the other hand, are only three steps away from your tenth beer tonight, the closest ditch, and a park bench to sleep on. You are getting a second chance. I don't know if God gives out thirds. You screw this one up and I'm thinking you're done. Done. You seeing eye to eye with me?"

I stop, hold up two fingers to my eyes then point to Billy. "So it's like this, bitch, why don't you go get me a beer for a change, huh? I like it cold and I like it dark. So wiggle your fat ass over to the bar and bring it to me on a tray like a good boy. Then, just so we're clear, if you ever, ever insult me again with any of your rude sexist, blonde-woman jokes again or you even fucking look at me sideways like you are checking out my ass in front of the crowd or you belch or spit or blow your nose up on the stage, I'm out of here. And you'll be back to sucking pee water out of the ditch out back again. You hear me?"

He doesn't answer. The crowd is silent, taking in every word I say, probably damning me for being rude to a legend. So I turn around in the silence. I lay my guitar down and I walk over where Billy keeps his stupid old baseball bat. I reach over and pick it up. I let it dangle in my fingertips while he smirks at me, his hand coming up to stifle his laugh. "I can't hear you, maybe you need to be a little louder, huh, sweetie?"

"You know what? I've been spending the entire time worried about growing a pair of balls like everybody says I need to do when the whole time, all's I really needed was a baseball bat and a damn good lawyer."

Then I lean back with that bat and I bash it into his priceless stupid drums as hard as I can until the drums, the chair and Billy Gentry make a wheeling turn off the stage.

"Maybe you hear me now?" I say, toss the bat on the floor, pick up my guitar, and walk off the stage. I hear Hobie just screaming at me: "What did you do? What did you do?" I'm stepping backward while he's coming at me. He has stepdaddy written all over his face. A beer bottle comes flying over my head from the stage and I realize he's got more things to worry about than me right then.

"I'm going to sue your little ass!" Billy screams at me.

"Sue me? Did you not hear a single word I said. I've got nothing, you idiot, except the shirt off my back." I stop (and later thanked God that I had on a tank top underneath my shirt) and I shimmy out of my shirt and toss it in the air at him. "There now you don't have to sue me. You've got what I got left." I launch into Hobie's office, snatch up my purse while I make a panicked escape out the back door.

Fifteen minutes later, I am sitting on guardrail off the side of the highway about a mile from Hobie's. My car won't start. The battery is dead and I can't stick around because people are filing out after the show. I can't call Delilah or Robert or Andrea. Brody and Bella hate me. I've really got nobody at all. And cars are parked all around my little vehicle so I can't even hide inside.

"Hey, Drew. It's Journey," I am sobbing into my phone answering machine. It is call number three. The other two, nobody answers. "I need you. I need you bad. I'm sitting on the side of the highway about a mile from the bar. I've got nowhere to go. Can you please come get me?" That is the message I left on the phone at the gas station where he works. I didn't think he would pick up. I figured I would sit there all night. But something clicks on the other end.

"Yeah, I'll be there."

Chapter –37

You're like a little dove that's suddenly free. Me, I'm like a robin caught in a snare. Baby, take my hand. Pull me out of here—

Drew has a cot in the back of the gas station. I stand there and stare at it. I am still hiccupping after my cry all the way on the motorcycle ride from Coalville to Dan Keyes Gas and Used Car Sales. "You can share it with me or sleep on the floor. Just so you know, there are cockroaches and rats. You know what a cockroach is right?"

"Yes, I do." I look at the old linoleum floor. I can't tell if it is supposed to be black or if that is just dirt crusted on it from years of dirty shoes. I'm afraid to put down my purse on the linoleum, but I lay it on the rickety, aluminum cot. "I'm sorry, Drew. I should have done things differently from the start. I'm just not—I guess I just don't know how. Everybody's right. I'm an idiot."

"I missed you, too," he tells me. It doesn't make sense, but he kind of smiles.

"Oh, God," I say and start to cry again. "Everybody is going to hate me, think I am the worst person alive."

"There are a thousand people better at this than me, Journey." Drew holds his hands out to his sides. "I'm not the consoling type. I just say, put this behind you. Move on." He points to the bed. "Listen, I have to get up early tomorrow. I've got three cars lined up that we need to pull parts from. I got to go to bed."

I want to tell him that maybe we can just hop right back on his bike and head down Interstate 75 until we just get too tired and want to stop. "Do you still think of going to Nashville or California or—" I ask instead.

I look around the dank confines of this room that is smaller than my old bathroom. It is like a prison cell and smells like old car oil and stinky socks.

"Journey, don't you get it? This is it for me. This is the end of the line." I realize then that any venture Drew was ever going to take into the sunset was only in my mind. "What happened to that boyfriend of yours?" he asks. "He had you set up pretty fine by my standards. Hell, you were driving a Corvette. Pretty dresses all the time, satin sheets to come home to at night."

"That all belongs to him so he can take it away from me if I don't obey his every command."

"Maybe you're just spoiled, Journey, I've got to be honest, I don't think Cal's going to like me having anybody here. I—can take you wherever you want. I just can't think of anything that would make me pick between that and this." He waves a hand around him, encompassing the room.

"That's fine. I get it." I feel empty inside. I realize maybe Drew is scared Robert will take something away from him now too. Even Drew doesn't want me around. "But just so you know there are worse things than dirty floors and dark rooms and sharing a too-small bed with a friend."

"It isn't a bed. It's an old army cot. I'll have to think about that one."

"Okay, he's all yours," I say, picking up my purse from the bed and turning toward the door. "I don't need you. I don't need anybody. Just be prepared, Robert has a way of finding those little wounds and poking them once in a while. He calls me dumbass and a ditz and tells me not to talk if we are in a crowd. My lips are too big, my head too small. I'm too skinny and I don't do blowjobs right," I huff.

"When I sing I sound like a frog trilling in spring. He gives me presents so he can take them away. He took the car and the house and my cell phone. He took my best friend." I stop to take a breath. "That would be you. Not the chick he screwed."

Drew is just staring at me with a bored look on his face. His eyes are shining blue beads in the room. "And when I found Brody Wells and realized what love really was, Robert realized I didn't have anything. So he stole their family farm from them to have something to keep me in his pocket. Last month, he said if I'd marry him, he'd refinance their loan. I can't ever tell Brody or anybody or the deal is done."

"You're telling me right now."

I push my hands to my head, feel like screaming. "You're the only person in the world right now that I can trust. And it is probably too late. It doesn't matter. Robert tossed me out to teach me another lesson. I'm sure he was never going to give the farm back to that family." I am so frustrated, my hands are tingling. "Drew, I've been sleeping in my car. All my checks are going to the bank Robert owns. This place looks like heaven right now compared to being alone and worrying about what I'm going to do with winter a few months away." I let out a high-pitched screamy growl, throw my hands into the air. "I shouldn't have to tell you. You know Robert. I'm just afraid he'll do something to you."

I don't really expect Drew to do anything. By his stance he is just patiently waiting for me to walk out the door. I shift my purse on my shoulder, shuffle my feet. I'm about to tell him thanks for the ride when he finally speaks.

"Journey, that's already been done," he says. "Robert's tornado of terror already clipped me, baby, why do you think I'm here?" Drew holds up his hands to display the bleak room.

"You think Robert paid Billy Gentry to get you out of my way?" I waver there, my eyes darting back and forth at the floor while the flood waters of realization surround me. "Robert was at the bar every night after he blackmailed me, shooting the breeze like they were best buddies. I bet it was Gentry who was spying, taking the pictures Robert used to coerce me." I look up, catch Drew's eyes. "I'm so sorry. If I wasn't there, you'd still have your job."

"It wasn't so great turning hamburgers until two in the morning and singing to the five same drunks who are in there all the time."

"Oh, come on, you liked singing with me." I laugh a little, look over his shoulder toward the door. "You liked it when we had washrag fights and mop battles. You liked banging new songs off each other."

"That part was fun." He points to the bed. "Just stay. I'd like to see him take away this pigsty. We'll figure something out. If Hobie fires you, we'll get gigs somewhere else. You were always so much better at dreaming than me. You're like a little dove that's suddenly free."

"Oh," I gasp, "that sounds like a cool song, Drew. *You were always so much better at dreaming than me,*" I sing softly, thinking what notes would work around the words. *"You're like a little dove that's suddenly free. Me, I'm like a robin caught in a snare. Baby, take my hand. Pull me out of here—"*

"Yeah, see?" he says. "Listen to you. You're an hour out of hitting rock bottom and you're already dreaming your way out again." I'm trying to remember the words, remember the pitch of my voice.

"I think delusional would better describe me," I kid with him. "Did I tell you I got to sing at the big kids stage last week with a real band?"

"Who was it?"

"I dunno." I shrug. "There were a bunch of people playing. They all sounded the same to me. I don't know if they even said they had a name for their band. That is not the point. The point is that if I can do it once, *we* can do it again. It doesn't' matter. I need a pen and paper to write this down. Go get your guitar. And paper. Grab a pen—I'm pulling us out of here."

I fall asleep sitting up on the bed with my guitar in my lap. I am halfway slouched over Drew who is trying to hum the song at four in the morning. He is laying down on his back behind me with his hands folded on his belly and snoring. I remember strumming my guitar to the beat of his snores, then the beat of his heart against my back before my eyes close. The next think I remember is the raucous sound of electric wrench seeping under the closed door.

It is Sunday morning. I awaken Drew at half past nine. "Would it be too much to drop me off at the Bacon Valley United Church out off the highway by ten?"

He looks at me with sleepy eyes. They scream *I just woke up with a crazy woman.* I don't think he is going to take me and maybe I don't mind too much. I've got nothing to wear but what I wore last night—blue jean shorts, tank top, and the cowboy boots I'm shoving on my feet right now. But I think I would rather turn a few heads with inappropriate attire worn to church than have my mother mad because I broke a promise, missed sitting with her in the pew after our talk. "That's okay, I'll walk or hitch a ride."

"Yeah, you won't be doing that." Drew is still wearing the clothes he wore last night. He runs a comb through his hair. He has gotten it cut. It is short on the sides and long along the top. He looks nice and clean-cut except the rips in his white t-shirt and his old tennis shoes.

We hop on his motorbike. For almost the entire ride, I wonder why he bothers to comb his hair if he is going to get it windblown anyway. Then I wonder what it would be like if he was Brody right now and I was hanging on to him, shoved up close with my arms around his waist.

It is 10:30 when we get to the church. Drew's motorcycle screams up to Main Street and stops just before the parking area, a small asphalt lot that almost abuts the white-wood church. He parks under a tree and I slide off while he cuts the engine. I hear the organ music already playing the first song, Amazing Grace, and I'm hoping Delilah saves me a seat. There are just a few late people filing inside. I try to catch up to them by weaving in and out of the parked cars so I can slide into the church, concealed somewhat by their shadows.

I don't get three steps away from the cement sidewalk when I feel a hand on my arm. It is a quick snatch that happens between a minivan and a white suburban. There are huge old trees above my head and their shadows are playing on the cars behind me and now, on Robert Ironwood's face.

"Where do you think you are going?" He snaps at me.

"Robert, let me go," I tell him. He is wheeling me back, making me take steps in reverse. "I'm going to church. I promised Delilah I would be here today.

"No, you are not doing this to her." He looks up, his angry glare settling on Drew by the road. "You're not doing this to my family. Do you even have a clue the embarrassment you are putting us through right now? Where the hell have you been for the last three weeks?"

"None of your business," I spit back. I am trembling, though, my heart is pounding horse hoofs on my chest. "What do you care, you kicked me out of my house."

I know Drew can't see us. He is busy poking something on his bike and there are rows of cars between. I could scream, but where would that lead? Robert has cut his hair, it is short like the ugly police buzz-cuts. It makes his ears look big and his eyebrows thick.

"I won't allow it," he spats at me. "You cannot come waltzing into church after one of your all-night binges whoring it up with whoever you bummed a bed with the night before. Look at you." He leans back, waves his free hand at my jean shorts and tank top. "You look like you slept on the floor, like you've been out drugging it up again."

"Let go, Robert." I am sweating suddenly. He is so much bigger than little me—I think by about a hundred and twenty pounds in weight and eight inches in height. I can feel his fingers pinch into the flesh just above my elbow. I always give in to him. Now is no different. It is like when Delilah's cat caught a little white-footed mouse in his teeth last June. The mouse just lay there still and dangling. He doesn't move. He knows at some point there is no getting away, no use fighting anymore.

So like the little mouse or a stupid, loyal dog I can feel my body instinctively stop pulling away. My arms lay at my sides. My shoulders fall and I just stand there waiting to be eaten by Robert even when he doesn't let go.

"Let's not make a scene," he says. "You go home, get yourself prettied up, lose last night's screw on the bike and we'll talk." But his fingers are starting to bite harder into my skin, his grasp slightly bending my wrist in an awkward position. I see him look to his left and right. Then he gives me a little shove backward.

I take two steps and almost fall. I right myself only to see Robert taking two steps toward me. He sticks out his pudgy hand and gives me another shove right on my chest.

I don't know what to do so I take the steps backward he affords me and start to turn to go to Drew's bike. "I'm leaving," I tell him. "Robert, lay off, I'm leaving." Still, I see him step forward again, spewing out a few whispered curses before his hand comes out to push me back.

He keeps looking over his shoulder to make sure no one can see him from the church. But he doesn't see Bella Johnson marching up from between the cars, her hands in fists and her eyes dead set on him.

"If you do that again, I swear to God, Ironwood, I will make you cry so hard they are going to hear you baying like a baby pig at the First Baptist Church in Winford."

Bella is standing not two feet away from his left side. She is wearing a suit coat and khaki pants and has a bible in one hand. I don't doubt for one second she is telling the truth. Maybe with that bible, she's got God on her side. Robert must have thought so too because when she takes another step, he automatically drops his arms. Robert looks up. I see his eyes span the distance between another set of cars. It is Bella's Aunt Rita and her husband and kids. I don't think he realizes there are always a few people that leave after Sunday school or who come out to smoke cigarettes between the services.

"Back off, Buttercup." Buttercup. That's what Bella used to call Robert in high school. It made him so mad. I could see the fury in his eyes right then. I swore, he was getting ready to wind up his fist. He doesn't though. Instead he pokes a finger at Bella.

"You better watch your step," he snorts.

"It looks like it might be the other way around, Ironwood," she says, nodding toward her aunt and another man who had climbed out of his car. "Hop off that throne, baby boy. Your days of being king are over."

Robert seems to soak in the hard gazes he is receiving. His eyes dart back and forth from the parking area to Bella. Then he takes a step back, waves his finger at me. "I'm not done with you." He threatens.

Bella just laughs, "Yeah, you are," she tells him. She stares at him, deep brown eyes expressionless. I think she scares him. He twists his lips, spits on the ground.

"Bitch." He turns on his feet, however, strutting away like he won some battle.

"Where are you going?" Bella growls behind me. "You're not even going to say a thank you for saving your life?"

I am winding my way back to Drew. He is standing near his bike, holding his arms out to his sides like he is asking me what the hell happened. I hardly turn to Bella's voice. "I could have handled him on my own."

"No, no you wouldn't."

"I'm not going to church, that's for sure. I don't even know why I thought I could."

"Why do you let him bully you?"

I stop in my tracks and pivot on my feet. "Why do you think, Bella?" I gripe. "Why did I let you bully me my whole life? Because I'm scared of you. And I'm terrified of him. Being batted around between you two has become a way of life for me. I realize that without it, I've got nothing." She is eyeballing me, not saying a word. "Oh, come on. How am I going to stop him? He is like a bulldozer rolling his way to me, taking out everything in his path. I can't take a sledgehammer to him in front of everybody. They'll have me committed. He's been telling everybody I'm on drugs. He's one step away from taking something from everybody I know. I don't know how to fight that. Hell's bells." I wave a hand at Drew. "I'm terrified now he'll take him away too."

Bella turns her attention to Drew. She narrows her eyes. "He's your boyfriend now?"

"No, of course not," I say. "He's just been taking care of me."

"Why don't you let Brody take care of you?"

I can't do any more than throw my hands into the air. "You know what is at stake here. And don't tell me I have to grow a set of balls. You were standing in that back room when Robert threatened me." I drop my hands, drop my voice. I know I'm waving my hands in the air to make up for the loud whisper so no one else overhears. "Every second I'm not with Brody, I'm buying time, don't you see? The second I reach out and try to touch him, Robert will know and he will take—take stuff away. You know what? I appreciate your help, I really do. But I can take care of myself."

"And how is that working for you now?" she says to my back while I walk away. I don't answer, just flip her off with my middle finger.

"Nice, Bacon," she hisses. "Nice to see some of your old self coming back. Maybe if you got rid of the whipped puppy look, you might scare off old Robert yourself. If I bullied you. You bullied back."

"Screw off, Bella." I turn again and stomp three feet away. My eyes are on Drew, I feel Bella's steps behind me more than hear them over sounds of a dog barking and the sounds of a church bell uptown.

"You know he would walk through fire for you."

I stop. I know she is referring to Brody. "I'm not so sure about that," I say. She didn't see the glares I got from him and the anger well up in his eyes when we talked last.

"I wouldn't even if he knew the truth and he won't. Because it would be a mistake to tell him."

"Why."

"Because he would either laugh and say I deserved it or do something stupid like try to get back at Robert."

"More stupid than what you are doing now?"

I finally put on the brakes, turn once more. I've got my hand out as if it would stop her from stepping close.

"Why are you doing this Bella? Why don't you just leave me alone? Brody doesn't like me, okay? Not once did we ever say 'I love you.' It was all just—a quick thing. I honestly can't fix something that isn't broken because it was never there at all in the first place." I am cringing inside. I'm just not one to open my heart one on one in person. On the stage, okay. But standing there staring Bella in the eye and talking about my feelings is insufferable.

"Because I think *it* was there. And I think you can fix what's broke."

Chapter –38

Note to Self: Meet Tina Lavelle at diner

I don't know why I am thinking about Bella's words when I walk out to the garage, hold my hands over my ears three hours later. I didn't have a single drink, but I feel hung over. I'm trying really hard not to think about what I'm going to do tomorrow or the next day if I'm fired. I just need to get away for a while.

"Drew!" I have to yell his name twice before he stops, looks up from the tire he is pulling from a car. "Can you take me to my car before noon? I'm supposed to meet with somebody in West Virginia tomorrow. I want to sneak in and get my car when there's nobody at the bar today."

"Yeah, whatever."

"Hey, let me ask you something." I kneel down, balance myself with a knuckle on the floor and look an impatient Drew in the eyes. "I told you about the dance card and the purse, right? Delbert gave it to me before he died. It belonged to a girl killed in a wreck."

"Uh huh."

"Well, I have this weird idea that the woman who actually owned it didn't die. They didn't find her body."

"Why would you say that?"

"Because her daughter called me the other day," I say. "But that's not my question. Even if it isn't and this lady is related to the girl who died, I want to give it back to the family. Do you think I should talk to Delbert's family first? It belonged to him. She gave it to him."

"Why are you asking me this?" Drew pulls in a breath, plays with the wrench like it is a gun and he is shooting me with it. "Does this have to do with you screaming at that woman in the church parking lot?"

"Well, when I talked to the daughter on the phone, she sounded exactly like Gayle Wells," I say. "It wasn't Gayle. I never heard Delbert or any of them mention any family outside Ohio."

"You think Delbert had another daughter?" Now Drew is interested, I see a spark in his eyes when I nod. "And you're just not going to let it go, are you." It wasn't a question. "Maybe you should just let it go. Maybe if Delbert did have a family, he didn't want anyone to know. Maybe that is why he gave you the purse in the first place. Maybe it wasn't that weird promise at all. He just didn't want anybody in his family to dig it out of some drawer some day and find out about it—oh—" Drew stops then. I see the comprehension on his face. "That's kind of what you do, isn't it, find stuff? And he knew that."

"Yeah, Drew," I answer, standing up. "That's what Delbert said I was really, really good at, finding stuff."

"I'm not a gambler," Drew says, then nods to the garage. "Obviously, I don't take many risks. I'm really more the type of person that believes in fate. There are a million things that can happen with every footstep you make. Go left, you have one path. Go right, you got another. The direction you go makes things either happen or not. But if I had to make a call on this and chance putting my foot out, I would think there was a reason he gave you the purse and it had to do with what he knew you did best. Here's something. Just don't tell Delbert's family right off. Just tell them you have a buyer interested and ask them to come along since it belonged to their family. If they do, they do. If they don't, let fate take care of the situation." He starts to wave me away, then heaves a puff of air. "And I'm not stupid. Part of this is wanting to see the Brody dude, right?"

"Is it that evident?"

He doesn't answer, just rolls his eyes. "Girl, I know you better than I know my own mama." Strangely, I realize I know him just as well. I suppose he had taken Andrea's place as Best Friend a long time ago.

Still, I really, really don't think Gayle and Brody will meet me at the diner. I just say: *Hey, I have someone interested in the silver purse your dad gave me. I thought you might want to meet and see what she wants for it.*

It is half past six when I get to the restaurant. The gravel lot has five or six cars parked around the perimeter of the building. Tina Lavelle tells me she has a white four door car with a bumper sticker on the back that says: I LOVE MOUNTAINEERS. It has a heart sticker next to it. I told her I was wearing ripped up jeans, red flip-flops and a pink tank top. I round the parking lot once just to make sure I didn't see Beady Eyes or Bushy Hair's black car. I do see Tina Lavelle's car. I'm really not sure if Gayle will show up. I don't see any of the vehicles they usually drive.

When I was about twelve, Delilah had this saying: *you're in for the shock of your life.* She said it all the time even when the person she was saying it to wasn't really going to be that surprised. *Oh, you're in for the shock of your life! Reverend Wilson's birthday is next week.* Or maybe in December when chilly, freezing weather was imminent: *You're in for the shock of your life! It's going to snow next week.*

Consequently, I never quite grasped what kind of jolt a person would really receive when the saying was actually used in proper circumstances. Like right now, when Tina Lavelle steps out of the driver's side of her car and extends a hand toward me. I am trying to think of a word that will describe it. Dumbstruck just doesn't cut it.

She is an exact replica of Gayle Wells with twenty or so years added on to her face. And she looks akin to the little girl in the picture tucked into the dance card purse.

"You must be Journey, the girl I am meeting about the purse?"

"I am." I can see over Tina's shoulder to the car behind her. I am watching as the window rolls slowly down. An elderly woman is peering out. I try not to stare at her. Her eyes are as wide as oranges, just like Delbert described Molly Lender. I don't know if she realizes that my own eyes are getting wider and wider by the minute, but she rolls the window back up. I quickly turn them away and focus on the daughter.

"Do you have it with you?" she asks. I pull the silver purse from my own purse. Thunderstruck, I am thinking. Yes, that is the word I am looking for to describe how I feel right now while I hand the purse to her. She takes it, rolls it around in her hand. "Now where did you get this?"

"Um, from Delbert Johnson. He was a friend who passed away recently."

"Um," she pulls out what looks like an old picture, gray and white and holds it up next to the purse. "Mom had a picture of it. See, here?"

I don't need to look at it. I do anyway.

"Mom always talked about her daddy giving her this old dance card purse. She lost it or gave it away. I really didn't know. She never talked much about her side of the family. For some reason, she didn't keep anything from her childhood. You know, the normal things like an old teddy bear or a picture of her family," Tina Lavelle is telling me. I'm just standing here, accessing the situation, wondering if I shouldn't just take the damn purse and run. Because what if Gayle shows up? What then? I have not really thought it all out.

"I couldn't help but think it was probably the only link to her past because her mother and father died when she was young," Tina goes on. "I just knew I wanted to find it for her. Maybe it would give her some peace or enjoyment. She would talk about it and get this misty look in her eyes. She said it had her initials on the front—M.L. for Mary Lavelle. I thought that maybe I could find it and give it to her for Christmas this year. I had no idea —no clue that there was any past connected to it so I ran the advertisement in a few newspapers looking for the purse. But somebody called on the phone while I was out shopping one day. Mom answered. It was someone looking for the purse too."

I hear the door to the car opening. I see the woman inside pulling herself up to a standing position. She is tall and although her hair is silver white, the resemblance of the picture from the newspaper I tucked into my purse this morning of the dead Molly Lender is uncanny.

"She doesn't know," the elderly lady says directly to me.

"What doesn't she know, mom?" Tina turns, tips her head to one side, turns her attention behind her to her mother.

"No, sweetheart, *you*. *You* don't know. But it is time that you do know the truth."

We are sitting at a table inside the little diner. It smells of bacon and sausage and hamburger. The little table we are sitting in has booth seats. I am sitting on one side, the mother and daughter are on the other.

We order coffees. Mary's face is pale while she takes the purse from her daughter to inspect it. It is then, I hear a familiar voice near the front doors.

It is Bella Johnson saying something to Gayle while they come in the doors. I turn. It is John, Brody and Bella first then Gayle tugging Cayce by the hand. They are all standing there, eyes working across the room to the table where we are sitting.

I know the sweat is beading on my forehead. "I didn't think they were coming," I say to no one in particular. "I mean, I asked them. I shouldn't have. I am so sorry. I just didn't think it out—again." I realize I should have never asked them. Was it not enough I was screwing up one family? I see Mary Lavelle's eyes wander to the front of the restaurant. She has a hand over her lips. "That must be one of Delbert's children? Oh, my."

Tina turns then. It is like I can feel the tension, the strange staggering quiet between the tables. It is surrounded by the clang of fork to plate, of chatter of the waitresses, a muffled country music song playing from an old boombox on the counter.

"Mom, what's going on?" she asks, her eyes on Gayle, never turning.

"That's Gayle Wells," I say. "She is Delbert Johnson's daughter." I can see all four of them staring at our table. The only thing I know to do is rise up. "Do you want me to go get them?" It was a rather stupid question. However, I feel like I have to ask it. I feel like I have been invited to a party, then asked a hundred friends who were uninvited to join me.

"Who is Delbert Johnson?" Tina asks.

Mary nods at me. "Yes, bring them over. I think we should all sit down and I'll explain it."

We all sit down at the table, seven people smooshed into a booth, clumsily thrown together with absolutely no elbow room. Cayce lunges for me, wraps her arms around my waist until I sit her on my lap.

I make a graceless attempt at introducing everyone over Cayce's head who smile cordially at each other. Now I am sitting between Bella and Mary and hugging my purse to my side for lack of anywhere else to place it.

"Well, I should probably let you know that I knew your father back when we were about seventeen," Mary starts out. She smiles softly like she has some wonderful memory, then reaches out and pats Gayle's hand delicately. "Journey here tells me you are his daughter."

Gayle nods, looks at John and then back to me. Cayce is running her fingers along my neck, tickling me so I take a moment, dig into my purse until I find a half-chewed pencil so she can draw a picture on a napkin. I wish I could crawl under the table and I'm glad I have Cayce as a shield while John Wells's eyes bore down on me with the lackluster expression of someone who despises another.

"I was sixteen when I met Delbert. He used to race cars along the back roads along with my fiancé, Ben Dodge. He was so funny, so sweet. It was fun for us city folks to come out to the country." She smiles, looks at Brody and Mary rubs a hand across her face. "He looked a lot like you back then." I follow her gaze and I see Brody looking at me. His face turns red and he fidgets a little in his chair. "Once in a while we would meet," she goes on. "But the timing was off for us. I was to be married in only a few months. My mother found out I was pregnant and she insisted I marry Ben. He had money, you know. He was very well off. I tried to tell her that the baby might not be his, but she simply wouldn't listen. She wouldn't believe her daughter had been with more than one man—or any man at all," she sighed. "She was controlling. Ben was very abusive. Neither he nor his family wanted me to marry him. Mother wouldn't listen when I told her he had raised his hand to me, threatened to toss me down the stairs to kill my baby."

She closes her eyes, opens them again and smiles softly at Tina. "I was so young, so naïve. I didn't know what to do. It was Delbert and a young man named Andy Fenton who saved my life. It was storming one night. Delbert came and picked me up. I climbed out the window of my house, shimmied off the roof. We went off to the races on Goose Creek Road that night. We had no idea that Ben would stop at my parents house after we left. He was supposed to be at some college function. When he found out I was gone, he chased me down, found me at the creek. They started to fight, Delbert and Ben. Then Delbert got into his truck. He was afraid if Ben got too mad, he would hurt me. Ben dragged me into his car and he started to race down the road after Andy Fenton and Delbert. Something happened. I remember feeling the car swerve and then pull hard to the right, then it was like hitting a wall when we went into the creek. I was thrown from the back, went right into the rushing water. I just recall not being able to breathe, feeling the cold just scooping me up like a wet blanket and smothering me. Then what seemed like an eternity later, I ran hard into an old tree that had fallen into the water. I think I wanted to die. I thought right then it would be my chance. I clung there to that tree for probably an hour, trying to persuade myself I would be better off dead than with Ben and his family. I tried to put my head under. I kept coming up for air. It was freezing, that water. Then, I heard voices, Delbert calling my name. I called back, then felt a hand reach down and pull me out." Mary pulls up a napkin, dabs her teary eyes.

Tina just stares at her mother. It freaks me out that she has the same expressions Gayle has, squints her eyes. Her nose is Delbert's nose, her eyes are his too, the same bluer than blue as Brody's. "I don't understand, mom," Tina asks softly with bated breath. "What is going on here?"

"That was the day Molly Lender died," I said for her. I tugged the newspaper article from my purse, held it on the table. "She became Mary Lavelle. That's your mother," I say softly to Tina, poking the picture. "She wasn't always Mary Lavelle. She was Molly Lender. Same initials. M.L."

"Delbert Johnson was your father," Mary adds. "He knew I wouldn't be safe so he made the choice to let me go."

Tina looks from the picture to her mother. I can tell she sees the eyes, wide as oranges. "Delbert took me to his truck, hid me inside with a blanket around me. I was so frightened and so cold. I was shivering hard enough I thought the truck was shaking with me. I thought Ben would find me. Andy Fenton went to his father's store and took every penny from the safe and gave it to me. After the police left, Delbert and Andy got me dry clothing, took me to the bus station, and stuck me on it. They called ahead to find a safe house, had someone from a church in West Virginia secretly take me in until I had the baby." Mary stops, takes in a couple deep breaths and puts a hand on Tina's arm. "Delbert knew you were his daughter," Mary says to Tina. "I wrote him a few years later. I sent a picture of you, but I never told him where I lived. It just wasn't safe for me. I think Ben would have killed me, killed you if he had known. I always hoped Delbert understood. At least, I prayed he would understand."

Tina still had the purse. It was sitting in front of her. She reaches out, touches it and then opens the tiny clasp to look inside. "So how did my—my father get this?"

"I gave it to him," Mary answers. "I gave him the purse to pay back the Fentons for the money the boys got me. I didn't think he would keep it." She reaches into the purse, snaps open the secret cover. The two wedding bands fall out along with the picture of the little girl.

"That's me," Tina says.

"When you were three," Mary says. "It is the picture I sent him. And the rings. Those were for Del and me. He got them. He asked me to marry him. I sometimes wonder what it would have been like if we had just run away, gotten married. But he was a good boy, had obligations on his farm. I had to find a place far away from Winford to hide my identity."

That was when I tug out the dance card and hand it to Mary. "Delbert told me you gave this to him too?"

A smile breaks out on her face. "Oh, yes, he was supposed to meet me the next weekend at our big spring dance. I told him the week before the wreck that if I had the dance card, all the boys would fill it up. There probably wouldn't be any dances for him. So, that bugger took it from me. He said he would fill it out with his name on every line when he met me at the dance." She sighed. "Of course, we never got to the dance." She looks at Gayle. "I know your father died in May. I'm sorry. I tried to keep tabs on him. I saw his obituary."

I didn't tell her Delbert's side of the story. That he told me she gave him the card and he would have all the dances. "So, my dear," Mary looks at Tina and then she looks at Gayle. "You have a younger half-sister. What do you think of that?"

"She actually has an aunt, too," I say. "Am I right? Brody and I met Della at the retirement home?" All eyes are on me. I suppose I could have kept my mouth shut. Perhaps I should have let the other information soak in for a few minutes before I brought up new.

"You know," I mumble. "Maybe I should go take Cayce for a walk. You all need to talk this out—among family." I didn't give them time to protest. I just gave a little shove and Bella stands up, lets me out of the booth.

"Journey?" Mary catches my attention before I turn. I stand there with my hands on the table waiting for her to say something.

"Della knows I'm alive," Mary tells me. "She has known for several years. We have not seen each other since the incident. We were both scared Ben would find out. That's how I knew to call you. She sent me your card."

Chapter −39
Note to Self: Try to let go

There is a little patch of grass between the restaurant and an old building that used to be a gas station. It is where I parked my car. I take Cayce out and we look for four leaf clovers in the grass. Then we sit with our legs crisscrossed. I take the little, white clover flowers, weave the stems together and make us each a crown.

"I used to do this with my mama," I tell her. "I would pretend I was a princess and I had a little white pony I could ride."

Cayce smiles up at me. She is missing her front teeth and I push a hand on my mouth. I can't believe I didn't notice this earlier and I tell her so. "You are the cutest girl in the whole wide world," I tell her. She grins even harder. I take out my phone and make her smile real big so I can take a picture. "That way you can be with me all the time. Anytime I want you, I can pull out my phone and Cayce is there." Then she starts to huff and sniffle and rub her eyes.

"Baby, what's wrong?" I ask her. She doesn't say anything, just climbs in my lap and wraps her arms around me. I just sit there and hold her, rocking back and forth. "I don't want you to ever leave. Daddy says you will."

I am struck mute for the moment. I don't know what to tell a five year-old while she softly sobs in my chest and her fingers wrap around my shirt in tiny fists. What did Delilah tell me when her boyfriends didn't come back? They were a piece of crap.

"I guess that gets rid of the ghost at Goose Creek." I hear Brody's voice just a few steps away. "Mary said a couple times she went back to where the wreck was at night.

She didn't think anybody would see her but she remembered a few cars did drive past. Guess they did. That was the lady in white." He stops, takes a look at Cayce, groans and asks me how I could possibly make so many people cry in a day. "Is it your thing? Mom's in there crying. So is every lady at that table. There were tears in Dad's eyes. Every time I am around you, somebody ends up crying. I come out here and you what, pinched my little girl?"

"I didn't hurt her," I say.

"That could be challenged," he says.

I ignore his jab and the irritation in his voice, reach over Cayce and grab a tissue from my purse. "Blow," I tell her and swipe away the snot. Then I roll it up and toss it at Brody. He shifts away from it so it hits his leg instead of his chest where I am aiming. It falls to the ground. "Make yourself useful." I point my finger at the tissue. "Throw that away." Instead, Bella sweeps an arm down and picks it up.

"Play nice, now." That is Bella who is poking Brody in the shoulder with her finger. I don't know what that means, but I can guess he's had some pretty crappy things he would like to say to me. I can see it in his eyes as he rolls them toward her. Bella saunters off toward a garbage can near the front door. I watch her leave and so does Brody. The silence is deafening between us. I watch the cars work their way along the highway mingling with semi-trucks.

"You missed the court date," he tells me, looking down at me with arms crossed. "You do realize that."

"Court date?" I ask.

"For the annulment. Zach sent out the paperwork." Brody mutters. "I went out and bought a suit for it. Even wore a tie. Stood there by myself feeling like an idiot. The judge postponed it. Nobody can find an address for you.

You've kind of fallen off the grid. It cost me a couple hundred bucks in court costs and fees. The court official said they can subpoena you. Now I guess I'm going to have to hire a lawyer?"

"I didn't know anything about it."

"The girl at the Country Fest Concert didn't give you the paperwork?" he asks flatly. "I handed it right to her. Told her it was important. I wrote down my number."

Was he really that stupid, I am wondering? "Where did you write it down? Because I didn't see it."

"On her palm. She didn't have any paper."

I am staring at him. "Are you really that naïve, Brody?"

"What do you mean."

"Let me just ask. Did she show you her tattoo?"

"Yeah and half her boob. She keeps texting me."

"Um," I say. "I would assume Courtney was more caught up in trying to get you to sleep with her than worrying about giving me the papers."

"I had a hundred bucks in an envelope."

"Well, I did get that. And I vaguely remember her telling me she thought there were two envelopes. But I'm pretty sure she was smoking something behind the booth with a couple guys, too." I rub my hands together. "Regardless, this whole mess was not my fault. However, I will be there next time."

"You need to get the court your new address then." Brody says.

I look up at the highway. There's a sign with the exit number and the name of the road we are on. "Well, right now its County Road 12. But I'm getting ready to move again really soon."

"Just let them know." He is looking down at me. I am squinting up at him. He doesn't leave, just stands there.

"Say what you want to say, Brody," I tell him. I know deep in my heart he hates me now. I know Bella kept her promise and didn't tell him. I wish I could change it. I don't know how.

"I can't," he says, nodding to Cayce who is still pressed against me. "There are cuss words involved."

"Like my CD," I ask him, "that you returned to me at the mall?"

"Yeah." Brody narrows his eyes. "Kind of. So, okay, how many guys were there?"

"I don't know. I don't want to bring it up. It is done. We aren't anything and obviously never were." He shoves his hands in his pockets, glares down at me does his swaggering rock back and forth in his boots. "Okay, Chase Smith? When I tried to find you about the court date, your boss said if I could find Chase Smith, I'd find you. That's where you were staying every night. That girl, Courtney, taking the money at the festival said it looked like you were real tight with a guy named Sam now. It's like your stupid song, Exes and Beaus and the reason I don't want Cayce listening to your album. You think I want her knowing someday I was one of those guys?"

I just laugh. "You're calling me a whore?" I know my voice has a sarcastic twang. "It was a stupid song, nothing more."

"Like the stupid song you allegedly wrote about your feelings for me?" He leans over, wiggles his fingers at Cayce. "C'mon, baby, it's time to go. Daddy doesn't want you around people who say bad words. Who have to have the words 'explicit language' on her CDs and still gives them to a little kid."

"Her lullaby didn't have any cusswords." I give her a little nudge off my lap. She's confused. I can see it in her eyes darting from Brody's to my own. I feel it in my heart because I remember the same expression on my own face. I feel like I am staring into a mirror. "We'll play again maybe next week. I promise."

"Don't make promises to her." Brody snaps, gently picks her up. His gentleness to Cayce is a stark contrast to the rage in his eyes. "Don't."

"Well, okay," I drop my voice, mocking. I push myself to my feet, snatch up my purse. "You know what? Now I know why your last girlfriend wanted to beat the crap out of me, why she hated you so bad. Because you're mean and hurtful and you won't let anybody get past that stupid suit of armor you've got around you and Cayce."

"Yeah, well, I opened it up for you and what happened?" Brody just stares at me after that, eye-locking, teeth-gritting anger like a wall between us.

If I didn't look to the right and see Tina flagging me down outside the restaurant doors, I think we could have glared at each other all day. Instead, I skirt around him, feeling horrible and wishing things were different, wishing Robert Ironwood still didn't have his damn invisible hands still around my neck, just waiting to take my last breath. I felt it was a tightrope walk, at best. I was stuck over a netherworld just waiting for the fall, knowing anything I did to piss Robert off would send him shaking the very wire I was walking. I really didn't have anything left, but I didn't want to add to it by telling Brody the truth. Maybe it wouldn't matter at all, but I wasn't taking the chance.

"I just wanted to thank you. I don't think mom would have ever told anybody about her other life. I'm in shock. I always wanted a sister and family," Tina Lavelle says.

"And I am reeling that now we have it. It is just mom and me and a big old house." She pushes an arm around my back, gives me a pat. "Okay, here's the big question. I would still like to buy the purse from you," Tina holds it and the dance card out in her palm. I take it lightly, almost cautiously. "Are you wanting to sell it still?"

"Well, there is a slight problem with that." I rub my hand on my head. It is hot. I'm wearing jeans and my bare shoulders are burning in the sunshine. "I have been hounded by the same man your mother was running from—Ben Dodge. Since he found out I had the purse, he has a couple private investigators and Delbert's grandson, Freddy Johnson, harassing me to buy the purse. It is bad enough, Freddy has been peering in my window, standing on my porch waiting for me. They even broke into my house and my shop. I just don't understand why he wants the purse so badly or what price someone will pay if he finds out your mother is alive and has it. I guess you'll have to decide if it means that much to you. Because at some point, this whole thing could get out. I would never tell, but maybe Gayle accidently slips one day and says she has a sister. Or—or you come to Thanksgiving and I mean, you look exactly like her. People are going to talk."

"He's dead." Tina says firmly. "Mom brought his obituary. He died last month."

"Oh, that's probably why it all stopped." Relief pours over me.

"She thinks he knew she was still alive. Maybe he wanted to track us down, make amends. Maybe he wanted to leave me a million dollars in his will. I don't know. It wouldn't matter anyway. I'm not his daughter. Even if I was, he never had anything to do with my life at all. Real fathers are the ones who are there or—can't be with you because they care so much about you."

She reaches into her purse and pulls out a checkbook. "As far as family. We'll just have to deal with it."

I look at the dance purse and the card, feel it in my fingers. It has always been like holding a piece of Delbert. Now while I extend my hand, it feels like I am losing him. It is almost like that very purse was some key to my destiny I would not have found if I did not have it. Yes, I was homeless and jobless. I had lost just about everything since the moment Delbert shoved it into my hand. However, I was free.

"Your father gave these to me," I say softly. I feel a lump in my throat, but I am not crying. "He knew I found stuff. He knew it was what I loved to do and he knew I did it well. He was the only person that appreciated it." I laugh a little thinking about our wild rides to one flea market or another. "He and I went so many places together finding stuff. Sometimes we snuck out while everybody was at church."

"I can't take it then." Tina pushes my hand away, refuses to take the purse and dance card. "It was a gift."

"No, no," I shake my head, shove both into her fingers. "I don't see it that way. I think he gave it to me so I would find you." I poke a thumb behind me. "And you found them. He believed in me. Sometimes I think he is the only one who believed in me so I have to do what my instinct tells me. He did it because of that."

I thought I could make it to my car, sneak away without confronting any of Delbert's family. I was tired. It was late. I felt the loss of Delbert in that little purse and dance car I knew never really belonged to me. In reality, I had to admit, I felt as if Delbert's and my own story had come full circle.

Delbert never really wanted anything more for me than to make sure I understood how controlling and callous Robert had been to me. He wanted me to date someone else so with my own little eyes, I saw the truth of how love really felt. I did. He knew I love to sing. Robert and I were finished. I found Delbert's daughter for him, brought out the truth. I should have felt emancipated. I just felt alone. I had to get on the road and back to the gas station in less than a half hour to get back before I was an explosion waiting to happen.

My hand is on the steering wheel. I am pushing the key into the ignition and praying that my car starts. It makes a sad chug-chugging sound. Air conditioning is not an option in my car so I have the window rolled down. It doesn't stop Bella from knuckle-rapping the two-inch sliver of glass sticking up that refuses to go all the way into the door.

"Nice car, Bacon. A classic." she razzes me. "Hey, Aunt Gayle and Uncle John want to buy everybody supper. You, too." I can see Bella raking in my car with her eyes, sipping it like it is a warm cup of coffee on a chilly day. I wait for her to remark about the dent on the side, the mismatched doors, the broken windshield or the pink princess comforter laid out like a bed in the backseat. Or the cardboard egg boxes and brown paper bags holding what is left of my life shoved to the floor.

"I can't." I turn the ignition again. Chug-chug. It still doesn't start. "I have to get back."

"Okay." That's all she says and backs away. Maybe she is going to say more. I don't know.

"Listen," I tell her out the window. "Just so you know when it happens again—"

"What happens?"

"When Robert pulls his fast shit and tries to take the farm. At least you know I did everything I could possibly do. I really, really did."

Bella is eyeballing me, then snaps a gaze behind her. Brody is walking up behind her. She turns around and gives Brody a really hard fist to his arm.

"Crap, what was that for?" he gripes, holding his fingers just above the elbow.

"You didn't tell her?"

"Tell her what?" Now he is eyeballing my car. If it wasn't embarrassing enough that Bella is giving it a lip-twitch, now Brody is looking it up and down.

"Jesus, Brody, you *are* a shit," she growls at him. Bella then turns her attention to me. "You heard about what happened, didn't you? About the farm getting paid off?"

I just stare at her. "No."

"Grandpa Delbert had some kind of savings account at the bank. Your friend, Andrea, found it while she was going through his old safety deposit box he kept there. She called, asked if they just didn't want to pay the farm off with it. Uncle John did."

"Oh." It is all I can say. "Well, good. I mean, great." *Dear God, please let the car start, please, please, please—* I turn the key again, easy on the gas pedal with my foot. "I've got to go." I should have been happy for them, ecstatic that I was finally free from Robert's control. I just want to get out of there. The car just makes that old sad grind. So I open the door, get out and start to give it a push with all my might. It eases along while I jump inside. *Please, please God, let it start!* God is listening to me. It starts with a blast that hurts my eardrums. And I take off in a spew of coal black smoke.

I can hardly wait to get out of the parking lot before I call Andrea on her cell phone. She doesn't pick up and I lose service. Then, the phone rings back.

"What do you want, Journey?" she asks. Her voice is low. "This has to be quick. I'm calling you from the bathroom. I told Robert I wouldn't talk to you."

"Did Delbert have an account or were you just bluffing? Is the farm paid off or is Robert planning something else?"

"I just paid it off," she whispers. "I used the money you gave me and the six-thousand dollars in deposits from the bar you work at. You have direct deposit, you know that?"

"No."

"It was that easy. It was enough. Please don't let anyone know this. Robert would be mad."

"Is this what you want?" I ask her. I imagine my hand reaching out through the phone and pulling her through to safety. But I can't help somebody who doesn't want it.

"I love him, Journey. I don't care if he only loves you. We are going to have the baby. We talked to his parents and we're getting married. Please don't call me back."

Chapter −40

Note to Self: 1) Thank Smalltalk for Saving my life

2) Buy another bottle of Bear Repellent

I still have the bottle of Econo-Size Bear Aware Bear Repellent in my purse that Smalltalk gave me. There were five or six times I wanted to take it out and put it in my bathroom vanity or throw it in the trash. The can is the size of a water bottle, bulky, and makes my purse bang against my hip. Every time I start to toss it, I imagine seeing the cautioning gaze in Smalltalk's eyes. So it is still in there floating around on top of my lip glosses, vanity mirror, and little purse with $122.17—what was left of my cash. And the words in my head that Smalltalk told me when he gave it to me: *Better not leave things up to chance.*

I really didn't understand what my mother and Smalltalk meant when each said it to me. However, on Sunday night while my car comes to a slow and grinding halt along the side of the dark highway and I am standing there with the hood up and staring dumbly inside, it all falls into place.

He comes out of nowhere while I am holding my phone in the air trying to get cell phone service. He is just a big guy with an old truck and he pulls in about twenty feet behind my car. Lots of other cars have passed by. Nobody stops. I can't even remember how far back the last sign said it was until the next exit ramp. There isn't a light in sight.

"Hey, I can give you a ride to the next exit."

"I don't have any money—"

"It won't cost you a dime." He is reaching into his pocket, pulling out a pack of gum. "No problem. Hop in. Want a piece of gum?"

How many times has Delilah told me not to accept candy from strangers? The one time I've ever had a real creep do it and like an idiot, I look at my car and then look at my phone.

"There's cell phone service at the top of the next hill," he says. "You can call someone there."

The guy has a thick brown beard and rosy cheeks. He smiles even when he laughs and his eyes are twinkly like Santa Claus. He asks me if I have a gun in my purse.

"No," I say. Instinctively, my heart starts pounding. *Oh, God, you haven't been listening to me in a while. My life is kind of going to shit. But maybe it's because you've been saving up for one big prayer on my part. And this is it. Please don't let me die tonight—*

He starts to roll forward toward my car, easing out on to the highway. I know I'm going to die. I just know it. And it isn't going to be quick and easy like my car blowing up because I got rear-ended. It is going to be long and painful and scary— He rolls his tongue over his bottom lip. "Open it up and let me see."

"I don't want to," I tell him and my voice sounds scared and shaky.

"You might be saying that a lot in a few minutes," he says. He reaches down and my eyes follow his right leg to his lap. He has a little black pistol. "You might want to just get used to doing what I say."

He makes a fist, hits me hard on the shoulder. I am suddenly woozy and faint. Something in the back of my mind tells me to put on my seatbelt. Smalltalk's voice I think. "Okay," I say. "I'll do whatever you say." I reach around put on my seatbelt like I always do. He doesn't question me. Then I unzip my purse.

"Slow," he says. "Let's see." My head is banging, my heart is banging and I swear I am going to faint. There is a dribble of sweat hanging on my forehead. My hands are trembling so hard they are jerking the zipper back and forth. I see him dipping his eyes into my purse. I slip my hand inside, "N—nothing, see?" Oh, and my stutter that has gone away for years returns in full force.

"What's that?"

That was the economy size Bear Aware Bear Repellent. That, I pull out and instantly jerk off the safety tab just like Smalltalk told me to do. Then, I pull the trigger and let the creep have from the tip of his greasy beard to the top of the head. He growls like a bear. His fist comes out hard and slams on my collarbone two times. I feel the car jerk forward, his foot impulsively hitting the gas so it is accelerating so fast, it sounds like a jet engine taking off for flight. I twist in my seatbelt, pull up my feet, propel them at his face and shoulders. I kick and kick and kick until I swear my head feels like it is going to explode in black. Then, I feel the sudden jar of impact as his truck smashes hard into the rear passenger side of my Pinto.

As the two impact and the truck makes a horrible deafening crash, I feel the seatbelt rip across my shoulder and neck. And the only thing I can think of while I watch my abductor flip forward is: *Oh, shit. We are going to die. We are hitting my car from behind. Boom.*

But his chest hits the steering wheel. It just smacks like a mosquito hitting one of those electric bug zappers. His head whips forward hard, seems to ooze up the steering wheel before it smacks against the windshield. It sounds like a potato falling from slippery fingers to fake wood floor. I hear a sickening crunch of his skull to glass watch in slow motion while deep red splotches dab the broken window.

The truck doesn't stop, it just slows and pushes around my car.

The sound of the horn blares into the air. I see I am sideways and swivel around in my seat, desperately trying to find the damn latch to the door. I can't think. I am numb. I am just reaching, reaching, slamming my body to it, trying to unlatch my seatbelt when I feel the warm summer air on my cheeks.

I am backing out standing there when a semi-truck nearly hits me and makes a veering wheel to the right. Thank God, the old truck had shoved my car out on to the high speed lane, the semi-truck was already changing lanes to avoid wrecking into us.

I don't remember much after, just the sound of sirens, throwing up, and sitting on the back of the ambulance to clear my lungs of bear repellent. And the cops smashing the creep over the top of his truck. His forehead is bleeding and he is screaming cusswords I could even hear over the traffic slowly filing past. My eyes sting just like Smalltalk said they would.

"No, I am fine. I don't need to go to the hospital," I am saying while the police officer finishes jotting stuff down in his book. "I just want to go home."

"You perpetrator is bagged and tagged."

"He's dead?" I ask.

"No, ma'am, he is handcuffed and heading to jail. He has a couple warrants already for his arrest. He jumped bail." My eyes were watering so hard, it feels like warm rivers on my cheeks. My shoulder hurts where he hit me and my neck is bruised and red from the seatbelt. "I just wanted you to know you are safe."

"I thought for sure we were both going to get blown up." I tell him.

"Um, your car. Yeah, the company came out with a recall and added a plastic shield to the tank. It must really be your lucky night. One of the owners had it fixed."

"Yeah," I say. "I guess it takes a village to raise me. Everybody keeps fixing stuff for me and telling me not to leave my life up to chance. If it had been left up to me, I would have tossed the bear repellent and never gotten the car fixed."

"Well, somebody's looking out for you, doing a good job." He points his pen behind him. "You called someone for a ride—"

"No," I am still not very clear-headed. I pat my side for my purse someone brought me earlier, getting ready to grab my phone inside. He looks up. "No, that wasn't a question." Oh, I am getting THE LOOK. "This is your family, right?"

"Oh, I didn't even know you—were here." I look up and see John and Brody Wells standing right behind me. "I was keeping my eyes down. Everybody in the passing cars is staring at me."

"It's okay. You're okay, right?" John Wells is leaning over, putting his hand on my shoulder. I can't help but note that he looks over his shoulder and sees the passing cars. He comes in a little like he is blocking the view. "Better? We've just been here a few minutes. We heard on the radio that a Pinto had gotten in a wreck with a semi. We were about an hour behind you." His hand feels comforting, gently holding my shoulder. He doesn't let go and it makes me feel safe.

"I'm fine."

"You don't look fine," Brody leans down with his hands on his knees so he is face to face with me. Now he is putting a soft hand on my leg, letting his fingers rest there.

It makes me feel safe too. "Your eyes are really bloodshot. Holy hell, your neck is red."

"Thank you for pointing that out," I growl. "But, yes, I am fine. My head hurts. My neck hurts. But I'm okay."

"I'm not fine." Brody holds up his hand. "Look. I'm shaking like crazy. I thought we'd find you in pieces on the highway."

"It wasn't that kind of a wreck. We weren't going that fast. There—there was a guy who gave me a ride—" I start to stutter. I keep reliving it over and over in my mind, seeing the man, the beard. I hate brown, scraggly beards right now.

"It's okay. We heard." John tells me. He is smiling. I don't know if I have ever seen him smile at me. "It probably isn't safe sitting here either. They are getting ready to tow the vehicles. The police said you are good to go if you're ready. How about we take you home, huh? We can get your stuff out of the car before they tow it. Do you have somebody that can meet you there?"

"Home." I nod. I'm not so sure about them dropping me off at Drew's. I guess I can just tell them I am visiting him tonight.

"Brody freaked just a little." Bella holds up her hands and pinches her forefinger and thumb together when I sit down in the car. I have an icepack they gave me from the ambulance and it is resting on my shoulder. "He told Uncle John that if he didn't drive faster, he was going to haul him out of the driver's seat and get us there himself."

"I did not."

"Yeah, son, you did," John says from the front seat. "And you cursed. We'll say a few extra prayers for you tonight."

"Well, you had cow eyes again." They all think Brody's words are funny and laugh. I don't get it.

"Cow eyes," Bella relates to me. "Are what Brody calls the stunned, wide-eyed look cows get when they run into an electric fence. The first time they do it, they kind of stand there stupid. One time, Uncle John and Brody and I were putting up an electric fence in the pasture and Uncle John yelled for Brody to turn on the electric to test it."

"Just so we're clear on this. I did not tell him to turn it on," John told me while he looked through the rearview mirror. "I told him to hold off. I found a split in the line. Big difference."

"Regardless, Brody plugged the electric box in and Uncle John got a good ol' shock. His eyes got as wide as fists and he got this stupid look on his face. Cow eyes. I saw it. I was standing right next to him."

"Yeah, I saw it too," Brody says. "But by the time he got to me, they were bloodshot red just like Journey's are now." He waves a finger in front of my eyes as if he needs to point them out. "He was so mad, I think he broke every blood vessel in his eyeballs." Brody keeps reaching out, gently touching my arms and then my legs while he talks. I don't know if it is for him or for me. He is shaking. I am just kind of numb still.

I know they are trying to cheer me up and I laugh a little. "Where's your tiara?" Cayce is in the front seat between Gayle and John. She is pointing to her little clover headband we made in the parking lot.

"I must have lost it," I reach up absently as if searching for it myself. "I'll have to make another one."

"You can have mine," she tells me, dragging it from her fine hair and bending her arm so it dangles against the back seat. Brody takes it in his fingers, plops it on my head.

"How does she look, baby girl?" he asks, adjusting it. I cross my eyes and stick out my tongue at her. Cayce thinks it is funny and giggles.

"Now, you look like a princess," she tells me. "Daddy can save you."

"I'm thinking this princess did just fine on her own," Brody says quickly. "I'm not so sure she needs my help. She's a kick-ass princess just like in her song."

"Oh," I cringe. "You listened to it."

"I did. Cayce didn't." he said. "Well, I made a copy of just the lullaby for her so she can listen to it before she goes to bed."

"You wrote me a song," Cayce does a little dance in her car seat. She can't move much, but she makes her arms wave in the air and kicks up her legs. "I'm famous."

Cayce dances some more and John tells her to calm down. Gayle tells John to let her be a little kid. Then Gayle leans over asks if I want a mint. I tell her I don't. "The last time I took candy, I nearly ended up in a fiery explosion."

They think this is funny. I didn't mean it to be. Then they all start chattering about one thing or another. Bella slumps back in her seat. She is trying to watch a video of cats running into walls on her phone. She keeps bumping me with her shoulder. I think it is her way of comforting me. She is laughing out loud and playing the video again and again. John hears a song he likes and turns up the radio. Gayle is singing along in a high-pitched voice. I think it is chaos.

"Is it always like this?"

"Pretty much." Brody answers. He plugs a pair of earphones into his phone and I can hear a solid throb of hard rock music. He is tapping a beat out on his own knee, looking like he just might start dancing in his own seat. He sees me looking at him and pulls an earplug out.

"You still okay?"

"Yeah, I'm fine. You listen to rock?"

"Yeah, I'm not a huge country fan. Um, I guess I go back and forth. Well, I like listening to your stuff."

"My stuff," I say. The poems of my heart are nothing more than *stuff*. I realize, though, he isn't trying to be mean.

"Yeah, your stuff's alright," he looks down and smiles at me. "You know what? I guess you really don't know me at all."

"Oh, I know you." I shift in my seat and rub my temples with my fingers. "I know you like the color blue because you always wanted me to wear that stupid baby blue tank top all the time. You are superstitious. You can't walk through the door without putting your right foot first and when you get nervous, you tap out a beat six times on your leg. You like old trucks and the way they make that throaty groan when they take off and you like comic books with superheroes. I know you think the stuff I pour out of my heart and soul is just *stuff*. You are wrong about that. You hate the number six because Cayce's mom left you for good on the sixth month of the year and the sixth day—June sixth. It was also the exact same date you escorted me to the courthouse and Zach pulled a funny little stunt on us." I am looking Brody in the eye. I don't know if he even realizes this until I say it. "And you're afraid to let anybody get to know you because some dumbass woman left you when you opened up a bit. I also know you're a bit stupid for thinking that it wasn't the woman and it was you. I hate to break it to you, Brody, but I know you. I see the whole picture inside and out and you're not something any girl in her right mind would leave."

"You did," he replies. His eyes are fine slits like he is trying to shut me out. It is another thing I know about Brody Wells. I just won't point this one out.

"She said any girl in her *right mind*," Bella pipes up. I snap my attention to her and then see both John and Gayle eyeing me in the rearview mirror.

"The conversation was between me and Brody," I bark. "Put your earphones back on, please."

"Okay," Bella says and she smiles at me. "But it is hard not to hear you because we are in a car, Bacon." It is weird. Has she ever smiled at me?

"Listen, you guys don't have to be nice to me," I tell Brody and Bella. "It's weird. Bella hasn't threatened to murder me in the last hour. Your dad keeps smiling at me like if he doesn't I'm going to melt like a candy bar in the sun. Your mom keeps asking me if I want a mint. It's like I'm dying or something."

"Oh, check this out." Bella turns a little and pushes her phone under my nose. "If you put in the words: 'cat, fight, video' and then if you accidently add 'bar' instead of 'barn', you get this—"

This. This just happens to be a cell phone video of me at Hobie's bar. The video is halfway through, but you can hear me screaming, hear me telling Billy Gentry exactly where I stand on his comments to me. It cuts off right after I walk off the stage and a chair comes flying at whoever took the video.

"You told him I didn't have to be nice to you," she says. "You said it was weird. Do you see this, Brody? Look at your princess."

"Ha ha," he laughs and pokes a finger at the screen. "I already saw it. I also saw the one where you were doing cartwheels on the stage before you thought anybody was there and you fell off the stage. Funny. Zach called me to tell me about them at four in the morning."

Great. I can only push my hands on my temples and slide down in the seat and wish this damn day —no, damn weekend— no, damn month would just end.

"Sweetie, the address you gave John is a gas station." It is Gayle's voice prodding my half-awake, half-asleep.

"Naw, it's right. I'm staying with Drew until I get another place to live."

"I thought you had that cute little ranch house on Maple Court."

"I couldn't make the payments," I lie. "I'm trying to find something closer to where I work. Until then, Drew's taking me in." But the place is dark. I texted Drew and got no reply. So I lie. "I sent Drew a message. He said he'd be here in a half hour."

"We'll wait with you," John says.

"No," I reply. "This will give me time to sort things out. I need some alone time."

Gayle tries to talk me out of it. So does John. I just push my way out of the car. I watch their tail lights head off down the old roads. I am trying to push the image of The Creep that almost killed me out of my head. I can only imagine what he would have done to me. Where would he have dumped my body? Even having Creepy Cal around at the moment would have been more comforting than sitting there by myself.

I slide down the glass of the door and sit there with my knees bent, checking my phone. The battery is almost dead. I laugh sarcastically. I am dead tired. I am terrified and the whole event is sinking in. I just want to go to bed at my little house on Maple Court and still—my mind is reeling so hard I can't even cry about what happened—about what almost happened.

A few cars pass. No sound of Drew's motorcycle though. Then there is about a ten minute span where it is quiet. Only the sound of crickets and frogs fill the air.

I'm hidden somewhat in the shadows. But not by any cars that would pull back into the lot again. Because I see John's car pull back in, his lights nearly blinding me sitting there. Brody simply gets out and saunters over, scoots down next to me. I watch him nonchalantly wave them away.

"Mind if I hang out for a while?" he asks. Like I have a choice. He sits there with his arms resting on his knees. "So who is this Chase guy you've been seeing?" he asks, banging me with his shoulder. "And how did I miss out on Robert being out of the picture again?"

"Chase Smith is an attorney," I tell him. "Well, William Chase is one attorney. Ed Smith sells cars off the state route. They have back to back billboards near the highway by Hobie's." I hold up my hands side by side to show him. "I'm not dating either one. I just tell guys that so they leave me alone. Hobie says the songs I sing make them think I'm looking for another relationship to screw up and they are willing to get beat with a stick if its with me. And it kept Hobie from knowing I was sleeping in my car in his back lot. I told him I was leaving with Chase every night." I take in a breath. "Robert decided he didn't want me around. He took my house, my shop, my car, my cell phone and anything else that was mine. He took my Drew away too," I shrug. "We think he talked Billy Gentry into setting it up to make it look like Drew stole money. We didn't think about it until last night. Oh, and you saw the video. Most likely I lost my job singing too."

"Sucks to be you right now."

"Not right this minute." I bang him back. "I kind of like sitting here with you. I think I'm freaking out more than I thought."

"Really?" Brody looks up at the sky. I do too. It is a clear blue with a million twinkling stars. A little warm wind blows the trees across the street. "Because the last time we talked in your shop, you chose not to be with me."

"Yeah, I said that. I do remember saying that."

"Bella says I should give you a second chance. I think she's crazy, right? I mean, would you if you were me? I mean who wants to be somebody's seconds because they got dumped? It's hard to get that stone-cold bitch face you gave me out of my mind. Damn, girl, you hurt me. You frigging ripped my heart right out of my chest."

I chew on his words. I think it might be his way of telling me he loves me. I want tell him that I didn't get dumped. I just didn't do what Robert told me to do. I didn't hang around with the people he liked. I got punished. I've got nothing left for him to punish me with anymore, do I? Or will he find a way to take him away from me again? I wanted to tell him Robert was in the other room of my store and I had no choice. Sometimes you have to do things you don't want to do so the people you love to stay alive, you know?

"I can only tell you that I don't love him. I love you. You were never seconds."

"I don't know if that's enough."

"What is enough, Brody?" I ask him. "I've obviously got nothing else. Look around you. I've been sleeping in my car for two weeks wrapped in a princess comforter I got from Goodwill. The only damn thing I wanted was to have my little shop and play my guitar to the bare walls inside it until you came in that day." I fiddle with my fingers gently. "And dropped off your grandpa's stuff. I'm rock bottom here except for the clothes off my back."

"How about the truth?"

Chapter –41

Note to Self: Life can only Get Better When you hit rock bottom.

"Hey, rumor has it you're looking for a new band."

I recognize the voice on the other end of my phone. It is Sam Littleton. He interrupts my conversation with Brody who just kind of rolls his eyes and tosses his hand into the air with minor annoyance.

"Oh, ha ha. I guess you saw the video," I groan. It seems rude to sit there and talk, so I walk the perimeter of the building.

"Me and a million others. It was on national news and BBC. Even the part you stripped to your underwear."

"Oh, no, really? And it was a tank top, not undies," I correct him. "You could tell I had a shirt on underneath, right? You know, you saw the worst of it. I'm not usually that irritable. Are the numbers really that high?"

"Yes, and counting. It's kind of blurred, but it makes the point. I got to admit, I'm surprised you lasted as long as you did with that jerk." Sam sounds like he is driving. I can hear traffic around him. "Gentry's been around a long time. He's known for being a real crud. Why'd your manager set you up with them in the first place?"

"I don't know. Contracts, I suppose," I say. "Because I was waitressing at the bar part-time, singing on the side to a handful of guys that were down and out enough they were already drinking at noon."

"Well, I got it here in front of me that you worked beauty pageants and you were Miss Ohio Kiwi Fruit Queen. Not your biggest accomplishment in the pageants, but I liked the picture of you wearing that emerald green dress.

By the way do they grow kiwi fruit in Ohio?"

"No."

"We didn't think so. And you graduated high school with a 3.5 average, and went to one of the colleges of music in Indiana. I have more details, but I don't need to tell you about—well, you. "

I open my mouth to speak and hesitate. How does he know this and why? "Okay, now you're creeping me out, Sam. How do you know this?"

He laughs. "It's public information. We actually pay a guy to check everybody we're interested in performing with. We don't want to make the same mistakes as before."

"Oh," I say and smack my forehead. I can imagine I am getting THE LOOK on the other end of the phone. He is just joking. "I thought you might be prepared on stalking me. You're funny. I thought you were serious. Really, I have never picked up a Louisville Slugger before and chased anyone around the stage. I'm so dense. I thought—what the hell is he talking about? I'm tired tonight. Not used to staying up this late."

He laughs. I look up at Brody, give him a I'll-be-one-minute-forefinger in the air. "Listen Sam, it was really fun playing with you guys and allowing you to call to make fun of the video. I hate to cut you short. I don't know where you are, but its really late here."

"Oh, I'm sorry," he says. "I'm on a different time zone."

"That's fine, bye—"

I close the phone, stand over Brody and bump my knees to his arm. "I'm sorry. It was a guy I sang with at the music festival. He saw that stupid video of me on stage with Gentry. It got on the news. He had to call to make fun of me. You ever heard of Sam Littleton?"

"Uh, yeah," he says. "Everybody knows him. He's with Witt. Or at least that's what they used to be called."

"Witt?" It starts to sink in then. I should have known it was a BIG band. They were just a little too good, too professional to be just some band that showed up to play at a little venue.

"Witt is Sam Littleton. When he first got started, he used the name Josh Wittler. Then he came out on stage a few years later and said he was hiding who he really was by having a stage name. The drummer is Ryan Carter. He's the oldest in the band."

"That would be Stoner," I mutter. "Oh, crud," I sink down next to Brody. "Man, I could have probably set it up so Drew could sing with them sometime. That's all he ever talks about. Witt. I had no clue. You know, not a single person at the show mentioned their name, not one."

"You didn't realize that's who you sang with at the festival?" Brody says. He laughs and calls me a ditz. I glare at him. I hate that word.

"Oh, come on. I don't know anybody who wouldn't think that's ridiculous. Who doesn't know Witt? Who just jumps up on the stage with one of the biggest bands and doesn't have a clue who it is?"

"Me," I say. "Nobody announced them when I was there. They just got up on stage. Just leave, Brody. I don't need anybody, you know?"

"*Just leave,*" he repeats. "That's your answer to every guy who pisses you off? You don't need anybody?"

"Yeah, why not? I don't need your shit." I'm waiting for him to get up, to walk off or out or whatever people do when they get angry, can't stand to be around someone else.

"Yeah, you do," He doesn't get up. He just sits there. "Everybody needs people to laugh with them when they do something stupid. It makes you feel like you're not alone. It's better to laugh with everybody, than feeling like you're being laughed at by everybody else. I do it all the time. So does Bella and Zach. We do something stupid and we all just laugh it off."

"Yeah, Brody, but how many people do you know who do it on national TV?"

"I suppose a lot more people would if they had the chance. You got the chance. Everywhere I go now, I hear your songs on the radio. The other day, I'm sitting in the kitchen and Cayce comes running in screaming even the lullaby you wrote her is on some religious station my mom listens to. She tells me that you're singing to her wherever she is because you're watching over her like some angel or something. I'm standing in the store buying groceries in Winford and the lady behind me is humming *Rebel Child*. Listen, Journey, I'm not pointing out some flaw you have, I'm saying it was a silly thing to do like me turning on the electric fence when Dad had both ends in his hands. You can look back on it and want to hide in the closet or you can just be you and laugh along with everybody else."

My phone rings again. I groan, open my purse to snatch it out.

"Can I have that?" Brody asks, wiggling his finger at a wadded up piece of paper inside.

"Sure." I answer gingerly, reach in, toss it to him while I answer the phone.

"It's one of your little song thingies, right?" he asks and I bob my head up and down.

It is Sam again: "I feel like I just got turned down for senior prom."

"You are stalking me, aren't you?" I tell him lightheartedly.

"In a way, we are," he tells me. "I'm not sure if you turned us down or you're just being coy."

"Coy." I repeat the word and laugh. "You saw the video, Sam. I am definitely not shy. Turned you down for what?"

"We want you to sing with us. I kid you not, we've looked at twelve-hundred vocalists in the last four years and not one of them connected with us. They were good. Some were great. But you've got charisma up on that stage. Hell, Stoner already finished up the song he was writing and wants you to sing it this weekend."

"I wish you would have been around when I tried out for the Ohio Wild Hog Queen about six years ago. The judge said I lacked 'a certain fairy-tale magic on the stage.' Of course, rumor was the judge slept with Entrant Number Seven. She won. It still hurt my pride. By the way, we do have wild hogs here."

"Will you think about it and get back with me tomorrow?"

"Well, there's more to it than just saying 'yes', you know? My manager got mad at me the other day for talking to somebody in another band," I tell him, the teasing gone in my voice. "I don't want to leave Bacon Valley and my mom's all alone. I don't want to let Hobie down. He believes in me. I need to talk to him first. He may not want me back —but he took a chance on me."

"Well, I'll just say those two at the bar are like a couple of leprechauns who know they are sitting on a pot of gold," Sam says. "And that was another reason we liked you. Stoner wasn't kidding when he said it gets tiring touring around, always moving. That song he wrote was about his wife leaving him because he wasn't around."

"She didn't leave in the song."

"In real life, she did." Sam lags there a moment. "It nearly killed him. He doesn't want to make the same mistake again. We're all walking that tightrope, don't want to travel that much anymore. We've got wives and kids and we don't know them at all. We want to settle down somewhere that's not the city, have a safe harbor, a dock where we can raise the family."

"If you are choosing Coalville, it is about as far out from the city as one can get."

"I know," he says. "We'll take the chance if you will."

My eyes work upward to the dirty old garage. Dark and empty, I know I can't leave Drew there to die.

"I've got one thing to ask." I don't realize it until this point, I almost feel high. The girl who hated crowds was feeling pretty happy about singing on stage right now. "I have this buddy, Drew. We're kind of a team, like your band. He's good, Sam, really good."

"I don't think we heard him when we were at your bar. I'd have to talk to the guys. I don't know if we are really looking for two singers."

"Okay, but will you listen to him once? Please."

"I suppose —"

"If I give you an e-mail address, will you have Stoner send me his song? I need the music and the words."

"I don't think he'll do that."

"You trust me enough to ask me to be a part of your band, but you won't trust me enough to borrow your music?" I ask. "I am telling you this. I will not steal it."

"So are you telling me that you won't jump on board without this guy?"

"I'm not sure. I don't know right this second. I just know that I am just very loyal, Sam. I'm a small town girl who has to stare everybody in the face every day if I hurt them. And he's good."

Brody is tossing the little piece of the paper in the air and catching it with his hand. I watch him while there is a long lull on the other end.

"I'll see what I can do."

"You know, I really missed having these little pieces of paper all over my dashboard." Brody holds up the paper between two fingers when I sit down beside him. "It was killing me leaving them there. It was killing me thinking that if I took them off, it was like you'd be gone."

"Well, you are an open book tonight." I lean over, reach into my purse and find five more scattered in the bottom. "Here. Stock up. The harder my life gets, the more I write these little buggers. I've got a trail halfway through Ohio from this past month."

"Bella told me that maybe if I opened up once in a while, you'd be more likely to stick around."

"You know, I'd never say that Bella would be right or wrong about something," I tell him. "It is a point worth considering. But honestly, I think you've told me more stuff about you than she thinks."

"So what's your excuse?" Brody is smiling and I know why. He led me right to the point I was trying to avoid.

"Oh, that was so wrong, Cowboy." Our shoulders are touching. Brody brings his hand up, sets it lightly on my bent knee. He wiggles his fingers around in one of the rips until he tickles the skin beneath.

"Listen, it's alright. I don't have to hear it. I know that singing up on the stage and telling people your life story isn't as hard as one on one for you," He bumps me with his shoulder. "You're not the one who should be given the second chance. It should be me." He swallows hard, looks a bit pasty around his cheeks. "Please give me a second chance to show you how I feel, would you? I mean, I'll get another job so I can buy you all those flowers and — and I can take you on an actual date."

"Stop. You don't need to step it up a notch. This—" I wave a hand between us. "What is going on has nothing to do with what you did or didn't do. It was the tree's fault," I interrupt him. "That stupid tree on The Hill above your house. I went up there the day you were loading boxes into the back of your dad's truck. I sat in the tree like I've done a thousand times before. I thought about not sitting there anymore. I thought about your family not living there and all the winters of sipping hot chocolate at the little fire your dad put out. How many people over the years have sledded down your hill or sat at the top looking out at the hills during the Fall? I used to have scout picnics at your pond and —and it was almost as if the whole town would shrivel up and die if you guys weren't there anymore. You know, I used to sit up there on that tree and pretend I was a part of your family. Because it was so real and normal and different than me calling my mom Delilah and having to do those stupid beauty pageants. I lost Delbert. I just couldn't imagine life without the old Johnson farm."

Brody is studying me hard. "But not me?"

"Well, that's where it gets a little blurry. That's where the trail of my songs begin, " I start, pointing to one of the little wadded up papers he is holding. "You started loving me like I've never had anyone love me in my life. I see your mom crying and your dad was getting skinnier and skinnier."

I let out a breath. I open my mouth to speak and nothing comes out.

"What?"

"Robert came to me and told me he had a deal. If I married him and forgot about you, he would finance a loan for your dad."

"Shit! I knew it." Brody pushes himself up from a sitting position. I jump, startled. He lets out a whole melee of curses and paces back and forth across the parking lot. "I could kill him right now," he is saying while he punches one hand into his palm. "I am going to kill him. That son of a bitch!"

He stops, stares at me. "How—how did it get paid off, how the hell did you get away from him —Journey, what the hell were you thinking?"

I know my eyes are wide. I realize I am grabbing my legs and pushing them to my chest like I can make myself small and hide. "I—I suppose your dad would say I wasn't thinking with my head—?" My voice is shaky. "Or maybe cotton candy and cocaine? Isn't that what Bella calls the goofy you get when you're stupid in love?"

I see him walking toward me and I reach out like I do with Robert when he is mad and wiggle my fingers like a little kid wanting an adult to hold my hand. "Please don't be mad at me." Yeah, I do. Stepdaddy. "Brody, I didn't do anything with him. I—I told him if we were going to get married, we would have to do it right this time. No—no sex until after the wedding. I know he didn't care. He had backup with Andrea and—then the night before he kicked me out of my house, he came over and started to kiss me and stuff. I stopped him and he got so mad, he left. I think that's what made him so mad.

But I didn't let him." Maybe I thought if he held my hand just once, step-daddy would like me, not pinch me or step on my toes when he was mad. He would see me as a princess, feel how soft my hands were. I didn't want to fight him because Delilah liked him so much. It was my only defense for stepdaddy and Robert.

"No, no, no—I'm not mad at you," Brody says. "Absolutely not. And that's not what I meant." He snatches up my fingers and kneels down in front of me. "And even if I was —well, you've seen the extent of how mad I get. Crap, you look like a kitten caught in a corner. I'm glad you used up all the bear repellent." He sees me grimace. "Oh, too soon?"

"Yeah, a little," I work up a half-hearted laugh. He chucks his arm around my shoulder. He is so angry, I can feel him shaking. "It is paid off and I am hoping everything is all done now. I had been saving up for the last five years to buy the Knick-Knack Shop. That's why I was working three jobs and singing at the bar and weddings and anywhere else people would have me. I had the money in the bank and Andrea used it to pay off the loan. Your grandpa didn't have anything in a safety deposit box. Please don't tell your mom that. Don't tell anybody."

"Don't tell anybody?" Brody growls. "Oh, I'm going to tell a lawyer. Don't you see, he's still got a hold of you, his hands wrapped around both our necks."

"Really?" I tickle his hand with my fingers. "Because I'm seeing it different. You've got your arm around me. I've got you. He doesn't have anything of ours. Nothing." Well, of course, Andrea. However, I think she was never much of a friend all along. It's almost like my words force the steam right out of Brody. I feel his arm relax around my shoulders.

"You know, yeah, you are right." He gets this little funny half-grin on his lips. "You remember when I came into your shop to drop off some of Grandpa's stuff?"

"Yeah."

"Robert was telling you you'd have to stop dragging around your pawn shop guitar and thinking you'd make money—"

"With my shrilly voice like I'm going to be a rock star."

"And you are—a star," Brody says. "Hey, how about we call Bella. See if she'll pick us up. We can crash at her house tonight."

"You and me —together?"

"Yeah, I'll even hold your hand."

"Hey, what would you say if Witt asked me to sing for their band?"

"Naw, really?" Brody looks excited. He is smiling. Then he rubs his forehead. "Did you tell them you would? Oh, no, that means I'm losing you again."

"No, not at all. They want to set up shop here."

"Here." Brody is holding out something in his hand. I can see instantly that it is Molly Lender's little dance card.

"How'd you get this?" I say so softly I'm not sure he can hear me. I push it to my chest.

"I just told her how much it meant to you," Brody said. "How much it means to me, too."

"You?"

"Yeah," he says like I'm crazy for asking. "If it hadn't been for this, we would have never—met again. And it's kind of like having a little remembrance of Grandpa with you right?"

"Well, for the last part, I got you."

Chapter −42

Note to Self: Talk to Hobie about Being Fired

"Hey, Hobie." I am standing outside Hobie's office. I am fidgeting, winding my fingers together and rocking a little side to side. He is sitting at his desk, poking a chubby forefinger on a little gray adding machine. He pokes a couple times, then curses. *Poke. Poke. Damn.* There are stacks of papers to his left, stacks of papers to his right. His cashbox full of crinkled and partially folded bills is propped up on the end like he started counting, then stopped without finishing. A contractor sweeps up behind me with a piece of plywood. I have to duck to get out of the way. It smells like new wood in the bar. Workers are banging walls with hammers and I jump at the sound of a drill.

"I don't know how I'm going to pay all these bills." He looks up and nods, barely catching my eyes. "What do you need, Bread and Butter?"

"Um, I was wondering if I still had a job."

"It's safe to say that Billy Gentry no longer works here," he tells me. "I've gotten calls from every women's advocacy agency from California to New York City willing to back you up on a lawsuit if you want it." *Poke. Poke. Damn.* "I've got a lawyer named E.B. Clinton calling me from a hospital in Cincinnati telling me he is going to sue me for Billy Gentry's injuries. I'm wondering—" he looks up at me from his eyebrows. "I'm wondering if I just can't pick up the phones with the advocacy agency on one and the lawyer on the other, shove them together." He lifts up his hands and cups them, then holds them across from each other. "We could let them hash this mess out."

"I'm sorry. I probably can work some extra hours and maybe clean up after closing," I tell him. "Then you wouldn't have to hire somebody. It would save you money."

"Look behind you," he says. "They are coming in today and building a huge patio that extends out into the parking lot." He pokes a finger at the papers in front of him. "I got this. Bills coming out my ass. If you want to help out here so I can pay these damn bills, you can sing. That's what I need you to do."

"Well, that's good." I feel some relief. "Um, I have another question. I don't have a band anymore, right?"

"Right." Hobie glares up at me.

"Well, I'd like to sing with Drew again."

"Well, I'd like to sing with Drew again." Hobie mimics me in a high voice. "Is that a demand? You're at that point now, I suppose. Your contract is up. I told Ducky we should have made it longer. He said it was too much of a risk. He was wrong. And I really don't want some dirty thief working here."

"He didn't steal that money, Hobie," I say aloud. "You know that. I know that. Look." I point to the cash register box full of money and wide open. "You always leave money sitting out. Anybody could have grabbed it."

"Nobody else but Billy was anywhere near it the night it was stolen. Five-hundred dollars is a lot of money. You think Billy stole it?" He asks sarcastically.

"Yeah, I do. He has a drinking problem. That's not new. He plays poker out here every night after closing."

"Poker? How do you know that?"

"Because I am living in my car in your parking lot, Hobie," I told him. "He didn't leave until four or five in the morning with the same group of men every weekend night. He was always losing because he was so damn drunk he couldn't stand up. I would hear them laughing about how bad they ripped him off. Drew didn't steal the money."

Hobie scrubs his chin. "I did have a lot of beer missing. It never occurred to me anybody was staying after the cleaning people locked up." He shakes his head like he is shaking off his thoughts. "Have you talked to the boy? Because he told me he was never coming back here. There was enough fire in his eyes to burn this place down."

"Well, here's the thing, Hobie." I am fidgeting again. "You ever heard of the band Witt?"

"Have you ever heard of the band Witt?" he mimics my voice again. It is really getting on my nerves. He seems to notice this and I see Hobie huff a laugh. "You don't have a Louisville Slugger baseball bat hidden somewhere on you, do you?"

"Ha ha," I say. "They know what you and Ducky are building here. They know you have the whole sound room and all the stuff to record. They are interested in singing with me. I told them I needed to make sure I still had a job. I'm interested in them. I like them. They are nice—"

"Baby, everybody's nice to you when they see what you've got."

"You're not," I say. Hobie looks up long enough to lock eyes with me. He says nothing.

"I need to know if you are interested too. And they said if I'm interested, have my people talk to their people. I don't know what that means, but you're my people. And Drew is my people. I won't work without him. Can you talk to them?"

"You're my bread and butter, sweetie. Just like I always knew you'd be. We'll cut a deal."

Bread and butter. It is also what I am eating at the Wells's dinner tables that same night. I suppose it was kind of a celebration. The local news got ahold of the story of Molly Lender. I think her daughter called them. They ran a piece showing her telling Peter Barker, the police officer who was on duty that night, that she had never died at all.

The both cried. They did a side piece on the Fentons and Junior Fenton got some kind of reward for helping her escape. He only wished his dad was still alive so he knew the truth that couldn't be told way back then.

After the show, we all come in and sit at the tables. I say tables because they have a big old dining table and then two card tables because their kids' friends have friends over and Bella and her dad are there. Some of them have sprawled into the living room in front of the TV. Bella's dad doesn't look anything like her. He's like a hippie with long hair and sandals. He told me a few minutes earlier he is planting organic crops this year.

"I thought you were kidding when you said dinners were crazy here," I tell Brody because it is chaos just like the car ride after my own car got wrecked, only ten times more. There are about twenty-five people passing around mashed potatoes, slamming the beans in front of me and every sort of silverware banging on mismatched plates. I'm used to just me and Delilah sitting quietly at her table while we both grab sections of the newspaper and eat in silence. If the cat meows, we both make a startled jump.

Zach is sitting down the table from Brody and me. He keeps giving me these weird little smiles and pointing at Brody and me like we have an inside joke.

"Make him stop." I keep telling Brody and Brody tells him to stop. But it doesn't. Then comes the icing on the cake, as Delilah would call it.

"So," Zach nearly yells from the far end of the table, "what was the reaction of your parents when they found out you two were married?"

Everything kind of comes to a standstill. I have my bread and butter in my hand, poised to take a bite. Brody is taking a drink and stops in mid-choke.

Only Bella looks from Brody and me and then to John and Gayle who are both staring at us with stupefied faces. John's mouth has dropped and his eyes are slowly veering toward Gayle. Gayle is getting ready to stand and she stops, sits down hard and goes completely blank. Even Cayce who is sitting next to Gayle quiets for a moment before stifling a yawn.

"Well, you're witnessing it right—now," Bella pipes up without losing a beat. Every eye at that table turns from us to John and Gayle.

"Oops," Zach says. There are two seconds there I want to clamber up on the table, walk right down the middle and kick Zach Metzler in the teeth. I swear sometimes he plans these things.

"What's the matter, Mamaw?" Cayce asks. Everyone ignores her.

"Um, it was an accident," Brody stumbles through the words like he is making his first speech. He is looking at his mom. She looks almost like she is going to get up, walk across the room and spank him. "I mean, we're supposed to get an annulment. But we can't because—"

"Why can't we?" I ask, turning quickly. "You told me we didn't have to do the divorce thing. I don't want a divorce."

"Well, *you* know." He looks at me like I know something that I don't know.

"No, *I* don't know," I say. "You mean because I missed the court date?"

"No."

"Because I signed my name backwards with the o's and x's?"

"No, I'll tell you later."

"Tell me now."

I didn't care that his eyes are getting big as if he is warning me to stop.

"I can answer that," Bella offers and laughs. Gayle and John seem to know the reason because I see their surprise turn to what I can only describe as indignant. Brody leans in. I can see his face has turned crimson. "Because we did *it*," he whispers. You know. We consummated the marriage. The judge says we had to—"

"Could you not have lied?" I say louder.

"You want me to lie to a judge? Really? I was in a bind, Journey, because you didn't show up. I didn't know if you were just running fashionably late or you were going for the arrest warrant look. I was trying to buy you time."

"Then why didn't you call me?"

"Your phone number changed."

"When did this happen?" Gayle interrupts our argument. My head shoots up before I realize she is talking about us getting married. "How long have you been married?"

I could see Zach was not going to answer. He had suddenly slipped down deep in his chair.

"June 6th," Brody tells her. "You saw the newspaper announcement. It was real. I told you it was a misprint."

John leans his elbows on the table, gets a reflective look in his eyes to the table. "Is it really that meaningless nowadays to you kids that you can just go out and get married and get divorced?" His gaze shoots up to mine, then over to Brody. "Do you not have any respect for marital vows? I thought I raised you better than that. I guess I should have known being out on your own wouldn't change things, make you grow up a bit."

I did not know what to say. I only know Brody latched on to my arm underneath the table really quick.

I was sure it was a sign not to say anything about Zach. Still, Brody shot a gaze at Zach that should have melted the butter on his own bread.

"Yes, sir," Brody says. "I do. I know we should have thought it out. We didn't." He looks at me. "I mean, I didn't. Journey had nothing to do with it."

Well, that didn't make any sense to Gayle. "It takes two to tango. You weren't drinking, were you?" Gayle asks. I thought Delilah had dibs on all the weird sayings. "Oh, my goodness, you're not pregnant, are you?"

"No," Brody says for me. "Mom! It just happened."

"Son, things like this just don't happen," John tells him. He starts to stand, tosses his napkin at his plate. "It is just another one of your dumbass moves. I'm getting too old to ride this rollercoaster ride again."

"It wasn't his fault," Zach mutters. "It wasn't Journey's fault. I did it."

"It's okay," Brody is just sitting back in his chair like he doesn't care. He waves a hand at Zach. "Don't worry about it. I'm never going to do anything right in his eyes."

"No, it isn't right." Zach looks pale.

"Zach, you don't have to stick up for Brody," John says, pushing back his chair. "He's got a head on his shoulders. He just needs to screw it on for a change and use it."

"He did use his head." Zach is sitting there with his hands folded in front of him. He suddenly looks like the six year-old in Missus Terry's fourth grade class that got caught cheating on his test. "He was trying to protect my job. I was the one who married them. They didn't even realize it. Journey just wanted to get her birth certificate. Brody was just there to help her get it because I'd been telling her I could get it, but I didn't. We haven't been able to find it.

I thought it'd be funny to go through the marriage vows because of the dance card and the promise Grandpa Delbert made Journey keep. It was a joke. Then somebody filed the paperwork. I guess it isn't that funny—now."

"Zach, it's okay."

"No, I don't want you leaving again because of something I did. Man, it's stupid. I'd rather go to jail than see what you've gone through for me." Zach turns around, takes in John's face like he's getting ready to suck up a sour lemon after drinking a sweet milkshake. "Mister Wells, I'm the one who burned down the barn. Brody never smoked. I did. I was smoking, we left, and it burned down. We were scared I'd go to jail. Brody just knew my dad would kill me if he found out. You—you would eventually forgive him. Not my dad."

John's eyes are just working back and forth directly on Zach's eyes. But his words are aimed at Brody, "Is this true, son?"

"Yeah. Does it matter?" Brody starts to get up. He wiggles his finger at me. "Come on, Journey, let's go." He looks over to Bella and she looks torn, her fork tapping its way across the plate. I rise like he says, unsure and feeling like I should do something or say something. But I'm at a loss so I just reach out and grab his hand, let him drag me away from the table. My eyes are on Bella's because I don't know what to do. I think she's figuring I've got dibs on Brody now, so I've also got dibs on his problems so she'll just sit it out here and not be a part of it. I figure if I can't reach her with my hands, I'll drag her out of there with my glare.

"I'm sure you'll find some reason to blame it on me anyway," Brody tells his dad while I watch Zach push back his chair and rise to leave. "Yeah, I shouldn't have let him smoke in the barn. Yeah, I should have told the truth.

It just didn't happen that way. I'm not even sure if you would have believed me if I told you the truth."

"Stop, Brody." I mutter hoarsely. We're almost to the door. Brody has Cayce in his left arm. Zach has just gone around Brody and is sliding his hand on the door to open it.

"Why the hell did you shame me with that eye-thing?" Bella stomps in behind me, whispers angrily at my back. She wiggles her forefinger in front of her eyes. "I had nothing to do with this. I wasn't around when the damn barn burned. Now my dad's going to think I was involved." Still, she slips in behind me like she's ready to follow.

"Oh, so now I'm in charge of Flight Risk now?" I ask her wagging a thumb at Brody. "I always thought you were his self-appointed bodyguard. You're just going to toss the torch at me when it gets tough now?" I just roll my eyes at her, grab a piece of her shirt and drag her along. "Screw that. I'm not going it alone."

Brody is pulling me with his right hand. I tug him back a little and he comes to a halt, but he looks like a pony that sees green pasture and he's ready to bolt. "I'm with you all the way if you walk out that door. But is this what you want? If you're thinking about moving in with me in my car, it was totaled, remember? My bedroom isn't my back seat, it's a rough piece of asphalt on Highway 50 or a three-way army cot with Drew." He doesn't laugh at my lame joke, so I sigh. "Brody, I'm just trying to say, they are all you have."

"They are all *we* have," Brody corrects me.

"You two can sort that out. I'm getting the hell out of here." Zach is looking at me then at Brody. I can see him leaving.

"Stop—" Brody interrupts him, slows Zach with a hand on his arm. "No, no you're not. You're not leaving me with your mess again."

He turns just enough in the open doorway to stare at both Brody and me. I don't understand Zach, but I do comprehend the pain in his eyes. He doesn't want to go. It is as simple as that. Right then, I realize he doesn't really mean to screw up. It just happens to him like crap seems to always happen to me. Brody always cleaned up for him. Now, maybe since he's got me, Zach figures it isn't going to happen anymore.

Bella finally intercedes. "What Brody is trying to say is that *we* are all in this, Zach. All of us here right now which includes you. And if you go out the door and he goes with you—and most likely, he will, you're dragging all of us. Because if Brody's going, she's going and I'm going. Then something broken doesn't get fixed. Maybe it breaks even more. If you stay, you've got the chance to repair it."

"Or you can do what Delilah always does and that's just pretend it doesn't happen," I mutter. "That works for her."

"I'm willing to fix it."

I jump. Until he speaks, I didn't hear John come up behind us in the small foyer. Brody's eyes go up over my head. His face is expressionless. Cayce leans in and pushes her arms around his neck and yawns. I can feel the tenseness, sense the apprehension in both men.

"What do you want me to do, Journey," Brody asks me. I am unsure of what to tell him, just stand there wavering between the two. I'm afraid he'll hate me if I tell him to leave, take him from his family. I am scared he will hold it against me if I make him feel caged beneath his father's rules.

"Why are you asking me? You know I can't make that decision for you," I finally say. "It isn't fair to ask me to do it and you know that. I will tell you this, though. Since you guys picked me up on the highway, I have not felt alone.

And I cannot remember ever *not* feeling lonely and scared all the time."

"You are kind of telling me what you want me to do." He leans against the wall, looks up at the ceiling.

"No. I just told you how your family makes me feel, how you make me feel around them. I'll stay. I'll go. I will sleep in the cab of your truck with you and eat peanut butter and jelly on day-old bread for breakfast, lunch and supper. I don't want to be without you ever again."

"Yeah, me too. And I don't want to do that," Brody says so softly I can almost feel it filtering down with the dust particles in the air. "Can we just try Delilah's approach and forget it ever happened?" Brody forces a laugh, looks at his dad and then to Zach.

"Your grandpa would have just said 'bygones,'" John said. "I say we honor Delbert and say that is all said and done. Bygones. Let's get some dessert."

Brody waves a hand at Zach. He still hesitates until John waves him back inside too. I can feel the sweat beading on my back while we walk back into the room. Everyone is staring at us. Then all of a sudden, one of the kids comes tearing through the room laughing. It is chaos again and nobody even seems to care.

"Is every meal like this at your house?" I ask Brody. "Because I'm thinking I'm going to have to limit the number of times I have dinner here. This is a bit too much drama for me to take in high doses."

He just laughs. I hear John laughing with him.

"Maybe we could do a couple a week for the next few months," Brody returns. "We can work up our stamina because at some point, you are going to have to tell your own mother that you've been married for quite some time. I bet that's going to fly like a big elephant in a small room."

Chapter −43

Note to Self: Call Stoner's Ex Wife

"Hey, we need to pull the plug on the song you and me were working on at the Country Fest."

It is Stoner on the other end of the line. His voice is low, quiet. "Okay." I answer. "Can I ask why?"

"Somebody sitting around with us while we were hashing it out, caught it on their phone. It was online and my ex-wife saw it. She hit the roof, said she'd sue us both if we sang it."

"Yeah, the phone thing hasn't been going well for me either," I try to laugh it off softly. It wasn't. Last Thursday, six teenage girls showed up at Hobie's and tried to get in with fake IDs. The bouncers sent them packing to the parking lot and they were out there crying and screaming cusswords at anybody who would listen. They had heard my song and drove all the way from southern Tennessee to hear me sing. I just pulled in and saw them. I got out my guitar, gave them a mini-concert in the parking lot off the back of some guy's truck. By the time I was into the third song, Ducky came out, shoved his way through the crowd and dragged me back inside. Somebody got a video of it and posted it online. I guess Ducky's shareholders in this new bar thing got wind and had a bit of a fit about it. However, I did gain a few fans.

"Yeah, there's no running away." Stoner sounds tired on the other end. "Damn, I worked hard on that. Two years, trying to get it just right, then scared to let my gut feelings out for the world to hear. It sat there so long. I changed it, tweaked it, then when we worked on it at the festival, it just worked. You know, I used to lay in bed and swear I could see it wiggling a finger at me to have somebody sing it.

Then, I couldn't find anybody who had the heart and soul. I finally get it going and —" I hear him snap his fingers on the other end. "Gone. Now, I can't ever get it out there. Maybe it's better."

"Can she really sue us for singing it?"

"Naw, I don't know," Stoner says. "But we've got kids. It just isn't worth another battle." He went on for twenty minutes, pouring his heart out about having the love of his life and losing her. I just listen on the other end. I understand him.

"Well, do you want me to talk to her?" I finally ask. "It sounds like you're still bruised, she's still got a skinned heart too."

There was silence on the other end of the line. I thought we might have lost the connection. "No, she'll think I told you to call her. I really don't want her mad at me."

We hung up. Twenty minutes later, Stoner calls back, gives me his ex-wife's number, tells me to call her.

I do. Her name is Meg. Still Meg Carter. She is mad like Delilah gets when we are at church and I drop a hymnal in the middle of the service. I can hear anger in her tone, although her words are subdued, hushed. They aren't aimed at me personally. Maybe just Stoner. Maybe the world.

"No," she says. "I don't want it anymore. It is always his side of the story for a million people to hear and think I'm crazy or a bitch. Do you know I had some woman beat my windshield with a tire iron because Ryan wrote a song about a woman who went out on her husband. Everybody thought it was me because it was the time we were getting the divorce. No. Absolutely not."

"What if I told your side of the story?" I offer. It occurs to me she is right. You only get one side of the story in a song most times. "Maybe we can rectify that situation and still, play the song."

"You're going to tell my side of the story before the song?"

"No, I'll sing your side of the story. I've got a guy I sing with. He'll sing Stoner's—I mean, Ryan's side and I'll sing yours." I tell her. "You just tell me how you felt, the hell you were going through. We'll do a duet. I'll stick up for you. He'll stick up for him. Your story is told and maybe we'll make a few bucks out of it."

"Okay, here's how I feel. He was my first love. He's a shit. He never came home. He spent more time with the band. I got sent pictures of him autographing a girl's tits at a bar. You know how that feels? I hate him—" She rants for a good three minutes, saying all those things girls say when they get dumped, used or their husband goes out on them.

She still loves him. I can hear it in her voice. Just like Delilah still loves me even though I drop a hymnal on the floor. "If you can make a song out of that, I'm all for it." she pauses, "But it's like this. You're a girl. You've had your heart broken. Don't let me down. Don't let every woman with a broken heart down. Because if you do, I will hate you—they will hate you."

Chapter −44

The big elephant in the little room that never gets out

"Hey, Drew," I am on my hands and knees in Dan Keyes Gas Station and Used Cars. "Come out a minute. Please."

I see the shadow, look to my left. Drew is standing there shaking his head. "How many times will Cal have to do that to you before you realize he's just doing it to check out your butt."

"Aw, come on." I push myself up, glare at Cal who is leaning against the register. Then I turn to Drew. "I need you again."

"Okay. But you're sleeping on the floor this time. You kick in your sleep."

"No, no, no," I say, pushing out a hand. "I want you to sing with me. I need you to sing with me." I reach out, hand him a large tan envelope. He opens the end and tugs out the sheet paper inside and CD within. "It's a song we're going to sing. Together. The CD is the instrumentals. Hobie's got sound room we can practice in and we'll sing it on stage Friday night. Tell me yes, please." He opens up his mouth to speak, but I'm scared he's going to say 'no' if I stop, let him get a word in. "You know the band called Witt?" I ask him. I know he does. "Well, they've asked us to sing with them."

"Witt." Drew just says the name and his eyes work back and forth between my own. His eyes narrow. I know he has probably seen someone's video online of me singing with them at the festival. He was always looking up their stuff on his phone. "Journey, you're doing just fine without me. I'm not an idiot."

"No, I'm not doing fine without you. I'm doing shitty. You know how I feel about singing in front of people. You know I freak out. I am being truly honest in saying that I really, really don't want to do it alone."

"It sounds like you've got a band, you're not alone."

I stare at him hard. We've known each other four years. We have dug crusty hamburger out of plates together at the sink at Hobie's at one o'clock in the morning, sat in his trailer when the electric went out in January and sang in the darkness and five degrees below 0. We've missed our cues together, gotten knocked off the stage together and he's stood outside the women's bathroom for me so I can pee and to make sure some creep doesn't follow me inside. "No, without you I am alone. I have felt so damn lonely since you left. I don't want to do it if I can't sing with you. It just isn't any fun. You know my dream was having my shop. It's gone and this is what I have left. But I can't to it by myself without you. I won't."

"Yes, you will."

I stand there and I can't believe he is turning me down. It is uncomfortable even if it is only Drew and Creepy Cal standing there staring at me in the silence following.

I don't know what else to do than turn and leave. I realize I am not lying. It is so great hearing people singing my songs. It is even better knowing they are splashed across the radio and Ducky is getting calls from all sorts of TV and radio stations wanting to talk to me. I'm just not so sure I like standing up there having all the attention focused on me. I don't really want to be a star. I liked doing it because I was up there with a friend who had the same interests. Maybe some would think this strange. But I had been in enough pageants. I didn't need anyone telling me I was pretty or talented to feel whole.

"If you change your mind, just give me a call." I turn then, make my way out the door. I feel like I've lost my real best friend. Not Andrea, but someone who actually shared stuff with me. "Maybe we can hang out, play guitar sometimes, huh?" I feel like I am going to cry. I don't. I just walk toward the door, push my arms against the glass to go outside.

"Dude, are you nuts?" Creepy Cal is the one who speaks up. His voice is deep and low in the drab garage. "Do you honestly want to work here instead of playing guitar? You're good, man. I hear you play every night after quitting time. You are messed up if you don't take her offer. Do it. Knock 'em dead."

That is all I hear before I step outside, close the door behind me, *Knock 'em dead*. Brody is sitting in the driver's side seat of his truck, watching me walk across the buckled asphalt drive. I know he can tell I'm upset.

I climb in, sit there quietly.

"You alright, Journey?" he asks me.

"Knock 'em dead. What's the real meaning of that, Brody?" I ask quietly instead of answering him.

He shrugs. "I suppose it means to—like do so well you leave folks so blown away they are speechless."

I sigh. "That's what me and Drew do together. I think we knock 'em dead. I've seen it sometimes where there's this long silence after we sing. I don't want to try to do that alone. I don't think I can."

Brody just pats the seat and I scoot over next to him. "You already have."

"Hey!"

I turn to Drew's voice shouting from the garage. He is standing there with his arms on the door, his head partially out of the door. "Okay, I'll do it. What time?"

"Right now."

Two weeks later, we did knock 'em dead. Drew got up on stage with me and Witt played backup. This time, Drew sang half of Stoner's song and I sang the other half. It was darn near perfect. What had started as a piece of paper with words on it at a picnic table at music fest, ended up leaving the audience silent for nearly ten seconds. We knocked 'em dead.

I never told Stoner I added words to his song. Everything from his heart stayed put. I just added in his wife's words between. It wasn't like I was keeping it from him. We just didn't have the time. Drew and I are hashing it out all the way to the end. I didn't change his part, not at all. I just shoved in Meg's feelings, her words between. I kept my voice low, soft. Drew belted out his feelings loud and clear. Then both Drew and I sang the chorus together, melding the words together. We both sat on chairs on opposite ends of the stage, backs to each other. It was dark all around us, except for two dim lights hanging over us.

"This is a song Stoner started writing when he and his wife were breaking up. She didn't want us to sing it. There was only one side of the story. It would have fallen to the trash can. It was too good for that. So I picked up the phone, called the ex-wife and she told me her side of the story too. Stoner, if you hate me for this, I'm sorry. But we're going to let you both get heard. So —here it is: *Both Sides of the Story.*

"Did I manage to lose two bands in one week?" I see Stoner standing there staring at me and Drew. We had just walked off the stage. He doesn't say a word. My stomach is gurgling. I went too far. Stupid me, again. Then I realize he isn't even looking at me, but around me.

"Meg," he says. I turn, see her standing there. She has a look on her face, I can't describe. It is sadness, heartbreak, happiness and then a bit of 'oh-my-God-I-haven't-seen-him-in-so-long.' She is like the words to a hundred different kinds of songs all wrapped up into one.

"Yeah, Ryan, it's me," she says. "I came to hear the song. That's why you wrote it, isn't it? You think I still can't read between the lines?"

"Oh," I just kind of moan and cringe. Drew is looking back and forth between the two. Awkwardly, that is.

"Maybe we should— go." He bumps me with his arm.

"If you would have done it three years ago, I would have stayed, you know."

"No, you wouldn't," he was saying. "Because it just wasn't working with the band then. We didn't have enough heart and soul for the song. It would have just been a — song. I needed the right person to sing it to make it come from a piece of a soul. We needed Journey. It took me this long to find it— find her. Is it too late?"

She just shakes her head back and forth while Drew and I try to slide around her. "Of course not." Still, she manages to reach out, snatch my arm and give it a gentle squeeze. "Thank you."

After our show, Delilah is standing outside the kitchen. The music is still blaring with another band. Hobie keeps the bands rolling in until he closes at two in the morning. Smalltalk is there beside her. He is not in his police uniform tonight, but is wearing a nice button-up shirt and khaki pants. "Delilah called and wanted me to escort her down here to listen to your show. We set up a couple chairs out here." He waves a hand outside next to his car. Sure enough, there were two folding plastic chairs sitting there.

"Out here?" I ask. I have a towel in my hand and I use it to swipe off my neck. "Delilah, you aren't going to burst into flames just by coming into a bar."

"I don't want to start something I can't finish."

"I don't know what that means," I say.

"It just means she doesn't want to come inside," Smalltalk translates for me. "You did wonderfully tonight, honey."

Delilah rubs her lips together. "Barring the cursing, it was quite nice, dear."

I feel Brody come up behind me. He puts his hand on my shoulder. I watch Delilah's eyes follow his movements, then turn slightly away.

"Delilah, you know Brody Wells, right?" I ask, introducing him.

"I do," she says. "I see his mother in church every Sunday." I know she is implying that she does not see *him*. However, I let it go. I am still surprised she complimented me on the show. Instead of rolling my eyes, I wiggle my hand into Brody's hand.

"I know you think Robert is the only one who will ever love me," I say softly. "I've heard you say it a thousand times. But it just isn't true. Brody loves me too."

"I do," Brody says to Delilah. To say I am pleasantly surprised at his remark is an understatement while my tummy does a flip-flop. He squeezes my shoulder and pokes me gently in the ribs. I just stand there like an idiot and grin. I watch Smalltalk grin back at both of us.

"You make it sound like I said you weren't loveable. I don't think that, Journey Dawn," she says. "I said Robert loves you like no other. It is different."

"I don't know so much about that. I just know he loved me in the wrong way," I answer. It is all I say.

I didn't want to fight with her tonight. "He told me you've got heart problems. Is that true?"

"I told him you were breaking my heart doing some of the things you do."

I open my mouth to spout how I really feel, but Brody gives me a little squeeze with his hand. I look at the ground, breath in, breath out. Then I look up again. Delilah is reaching out her hand. In her fingers, she is holding an envelope. I take it and look at it. It is blank. "What is this?"

"Just open it."

I do what she says, tugging out the thick paper within. "My birth certificate." I'm not so sure I really want to see it. She looks up at Smalltalk. He just shrugs with his hands in his pockets.

"Open it, dear."

So I open it, let my eyes slide down the page. Brody is behind me, his chest against my back and his hand resting on my shoulder. I pause at Delilah Jean Bacon. Then I look underneath. I swallow hard, narrow my gaze. William James Hobert.

"William Hobert?" I whisper. "Do I know who this is?" Then it occurs to me. My eyes widen when I look up. Smalltalk is staring at me hard. "H—Hobie is my father?"

Delilah has her own beauty pageant face. She is wearing it now. It has the same expressionless features as an old China doll. "We met in high school. I barely knew him. But I saw him many years later in Nashville when he was first managing bands. He also helped models find jobs with local companies looking for pretty women to sell their products. I was one of those women. He was very handsome and quite charming. He got me a job as a flight attendant.

I thought he was a hometown boy and I missed home so bad. He was like seeing a little piece of Bacon Valley when I was so far from home. I worked there just a month or so before I got pregnant. Marriage was not an option for me or for him. He was—he liked pretty women and lots of them. And I was so naïve. He wasn't the type to settle on just one and certainly not me. It took me a while to realize that, but I finally did. His uncle owned this place years ago. Hobie retired here. I kept you away from him."

"Does he know I'm his kid?"

"I'm sure he has a good idea."

Chapter −45

You're the closest thing to a daddy I ever got. Took me fishing at your secret spot—

"Hobie."

Hobie is directing stage hands in putting the band equipment away. "The show went well tonight," he says, looking up long enough to give me a little salute with his right hand. "No, it went better than well. I think we've got something here."

I know he can tell something is going on because he is still staring at me. I walk up, hand him the envelope. "It's my birth certificate."

"I'll make a copy of it for the files." He takes it from my fingers. I could tell it was just an unconscious effort on his part to open it up, scan the document with his eyes. I wait, wait. He stops at the bottom, his eyes lock in. Then he closes the envelope, folds it up and stuffs it in his breast pocket. "I'll make a copy, get it back to you on Monday." He starts to turn. I reach out my hand, lay it on his arm long enough to stop him.

"You knew I was your daughter?"

"When you walked in the door asking for a waitress job, I wondered if there wasn't more to it," he told me. "I thought maybe your mama sent you. Maybe you were trying to get some money from me. I've had more than one of you knock on my door."

I am staring at him, thinking I should look at Hobie in a different light. I don't. It occurs to me it really wasn't any different this very moment than ten years ago or four years ago or even five minutes. He isn't much of a dad.

"I didn't know," I told him. "Delilah didn't know I worked here." It didn't seem so important. I realize I am almost disappointed. I think of what Smalltalk told me. He really wishes I was his little girl. And I realize I wish he was my dad too.

"See you on Monday, right?" Hobie says when I do a little turn on my feet like maybe I'm not going to show up now.

"You are my people, Hobie," I say. "Sam wants to practice every day for a few hours until we get things going. He wants to make an album."

"I'll make sure the stage is set up. Ducky's got the contracts."

Smalltalk's still waiting for me at the back door like he always is. "I walked your mother to her car. It's your turn. Where are you parked?" he asks me. I don't tell him that Brody is waiting for me. I kind of learned to like these little walks.

"So did you talk her into this or did she plan this herself?"

"I asked her out on a date, Journey," he answers. "I've asked her out seventy-two times. Every time, she turned me down. The other day, she called me for the two-hundredth time trying to find out where you were living, where you had gone and why I wasn't calling in the National Guard to find you." He rocks back and forth on his feet and has a cocky tip to his chin. "I said to her: if I find Journey, will you go out on a date with me? She said she would. This was our date."

"No kidding." I laugh. "By the way, I got to use that bear repellent you gave me the other night," I tell him. "I need some more."

He is looking at me, his eyes looking concerned, his brow furrowed.

"You might have heard it on the news. They didn't use my name. It was just a little piece at six o'clock and ten, then they talked about safety on the highway for women driving alone."

"I did hear it." Smalltalk stops me, his hand on my shoulder. "I actually taped it and put it on a CD for you. I had no clue it was you. Are you okay?"

"I learned not to accept candy from strangers. But you told me that as a kid about a million times." I laugh. I know it isn't funny really. I'm just thinking about what Tina Lavelle said about fathers are the ones who are there for you. "But your bear spray saved me. You saved my life. I did everything you told me to do if I was ever in a carjacking. I got in like the man said. I put on my seatbelt and then I grabbed the bear repellent and then the steering wheel and let it run into the first thing it came to. If I didn't have it—" I chew on my lip a minute. "I would probably be dead right now." I think he is going to hug me. He doesn't. It isn't Smalltalk's way. He just nods, looks serious just like he always was when he helped me put a worm on the end of a hook. "You had a lot of people swarming you tonight," he says. "I'll talk to Hobie about getting more security."

"That's fine. I obviously need to listen to your advise more, I suppose." I wiggle a hair band off my wrist, tie up my hair in the quiet between us. Then I reach into my pocket and pull out a folded sheet of paper. "I've been working on this song for a little bit. It kind of says how I feel. It was for you. Now I think I probably won't sing it so I don't hurt Hobie's feelings." I stretch out my hand, give the paper to Smalltalk. He opens it, peers inside.

You're the closest thing to a daddy I ever got.

Took me fishing at your secret spot.

There were movies on Friday night. While mama dated

other guys. I asked mama if I could call you dad.

She said no. It made me sad.

I'm older now, don't need her advice. I'm skipping over her

and asking twice.

Can I call you daddy, daddy? Can I, Can I?

I remember walking in the woods, looking up to big old you

and holding your hand

And thinking someday I'd marry a man—

Like you. Like You. A man like you.

Smalltalk just stares at the paper. I'm thinking I overstepped my bounds. "I'm sorry," I fumble with the words. "I probably shouldn't have given it to you."

"No," he looks up. Smalltalk's eyes look red, a tear is welling in one. "I mean, yes, you can."

"Really?" I ask. He nods, swipes away a tear. "Then, I was thinking maybe you could take me fishing tomorrow down at Goose Creek," I say to him. "I remember you used to have that special hole where we could catch bluegill."

"I still have that little pole you used to use hanging in my garage."

"That would be cool," I say.

"After church," he says. "Your mother asked me to pick her up for church tomorrow."

Holy hell. I just stand there staring at him with a smile on my lips. He's still got that cocky tip to his chin. "I think you used me to get to Delilah," I tease him.

"You think?" he says. "Maybe, when you were little. Then you and your ornery little self grew on me. You went from this little pampered, prissy princess making that sour face when I stuck a minnow on your hook to this little rebel who would cuss and run away with the pole if you couldn't stick the gooey worms on yourself. That kind of stuff makes a man proud."

"You were the only one who let me be myself," I told him. "You were the only one who let me spread my wings and fly. And caught me when I thought I might fall."

Brody's mom hasn't quite embraced the idea that we're married. She tells me she would feel more comfortable if it was done before the eyes of the Lord in a church with her son in a tuxedo and me in a white dress. I am staying with them. He sleeps on the couch. I get to share a room with Cayce and his little sister.

That's what I'm expecting when he drives me back to the house that night. It is late, nearly one in the morning. But Brody doesn't pull off in the driveway of his dad's house. Instead, he keeps on going and doesn't stop until he's right in front of Delbert's old home.

"I want to show you something," he tells me. "In the barn." He points to the huge, sturdy barn to the left of the gravel drive. Delbert once told me it was over a hundred years old. But it had withstood the test of time and would be here a hundred more. His great-grandfather and his grandfather had built it out of the wood on the land. It is a huge old barn, freshly painted a couple years ago in a pretty red with white trim.

"Um," I grin while he opens my door. "I've seen *that something* everyplace but your grandpa's barn."

He laughs, then comes up in front of me and gives me one of his perfect, long hard kisses. "This is something else." He tugs me by my hand toward the barn. "Not as exciting as that particular something, but something nice."

"You bought me a tractor?"

"No."

"A horse."

"Nope." Brody pushes the doors open, they are the kind of doors that slide across. They are thick and huge and he has to shove them hard. I wait outside until he turns the light on. It doesn't exactly douse the room in light, just gives it a spray of orange and yellows. They are high on the ceiling and I watch the dust trickle down to the cement floor below. It is nearly empty, the huge barn. There are no longer any stalls inside, just a huge area that appears recently swept clean. I can see some boxes in one corner and a lone, wooden chair in the center.

He tugs me inward by the hand. I follow behind like a kid in tow and he stops just short of the chair.

"Here." He points to the wooden chair and I hover over it, wondering if I should act excited. I look at the chair, then to Brody. "Look *on* the chair first." He points to the seat and I see a small box on it. "Go ahead."

I reach down and pick it up. It looks like a ring box. "Don't open it just yet," he says and I see him getting down on one knee and I suddenly realize what this is all about. And I'm thinking that we never got to this part, we kind of skipped over it. I don't even know if I thought about it. Maybe I just figured this was the way it would be because we had not broached the subject, never quite grasping the magnitude of what it meant.

"Journey Bacon, I know we're married, but you didn't have a choice when it happened," he says softly. I see his eyes twinkling as I look down and I'm screaming yes already in my mind. I see him shaking and his voice is quivering. I wonder if he thinks for one second I would decline. "I know you could have any man you wanted, any man. I see a hundred of them looking at you when you sing and I wonder why the hell you're with me right now instead of one of them. And I also know Grandpa Del made you promise to go on nineteen dates, fill up the card. But I'm thinking we got something here. I want my name on every one of those lines, every one of those dances. I don't think Grandpa would mind." He waves his hand between us while I nod my head. I've gotten the feeling this was what Delbert Johnson was aiming for the entire time. "I'm asking you to marry me in a white dress and me in a tux in front of anybody who'll come and to make my mom happy and your mom happy. Before you answer, though, please open the box."

I do. It is a small brown velvet ring box and I lift the lid. But there is nothing inside. "There isn't anything in here." I think for a moment it is a joke. Brody rises and smiles. "You like to find stuff and everybody I talk to says you always find exactly what they are looking for. I thought maybe you and me, we could go hit some antique shops and all those places you go alone and find our rings together. That was so much fun the road trip we took with Bella to get mom's ring and old Jack."

"Oh." I have my fingers on my lips. I can't answer more than a peep because I'm starting to cry in a good way.

"Here's the other thing. Dad and I started fixing up the barn. He realizes how wrong he was for judging you before he even really knew you, Journey. He's not one to apologize out loud. But he'll show how he feels, like this."

Brody smiles softly, looks around the barn. "We thought you could make a new shop out of it, a big shop with all the antiques and stuff."

He stops and points to the far side of the room. I squint and peer to where he is aiming. "Bella, Zach, Dad, and I went in the back door of the Knick-Knack Shop and pulled out all of shelves, you know the ones that kept falling. A bunch of people downtown started collecting the stuff out of the dumpster and putting it in boxes and dropping them off at the post office where mom works. We collected some too, after dark."

I'm just standing there staring at the stuff. All the stuff I thought Robert had taken from me. The tears are pouring out of my eyes hot and fast and I am clinging to Brody so hard, I think I might take away his breath.

"One more thing before you answer. I'm going to lay this on the line. I work at the feed mill. It isn't much money. And you are right. I am a farmer and always wanted to be one. Even when I try not to be one, I always come back to it. Dad says it might be hard, but we can build up the farm again. You're a big part of it because some of it belongs to you now for paying it off for us. I just want to lay it on the line so you can back out gracefully if you —" His hands are trembling and my hands are trembling.

"Yes." I push out my hand stop him. "Brody Wells, you would have already had a *yes* the day I locked the keys out of the car and you kissed me waiting for Zach." I feel his arms around me, feeling him pulling me tight. I'm thinking that it all started with that stupid dance card and his stupid best friend whose intentions were a bit misguided. And it ended, like this.

Made in the USA
San Bernardino, CA
12 January 2017